Amuc

by

Mo McCarthy

Copyright © 2016 Mo McCarthy

All rights reserved, including the right to reproduce this book, or portions thereof in any form. No part of this text may be reproduced, transmitted, downloaded, decompiled, reverse engineered, or stored, in any form or introduced into any information storage and retrieval system, in any form or by any means, whether electronic or mechanical without the express written permission of the author.

This is a work of fiction. Names and characters are the product of the author's imagination and any resemblance to actual persons, living or dead, is entirely coincidental.

ISBN: 978-1-326-77094-5

Introduction

Like ants we pour in daily from various corners of the globe, all seekers of something, some with clear ideas and solid plans, and others with just the destination in mind as a docking station or stop gap to their real dream. Like the ghost of nobody we move amongst you, we have no meaningful shape or form yet, so you don't notice us, we clean, wash, serve, build, care for you and your nation staying under the radar until the 14 years illegal presence makes us eligible to request to remain here lawfully. We live like rats and rabbits during that time, working in the black economy, never going near your social security funds, finding ways round red tapes, greasing palms, stealing identities, paying strangers to take us to the Registry who then demand more money just before the ceremony or sex without which they threaten to call Immigration services and report us, women and men enslaved for the rubber stamp stating.....Indefinite leave to remain in the United Kingdom.

My friends and I headed into the world famous city called London, different dreams same aim, get away from our various demons and dead ends to live work acquire and return home with the cargo goods of success just like others did before us. Not once did we ask ourselves about the indigenous people and the reception that awaits us but head here we do, pouring out of the likes of Heathrow, Gatwick, Stansted Airport or by road maybe sea with documents that have details that may be ours or bought, sometimes borrowed just to get us into Great Britain...... once in how we fare is up to the God's.

Chapter One

The traffic on Wilshire Boulevard crossing unto La Brea is crawling, I love living in LA, it's the place to get lost or find yourself, you can have as much or as little as you want from the drug scene to the sane scene. Money makes money here, you're either it or you're invisible. You're either in or no one's heard of you nor gives a damn.

LA is the place to hide your madness, anything goes as long as it's within the city lights and you don't get caught. I'm a 60's child and cruise along to the sound of George Benson crooning 'Give me the Night'. I people watch as I drive, nips and tucks, that is so yesterday, today designer vagina and penis enlargements are the rage, such a bloody painful hellish procedure but waiting lists as long as your arm.

LA is the place to get laid by a different partner every night if that's what rocks your boat. Been there done that, after a while you count the heads while pretending to sip your cocktail, rate performances between the sheets as you circulate, air kissing and being very LA.

Tonight I've ordered a Cuban, to arrive at 9.30pm, a late dinner and we get down to the business of my satisfaction, my needs at a cool grand I expect to be worshipped for a couple of hours, the ringing of the phone interrupts my delicious thoughts as I press to pick up I see the number and groan inwardly, 002348 it's Nigeria and can only be my god awful sister Tayo calling, it is.

That hurried, harsh, pressured speech begins, "can you talk"? She doesn't wait for an answer before continuing. "Mum's not great the hospital is saying she won't last the month". I try to keep my voice steady and get my pitch right, I make all the right noises and assure Tayo I'll make arrangements and be home next week. In the same breath the silly cow is telling me she has to fly to India, work related she can't cancel or postpone.

I've being expecting this call, spent the last 40 years praying for this day, planned re-planned, adjusted, saved and patiently laid in wait for today's words, you see I am the rejected corner stone that made good. Like an elephant that never forgets I have simply waited secure in the knowledge that one day I will ensure what my mother sowed is reaped. I am so going to kick her ass.

I park the car and go in, all thoughts of getting laid vanished, I head to my safe, my little black leather bound book of instructions, written and re-written totally fit for its purpose. I caress this book that has kept me going over the years a blow by blow account of what I will do when this glorious day arrives.

I shiver with the delight, it's exciting almost sensual, I finally feel as they say, 'like the cat that got the cream'. But first things first, I need to destroy this book; fools who get caught leave evidence lying around that lead back to them. I stroll downstairs and fire up the gas barbeque, my note book is ashes within a minute. I know the content of that little book off by heart.

Heading into the downstairs study I send several emails to my PA with instructions regarding imminent departure and work related stuff. I am buzzing on pure adrenaline. Another email wings it's way to the only four guys that I can be bothered with, my childhood hanger-on's Moses, Wale, Pitan & Ayo, we all agreed to meet up in Lagos to catch up and reconnect sometime this year, they are in Europe so easier path for them.

I send the dates and choose Federal Palace Hotel as the meet-up venue. Beautiful thing money, my thought as I log into my BA account, I can move whenever, wherever. I book my flight for departure in 2 days via New York and London, calling Tayo with instruction to send someone over to open my house up and air the rooms.

I have a lovely 4 flat building, 3 bedroom duplex, I keep one half of the building empty for my use, on the other side I lease out the ground floor to a dirty Lebanese pervert, he is no trouble really and does not realize he provides me with free security. Over the years he must have slept with all the available females/males within a 5 mile radius. The top floor is an elderly expatriate who spends her time helping out at the local schools.

I book myself a session with my therapist midday tomorrow, it's part of the agreement we have if I am to have contact with my mother. I have to be careful, if she senses the real reasons or as much as suspects I have any other motive she can pull the strings that will ensure my plans do not go the way I want. She is the only person who knows my mum may be in danger, serious high risk from me.

Chapter Two

Reason for heading home. Mum is dying, at 78 she has become frail, several falls and a stroke has taken the wind out of her sail physically yet the old bat's mind is as sharp as a button. She's clogged up a bed for some time at St Nicholas hospital on Lagos Island, well now it's time to go home and die no doubt her wishes all nicely documented and filed prior to her losing much of her power of speech.

I think of Tayo the spoilt one, apple of my mother's eyes a total waste of space in my estimate. Grew up on Lagos Island an Accounts graduate of the University of Lagos, married a Lagos boy, a successful commodity trader with enough money for them to do the usual route and occasional turn up in LA with their 4 greedy kids, all into designer names, nil sense of real style.

They live in Victoria Garden City amongst the other entire pretentious isolated look at me I've landed in money souls, who are actually prisoners behind their own front gate. Christ, these guys make my blood boil.

I'm no longer in the mood to get laid, but I am excited, too excited to keep still, I'm going to dismiss my staff as soon as the Cuban is paid off, easy money for nil sweat. I hear the soft opening of the door; the Cuban is surprised I'm not in the bath or already in bed. I give him his envelope and walk away without an explanation, he waits for a moment and leaves, I briefly have second thoughts, shall I call him back? nah I'll save the orgasms for another day.

I can imagine the shock and horror in the Nigerian community that a Nigerian woman knows her g-spot and exactly how she wants to be laid, folks will be scandalized by the fact I pay for sex, I laugh out loud and long at the pretentiousness of it all. In the West I learnt to tolerate sex as long as it's my way but also to avoid the Nigerian social gathering.

I mix a large Pina colada and fire off more emails, I check my Naira account 759 million will do just fine for three weeks, I will take $9000 as back up. I send instructions to the office, a pleasure to own your own business. I don't need permission to take off.

Actually I could fly tonight if I wanted to but what's the hurry. I have waited this long I can wait a little bit more.

Besides I have to route my travel through New York with another 2 days stopover in London. Heading to New York first as I have something very special to pick up from Flatbush in one of the Haitian shops, where statuses of Jesus, Mary and Muerte the patron saint of death all face each other available for sale.

I call London and speak to my childhood friends, Moses, Wale, Pitan and Ayo (previously four hunger filthy poor losers) to firm up plans of meeting up, reflecting again on the fact I really don't have female friends all a waste of time, effort, money and head space.

What I do have is a husband and a daughter. Tunde my husband is happy to play golf all day and is currently in the Cayman Islands with his latest squeeze, our daughter Ife is happily married lives in Arizona with no sign yet of having a child! I got married because I wanted a child, just one so I don't have to share my love or have a preference for one above the other. My thoughts slip back to my four friends, bearers of the only laughter period when growing up.

Over thirty plus years ago the four musketeers and I we sat on iron pails with pillows on top to stop the iron from cutting off the blood circulation in our bottoms and talked about what we would do in the West, we are in my compound as the most affluent of the lot the boys prefer to come to my house for the comfort and food. Moses spoke first "I will use my prick to make money" he said it the way it is; he is not academically gifted but apparently has a manhood to be proud of. Wale dreams of having a trading business in the UK. Pitan wants to be lawyer and Ayo dreams of becoming a journalist and working for NTA (Nigerian Television Authorities).

Me, I just want to get as far away from Aguda as remotely possible. We all thought these were reasonable goals no inclining of what awaited us abroad. We'll be catching up soon; my contact with them will be the respite I need for the gruesome task ahead. That reminds me I need to pick up essentials travel bits and pieces from Duane Reade and the grill store.

You have no idea what big brother is watching you means until you live in the USA. I tell you, it is almost impossible to get in or out of places without countless cameras you can't see taking pictures of you. My main item is 6 freezer ice packs, I pick these up with bits and pieces I don't need just to make it look like I'm planning a barbeque.

I buy gifts for my sisters greedy children, they mill round like vultures each trying to outdo the other, bloody fools, you send them on an errand and they add thousands of Naira to the cost. Me an Ibadan girl you want to cheat me, you have to return to the drawing board, the sharp noise of a car horn and swearing brings me back to the present.

The Mental preparation needed prior to meeting with Claire McCluskey Clinical Psychologist returns me back down to a dose of reality. I have to make her believe my trip home is to heal things between my mother & I, lay the ghost of the past to rest as they say. I'm going to have an early night; tomorrow with Claire will be an Oscar winning act. I think back to my childhood and when the pain began.

Chapter Three

My guess young way too young, even at that age I understood I was privileged, we had estates where we had countless tenants, we wandered where we wished and small as I was I felt safe, treated with respect. That day I had walked into one of the tenants room, he was ironing, I stood on the other side of the iron and said hello, he must have being in his 30's, he smiled and through the space in the ironing board stuck his leg through and used his large toe to lift my dress up he then pushed my legs apart and pushed his toe between my legs. I stood frozen, even at that age I knew something was wrong but was too scared to move, eventually I ran, confused and worried I would get into trouble.

He must have told his friend another tenant Theo; initially he would ask how I was, always with a smile which I later learnt to interpret as a predatory smirk. Theo asked if he could send me on an errand, I felt so special, I send people on errands for what I want; to be sent to carry out an errand made me feel amazing.

I followed him full of excitement, in his room he pulled out a piece of dirty handkerchief, the terry nappy sort, he puts my hand on his crotch and tells me to keep it there while he made strange noises quietly deep within his throat, his eyes start to bulge, he breaks out in sweat, I'm thinking he is ill, all of a sudden he doubles over, I am told I'm a good girl and sent on my way.

I sit out in the open yard, something is wrong something has changed, I don't understand, I feel everything yet I feel nothing, I have everything yet feel I have nothing. I am a child of wealth yet no one is as poor and destitute as me right now. We have money yet the children of the poor enjoy more protection than I do.

I am young yet within my living space where I should feel safe, I have been violated right under the nose of all the servants, the cooks the home help, house girl house boy, my parents, sibling, and grandparents. Can nobody tell, why has someone not noticed?

I begin to run a temperature and I'm rushed to LUTH the nearest hospital, the pattern of becoming ill at weekends soon becomes well established and yet no one notices no one queries why this little girl is ill every weekend with sky high temperature.

My mother is her usual dismissive self, don't mind that child she is an attention seeker, was her response. I hated her, how I hated her, how can a woman have two children and behave like she only has one, frothing at the mouth to please my sister with barely a tolerant glance for me. You will get to know my mother more if you continue to walk this part of fire with me.

Highly intelligent she obtained her Doctorate at the age of 24. My father was simply referred to as Ola, meaning wealth or affluence. Folks bowed and scraped down in front of them daily. Everything was big, the cars, the houses, both my parents are featured endlessly in magazines, what she wore, where they went what he said who they met, real socialites.

To date my father is one of the few men in my life who held me cuddled me played with me laid next to me to comfort me when I was ill or felt sad, he is the only man I felt safe with. He died in a car crash on the 3rd mainland bridge when I was 8 that is when the real nightmare began.

The next person to get in on the act was our main houseboy Otis, he called me to the living room one quiet day, sat me on the side board and hugged me in a hard hold for long periods, I sat there quietly, totally desensitized and disconnected from the act going on, I had thought if I avoid going to the estate I will be safe but here in the house is the boy who answers, yes little miss to me if I ask for a glass of water , somehow he had found out what Theo was making me do and was getting in on the act.

I remember they smell slightly different, all musky and malodorous, these were not refined people who knew their way around cleanliness and aftershaves. All this in opulent surrounding. You can't begin to imagine our lifestyle, with parents who travelled abroad like they were visiting the local market, parents with friends in high places, but nil common sense.

To leave two daughters to the mercy of servants, some rich children certainly have the poorest quality of life.

I feel myself tumbling, I am in that dark place, it's a dangerous place, it's that corner that recaptures things in tri-colour full screen, I need release, I want to cut so badly, I haven't self harmed in 15 years,

If I do so now I have to make do with methods that leave no visible mark above the cloth line.

I head for the bathroom and stick my fingers down my throat, the hot stingy bile gushes up followed by everything in my stomach, my teeth are all capped, rotted away by stomach acid, it was one of the first cosmetic procedure I had done as soon as the money rolled in, rotten teeth is such a giveaway.

I notice a small streak of fresh blood in the toilet; fresh blood is okay, its dark that would cause concern. I don't feel better and can tell it's going to be a long night. Before the morning dawns I would have made myself sick at least a dozen times, drinking eating and heading to the toilet.

To look at me heading in to the office you have no idea, I am made up and totally immaculate, I am an expert at camouflage make up. Tanisha my PA is waiting with a latte, I tell you money is good. I have money I make good money and enjoy sending money, like all coins the other side is I cannot forgive I will not forgive, if you hurt me, disappointment me cheat me or whatever it is you do I will get you. That is my promise to you.

Chapter Four

I run a tight ship, I have to so delegating and clearing appointments is child's play. My long distant haulage business can practically run itself, I have a Mexican managing that, you cannot go wrong if you give opportunity to men down on their luck, they will serve you faithfully.

The bulk of my wealth comes from the Prison Services; I have the contract for their staple wear, that suit you see in the movies and laugh at escaping prisoner, well that's my work and money. I get these made in China everything ties in well. I guess in American terms I have shitload of dollars.

I call a quick tele-conference and hand over to my board members. Weekly conference calls unless there is an emergency; I am free to switch off work.

I practice mindfulness as I head to Claire's appointment. Should I have a hit list she would be second on it, she knows too much about me. My biggest mistake is forgetting who I am and making use of a therapist, it is all the rage here and has helped in the past but these guys keep everything you say on record locked away.

I had made my first appointment when I started to burn myself with caustic soda. The pain and smell of sizzling flesh gave me release when images of my early days will not let me sleep, occasionally I used small droplets of caustic soda targeting areas always under the cloth line as near the private part as I can get. The raw wounds, the pain factor, the release kept me going confirming I am here, alive feeling and ripe for revenge.

Claire McCluskey is well experienced, she welcomes me with that smoothness educated Americans have, her office setting is what you describe as lush.....I begin the session after pleasantries, after all I pay $800 to chat for 50 minutes. I bring her up to date with me, my family, my well-being business and the recent decline in health of my mother. Claire asks how I feel about my mother, I'm on dangerous grounds this is where I start crying softly, if I overdo it she will become suspicious.

I say how vulnerable and scared I feel, I focus on my recovery journey, I have to convince this bitch I am recovered and not a danger to my mother, I have to make Claire put aside all I have said I will do in the past as trauma. She must be convinced I see my mother as someone to forgive! and that I have moved on. The danger with therapy is you go in, you feel safe and start to run your mouth off because someone is finally listening to you and state they believe you.

Too many threats made towards my mother to ignore, but today I am the forgiving daughter reflecting on the fact my mother may have been a victim of circumstances herself and without specialist training to spot an emotionally distressed child how could I continue to blame her.

I talk about my cultural background; children are seen and not heard. I miss father and have to forgive my mother while I have the opportunity. I finish with the word; I want to be able to exhale without a constriction in my chest.

Claire listens silently watching me like a hawk, she expresses concern about what will be my third and final contact with my mother in 31 years, what support I will have in Nigeria if I become distressed, how do I think I will cope with bereavement. I watch her with the looks of a little girl lost and ask what she thinks I should set up.

Claire thinks she is a step ahead of me, she gives me contact details for an attaché at the US embassy in Victoria Lagos, Kirk Stapleton is a trained Psychologist. I thank Claire and ask for an appointment on my return, I need to disarm this woman totally; she is one of the only people who have listened to what I will do to my mother if I know I can get away with to avenge myself.

Claire wishes me well, having arranged to meet on my return I'm again very mindful of my presentation as I make my exit, walking to the car I maintain my heavy shoulders and a sad look, I drive off and know I'll catch a flight to Europe via New York, nil restriction of movement.

The trip from LA Lax into JFK is uneventful, I have 6 hours to conclude my business before the flight for London and it's more than enough. I grab a cab and head downtown into Flatbush. I make the cab drop me off outside the subway. Pulling my coat close I walk up the road, I had discovered this place by accident years ago when I searched for designers suits amongst their fashion outlets. You could pick up a $300 suit for $29.99.

Walking along one day I saw shops which appeared religious focused on buying a small cross I walked into one and stopped dead in my tracks, inside was crammed with religious images depending on what you want or if you want to mix it, you name it, they had it there from Christ to Voodoo to skulls, as I made to walk out a very attractive lady came out, with a smile that lit up the shop, she explained they believe in the powers of the ancestors, voodoo, the Catholic God and many more. I stood there half petrified and fascinated.

I stare at her with my mouth open as she continued speaking and I think if this is fraud, she is the greatest. "You've been hurt, hurt bad by loved ones, I see you will get revenge but not for many years, you will become rich very rich, you will have a sickness rich people have. Only one child I see you have. The spirits tell me to tell you this when the time is right you come back, you will know when to come back when you do return Lola-Bella/ma will give you something special to take with you when you go to Africa". I bolted through the door as her voice followed me, "no need to be afraid" she called out.

I cross the road trying to remember where the shop is, so many of this Haitian shops, crazy of crazies, it's there with the same pictures of Christ and multiple saints in the window, you get the skulls and strange candles when you go in. I open the door, there are three people at the far end talking a young lady comes over to ask if she can help me, these people are incredibly beautiful, cat has got my tongue and I stand looking at her, the man and woman stop their conversation and come over.

I feel overwhelmed and slightly unsafe, the incense is sweetish and heavy in the air, no one knows I'm here, the man begins to speak, "you are on your way to Africa you are the one the oracle spoke about, come", like one hypnotized I follow and sit in the chair, the older woman disappears and returns almost immediately with a silver looking ring set with fake amber.

To my surprise she flicks something and the amber lifts to reveal a tiny compartment, inside are two tiny bits of rolled up paper. I am concerned about narcotics and for the first time find my voice, "what is the paper for"? The reply shocks me to the core but is it not what I wanted that thing that special thing the oracle said I will take with me.

"The white paper is soaked in puffer fish poison and dried, to activate you put the paper in with a tea or coffee drink hot water will activate it, no need to worry, the person within a few hours will sleep deeply slowly no more heart beat, dead, alive, but no heartbeat. The black paper contains a few grains of the same poison you put in drink or food same result".

"Don't touch", he warns and with that all three walk to the back of the room and leave me there. I wait a few moments when no one returns I leave $500 on the counter and walk out.

I walk a few blocks then hail a taxi to Grand Central from there I hail a different cab to 34th and head into Macey's, I buy $1500 worth of Amber and Silver jewelry and head back to the airport. If the ring was not staring me in the face in my purse I would put the last 30 minutes down to hallucination but the ring is here, I flick it open in the safety of my handbag and look at the tiny papers, closing it I add it to the other amber purchase, it fits in nicely. It then dawns on me I have a poison ring, I'm blown away.

Chapter Five

Arriving back at JFK, I check in and go and grab a bite to eat all the time wondering if I dreamt the past few hours, I am glad to get on the flight without my ring getting any special attention.

The flight into London Gatwick is dull and predictable like the English weather, nothing as boring as first class travel, such money bores, they are curious about me, I get a slight thrill from ignoring those sitting around me, going to the upper deck for a massage and then turn in.

I'm spending two nights at the Anthenum Hotel on Piccadilly; it puts me in the heart of all I enjoy in London. I sleep all day and dine at Faroukdin an Arab restaurant a few doors away, tomorrow I chill, shop and then head for Lagos...show time.

Hurrying down Bond Street I walk up and down several times before I realize F.Pinet is not where it should be. I find a shop Clio and purchase a few pairs of shoes and handbags, I head to Marble Arch and stopped dead where I expect Pin Pin another of my favorite shoe shops to be its disappeared such a shame. Harrods's will have to do as Ivory plus Russell and Bromley shoes already cram my wardrobe.

Good quality Italian shoes to suit my taste is not easy to come by in LA I've got to the stage where I can only wear so much Escada loafers. London, this little island that makes so much noise, and gets involved in all other countries business. What has happened to the Italian outlets that made shopping such an aphrodisiac you can't get enough of here the likes of Grant?

London is a strange place I lived on Stockwell's Binfield estate for 6 years, long enough to pay £120 for an arranged marriage with a guy who was off his head on cannabis most of the time, once in receipt of my stay, I nationalized and took off for the USA my real destination.

Thinking of Stockwell a funny thing happened one evening while waiting for the traffic lights to change outside the train station an Italian guy came up to me and asked if I wanted to go for a drink at one of the many wine bars in Clapham, I said yes, it was nice to get some attention, we had a couple of drinks and tapas both quite merry headed back to his flat which overlooked the common. Attracted to each other I secretly hoped I had found a boyfriend, the sex was out of this world, nothing like the things I had experienced, this was fun, different, he woke up nerves I didn't know existed, touching gently and sitting me on top of him which he realized made me get into the sex itself.

The feeling of control sent me into orgasm after orgasm, I learnt that day for me to enjoy sex I needed to feel in control. Reality dawned when he gave me £40, the bastard thought I was a prostitute. I had indeed behaved like one. I took the money and walked out £40 is a lot of money in 1979 and we had used a condom.

I started to look closer at my environment and realized I needed to move to a better part of town, between Stockwell and Streatham if you know what you're looking for can be a hooker's happy paradise. I soon found a tiny attic bedsit in Fulham: home until I moved to the States.

Today I walk along New Bond street, go in and out of Selfridges, stroll into Harrods in Knightsbridge, bowed in because moneyed people have that effect on others. Folks respect me acknowledge me want to be my friend view me as a fantastic role model, not having an inkling of the demons just underneath my skin nor the pain torture and misery I can inflict.

I head to the Ritz for afternoon tea, a mixture of transparent cucumber sandwiches scones and miniature cakes, again money talks, it's how you dress hold yourself up walk and look at people from an angle that appears you are doing them a favor that acts as a caution to institutionalized way of color coding reaction.

It is true color of skin begins to take a back seat when money is talking. Nil dinner tonight I'll eat on the flight, while I relish what lies ahead, don't be mistaken, this is about me settling scores.

BA is really quite okay if you're in 1st class and have all the extra perks attached to frequent flying. I call and speak to Tayo before boarding, things just get better and better her trip has been brought forward, as a banker with a leading Industrial Bank she has being asked to go to Delhi for an audit of the books, she leaves as I arrive and will be gone for 5 days. I only have 48hrs with mother when she is brought to my house from the hospital before Tayo is on the scene.

48 hours is grand. Things can only get super better, I am in a great mood, the darkness sent deep down within me for now, so good am I feeling it radiates off me enough to attract the attention of one of the well know Naija Billionaires travelling.

I smile deeply at him and he ambles over, I won't touch this fat lump of lard with a broom for all the sand in the Sahara, I feel repulsed, but bored use him to relax and pass away time during the flights, he wants to see me here in Lagos anywhere he says, he gives me his card and contact number only immediate members of the family have.

I ask myself looking at this man who is so fat I wonder how he keeps himself clean after a bowel movement his ham hock hands certainly don't look capable of reaching round, the fool carries on taking not missing any opportunity to touch my hand or brush near me. The six hours twenty minutes pass by pleasantly, I ignore him once we are on the ground, fatso is flustered and puzzled.

Muritala Mohammed airport remains what it is an airport, the air conditioning is working big deal, such a shit load of people all milling around, welcome home, I will not waste my time travelling to Naija and present a United States passport it attracts too much attention. I present my Nigerian passport and use the American passport in Europe and when leaving or entering the USA.

Welcome home madam anything for us, I would love to give something, Aids, Typhoid, Hepatitis a dose of the clap maybe but give the idiots a $20 dollar bill instead, sada and all that stuff and nonsense. The driver is waiting outside, my car is in the diplomatic car park I am neither a diplomat nor is Tayo but this is Lagos grease the palm and you can park on the tarmac.

We head towards Ilupeju in the early morning traffic, I ensure I say nothing to the driver apart from returning his greeting; workers like this turned me into the monster and hater I am today. We pull in to my compound, I have given instructions they are never to repaint the outside of the house, it looks dull and uninteresting but walk in and my home will take your breath away, the finest Italian furniture, simple and tastefully done, nil clutter, minimalistic touch, light and airy just the way I like.

I have an en-suite room on the ground floor, jokingly planned that way for when I am too old to do the stairs. This is where my mother will be nursed, this is where for the first time in my life I will have the upper hand, I will show my mother the fruits of not looking after or protecting her child the way she should have.

It reminds me of my grandfather a hard no nonsense man who sacked a houseboy on the spot because he lifted me up without being given directive to touch me. One minute he was there next he was gone, we had just arrived to visit and were all still standing outside the house in the driveway, I wanted some cashew fruit from the tree outside my grandparent's house.

Grandpa summoned this young man who proceeded to get some down having done this for some insane reason known only to him he then picked me up, I must have been about 9 years old, my mother said nothing totally into herself to notice something was amiss.

Grandpa is old school, the classes don't mix and all must know their station. He roared something at the guy who quickly dropped me apologized profusely and disappeared not to be seen again. I was pubescent, breasts were already visible, short and dumpy, and I was developing quickly. My grandparents I recall were very nice people.

I shower and ask the driver to head to Eko Hotel in Victoria Island, I'm having an early breakfast with Moses, though we're getting together later I plan to meet each of my close childhood friends separately before our meal at Federal Palace Hotel. Moses is waiting just inside the reception we hug and hug, my friend my brother one of the few people who knows what I've been through. It's been a long time and we quickly settle down to eat; Moses fills me in on the years.

After our famous chat on the bucket as I call it he had by sleeping with several Lagos seniors girls gathered the money together to head to London with the glorious sum of £980 in his pocket after paying 210 Naira for a return ticket he had no plan of using for the return leg, at that time you didn't need a visa just turned up at Heathrow and told immigration how long you planned to stay. Now he warns me, 'I know you don't like or do bad language but you have to let me say it like it is, I can't do my head in trying to stick to your polite language' I smile back at Moses I see not much has changed, I am in for lots of f-words I gather from his warning.

Chapter Six

Moses talks.

I arrived on a cold November morning, to crisp fresh smelling Kent air of Stanstead Airport that gradually changed to a vegetation rotten musty odour when we hit the south east. I was met by my cousin, his home address is Kemble Court North Peckham Estate, SE15 my dear any mention of that area still breaks me out in a sweat.

Kemble Court is scary, like the houses in Barracks near stadium but close together and many floors, lift and long walk ways, if someone is chasing you to hurt you, you are dead, nowhere to run and no chance of anyone opening their door to you. On arrival I was allowed to sleep all day. At 7pm sharp I was woken up, it's time to go to work.

I purchase a £2.80 bus pass as instructed this covers all zones. We jumped on the no 36 bus heading into the West End, I loved the lights the sounds, people milling around all looking prosperous. I am your typical Johnny just come. I love standing close to white people, they look and smell different. I am fascinated by everything around me.

Work is in a top London hotel, I am taken to the Nigerian Housekeeper who will help me, first things first we complete a form to apply for a National Insurance number, I don't need to change my name, it will remain Moses, my cousin Kofoworola is called Tony...to live and work abroad be easily accepted and blend in you have to be John, Tony, Henry, Jennifer, Alison, Trina or Sue. I am paired to work with my cousin.

Until my NI arrives I will be using an emergency tax number, all sounded great to me until I was shown into the 1st of the rooms, I am to clean and make up ready for the next guests. That 1st room had a double bed and two single sofa beds, the room was littered with cigarette butts, half eaten food and discarded bags from shops like Selfridges, those who stay here are clearly rich but filthy, the state of the toilet and bathroom bore witness to that, so dirty, urine spots where they haven't bothered to aim well and skid marks in the toilet, that my dear was my welcome to England.

For today to break me in Tony and I are given 25 rooms to do. We set to work straight away, when we clock off at 07.15hrs, I know this is not what I can do for long, my back is so sore I can't stand up straight, Tony won't stop talking about our haul, what haul, half used perfumes and lotions, shirts and few other items of clothing left behind by guests, a leather belt, big deal.

It becomes clear to me later there is a thriving trade going on in all this designer junk left over's. We get home a few minutes to 08.40 hrs Tony as I have to remember to address him, tells me how lucky I am over a bowl of rice and chicken, served to us by his girlfriend who promptly departs to work, whatever that is, I am so tired I do not have the energy to ask.

I am apparently lucky to have a room to call home and a relative who didn't mind me staying as long as I need to, based on the understanding I pitch in with all the bills. We work side by side for the next fortnight; there is a lot to learn, from the English accent to standards expected in a top hotel. Week three and I'm told I'm so reliable and hardworking I am needed on the early shifts for the next 6 months. I curse my luck, not for once imagining that this is what will set me free.

London is a strange place in the morning, ugly and cold, hard and heartless, do me I do you world. Bus 36 at 06.00hrs might have a white driver but 99.9% of the passengers is a mix of Nigerian's Ghanaian's and Ivorians. I heard a Nigerian woman refer to herself as a crew member of 'good morning Britain' a term for early morning cleaners.

The first few days were uneventful and then day six I am allocated the entire 9th floor and left to my own device. Knock-knock; "may I come in housekeeping", I call out as taught, a woman gave permission. I go straight to the bathroom to start my work, just as I'm finishing she walks over to the shower naked as a jay bird, brushes past me slowly and I mean slowly, the uneducated fool between my legs swells in an instant, I am sacred, I have never been this close a proximity to a white woman never mind a naked one.

Breathing hard and trying to clear my head, feeling hot, cold and prickly all over, I hurriedly start on the bedroom while she's in the shower. But she's out and heading straight for me naked, I'm frightened, my heart is hammering away against my rib cage, I start to beg her, please madam I don't want any problem, please lady I can leave and come back, I'm thinking fast, that bloody Tony has not told me how to deal with situations like this, I don't want to be deported back to Nigeria, what do I do I haven't been in England long enough to understand the score, I don't want her crying rape.

It's as if my thoughts are transparent, she talks to me, "it's okay", she says "it's okay", attempting to reassure and calm me down moving close to me she gently begins to caress my cheeks then neck then chest followed by my waist she is touching me all over, moving even closer to me.

She smells fresh from the luxurious body wash items in the bathroom; her short hair is wet and smells of a sweet tasting fruit I will later identify as strawberry. I stand perfectly still while she touches me, strokes me gives me little kisses all the time telling me to relax, "I really like you, dig your style if you know what I mean".

She kisses me on the lips, I open my mouth and truly understand for the first time what a French kiss is, she kisses me slowly, leaving me room to breathe freely without needing to pull back, her tongue traces my teeth while her hands move all over my body, though I haven't pulled away I also haven't touched her.

"Hold me", she says "touch me", for a boy who wants to shag himself rich I can't understand my reluctance, then it comes to me, I see me sleeping with easy women, women who work in the industry not a clean high ranking obviously wealthy woman. She has to be rich; the suite she's in is £490per night. I begin to touch her, it feels different from the girls back home, her breasts are just about enough for a handful whilst the girls back home you need both hands to cup one.

I sneak a peep, her eyes are closed so I keep mine open, her skin is not white rather a pale wheat color, you can see her blood vessels in some places, her hair is sleekly, I like the texture, I am distracted when she unzips me and eases my trousers down, I can't remember when she took my shirt off. In a moment she took me in her mouth.

I worry for a moment she might change her mind once she's felt my size, I am well endowed, I touch her back and gradually take control, she moans making strange little noises clinging to me like her life depends on it she's kneeling in front of me again worshipping me, I have had blow jobs in Nigeria this is different, fear of been bitten has made me watch like an eagle, Naija girl vex with you you'll find out the hard way with a nip perhaps anyway once you've had the little bit of a blow job at the beginning that's your lot.

This is different delicious, she's getting it right touching me in all the right places, I need to shag this woman but I'm unsure if it's skin to skin or she has a raincoat as I call condoms. I have forgotten what I came to do, I look at this woman and marvel at the smooth silkiness of her skin, the shape is familiar but different unlike Nigerian women with their beautifully sculptured behind this woman has no ass it's totally flat behind her, I'm reminded each time I reach round to cup her ass cheeks.

Her nipples are rose pink almost blending into her complexion, I'm touching her and touching her, but fear is not letting me do anything else, I am on alert to stop as soon as she makes it clear no more.

I'm surprised she doesn't expect me to go down on her, clean from a shower I am quietly aware she smells different from black women, not bad just different not the heady scents I'm used to. She stops for a moment and rips a condom open slides it on me and offers me her back, I panic, I've watched videos of women wanting sex in the other hole, I don't think today should be my introduction, she touches her toe and guides me.

It is 08.00hrs and I am having sex with a strange white female. This petite woman is energetic and I'm soon lost in the translations of raw sex, but over alert and slightly detached from what I'm doing I feel I'm watching myself from a distance, she shudders over and over and then collapses on the floor...fear grips me again, "please are you okay", I ask, she smiles dreamily replies "I've died and gone to heaven", followed by can she see me tomorrow morning same time, "go", she says "you don't have to do the room", handing me an envelope.

I clean up willing my manhood to relax itself, I had been so uptight I haven't climaxed. I quickly get dressed, keeping an eye on her to ensure she doesn't reach for the phone to call the police leaving the room I move on to the next room.

Thankfully it's empty, I go in the toilet and use the liquid soap to create the lubrication to giving myself much needed release, I check the envelope £600, I rejoice then felt scared waiting all morning to be accused of theft, nothing happens. I sure as hell will not be sharing this with Tony; if he is making money this way then I'm bad for business. £600 if I can get several white women like this I am made, no more thoughts of making blue movies in Amsterdam.

After my shift I head to National Bank of Nigeria in Devonshire annex near Liverpool street, open an account and pay in the money, I throw away the receipt. I need to get back to work; I hope the lady is there tomorrow I am so desperate for this not to be a one off. Now that I've had sex I am rearing gagging for more. I check myself as I approach the flat, nothing must be different about me, my new boy on the block just arrived from Lagos image must not slip.

There is a God I am given the same floor and she is still in residence, this time I don't waste time this is what I came to the west for, Naija girls run from my bigness, it will seem this is not the case so far. I am no longer scared but find myself asking her would you like to make love as I hear them say in the movies, to ensure its consensual you see, she says yes, I shag her the way I handled girls backs home, in a way this is me giving her my CV of how I perform.

Its wild all the trashing about when I see she's exhausted I allow myself to finish; it has been 15 minutes of hard strokes, work wise I'm still on track. I quickly rush through her room while she lies slumped. She musters the energy to hand me another envelope then asks me how much I would like whenever we meet. I say whatever she can afford I will be delighted, well with that she asks for the envelope back, shit I've blown it, but she hands me another envelope, I say thank you and ask if I can kiss her, no she says, during sex yes, kissing outside sex no. I take my leave.

No luck of empty rooms today, I can smell sex on me so use a disabled toilet along the corridor to clean up. I don't get a chance to know the amount until I got to the bank a cool £600 again. I am delighted but need to stop thinking of her.....I still don't know her name. How do I expand this, where do I start.

I'm so deep in thought I bump into a tiny petite lady, her shopping scatters all over the pavement I apologize and help to pick things up, she's young probably in her 20's like me, she's smiling at me like she knows me, I am confused as she reassures me all is well then asks if I'll like to join her for coffee. I accept as long as she lets me pay, she then suggests salt beef sandwich, the best in the world is apparently served in Petticoat Lane just round the corner from where we are.

She's Julie, talks and tells me about herself as we walk, she's a designer, designs ball gowns whatever that is, I smile, and when she says evening wear I understand a bit better. I carry her small bag of shopping while we walk, she is asking questions about me and apologizing at the same time, English folks are strange that way. We get the sandwiches and coffee and walk over to a little park she knows, I am in Shoreditch.

Salt beef is pretty nice, Jewish thing I'm told. I tell Julie a little bit about myself not sure why but I tell her my dream of making money using my body, she thinks I mean modeling, when I explain what I meant she turns bright red laughs and states "we are going to get on just fine, you have no idea what a rebel I am".

Julie is my first non- Nigerian friend, I find out she is the daughter of a titled family, pot loads of money, country seat and land and business, but Julie rather than marry into a titled family as expected heads to London and is doing her own thing. I am invited to a show next month, it's called London Fashion week, she will be showing her gowns.

Julie gives me the only sound advice anyone has since I arrived in London she tells me to enrol at college part-time if that's all I can manage. I thank her but I don't want to study I want to shaggie my way rich. Julie goes on to become my best friend, helper and door opener. I begin to see her every day after work, for the first time I am with a female who wants nothing from me but friendship,7 weeks later she gives me a lifeline, she will marry me so I can stay in the country, her flat mate is leaving to go backpacking in Australia, I can move in and split the bills.

We pay £70 for a special license to get married as there are no time slots at her local registry in the next month. We get married at

Lewisham registry, pulling a couple out of a nearby pub to act as witnesses. I tell no one of my marriage. The evening of our marriage I find out what I've always suspected Julie likes women. Julie encourages me to sign up for a workshop to improve my English; it's all about the accent she points out.

I continue to shag my way rich at work, there must be an underground network as the number of wealthy sex starved women slowly grow, within 4 months of starting work I have thousands of pound in my account, in the scheme of things this is chicken change. I want women who will give me tens of thousands, who will take me on trips who will gift me, things that will make me whistle.

I continue to work quietly and diligently my accent also improves, somehow I come to the attention of the Senior managers they would like me to train as a floor supervisor, have I got any GCSE, I have 4 all Passes none of which links in to study anything concrete at University, but this is enough and I am put on the in-house program, Tony hides his unhappiness well.

The college is a farce, I pay £700 per annum and don't attend a single lecture, now that I'm married I send my papers to the Home Office and they promptly returned it with an indefinite leave to remain in the United Kingdom, I have been in London less than a year.

Telling Tony I am moving on is a relief, I have had to hide my new found fortune from a small minded nil goals narrow vision cousin. He gave me all the scenarios of things that will go wrong as an illegal immigrant. I tell him I'm married and have secured leave to remain, he arrived 4 years before me and is furious I have not included him in my plan, we part on rotten terms him feeling used, me happy to get away.

The goodwill gesture of £2000 pounds only adds to his anger but he doesn't refuse the money. I'll be back he says you can't trust white women, you will be a modern slave, dick on duty and on and on he went. I celebrate my departure from Peckham by calling home and giving instructions for the purchase of six plots of land at Eti Osa Local Government at 40.000 Naira a plot, with the exchange rate at 25 to1, I'm good. I tell you for me nothing good can come out of living in South East London.

Shoreditch is a vibrant part of town, with wine and tapas bars, it's collection of old money and new thrill seekers, wealthy Jews and their numerous shops, Brick Lane and the Asian supply of tasty dishes, the endless flocks of Africans shopping in Petticoat Lane market on a Sunday, all is well.

I am nobody, yet slowly I am becoming somebody, with Julie's guidance I began to dress in a manner I noticed quietly commands respect. She shows me the do's and don'ts of London society, I am being polished, groomed and I love it. I struggle with the gay scene which is inevitable given Julie's professional circle of friends and lovers, it is not something I am familiar with, my world has been Epe-Lagos-London. I get a thrill from wandering around shops like Selfridges, Harrods, Harvey Nichols to see Julie's designs on sale for thousands of £'s. Her parents still don't know she is married.

I ask Julie for help on how to crack and access my way to a rich sugar mummy, Julie's hatred of the upper class is such she says it will be her pleasure and revenge. We begin to attend movie and magazine premiers, art gallery functions private parties and races...

This is another world for me a local boy, Julie guides and advices me she gets a crazy thrill from watching upper class idiots fall for my story of an African Prince wishing to go it alone, I am connected to Royalty back home if you count the fact my mum is occasionally summoned to help with the cooking chores if there is a large function at the local Palace.

I am a project for Julie, she has all sorts of hang-ups' about her social status, slavery modern and old, class barriers sexuality equal opportunities, her list of gripes is endless. As for me, I am screwing rich babes in classy surroundings five days a week. Making oodles of money, nil set amounts I simply take whatever I'm given after an encounter.

I am learning about needs, each woman is different while some want me to talk dirty others want complete silence and can't wait for me to leave, some are disgusted by their need for me and will have rough sex in total silence shove an envelope at me and want me out of sight, yet there will be a voice message on my people phone, a mobile which I acquired for this very purpose, always short and to the point, "it will be nice to see you".

I open another bank account, making sure it's at one of the city branches as advised by Julie, these have big money accounts that a little person like me will draw no attention to frequent low deposits.

Exiting the bank one day the senior citizen in front of me stumbles as she's getting to her chauffer driven car, I help steady her and quickly apologize for touching her, stating hope you don't mind me touching you as Julie has coached, "not at all my dear", she replies in that drawl, "it's been a while since anyone, apart from my physician has touched me".

She complements me on my ebony skin, strong facial features, this woman must be 60 years or more, she waves the chauffer away and asks if I will like to join her for tea, she's heading to the Ritz, I don't think so it's one of my usual hunting grounds, I ask if there is anywhere more quiet, she smiles from that smile she knows what I mean.

We get into her car, my 1st ride in a Rolls Royce, I avoid the eyes of the uniformed chauffeur and ensure I speak slowly and clearly pronouncing my words the old English way as taught by, who else but Julie, she buys the story of African Royalty living incognito.

We have tea in a little cafe off Kensington High Street. She is a Lady, her late husband had a seat in Parliament, she has done lots of charitable work in Africa hence her relaxed attitude, I have no doubt she has screwed her way around Africa, the old dame is rubbing her leg against mine under the table, I get her message loud and clear, but can I sleep with someone the age of my grand mama back home.

She cuts straight to the chase, she wants my company discreetly on a regular basis, she laughs at my expression, I clearly will not be her first sugar boy. I tell her I would like that very much, I am given her card and home address, Church Street Sheffield Terrace is marked, I notice a Knightsbridge and Cheltenham address also. I am told to come to Sheffield Terrace. I will do whatever I need to make money I decide, I did not come to England to sightsee. A hole is a hole. 'Oh God, stop looking so shocked woman, I know you're all posh and things but I have to tell it my way not use fancy words to describe what I went through' I nod that I understood wondering how much more of front and back bummie story is remaining'

Julie is great I wish all marriages could be like this a warm relaxed friendly atmosphere. Julie is travelling a lot, I have since met her partner a pretty young woman from the Island of Martinique, they make a lovely pair, I am still rolled out as and when needed. I have heeded all Julie's advice, I make friends with those she gives the nod to, I say and give little or no opinion regarding her business, I value her and she knows it, I am her weapon of mass destruction for the two faced facade of the upper class circle she grew up in.

She is a good judge of character in two years I fail to recognize the Moses who stepped off a plane, I am totally transformed, I smile as I remember her lessons, pick out the fish knife, now the butter knife, wine glass water glass and on and on. Today you take me to any fine dining and you'll think I grew up in that environment. I am bowed in at nightclubs such as Thursday's on Kensington High street, Gulliver's off Oxford Street, me the little back street boy with a big staff.

Chapter 7

I head to Sheffield Terrace her ladyship is waiting, a negligee this scrap of clothing is called, tiny little see through material with a matching flowing top in pastel color, she is lying on a chaise lounge, I kiss her hand as the livered man pours champagne and is dismissed for the night. Again I wonder this might be an abomination in my culture, but she's willing.

I struggle to stay focused as she talks, she is interested in writing a piece on the English dream from an African prospective, to this end she would like me to do some work for her, interviews and help put together the article, those who participate will be given a token amount, my monthly salary will be £4000, I nearly choke on my drink, she's still talking "we must be able to explain your presence", she says and reality dawns. I will provide sex as required on a monthly retainer.

I have no complaints, I explain my work schedule, she smiles, knowingly, that smile of her unnerves me a bit, this woman has seen life, I wonder if I'm about to get played, she asks for my account details and sets up a direct debit there and then, I sign the one page documentation saying I'm a research worker for her said project. No sooner do I put the pen down that she leads me to a lift.

To understand these properties you need to visit Sheffield Terrace, no front garden, a massive communal back garden and lifts inside the house. We arrive in the basement, the entire length of it holds a pool a bar changing room, bathroom with a Jacuzzi bubbling away next to the pool. Lady as I think of her slowly undresses me, she shrugs off her negligee and leads me to the Jacuzzi, no sooner had we stepped into it, she sat me down then sat on me legs astride, for a woman in her seventies, she has the body of one in her fifties, I thank my lucky stars there are no major saggy bits, her breasts are full and a delight to cup, her nipples surprise me, full and thick like an African woman, she is touching me and in no time I am fully aroused, this is a new experience as she is not encouraging penetration but rubbing me on herself, now fast now slow, in no time at all she gasps and falls against me panting and out of breath, I ease myself inside her, I don't move much and can feel her clenching her walls against my manhood, this woman is blowing my mind, money is good, different. I don't move until she starts to rock and drive herself on me.

If you can't swim don't get in a pool, this is not applicable to a Jacuzzi, I can't begin to describe the sensation of water gushing all around and over you while you are been driven crazy by a muscle clenching woman on top of you. It seems like minutes, but I've being screwing for 2 hours it must be the buoyancy of the water. This delightful Lady is going to rock my manhood to death and I am a willing partner all the way.

We head upstairs where she mixes me a drink and lights a joint, Mary mother of Christ I have never in all my years done drugs, here I am in the home of a British aristocrat and she is doing cannabis. She takes a deep drag and smiles at me, she blows the puff on my dick which I think is funny, she leans in and kisses me, slowly at first then intensely, she traces my teeth with the tip of her tongue and then the roof of my mouth all the time caressing me pinching my nipples, running her hands all over, even my arm pit is deliciously sensitive, I didn't know I had so many erogenous zone.

I kiss her back hungry for this level of intimacy that has been denied me for a long time. Only in the West can women have sex with a stranger but refuse a kiss, it is apparently called intimate! I unwrap her from me and lay her on the chaise lounge, spread her legs and slowly begin to massage her labia, I do this without using my finger to penetrate her at any point, I know the nerve endings around the vagina coupled with the clitoris if handled properly will bring a woman to a climax, squirming and speaking the gibberish language of sex in no time, lifting her hip off the bed and urging me on, she starts to tug at my me, I let her but I'm not going to penetrate, she beings to shudder.

I add my tongue to the experience licking and sucking gently getting the pressure just right as she begins her climax, I put my middle finger in her and settle it just behind the head of her clitoris, I am getting something right because this old broad is jerking and twisting and contorting her body all over the place, my hand is at a crazy angle and will lose blood supply if she carries on any longer, she falls back satiated, breathing in a manner that makes an image of her dying during sex flash across my mind.

For a brief second I break out in a cold sweat, when my parents had asked where I was getting large amounts from I told them I won the pools, invested the winnings now sending the dividends home slowly. If this broad was to die I would be on the front page of that paper the Sun and the News of the World, excavation of the world it should be called always exposing something. My ladyship is talking, thanking me for a wonderful evening, she hands me a white envelope, I guess I am dismissed. Would I come over tomorrow there are some people she would like me to meet. Dinner will be served at 7, cocktails at 6pm. I confirm my attendance. I ask the dress code, black tie and jacket.

It's time I will buy a small car, I am in England legit now so nil to worry about the police stopping me I have my Naija international drivers license, I check how much she's given me as the cab carries me towards Shoreditch, £10.000 pounds neat and with the bank band intact. Oh boy I don arrive be this.

Chapter 8

I continue to work as a floor supervisor, the work is easy, the lay is great and funds welcome. I can tell the young men who are also screwing the room guest, the difference is I am so hard faced no one would dare let a thought like that enter their head. This week three of my five floors are booked out to one of the families from the oil rich country with their numerous entourages of family and servants.

I think back to two years ago, I would have been thrilled looking forward to the rich pickings of clothing perfumes and sometimes money left behind. Today I'm uneasy and don't know why, perhaps it's that thing when you're in a room and another language is being spoken. I have been to introduce myself to the headman, a man the shape of an onion who must have been dashing looking when younger.

He is surrounded by others in flowing robes and a lot of chatter is going on, the younger generation who had all arrived covered up in hijab are now milling around dressed in Chanel and more Chanel. There is money, pile after pile, bundles of it and the kids are helping themselves all echoing Harrods. I wait as I have not been dismissed.

One of the younger men addresses me quietly, my friend he says when others have left, where can I catch some fun; I'm in 503 come and see me in 20 minutes. I bow myself out of the room, thinking I need to organize ladies for a private party, Ismael the door man will sort that out once I have clarity regarding what his taste is.

I knock on 503 promptly, this young prince is at most late twenties, he gets straight to the point, I like you, well I like you I say, not quite realizing where we're heading. You are very sexy, like I like you, are okay with me liking you. I say I am, what can you say in these circumstances, he begins to disrobe while talking, "We are here for 5 days you good to me, I good very good to you, you like I give for you".

What is my view on homosexuality zilch, I never thought I would ask myself that question, women yes men, hell I don't know and don't have time to question as the prince, as I think of him in my head, is now unzipping me and worshiping my balls kissing each and caressing the other in turn, he takes one in his mouth and gently sucks, I am shocked senseless by the sensation of a man with soft womanlike hands nuzzling me, is this not where I kick the shit out of him and storm out, what is keeping me.

My massive erection the buzz of wealthy folks who can't get enough of me or am I into everything, I correct my mind and tell it it's all about the money, this is just another errand just as he clamps his warm lips on my hood, the effect of this feminine man is driving me crazy then I start to panic, I cannot go through with someone banging my ass, I tense and he senses it, "not me", he says "you", I don't understand, he pulls a condom and puts it on me, reality dawns I will do the shagging.

The word virgin comes to mind, pushing and pushing until you gain entry, well that's what it was like, except this virgin had a smooth body and a set of male genitalia, as I begin to move he rocks, trashes, moans contorts and gibbers away in his language. I keep my mind on the busy hard long strokes, I realize I am punishing him, enjoying myself excited but puzzled by my lack of disgust, all this different questions in my mind at once, if he senses it he doesn't show it, within 5 minutes he's done and collapses on the bed. I take the condom off ensuring I flush it myself, he is waiting smiling coy like a girl would, he offers me a brown envelope, please he says in halting English "come tomorrow morning", I say yes and leave,. In the staff toilet I look in the envelope £50.000 I shit myself worried he's made a mistake with the amount, I wait in anguish for the call to come through asking me to return to 503, nothing happens and the shift ends with me servicing one of my regular ladies the £600 crew as I refer to them.

I seem to have a semi hard on these days and only need a recipient to harden.

Julie is home, I ask her advice regarding money, I want to clean my money up by investing it, she suggests setting up a business that will link in with the Nigerian trade in Petticoat lane market, I can't imagine what but she has links via her own fashion work.

She makes a couple of calls and declares I need to set up a courier service for those buying large quantities of materials to ship back to the West African countries. That week I am Julie's home work, we submit paperwork to register a limited company in her honor and to say thanks I used the name Julie's. Each textile trader Julie knows has agreed to recommend us, I find a small room under the arches in Shoreditch, I call in a favour with a friend at Nigerian Airways, he talks me through what to do, in no time I have all I need, all my cargo's will go via Nigerian Airways, smoothing the way cost me less than £5000.

I speak to Tony, I need two older men, possibly semi-retired who need the extra funds, I arrange with a local taxi firm for a hatchback and a dedicated driver at the firm to do my runs. White van, Industrial scale, packing boxes, tapes, and markers all purchased and ready. We will work Sunday's to Thursdays. All airport runs will be on Fridays. To ensure nil difficulties my company will only ship collection with be via paperwork from Muritala Mohammed, I have no intension yet of having a Lagos office. I have been in London less than 5 years from a polygamous home I don't need any unwanted attention. In a nutshell this is how my freight company started from that 50 grand fuck money.

I continue to work at the hotel the money I make there a week is crazy, my safety net is I keep to the same client list; any new lady gives me that smile I ignore, not putting anything past undercover cops or the News of the World tabloid.

Chapter 9

I continue to visit her ladyship, the surroundings in her home can only be described as opulent, and like all predators she had a surprise for me. Summoned as usual I turn up to find there are two dinner guests, lady this and Duchess of something or the other, it's as if I'm the guest they need to honor, I am regaled with their escapades from round the world, I listen attentively and make all the right noises. Champagne flows freely followed by cognac after dinner, I am loose and don't protest when the Duchess starts to rub herself against me, It finally dawned on me I'm desert.

It's the first time I will have multiple sex, there are arms and legs, tongues and fingers breasts and pubic hair in my face, losing touch of what belongs to whom I have sex with whatever is presented, I am a little shocked to see they are also pleasuring each others, without knowing their age you will make them late 40's. I truly lived up to the daft image Western women have of black men, I reverted to the primeval man cocked and wild, I screwed like tomorrow was not going to come. The ooh arghs sighs, screams scratches and body plunging spurred me on. There is nothing as heady as women appreciating being handled, no pretence just pure straight enjoyment.

I watch as they lie sated in that post coital glow, their combine age comes to my mind and I almost laugh out loud, but they are throwing money at me and I couldn't care less, besides these were not women who screwed around they are frustrated widows all making do with dildo's until I came along. I am making serious money now. I am okay if they want to patronize me, you see it's about taking as much from them as I can.

Tomorrow I am opening a dollar account as instructed by one of the American ladies, it will make it easy for her to gift me whenever she wants.

In 5 years I have come a long way, the first thing I did right was to avoid the Nigerian crowd, there is no way you can do what I do and keep it quiet. From time to time I envy Julie and her partner, there for each other day in day out, me on the other hand giving sex on demand to ladies of all ages, most of whom wouldn't acknowledge me outside the shagging arena.

You know what I am content, my account continues to grow, my small business has taken off I have an accountant, the one way you can piss her majesty off is not to pay tax, I am making enough cash in hand money to be honest with Inland Revenue. I treat myself to a Peugeot 205 small and inconspicuous.

My phone pings a message, I check's it's my little middle-eastern friend flying in tomorrow wants to hit the Casino on Edgware road. I am game, the thought of this little harmless begging man no longer frightens me, despite all his money, I am in control when with him, he says yes to anything I suggest and introduces me as an associate. Not sure associate in what.

Last time we went to a casino, it was a private place in Berkeley Square, I sat quietly while he wasted £350.000 in 2 hours, next morning he still gave me 50 grand, endless money these oil rich guys, I'm appreciative of his gifts, I have several watches from him all ranging from $15-60.000 it's always a watch. I look forward to seeing him I enjoy the control and forbiddances of our actions.

What have I become, I am not a male gigolo, I do not make the first move, I am a machine, tune me and I function tell me to go and I go say stop and I stop all dick and little choice because of my focus, I want your money, you can call me what you like.

Things cannot continue in this manner without a hiccup, I have been expecting it but the source throws me, If you know England you will know the country is ruled by a few elite, their network is scary and powerful, if you're one of them they take care of you all obstacles removed.

I am summoned by the Area team manager Mark an aggressive male, he tells me to take a seat and offers me coffee, if white man offers you a drink in his office begin to beg him ask what you've done wrong. I decline, he stands looking at me for a long time, I return his gaze with respect occasionally casting my eye down to show subordination.

Two feet appear in front of me, Mark pulls me up and smiles at me, I begin to feel dread, I like you, I like what you've being doing, this is the score, you cut me my own action and we're cool. I ask how much he wants; he laughs and caresses my chest, then cups my balls. I want you.

I have been with the prince how difficult will it be with Mark, he is still talking, "all I want is once a week in my office, I won't take too much of your time". I am trying hard to gain control and say "yes, okay, no worries whatever", I am panicking and blabbing, something is not quite right.

I am too muddled in my mind to make sense of things until Mark unzips me and takes me in his mouth, this is nothing like the prince, I feel revulsion, this is different at 6"3 I am a good build but something dreadful is going to happen to me right now today.

I am panting with fear, if I attack him I am done for, this is London. Mark lubricates me puts on a condom and then the most excruciating pain begins, I clench my fist as the pain hits me, he is not gentle but violent like his nature.

It's over within minutes this hole that was designed for things to pass out of not things go up, I am in pain and a blind rage, I can feel a leak from my back passage, I use the wet flannel he gives me to clean myself and hold on to it, even in the depth of this craziness and violation I am thinking of how to survive and preserve myself. I pocket the flannel. He is looking at me like I'm dinner, I leave without a word knowing if I stayed any longer I will attack him, as I walk out a plan comes to mind despite the immense pain I'm in. I can hardly sit down and spend the shift on my feet.

What do you do when one bastard is abusing you, go for a man higher up the rank than him? Simple but effective, one of the directors, the pink shirt type had tried to befriend me some months back, I'm going to seek him out and use him to keep an animal away from me. It takes me a good 4 days to be able to sit comfortably. Julie is away thank God as I would have to explain why I'm standing even to eat. I seek François my pink wearing shirt director out, he is delighted to bump into me in the corridor and accepts my invitation to come and try some African food.

I take François to mama Calabar, he swears edikikon is to die for and wants to try lots more dishes if I will bring him back. After 3 bottles of Gulder he is ripe to hear what I have to say, I tell the fool I'm not sure about my sexuality, that I've slept with women and one man willingly, I'm in an open marriage and have a problem. He is more than eager to help, I explain about someone at work harassing me for sex, I ask for his advice and protection, I am careful not to name who it is. Francois suggests a simple solution if I won't name names, have lunch together in the staff canteen, so whoever it is sees we are an item and backs off, simple yet I know it will work and it does spot on.

While Mark was watching me like a hawk in the staff canteen I make sure I touch Francois's hand and act like he is the only one in the room giving him my undivided attention, Mark catches me on my own just as I left work and called me a bitch but leaves me alone after that. Now I think I am saddled with Francois, but the reality is he goes on to become as important to me as Julie.

Yet I can never be the same again, I continue to service my ladies the prince and an unending repertoire of sex needing women, I have money, I am quietly laundering my own money via my business, the 6 houses in Lagos are complete and given out to an oil company for rent as accommodation for their directors we have a tenancy agreement for ten years.

I am old in my mind and spirit. I am lonely and isolated from my people; I have no visitors from home nor am I guest to others. My spirits dip. Both Julie and Francois notice and try to cheer me up.

Chapter 10

Salvation came in the form of a Nigerian babe called Helen, some Nigerian politicians were in town and camped at our hotel, and where they are the babes will follow. I have lost my Nigerian accent and blend in name and manners. Helen was trying to locate a suite on my floor I showed her the door, I am amused when she hands me a £50 note, this is not the norm.

An hour later I am doing the rounds when I see the door to the suite open and then close as if in panic, I knock on the door, Helen opens it, she's panicking and drags me in, can I help, he was alright now he's gasping and saying his chest hurts. I run in the bedroom a very prominent Nigerian man is lying naked on the bed, taking shallow labored breaths.

I tell Helen to get dressed and get out; I seat him up and then lay him in the recovery position and cover his modesty. Helen is out the door before you can say bob's you're uncle. I call the in-house doctor and health team, they are there in minutes once they take over I leave, my story is I was walking past and he opened the door in distress. I finish my shift and go home.

Next day there is a message to go to the suite, Helen opens the door she thanks me, Mr. big clears his throat and commends me for my fast thinking, I like you young man, you are the sort of person I would like around me. I thank him and back out of the room with a grand hand shake. What is wrong with rich people, why is thank you not enough, it's like a fear of them owing you something so give money and we're even.

Helen shakes my hand and passes her details to me clever girl. Helen will be the only Nigerian girl to get close to me, physically mentally and psychologically, I hide nothing from her but today she is in a long stay secure mental institute.

Helen an incredibly beautiful girl was working the diplomatic and rich Nigerians would you call her a call girl, no, she was me in a female version; wanted money knew the fools would part with it sex or no sex and milked it. A Yoruba girl the sixth child in a family of eight she lived a life only some can dream about. Her one mistake in life was to fall in love with a married man.

I called Helen out of curiosity and accepted her invitation to dinner at her place. Helen lives in a flat known as the Tower one of her wealthy suitors had bought it for her in her name so nil worries of homelessness.

She tells me about herself over dinner, I find her honesty refreshing, a product of a broken home who had being lucky to be born in England she took off back here when she was 18 under the promises of a Prominent Hausa man who spoilt her rotten but only screwed her back passage. She got a flat and enough money out of him before he tired of her and moved on.

Other wealthy Nigerians followed, she milks her beauty and shagged herself rich just like me. Helen asked me to spend the night, for the first time in 7 years I cuddle up to a female and sleep a dreamless peaceful sleep, that resulted not in sex but the closest I will come to lovemaking in the early hours of dawn, Helen cried nonstop, I understood where she was at. In our line of business emotions are forbidden, besides I don't want to be her next money target.

I have been in London seven years and have added no qualifications to the O'levels I brought from Naija apart from the managerial course at work. I try my luck at London University; I am accepted for a part-time degree in media studies based on passing a foundation course. Julie is delighted, this amazing English woman who gave me stay, a home and goes about everyday life peacefully with me but feels not one ounce of attraction to me, I am in awe of her.

I continue my work at the hotel and expand my freight forwarding business, opening a small office at Cemetery street Ebutte Metta, just one room in an office block, for an extra amount we will do the clearing and folks can collect locally. I am able to do this because one of the old men wants to relocate to Lagos, his role will be required for one day only pickup from airport on Saturday morning, customers pick up between 1-3pm leaving an empty room not needing security staff during the week.

I have a difficult conversation with Julie I would like to buy a house. Her reaction is positive we begin to go house hunting, advice rained at me about locations, having the right postcode. Ironically we find a 4 bedroom detached crumbling place in Notting Hill, not yet a fashionable postcode but up and coming, I can easily afford the asking price, it will need almost the same amount to bring it up to scratch. I have come a long way. I continue to shag me rich as I put it, except I am rich but not enough, at work I am now a supervising manager, I know François pulled strings for this, it is now impossible for Mark to mess with me if anything he looks terrorized whenever he sees me, he's made a big mistake and I am waiting for revenge my day will come and it's sooner than I imagined.

François and I are sleeping together if you can call it that, he gives me head and I shag him. I am hardened to my way of life I am also ruthless and will do anything to ensure nothing less than £5000 is coming in via my shag me rich role weekly. Elderly senior girls, maidens, titled, self-made, inheritance winners, oil rich Texans, shag the husband kiss the wife you name it I'm doing it.

Francois is a gem he introduces me to a buddy of his in Harley Street, make sure you are well he says. I heed his words and get a full health check up every 6 months. Life continues at much the same boring pace, occasional I'm invited to private parties in London or the home country, it's on one of these occasions I exert my revenge on Mark.

A famous film star is in town staying at our hotel but with several homes in London, he is into babes but is also a voyager, he asks if I would like to attend his party and put on a show, my fee is £60 grand. I eagerly agree and call Helen. Helen will supply four ladies she suggests I get six men, three of them must be gay or ACDC. I easily find these in Soho, making sure they are over 18 I tell them it's a private party they are up for it, I will give them a grand each, and pick-up is at 10pm. Helen will drive down with her entourage keeping in touch by phone. Not sure what to expect we arrive at the given address to find ourselves outside a country estate. we are directed to the outhouse and quickly setup things, there is a small stage and the lighting is dimmed.

A little after 1am people begin to arrive and take a seat round the little stag, and who should walk in with the other guest but Mark. Keeping my voice low I tell Helen my plan, she walks out on the stage naked with one of the sweet boys and asks for a volunteer, just as I expected Mark is desperate to get his hands on the new flesh.

He is lead on stage undressed and quickly blindfolded, lent across a chair hands tied together and then to the chairs, legs spread and each tied to the chair the chair is then tilted forward to rest on the table, chair legs are then tied to table legs. Mark's boxers are stuffed in his mouth then the fun begins.

I am going to humiliate and make this shit of a person suffer; he is a big man so I make sure he is securely tied. The room is silence with anticipation sexual tension cuts hard, I beckon the boys forward while Helen has started to rub herself on Mark something I know will disgust him no end, the boys start to touch him he is making animal noises not sure what or who to respond to, he gains an erection and looses it equally fast, his brain and body in over drive.

This continues and those in the room quickly pick up the tension but are unsure what is causing it, the girls start to circulate and work the audience the boys leave Mark alone and seek out lovers in the audience, I put a condom on, I jock Mark without laying a finger on him and move for each of the three boys to take a turn, I check Mark to make sure he is okay, he looks outraged and a little frightened, while the room has descended in chaos of shag me shag you, I ensure for the next two hours there is someone touching Mark. Mark is outraged, that is all I needed to see a larger dose of the medicine he dished out.

Sex, Charlie, Alcohol, Spiff, a great combination for most party folks to fall asleep. We departed just before 4am, with Mark still tied blind folded and spread like a dual carriage way. The Soho boys are happy, Helen and her girls are happy, I am ecstatic. I spend the night with Helen. Opportunity to revenge is the best sleep aid.

Chapter 11

A State Governor is in town next week Helen wants me to meet him, this big boy needs to move money out of Nigeria and needs a discreet person/s who can help, he will reward them handsomely. I am up for it. I meet Mr Governor a few days later, a tall pot bellied rather loud alcohol consuming man who confused me when he excused himself to pray. Helen and I grinned at each other like a pair of play ground chimps, the hypocrite.

Do you know how to buy house here he asks, I confirmed I have recently purchased one, he would like me to purchase several houses and gives me the location, this Northern fart can't pronounce the names of the areas, he will give me £15.000 for each purchase. I am game. The first property is in Barnes, in no time I have the promised money. I purchased a total of 14 properties ranging from Chislehurst in Kent, Central London and a pokey little flat in Star street off Edgware road that came in at a cool £700.000 the heart of Arab London.

Helen and I are still have the occasional sex, we talk most days, when I try to broach the idea of investments she shrugs me off, I can see the bulk of the money she makes goes on her appearance, this fine babe was doing weave-on before south east babes knew what a weave-on was. I looked at her £300 YSL tops Chanel shoes, top of the range perfumes, she will not listen and I do not push.

Then she gets involved with an Oba and drags me in, I begin to question my association with Helen, on my own I was doing great with my scheme, in Helen's company I am slowly becoming a do this boy for the rich it doesn't sit well with me. The Oba has several of his wives with him, the house in Hampstead is on a private road and when I asked to use the bathroom I had difficulties finding my way back so many corridors and twists and turns in this house.

The Olori's say nothing as Helen scrimps and scraps to the Oba, I watch silently as he praises her telling his wives this young girl is a mover and shaker, everything that needs organizing she will do without me moving an inch, I watch as this man who is old enough to be her granddad salivates after her.

The Olori's take their leave they are going out, no sooner does the car take off that he has Helen's nipple in his mouth, her ass latched onto his small stumpy manhood; I nearly laugh out as I quietly excuse them and go to another reception room towards the back of the house.

Watching them has given me a hard-on I became aware of being watched , there is a 5th Olori, young fresh and clearly gagging for sex, she walks across to me without a word, hikes her dress up and eases her pant aside, I get behind her and penetrate, now I'm getting it for free, this young ebony beauty, I'm blown away as we come together, is she faking or am I so used to being a show boy I make sure I match her rhythm, she moves away from me, this woman has not said a word the whole time.

I clean myself up and move to another lounge, this one now smells of sex. A Thai looking man comes in with a tray of coffee and finger food, this is where the Oba finds me. I look at this giant of a man, and know that traditionally what I have just done will cost the life of both the Olori and I but as they say in the west only if you get caught. The Royal family are here to prepare for a wedding; all the goods will need shipping am I up to it. I assure the Oba I will not disappoint and take my leave.

Helen continues to introduce me to the movers and shakers of the current regime back home, to refer to them as money bag is an insult as a bag can contain money; these guys have shitloads that bags can't contain. The big girls were no better; slowly I had started to get drawn in on the big babe scene. I realize the reason I've kept things to white foreign women is the care they take of their physic, I can lift any of them up and impale them on me, if I try that with any of the Nigerian senior babes I came across I will need a back brace for the rest of my life.

I am no longer an ass person and to have these mass wobbles which is highly favored by Nigerian men being rolled for me is difficult as it does nothing for me. Try grabbing an ass that means you have to spread your arms to accommodate it, then try finding the opening, I am convinced there are times I have simply shagged the top of thighs. But big babes are not complaining and their generosity is scary, through the Nigerian senior babes I begin to acquire shares, land, stocks, you name it from Coca-Cola, PZ, Shell, Elf if it's floated I have shares.

Chapter 12

Nigerians give away national treasure like it's their personal collection. I am invited to my 1st Nigerian Embassy function in New York; Helen who was kicking it with a big boy solider had also being invited. Arriving in New York I am met by my current squeeze, she is Ambassador to some country or other to me she is a drain, I have had women with healthy appetites, this woman is like an every ready battery, I made sure I got plenty of sleep on the plane.

We are in a hotel where from the suite I can see the ice rink of the Rockefeller centre and the flags of the united nation, we are off as this woman on heat is already sliding her hands between my legs, business is business, she gives I deliver. When I picked up my travel document an envelope containing $9500 was waiting. In the limo ride into town she gave me another envelope a fat one this time as she hasn't left me alone I can't check the amount, it will be crass and tacky to check money in front of the giver.

I begin my slow shag to China, if I don't pace myself she will be cranky, most effective thing with her is to let her sit on you and ride, face me face away but her on top doing all the work, she'll work up a sweat exhaust herself and I'll still be asking her to give me head when I know she's pooped.

This is how I want to live, surrounded by opulence, lying on pristine sheets, eating and drinking food that would cost others a week's wage at a sitting. She orders dinner and attends to calls while we eat, an octopus woman her hands are constantly caressing me, my nipples get sucked with wine in her mouth, it's an unusual sensation and she's delighted with the response, food is abandoned as she climbs on me.

A call from the Perm Sec does not halt her grinding in a circular motion that she likes so much. I am young and in my prime, Viagra has not yet being invented if it was available I would fall back on it as insurance I am in for 5 days of rough sex, I hope she has a few meetings which will give me time for recovery.

My sleep is broken just as I expected, this woman in her late fifties with such high energy, I breathe a sigh of relief when she hurriedly get dressed and leaves for a meeting, she's be back at 3pm. I get up and shower then move into the small room in the suite to ensure the cleaning can be done without disturbing me, I put in a wake-up call for 2.30pm. I sleep the sleep of the dead and I'm up dressed and ready when she returns.

We are going shopping and head to the Jewish shops on 47th street. Babe buys enough jewels to bring home the stark fact that Nigeria is a stinking rich oil country and no one in the government can finish spending the money however much of it they help themselves to.

She insists on a diamond and ruby encrusted chain and cross for me, at $47, 000. I am not impressed but accept gracefully, I am in for a lot of shag me happy.

We head to Saks on 5th Avenue and continue in much the same manner, how many handbags does a woman need? Dresses and suits that came in at several grand each. She buys a Judith Lieberman crystal purse for $15.000. I quickly lost count of how much she is spending, all raw cash with bundles of travelers checks should they be needed.

This babe will draw the attention of the law to me in an innocent way that spooked me. The following morning she gives me a bundle of traveler's checks, in meetings all day would 1 like to do my shopping. $70,000 in traveler's checks. I decide to use the bank at Macy's to change some. I present $10,000 and my passport, I am clearly not alert as at no time did I see the man reach to press any alarm, but press he must have because two security agents and a senior member of staff ask to speak to me.

How did I acquire my checks, I keep a cool exterior and ask them if they have checks missing, my coolness pays off, I explain I am with the Nigerian team here for the Independence day function tonight should they want to check with the High Commission, thank god I was listening when Ambassador babe stated to whoever she was talking to that Central Bank had issued the travelers checks. I quote this to the team in front of me and made out I'm feeling just a tad discriminated against.

Nothing scares an American like a law suit and bad publicity while talking they've been doing their checks, I am thanked for my patience and the teller is told to go ahead and cash my checks, I inform them all I have a total estacode of $70,000 so I will be back, the fool manager practically bows to me. I went back and changed the rest there as I had threatened and was treated with excellent customer service, I put all this money into my $ account.

The few days in New York flew by; at the dinner and dance at the embassy I ensure a low profile and stayed out of the camera lenses. Time to depart, I thank my senior girl and head to the airport, I am grateful for her booking 1st class, if she hadn't I would have paid the difference to upgrade. I don't know why but I feel rough slightly feverish.

By day three of my return I realized I'm not jetlagged or exhausted, I feel really rough, I'm not going to my GP, I make an appointment at Harley Street, blood screening showed I have STD, I don't get it I have always used a condom, New York babe must have the infection and passed it on pre-sex with all the rubbing round on me. In less than a week she spent almost $200,000 on me was I naive to think she's not screwing other guys and they're clearly screwing others and so on.

The news of Aids/HIV has just broken and it's making me jumpy we associate it with unprotected sex and blood transfusion. I start a course of anti-biotic and have an Intramuscular injection to boost things along, I am told to abstain from sex, impossible with the hungry birds at work. I call in sick; it's the first time in an 8 year career so it's okay.

I call ambassador babe who thinks I'm calling to thank her, I give her the courtesy of asking if she can talk freely, I tell her my symptoms and the visit to the doctor, diagnoses and advice her to get treatment, I keep it sweet, she apologizes profusely and doesn't try to hip blame on me. Be more careful my darling I say. I need an Oscar nomination, what I really wanted to do is cuss the bitch out but one does not bite the hand that is currently holding food.

Chapter 13

Speaking of food the breakfast Moses ordered finally arrives we've asked for yam pottage, it's clear they cooked it from scratch with the famous fried palm oil stew with assorted meat cut small. I look at Moses he's aged while telling me his journey, I reach out and squeeze my friend's hand, shocked at his language and too much description but accepting it as this is how events went for him. At 54 our lives has been an absolute nightmare but we're still standing as they say, just with a different set of reasons and strength propelling each person.

We tuck into our food enjoying the deliciousness of proper Naija cooking. We eat in silence for a few moments, Moses had opened up and I can see him trying hard to put some new protective layers on. I reach for his hand again, bros it's me I say, if we can't talk to each other then who can we talk to. He smiles in appreciation and we continue eating drawing admiring glances from both men and women. We are affluent and it shows.

Moses mention of STD has put me in a bad place, I have had these infections a total of seven times, the first at the age of 16, I had no idea what was wrong just that the bastard who was forcing me to have sex took me to a local clinic and insisted I had to take the tablets given to me for ten days and accept the course of injections.

I itched like mad and smelt like rotten fish down below, the discharge a nasty green color. The second time I deliberately give it to as many men as I could, I wasn't asking or looking for sex, I had no choice, once the bad fish smell started I knew what had happened I then went with the flow, all the men who slept with me I went to one by one, they used me as they normally would, except this time I had a secret let them try and explain it to their wives and girlfriends.

At the end of the second week when I couldn't stand the smell and itchiness anymore I went for treatment, when asked how I contacted the disease, I told them a visiting relative who has since returned to Italy had forced me to have sex and denied sleeping with anyone else. I shake my head to clear it; I really need to return to the present.

In keeping with the home tune, I order Bournvita, Moses begins to laugh, you can take the girl out of Lagos but no fit remove Lagos from the girl. My friend and I are back from our dark place. Moses rubs his elbows and arms then crosses it across his chest, I know that defensive posture and my mind wanders briefly to a very sick person deliberate self harm, suicide attempts, and rock bottom.

I'm tumbling into that dark prison with no key while sipping my drink in silence, I try but I can't pull myself back, Moses is quiet, lost in his own bubble. As for me between the age of 7 and 10 I was used. An array of uncles, relative's acquaintances of my parents, the toughest thing in life is a mother who does not believe and calls you a lair in front of your abuser, thus giving them the go ahead to carry on, almost legitimizing and giving consent to it. I become familiar with man smells different but all had one thing in common their ugly act on a defenseless child.

My small hands learnt to hold different size body parts. Age 11 I got some light relief sent to boarding house at a Federal Government College, a mixed college where the senior girls were cruel but kept us safe from the boys. I began to dread school holidays, it meant I had to go home, home meant abuse under the nose of a mother who didn't see it or chose to ignore it.

She would send me to visit various relatives as if she couldn't bear to be under the same roof as me. Each destination I went to an abuser was waiting if not the man of the house, the male children of the house or the servants of the house. It was like a punishment if your family didn't want you then you get what you deserve.

One elderly divorced woman comes to mind, I didn't know women could be cruel, she would ask me to rub her legs as they ache, one night she laid on the bed I rubbed and rubbed until I was practically rubbing her buttocks when she rolled over the only thing I didn't do was put my hand in her vagina I rubbed everywhere she said ached.

Her granddaughters are holidaying the same time as me she doesn't ask them to fetch a cup more less rub her legs. I struggle to understand my crime as her foreign home help from Cameroon puts a Bata shoe carrier bag over himself and rubs himself against me until he gets the release he wants. My life really is over I am empty and walk around like a ghost. Was it going to get better hell no.

I meet Bassey, his nickname during one of my school breaks. My first male friend, we talked and talked on the phone, went to Falomo shopping centre for ice cream sundaes, I feel the closest to normal, we correspond when I return to boarding school next time I will see him is the long summer break.

Bassey and I picked up where we left off talking laughing discussing music likes and dislikes, a favorite one is my fear of earthworms, choosing to remain indoors when it rains for fear of encountering one. Bassey invites me to lunch his sister and step mum will be present I have a safety net so I say yes. Lunch is simple rice beans dodo selection of meats nothing fancy; desert was the little cupped iced cream from Samco.

Bassey his sister and I went to sit in a lounge demarcated as the children's lounge. I thought I had spots until I saw his sister, face like an un-tarred road, at some point she left and we continued to listen to music. I was so caught up in my first human contact that didn't frighten or abuse me I was in some sort of euphoric state until Bassey shoved a container of earthworms under my nose.

I sat trembling; don't make a sound he hissed. Follow me, I followed him to his room, he made me take my clothes off and lie on the bed, he took his off after leaving the container of earthworms on the bedside cabinet near my head, he them forced himself on me careful to keep a hand over my mouth, I couldn't scream if I tried, I laid there a piece of shit I had become a sex object, he didn't want to be my friend he wanted to abuse me, I was 14 and he was 16.

When he finished he told me to stop crying and stated he was surprised I hadn't done it before as I was so tight. Then he raped me again. I got dressed and went back to the lounge, I realized at that point he had locked the door to the stairs and pocketed the key, I went to the balcony it was here he found me, I told him I wanted to go, he said he had to do it again before I left, I climbed over the railing, "I will jump if you don't open the door and let me go" I said. We were on the first floor of their huge 2 story building.

This appeared to frighten him and he begs me to come in, he will not touch me and I can leave. Thus worm-man as I named him ended my foray into friendship with the opposite sex. Today he is a big boy in Lagos, only I know the Psychopath he is. If curses are answered mine was, as I rode home in the taxi that faithful day I asked God not to give him children. To date he has none from his marriage.

An image flashes in my mind I must have been about 8 years old, an uncle of my mum came to visit, this man is well known and respected, a decision maker who nothing happens in the realm of politics if he doesn't give his nod of approval, I walk past the sitting room and see him leaning his back on the side board, he has my mum in an embrace, I wonder for a split second if she had also been sexually abused but can't imagine her putting up with that nonsense.

This was about the time I tried to tell her something was wrong, a foreign photographer was flown in to Lagos to take pictures of all the prominent families, when it was our turn I was asked to go with him and the driver to see Mum at work, in the lift he rubbed his hand under my skirt all the way to my bottom and back, I told mum as soon as I went into her office, her reply was "you must be mistaken, he would never do anything like that", as if she knew this piece of garbage personally. Kolo mentality at play a white man would never do such a thing. White man next to God. That woman is so going to get it once I get her home from the hospital.

Chapter 14

Moses is speaking and I drag myself back from the depth where I've gone.
Something has to change he says, I don't catch gonorrhea in my youth can you imagine! Anyway I got over it but things pitted out with the senior girl who was generous to the last to ensure I kept my mouth shut.
Around this time the 1st of many Naija gossip magazines started up. How I managed to be photographed and end up in Hello Magazine, Timeout and the News of the World Sunday supplement is beyond me, be there I was at the premier of Superman the Movie and the private party after at Brown's. I am with François and a few others of the regular guys and ladies. I stand out only because I am the only black dude, at 6"3 I am not easy to hide.

Tony my cousin tracks me down, he turns up at the hotel unlike me he is constantly on the move still has no papers and is waiting until he has been in the country illegally for 14 years to apply for his stay. Small guys small dreams. Tony who had helped and supported me on my arrival needs my help. I offer him a job at Shoreditch with the shipping and forwarding.
My cousin is a bastard and an asshole, first he vex that I have a company and couldn't ask him if we could go halves, within a week he is talking about expansion, an office in Peckham, Brixton, Dalston to capture the Najia trade. I tell him things are good the way they are, I am under the radar of the tax man and wish to keep it that way.
I speak to Francois he can get Tony a job at Heaven's Nightclub under the Arches at Charring Cross fulltime 5 days a week if he pulls strings, Tony looses the plot, him! work in a gay night club God forbid.
I stick to my guns and offer him £300 a week working in Shoreditch anything else would have raised his suspicion. I tell him nothing about my private life and feel cornered when he invites me to his daughters naming ceremony. I have to go, nil choice. If you have even been to a party in Peckham you will understand my dread.

Over the hill senior girls, desperate young ones, hungry young men who will drop you where you are for a few bucks. All loud dancing to Fuji Garbage and Shine Peters with a dose of Kollington thrown in.

I arrive with Helen on my own would make me a target, we are laden with presents for the baby including the custom of an envelope for the baby. Helen and I have a great night, we reconnect with all we don't want and use the evening as an exercise to talk through what we don't want to return to. Southeast London is one of them the Yoruba scene is one of them, parties every weekend is another, friends from the Naija circle is a no no. We watch as people who can barely afford it spray $ while someone has the job of gathering it in a black rubbish bag.

The food is good and there are some refreshing people but conversation quickly dies out as there is only so much you can talk to a bus driver or security guard, kitchen help and key job cleaner about. I see a few faces from the chamber person service but keep my distance.

Surprisingly Tony causes me no problem he's getting paid £300 for 28 hours work each week. My contact with him makes me realize it's time to visit Nigeria, I have been away for 12 years, Odo Otin village is not exactly my cup of tea but that's where my parents insisted they wanted to return to live, in Epe local Government so that's where I built a house for them.

Chapter 15

In the years I've been away I've sent money home to my parents monthly, covered their bills and educated my remaining siblings, my father is apparently very proud of the house he built with the money I sent. I am dreading it but feel it must be done, I ask Helen if she has plans to visit Lagos, she will go for the fun of it if I'm visiting.

My Sheffied Terrace lady is frail but still requests the pleasure of my company once a month, we never did write any article but interestingly Julie and her were the two guests at my graduation. Now when I visit my role had changed, she still likes sex but a gentler form, touching caressing, holding her and occasionally when she feels able I penetrate, her sense of humor makes her great company, I have a soft spot for her and sense she feels the same. Her two friends have passed away so her secret is safe. Her staff are used to seeing me.

I ask her about relatives, she laughs and describes nieces and nephews who have no time for her but eagerly wait for her demise, they are in for a shock she smiles knowingly always the same statement they are in for a shock. I fantasize about her leaving me the Sheffield Terrace property.

When she goes into a hospice I am her only visitor, her staff dismissed back to the various agencies they came from. It has been a strange relationship, shagging, caring for and nursing a woman old enough to be my grandmother, I am grateful, in the years I've known her nothing short of over a million bucks of her money has passed through my hands if I am not mentioned in her will that is fine.

When she passes away her will confirms what I have always thought, white folks are crazy with a capital C. I am described as an adopted son from Africa and given a property in Bulawayo Zimbabwe and a cash amount of £300.000 I sat quietly and watched the drama unfold, her estate after taxes and whatever is worth a staggering £98,000 000, she gives all the nieces and nephews who have crawled out of the woodwork the same £300,000.

Millions to various churches she's being affiliated with then the word Battersea Dog's home is mentioned I sit up straight with the others in the room, the Lawyers are the only ones with a blank face, I know it's time to leave and make my exit as the room erupts in shouts of contesting the will, was she sane and of sound mind, where is the proof she wasn't coerced, did she have mental capacity.

I left feeling sad for a long time, at least I was honest in my dealings with her, I gave her time she gave me money, these guys had not done one visit to her in all the years I've known her, well her revenge is as spectacular as her. I never returned to the neighborhood and found a guy Fidelis, who was happy to take what turned out to be a 17 bedded farm house with endless acres of land in Bulawayo off my hands for £50.000.00

Moses' mentions of the will makes me think of the other woman, Mummy Funtan, a childhood friend of my mother who truly loved me and gave me glimpses' of what a loving mother does, my stays with her were short, she protected me like she knew what was wrong, she fed me, kept me close and talked to me, she acknowledge what I had to say as important.

Once my mother realized how much I had come to mean to this woman, who had two children of her own she ensured my contact with her was limited, till this moment I don't know where she is, my mother makes out she can't remember where this amazing woman now resides.

The lazy days with her shopping, cooking, gossiping and seeing the gentle love and affection between her and her husband and their endless guests, who like me adored them showed me how I know my life would have been so different if I had grown up in that environment. On my return home my mother would go through my things and take away the best, whatever money I was given went in her pocket with a token small amount given back to me. Daddy and Mummy Funtan always said as one of their child all they have also belongs to me. That statement sure made my mother mad, she looked down her nose at me in that familiar way, shit filth, get out of my sight is easy to translate.

It's so hard to drag myself back to the present with Moses, hoping I hadn't missed too much; he's talking about a degree.

With my degree in media studies Francois, who has tentacles in all networks, tells me about a crew putting together a script for a TV series. They need someone to help advise, write the dialogues for the black on black relationships of an African and Afro-Caribbean family, the tensions and discrimination between the two cultures, the undercurrent of tension whenever both sides come across each other.

I agree to meet with the writers and a meeting is set up at their studios. I step into a world where it would appear all have an unhealthy appetite of some sort. It is like a giant corridor of flirting, boys to boys to girls to both; I gave up trying to make sense of things that day.

Within weeks I'm caught up in their foolishness and banging both male and female door openers as I refer to them in my head. I'm not actually writing much but sit around reading the dialogues written highlighting the areas and contents black people would never use or say then providing an alternative. I am referred to as a consultant.

The party and launch of shows invitations begin to kick in. I'm am struggling to meet the demands of my early birds at work, on an average morning the minimum I have sex is twice, there is always someone wanting to get laid. I'm tired from the late nights and champagne, I have managed to stay away from drugs, not meaning I was not once involved in shifting the stuff.

This came about by accident, I had just finished having sex with one of my Latin-Americans can't get enough of you feisty babe, when there is a knock on the door, I step into her bathroom as she says give me one minute, she drags a dressing gown on and opens a small carry-on type bag, it is packed neatly with 2 kilo bags of cocaine. I hustled into my clothes without cleaning up, praying it isn't the police about to bust her. She comes to the bathroom within 2 minutes and kisses me, long and deep, my mind is far far away for this shit.

On the coffee table is a larger bag, she opens it to show me the most I will probably ever see of £50 notes in one place, she has just done a £60,0000.00 drug deal, I seriously need to get out of there, she gives me an envelope thicker than normal, "I don't stay here anymore" she explains, "not when making drops, I don't use the same hotel twice", she offers to call me when next she's in town.

I give her my number but ensure a mix-up of one digit. She senses my fear, "no problem" she says, "we Colombians do good business, no problem, every room for three sides of me staying my Colombian brothers, nothing going wrong". I smile thank her and to come across real I bend her over the coffee table holding the money and shag her before I leave knowing it will be the last time. Out of curiosity I check the names of the occupiers in the rooms she mentioned babe was not telling tales. £20.000 for witnessing a drug deal, hotel work should carry a health warning sign.

I interrupt Moses to tell him of my one brush with drugs, I had gone to Nigeria, flew in from New York and planned my return via London.

How word got around that I lived in New York I don't know but the son of an equally wealthy family that lived across the road unbeknown to me is a big player on the drug scene and operates out of, you've guessed it NY, he's friendly and I assume it's the spirit of the Fanti festival that day.

Anyway two weeks later I arrive at the airport for my night flight and who is at the airport but this guy, he introduces me to the man with him who said no need to hang about in the queue, the guy has contacts and will get me checked in quickly, so like the village idiot I am I hand over my passport just as I begin to tire of conversation with my neighbor and worry what was going on, the friend reappears and leads me to the front of the queue, check in is smooth.

We get to the departure immigration customs entrance and my neighbor is standing there with a bag, "give me a hand with the bag, it's heavy", he says, I don't ask what is in it simply lifted it and carried it through, as we go through customs the armed soldiers ask me what I am carrying before I could reply he said "food stuff and fruits".

I carry this heavy bag all the way to boarding gate 35, where there is a BA flight for NY, at gate 34 is my London flight. I put the bag down to take a can of coke he bought for me and bid him goodbye, even then I wasn't suspicious of his behavior, he said "what do you mean you're going to gate 34", I said "I'm heading to London", "but you are going to New York", no I replied like I'm talking to a child "I don't live in NY I flew in from NY and live in LA but will be spending a few days in London", and with that, and the stewardesses hurrying him up to board I walked away.

Chatting to my cousin a few weeks later he mentions guy, I don't click until he says the story is the guy got some stupid chick going to NY to be his drug mule but things fell apart when she boarded a flight to somewhere else. He got a 7 year prison sentence when caught with the cocaine at JFK. I didn't dare tell my cousin it was me but out of curiosity asked him how these guys operate, this is the low down.

The guy who took my passport, the check in, the customs the police all are in on it, having had their palms well greased. When the guy took my passport away it was to show all involved I will be coming through with drugs and not to stop me. I thank God that I didn't end up in a Nigerian prison for drug trafficking, I look at Moses as I talk but think of my mother, "can you imagine my mother, she would have a field day, that would be confirmation that I am everything bad and rotten to the core".

Moses smiles "only someone like you will make a good drug smuggler as you will walk confidently through the airport not knowing you had drugs on you".

Moses continues his tread of his escapades in the UK. "I'll give you an example of what I mean by health warning, on my round one day I hear a muffled noise, muffled but distressed, I knock on the door, four women faces only showing they are dressed in flowing black robes, I ask if everything is okay, yes please yes go, I am presented with four sweaty faces telling me yes go" in an air conditioned room, something is not right.

I radio for security, they start to gibber away in their language, security arrives always one male one female, I ask to do a room check they said no, I suggest calling the police now they look petrified, I am at a total loss but something is really wrong here, as it's all female I ask the female officer to do a well-being sweep of the room, if nothing is amiss we'll leave them to their devise.

The bathroom door is locked from the inside, it took another threat of calling the police for the door to be opened, inside is another black clad woman with a young girl, eyes filled with horror, "are you okay" she says "yes" all the time clamped to the women in the bathroom, we ask her to step forward and see the woman was holding her by the flesh, "can you speak English" "yes", "what is going on here".

I radio the in-house doctor and ask for a female, the young girl is now talking speaking fluent English associated with the upper class, she is 12 years old a princess at a boarding school in Cheltenham, this team of women were sent over as she has reached the age for circumcision, that is what they were about to do. I hand over to the medics and security and leave, I know the police and Social Services will be called, there will be trouble, what I did not expect is how it would affect me.

Next morning I am summoned and told by top management that was a good piece of work as the child is a minor the problem we now have is a foreign royal family kicking up a stink about a member of staff, male who was with their women, this was unacceptable and recourse is sort. This foreign Royal family keeps a floor of suites whether they visit or not, our hotel makes 1.5 million per annum as a standby fee, and they were not going to lose this over a black boy. The solution, I am to be moved with immediate effect to the Knightsbridge branch.

Now or never I pluck up the courage to ask about my promotion, which was imminent, It is confirmed I will be going as a Jnr executive, a glorified section manager with a cubicle for office. If I have any concerns in the future to check with my superior, we do not want any further culture clash. My exit from a location I worked for 10 years based on an incident of female genitalia mutilation, either way you view it, I am moving on because of genitals.

Chapter 16

I have done well you know, the shares I have in BT, Boots, Marks & Spencer's, BA and H Samuel bare testament to that, the 20 grand from the Colombian went into Shell shares. For a two bit nobody from a tiny village you will drive through without considering stopping, I am on track for making enough money to retire at 40. I am lonely, life is lonely, my current circle is work, shag, party, I have no doubt I can keep this going for a few more years.

Francois is inconsolable about my departure but assures me Pierre his counterpart at the Knightsbridge hotel will take good care of me. The hotel lay out is the same so orientation is not needed, I put in for two weeks leave and ask Helen if she would like to go on a cruise.

We fly out to Florida and cruise the Caribbean for ten days, not once did we have sex, our relationship is like that but we worked that cruise liner, Helen was shagging tycoons within hours of arriving on the ship, big Texan oil men with fat cigars clamped between their lips all trying to outdo each other. The first night she walked in with a necklace that had been in the Cartier display window at a cool $175.000.00 she wore it all night and dully informed me she is heading to Hatton Gardens as soon as we return to England to turn it to cash.

The old birds begin to give me the eye, very subtle, I begin to do the rounds, quietly and effectively, the only one who cottoned onto to me is the sales girls my buying condoms in bulk. For the fun of it I tip her a $1000 and again shagged me rich in the 10 days, my $ account is growing, you cannot find cash on me to raise eyebrows. Between Helen and I, in ten days we figured we got close to a million dollars off the moneybags.

One evening the captain got me on my own, I put on an Oscar performance as a man who couldn't control his partner's sexual appetite who himself preferred mature flesh, the man looks at me in astonishment, he introduced himself properly and gave me his contact card, I get a slap on the back and male bonding is born. He offers to show me starboard, whatever that means, it's late and I really want to get some sleep but I follow him up, the view is stunning if you're into that sort of nonsense.

I feel his hand on my crotch before my brain registers it, by now I am desensitized to this stuff, the Captain of a cruise liner is on his knees undoing my flies taking me in his mouth tea bagging me, greedily, I picture his elegant wife, does he know I've shagged her is this revenge or do they share. I let my mind wander so I stay erect longer what harm will it do to have a Captain in my retainer.

For an older man he is good, I slip a condom on and pull his ass towards me, I sense he likes pain and slap him on the ass cheeks, gently at first then hard enough to leave read marks, I am performing and watching myself and this man with his pink flesh hairy back and hot angry backside, his language is the same, harder, don't stop please harder. I try my best to hit his prostate gland hard, he explodes hard and fast making strangulation noises, red in the face and referring to me as a jolly good boy.

I'm glad it's a day before the cruise ends his build reminds me of the Naija heavy set women, this thick set man is not my usual cup of tea and has nothing to offer me. I get dressed when I try to leave, he is hangs on to my arm with vice grips, this is his last command he informs me he is retiring to the country but will be spending time in London, would I like to meet up, he will spoil me he promises, I'm not listening I just need to leave and agree, Admiralty ... at this point I must be due to sleep with a President.

On the way back from Southampton Helen suggests staying at my place, I say no, however good it is I have never let anyone stay at my house, no visitor ever and don't plan to start now. Julie and my employer are the only ones who know my address.

I receive a text from Tony, his parents are applying for a passport would I like them to include my parents, the total cost is £500. Bastard if I say no it will get back to my parents, if I say yes then at some point they are coming to England. I say yes, they do come to England arriving sooner than expected.

Chapter 17

My new role is much the same no difference except more areas are open to me I come and go as I please, my first hit there is a pop star, I can only describe her as portable, pintsize and incredibly beautiful, amber skin to die for and a voice to match, she is topping all the chats and has two bodyguards the size of Mt Kilimanjaro with her, she say's "good morning" declares "I'm harmless", as the four of us troop into the lift.

She giggles like a little girl and rolls her eyes at the two men who are not even permitted to have a facial expression. I ask how she's enjoying London; apart from performing looking at grey skies she's seen nothing else. I ask what she would like to see and she states "the real London, people, downtown, food, swap meat". I ask what a swap meat is, she laughs and say's "market not Harrods". AJ formally introduces herself, I shake her tiny hand and get an instant erection, and she knows and holds on to my hand unnecessarily longer. She says she would like to see London, and is free for the next three nights. Her next concert is midweek in Hyde Park.

I call Tony and ask where it is happening on the Naija scene, some park boy is in town at Downey hall in Hackney, a new Najia restaurant on Walworth road, another option is the Palm Beach opposite Waterfront in Woolwich. Long and short of it is Southeast London.

I call AJ's room she practically snatches the phone from her PA. I'll be waiting for her outside the hotel in a black cab at 10.30. Dress code smart casual. She's thrilled. On the dot she walks out as I open the cab door she bounces in and barks at the driver to drive, I am shocked until I see the two Man Mountains emerge looking frantically left and right.

We pull away and disappear into the Knightsbridge traffic, the cab driver is surprised by the Walworth road address. I have an arrangement with him for the night, he keeps his meter off, I pay him a grand, and it has always worked well in the past.

AJ is 24, worth money she herself is unsure about; her parents are her managers and suffocate her, for the next three nights she wants to have fun. We get to Walworth road and the shops of course are still opened, she has an idea, we purchase a mobile and pay as you go sim, her direct line to me.

Tropicana restaurant lives up to its name, tacky chaotic fabulous food and the Najia music from modern to old highlife rock like Wura Fada and Victor Olaiya. My pintsize quest is enjoying every minute she tries several different dishes, for a tiny woman she can eat. She tries Naija Guinness and declares she wants to ship it to the States including the chicken suya.

I am enjoying her innocence, it's one I never had, she's refreshing and the fact she trusted me enough to give her security team the slip makes me feel good, maybe there is something about me worth spending time with and it's not my penis. We danced and she can move, she draws attention but only in a respectful way, there is the constant double take of people, is it isn't it AJ?

She had fun I can tell and when it's time to leave she asks to meet the restaurant owner who comes out with his family, the camera's start clicking, I stay well out of the frame, autographs are signed and hands shaken, all the Naija men suddenly want to say hello, I hang back bemused at the content of their conversation most repeating the same "ah if I can get a girl like this to marry I am sorted", I drop AJ off at 05.00hrs, it's been a good night.

I get home and the answer phone is flashing, the passport and visas have been approved, my parents are arriving in a fortnight, Tony is making noise about difficulties in housing his, he continues to live in Peckham in a 2 bedroom flat with 2 children.

I need to think about this do I want extended family to see what I have achieved Naija mind is hard, their son arrived before me helped me when I arrived, I have made all this and not invited him along on the good luck I found, the fact his dreams and wants are different from mine will not matter, there will be wonders by my aunt and uncle could I have somehow stolen their son's bright star when I arrived, it will go on and on the whole family will eventually be in uproar.

I speak to Julie. Have I ever used my staff discount no, now is the time to use it. Time to tell folks about my marriage, Naija will buy the 'can't stay with white in-laws' story.

I call Tony he'll be up getting ready for work. I explain I am managing myself and would like to book the family in at the hotel for the six weeks they are here; I will use my 60% staff discount and pay the rest. Tony is delighted with this as soon as he knows he doesn't need to part with a penny. I make the arrangement 1st thing in the morning and arrange for a 7 seater to pick them up from the airport; Tony will make his way to the airport and return with them.

We will all meet when the folks arrive. I ask him to please warn them not to bring all the smoked fish for sale in Epe, he laughs he's already sent his list. I wait with dread and excitement, my parents are good people they did the best with what they had, my father worked at a ply wood plant and my mother sold foam mattresses opposite command school, a win win situation because of boarding schools in the area.

Tonight I'm taking AJ to Waisu in Hackney. I wear a white linen shirt and Black leather trousers finished with black Hugo Boss slip-ons. We head there at 1am any sooner and we'll be sitting around. Having experienced luxury via my dick I find the desperate dressing and hustle of my people nauseating, to prove you have money the loudest lace largest jewellery and multi-color shoes by Lanzoni is a must, the men are no better.

AJ is in her element she taking pictures and making short recordings. Surprisingly the music is catchy something about American Beat. AJ is fascinated and wants to get in on the act, she wants to spray Wasiu, I call over one of the boys, get $200 in $1 bills and off she goes on stage with a warning not to mention my name. Within minutes Wasiu is screaming AJ's name as she rains the $'s down. I laugh at the spectacle.

Funny enough Wasiu himself worked out who she was and made a slight attempt to rap with her, it went down well. We walked out at 6.45am while those inside were still jamming. AJ wants Naija clothes, tight fitting ones, bubu's, lace whatever we can buy off the shelf. We agree to meet at 3pm.

We head to Dalston that afternoon and make her way to Checkbuy, it's full of linen and ready to wear Naija clothes. AJ avoids the linen like a plague and opts for Ankara, brocade and Adire, a tailor next door will make the adjustments and have everything ready in an hour, we pay £200 for them to stop what they're doing and concentrate on AJ's stuff. We have a wander up the road to Grant' s with its good quality Italian designer shoes & bags, AJ loads up, I haven't much experience of shopping with a friend I'm really enjoying myself.

I lead her into Dalston Market, the smell the noise the pushing impatience around us is what she wants, the real people going about their business, suddenly there is an uproar, two women are shouting at the top of their voices at each other, I translate for AJ as she stands totally transfixed, they are fighting over a man one the wife the other a lover, to add spin to it the man appears with yet another girlfriend, it descends into total chaos and the girlfriends start to fight each other while the wife turns on her husband , no one bats an eyelid, this must be the norm.

We wonder round and AJ makes purchases such as Du-du Osun soap in its natural form and Ori, pure shea butter. I call ahead to Palm Beach bar in Woolwich as they insist you do. I order pounded yam and efor riro.

In high spirits on arrival she attacks the food without asking what is what and there and then wants to buy yam pounder to ship back to the states, I tell you this young multi-millionaire is making me feel young alive, fresh a feeling I have forgotten, she tries Unkwobi and loves the fiery peppers in it and wolfs down her plate decides to order another and asks what she's eaten discovers it's cow foot and calls a halt, I laugh until I cry.

Next she tries turkey gizzard, loves the meaty game taste until I explain it's the stomach. On to palm wine, I have to tell her to steady on; at about 10pm when I was going to suggest leaving music starts downstairs, I didn't know there was a basement.

Chapter 18

We head down and dance with the others like there is no tomorrow, funk fuji, makosa, rap, afro -juju you name it. Again it hits me that at my age the only time I socialize it's to make money and it involves the use of my willy, being with AJ is nice.

I push that thought from my mind as we walk out, same moment hell breaks loose, the camera flashes off the paparazzi catches her unaware then kudo's to this feisty woman, she brings everything under control by asking them to talk in an orderly manner, she gives an interview there and then, stating "she wanted to know the real London, not the inside of a hotel room in the West end", she speaks of African food, Wasiu, Dalston Market the Palm Beach Restaurant and Walworth Road, Tropicana and states "her love for all things African and original".

I walk ahead and wait for her in the cab, when she's done signing autographs she asks the news men who alerted them, her publicity crew who had hired someone to trail us all along. I see a new side to my pintsize friend.

The minute the cab pulls away she's screaming into the phone, no doubt heads will roll. Rather than head back to the hotel she asks the cab to head to Piccadilly, at one of the traffic lights we jump out and quickly disappear into the crowd.

I'm tired and not interested in ducking and diving. AJ must have sensed this, she turns me round and asks if we can go to my place.....she just wants to be normal for a bit longer. I hail a cab and we're at my place in 10 minutes. She whistles when she walks in for the first time, I try to see my home through the eyes of another, she is clearly impressed.

Not sure why I tell her a little about my business, shares, and the little consulting role with BBC drama. I make her hot chocolate and offer her one of my shirts, she drowns in it. I'm tired and tell her to feel at home heading to the shower.

Washing my hair I feel her hands rubbing the suds into my chest, she must be standing on tiptoe for the first time in my life I don't want sex, I want friendship this pintsize woman has opened up a wound, I am lonely. My house suddenly feels too big. I gather her to me and wash her all over; she washed what she could reach of me.

With a towel wrapped round her head we head to my room fall on the bed and fall asleep in each other's arms. I wake to a soft caress and coffee. My guard is down and I lean forward and kiss her, she does not resist, I am 32 years old and making love for one of the very first time, I will have several first times.

I have conditioned myself to be silent so as not to call out the wrong name. Today I feel what I am doing, I touch, I kiss, I caress, I rub, I wallow, I connect, I feel. When she climaxes I stop myself, a mixture of punishment and not wanting this delicious sensation to end. She offers me her bottom, instead I turn her over and keep her on her back, I use my elbow to support myself and slowly glide into her, she's warm and embracing.

I like the smell of her in the morning, I love the way she is looking at me eyes wide a part of my enjoyment, an equal partner in the moment. When I finally allow myself, I shudder and afterward feel slightly feverish with the intensity of the emotions, we have not used a condom, I will pay for that dearly.

After a simple brunch I walk her down to Ladbroke Grove to catch a cab, I do not want to give my home address. I am confused by what I feel in three days, I have come alive, felt young, free, exhaled, being myself through my pintsize lady.

She calls me on her mobile one of the few women to have my real mobile number, she thanks me for a wonderful time, explains there will be hell to pay if her parents and team find out I'm her link hence she's making the decision to move, same hotel but the Regents Park branch.

I don't ask if I will see her again, something in her voice tells me I won't. I walk past the newsagent she's front page, I buy all the papers to see if the camera caught me, unless you know my hand that's all you see just beside her. I breathe a sigh of relief. Her concerts are a sell-out and she moves on to Europe, no doubt another black mugu like me waiting.

I remain in this state of anger, tight, boiling when I went to my Consultancy stint, a politician makes a point of saying hello, today I stop and talk to him, he's delighted, when will I finish, should he wait, I would like that I say.

We go to his pad a flat in Swiss Cottage; I am brutal with this man. I am back on familiar grounds not a word during sex, just bang bang bang and bang, this man is married with grownup kids keeps a secret flat for his personal pleasure. He gives me £5000, today I truly feel what I am, a part time male hooker, dickie for rent, yours if you can pay the price.

What is happening to me? I call Francois, he is delighted and can meet later tonight. I talk to Francois he speaks to his friend in Harley Street, I am to start a magic tablet an answer for depression. I'm depressed!!! I didn't know I was depressed I thought I was paying the price for the life style choice I made. I duly picked up the tablets took it for a week felt like shit then feeling an idiot binned it. End of depression or so I thought.

Chapter 19

My parents arrived on a Thursday morning, I watch as Tony gets both sets of parents checked in, I am on duty so pop down to visit them once they are in the room, already I can hear my aunt and Uncle telling Tony he should have stayed working in the hotel business, my parents cry and cry while blessing me they curse all my enemies known and unknown.

My parents look out of place in the setting of a 5* hotel, they admire my uniform of double breasted navy suit, tie and crisp light blue shirt. My father is in awe of me and I feel sorry for him, for the hardship he's faced for the burden that's made him grey haired, I hug him and hug and hold my mother for a long time. I order a simple breakfast of bread and eggs, tea and coffee; I will catch up with them at Tony's after work. I walk away feeling strange, it is not nice to be faced with one's wretchedness.

My mum watches me woman's intuition they call it. I will not take Julie to Tony's but will take Mum and Dad's to Julie's. I have to protect myself, if they see my home they will boast of what the Lord has done for their child and I do not want to make an enemy of Tony.

Every time I visit southeast I feel like I can't breathe, I look at the poverty and people moaning but not finding a way out of their gutter except for drugs benefit and bank fraud then each year they add to their tally of children, mum dad and 4 children living in a two bedroom flat and still the babies keep coming. Peckham High Street is an Isaleko Muslin Ajegunle combined madness.

I take my Peugeot, I change it every 3 years same model nil attention, the usual good for nothing youths are hanging round downstairs, they are the bicycle drug runners and the local lilo-lils who believe guys want them because they are beautiful, white girls talking black acting black all mixed up.

I am my usual over alert self, Tony has told me he's broke so I give the spending money. I give all four a grand each. Tomorrow before the airport run I will take my parents to Shoreditch so they can see how I make my money. I give Tony's wife an envelope out of sight.

What do you do with parents you haven't seen in yonks, where do you start, I needn't have worried? When I turn up in my parents suite in the morning I realize there and then I must show them my house and world, in my mum's words as long as you haven't stolen to acquire what you have then it is well. I tell them all you can tell parents how I have found help and the angel Julie has been. My mother asks about Julie's fertility is there a problem. I explain we have never slept together.... just Julie helped me.

That afternoon I drive them down to Alhaja's in Deptford High Street, they are astonished by the quality of Nigerian products available. My mother is quiet and watches me a lot. We pop into one of the many caravan Nigerian restaurants for lunch, when father goes to the toilet she says "it has been hard I can tell you have done whatever you have needed to do, as long as you have life there is hope", I burst into tears I am a kid again, I cry for the lost adulthood for my innocence for the path I chose the things I will never have the things and opportunities I've lost, I cry for Moses.

I decided to use the toilet before the drive back to Knightsbridge, I feel them then, little tags on my willy, I haven't really paid much notice to them, thought they are age tags, I also haven't seen them on others, so now something tells me they are not skin tags. I book an appointment there and then with the Harley Street guy, I also book both my parents in for a well-being check, he can see us tomorrow.

My worst fears are confirmed after a sleepless night I have genital warts, I am furious at AJ, they would need freezing or burning off, because of my hairy thatch they have taken hold well, my pubic hair is shaved and I am horrified, I practically have a colony of warts in my crotch, treatment starts immediately.

That is the benefit of money; my parents are in the same building for the day, well-being and spa treatment. I feel the need to strangle AJ, the filthy so and so, spreading genital warts all over the world. I know I am filth but I feel filthy like when the ambassador gave me STD.

As we exit and stroll towards Oxford Street my dad joking says he would like a beautiful white woman to rub him down every day and plans to marry one if mum doesn't shape up, who will scream my name and fling herself into my arms, it's been a while and kisses are rained down on my face and cheeky innuendoes pour forth nonstop it takes Helen a moment to realize I am not on my own.

My father is bowled over my mother tight lipped, all hellos are done, Helen wins my mother over by kneeling down properly the Nigerian way to greet elders and invites us back to her flat. We say yes, will drive down shortly. Mother wants to know why I haven't settled down with a nice girl like her, well- mannered, she will make a good daughter in law, I chuckle to myself, thinking how Helen is like the Blackwall tunnel so many cars have passed through.

That evening we are tuck into eba and mixed meat ogbono, my parents are impressed. Helen is a good hostess and by the time we leave my mother has accepted the brother sister relationship and promised to speak to Oba Kassim of Epe regarding an eligible husband for Helen.

I show my parents my home the next morning, my father took his shoes off then prostated in the garden he talked to the earth the way we do at home, once inside he asked for a bowl of water, praying and shouting his command to the wall flicked water in all corners completing the rituals expected when one goes into a new home, I tell them to look round but they insist I accompany them, I show them round and they offer me the best advice ever, don't let others know you live here they will be envious and bad things will happen.

I hyped this up by telling them that's why I haven't, I have been waiting for the day when they will be the first guests, and they are both delighted. Shortly after my mobile bleeps, my Arab is in town and wants to see me, he is around tonight only. I text back I will see him later.

I drop my parents off just before 11pm and make my way to the Arab, tonight is going to be tricky, I will not let him touch me, nor see my willy. I am angry again.

He opens the door, gushing as usual, I have been shagging this guy for 8 years now, in that time he's got married to four women, and still I am on the menu. I kiss and undress him roughly, he purrs thinking I have missed him, I jerk him to me I slip a condom on, he sees I'm shaved and mutters something Arabic, tonight I use sex to punish him, if he is in pain he mixes the noise of it with pleasure, it takes me a bit for his words to cut though me, he has had enough, but

I won't stop I am fired up and every attempt he makes to pull away from me makes me jerk him back, he begins to cry softly.

    I do him nonstop for 17 minutes, he collapses on the bed after and asks "you not happy with me", as I zip myself up, I slow my breathing and explain in a childlike voice that I have missed him so bad I lost it, would he forgive me, I am astonished when he jumps up and hugs me showering little kisses on me and confirming he has missed me badly too in broken English, "it is bad being married having women, makes me feel bad, I happy very happy only happy with you", I stand rooted what the hell do I do my love of money has totally entrapped me. I leave with various gifts and $50.000

Chapter 20

I am restless, feel I can't breathe, I need to get out of London, I offer to show my parents, Aunt and Uncle the English Country side, my aunt declines she's on baby duties, my dad and uncle will share a room I will buddy up with my mum. The first evening is in Maidstone, I book us in the Dales a hotel in the shadow of Leeds Castle, when we visited the Castle mother can't get over that it was once someone's country home, why would one family need so much space she repeated several times.

When she sees the original clothes and shoes displayed in the bedroom she laughs herself silly, lunch is a large steak burger, I have brought along suya pepper purchased in Peckham we eat a lot of pepper in Epe, I don't want any one feeling sick.

We spend two days in Brighton, I feel a fraud when went out in the evening my parents and uncle cannot hide their astonishment at same sex relationships, apparently there is medication and sacrifices at home that will cure this sort of illness, things descend into chaos when I took them too far down the beach and we arrived at the nudist section. We mainly had a good laugh.

The bright light of Bournemouth, game arcades, ice cream on the pier, tea and scones made me feel I had just arrived in England. Picture after picture was posed for evidence for Epe people of the trip abroad. In sharing a room with my mum I am given something of an identity back, she talks to me rubs my head, prays and praises me until one evening I break down, I cry and cry and she simply holds me and rocks me, it reminds me, money we didn't have, but love I had by the bucket full from my parents.

I am 32 years old and fall asleep in the arms of my mother. In the morning she gave one piece of advice, if there is something I am doing that is making me unhappy I should consider what I have to gain and what I have to lose, weight it against peace of mind and make a decision. Before my mother leaves I ask her to find me a nice girl back home.

My father was so consumed by my apparent success he failed to see the cracks my mother had picked up on. My father makes a request, he would like to do one day in Shoreditch from helping to receive and offload the goods from the taxi, to packaging and the airport run, "I want to work one day in my sons business", my uncle is game. I jokingly agree a set amount per hour and to add delight to their experience I write up a short term contract, conditions, pay agreement and job description. Men will be men.

Too soon the time to board a plane back to Nigeria is up, my mother is inconsolable, my father and the rest of the family long given up comforting her, parting is difficult, only this woman can see there is something deeply wrong with me in that I go through the motions putting a mask in place, saying the right things, doing the right thing at the right time but feeling and enjoying nothing, a part of the crowd yet alone, in company yet totally isolated. I am a shell and she's managed to see beyond the facade.

She's made me look back on my journey, the choices I've made, and the various paths I choose, all money propelled. I live a life that is totally against my culture yet in a way I am comfortable with what I do I have access to a part of people's life that makes me feel powerful, I know their little secrets and in my ignorance at my age I think it's limited to the west. I am about to meet a group of Nigerians that blow my mind and any myth I have about bi-sexuality.

Helen calls up and asks to meet at Harvey Nichols, we have a few drinks and then head to Selfridges, as we leave Selfridges a man clad in a full length mink coat with the most twinkling eyes and refined manner beams at Helen, she goes over and kisses him they hug and he asks me to come forward. We are invited back to his house, a stone throw from mine. He is a law maker and political figure, born with a silver spoon a mover and shaker both here and in Nigeria, educated at Oxford he speaks with a chipped English accent. Married with 6 children he chats to Helen like she's family.

On arrival at the large detached house we walk in he drops his coat and pulls Helen close, he then holds out a hand for me. I stand there rooted to the spot. Arab's, British, white, Latino I've done but a prominent Naija man no no no! Helen had given no indicator threesome is on the card. My treatment is over nil warts besides I'm bored.

In no time we're in the main bedroom, mirror on the ceiling a water bed to slop on and the action begins, shortly after the bedroom door opens we are joined by an incredibly black man, black as in black skinned, so dark if he doesn't smile in the dark you will not know he's standing there. This small aggressive man with his little stump of a willy brings the only frown I have ever seen on Helen's face, she later explains he bangs it against her, has never achieved penetration but bangs so energetically she is sore for days.

Three men and a lady, I submit to all ways I'm turned, I do the banging but accept the adulation from the men, switching off and performing the way I've taught myself to, the men discuss me like I'm deaf, two very wealthy married middle aged men probably in their early 50's, I can tell they are not new on the gay scene or bi-scene.

In a way I am gutted all last pretension that my culture could not sustain homosexuality gone. If these men are behaving like this there must be an active market back home. To add to my agony they put out lines of cocaine to snort while Helen snorts away, I decline, I accept a glass of Remi Martins, it's not often I drink but something about this two, revolt, yet fascinate me.

Final insult on injury when we are ready to leave we are each given a check for £200, I laughed, I guess on the Naija market the going rate for sex is £200. Helen offers me her check, she explains through this lawyer she has accessed moneybags, real moneybags, movers and shakers, to her he is like a favorite uncle who ensures she's at all the right events. I am pissed off for a long time.

There is someone Helen would like me to meet she is in love with a Nigerian Airways Pilot, I humor her and meet the guy, long and short of George the Pilot he's using her, laughing at her, would never leave his wife and children will enjoy Helen's package as long as it's available. My words of caution fall on deaf ears. Interestingly she later names this relationship failure as one of the reasons for her breakdown.

I am back in my world of same same, I continue to carry a small client list, twenty women at a time all flying in and out of London on business making sure they are those who need to be in London a minimum of thrice a month, I accept invitations and spend weekends in the lap of luxury in places like Venice, Rome, Zurich where there is money there is an endless need to create fun.

Chapter 21

I continue to be paid handsomely for my company, service and discretion, listening to money advice I invest, buying shares when prompted only to watch the value go sky high when there is a takeover bid. I am wealthy by all standards, I have millions ferreted away, keeping a low profile I stay under the radar of the law.

I have no convictions nor have I ever been cautioned. In a way I am living the dream. I frame and keep the Nigerian law makers cheque the only decor item on my toilet wall; I ensure our paths don't cross again though Helen passes on messages periodically.

Julie wants to talk, her relationship has been steady and she wants to make an honest woman of her partner we need to get a divorce. I thank Julie, without who nothing would have been possible. I sort out the divorce and accompany her and her partner to San Francisco the only witness at their same partnership blessing.

I fly back to London feeling dejected, only on the flight is a presenter who's ratings are sky high, he is seated next to me in the 1st class cabin, what is it about me, do I carry a sign on my forehead, no sooner are the cabin lights dimmed I feel his hand on my leg, I ignore it until the fool gives me a hard on I can't ignore. "Heard of the mile high club", he asked, I have, would it be something I would do, maybe but not with a man in mind.

But hell that's how it worked out; if the hostesses and attendance saw us go into the toilet no one battered an eyelid. As he leaned against the wall I took my stand behind him, it lasted just long enough for both of us as we hurriedly get back to our seat for the fasten seat belt light on from turbulence. When the duty free trolley came round I pick out a £15,000 Cartier watch, he paid without blinking, as I speak I still have his business card somewhere.

My dear this is how my life went on, hotel work, script consultant, forwarding agent and sex aider. I went to the best parties, had a house full of the best, accounts that meant in reality I didn't have to work anymore and a client group who behaved themselves well towards yours truly, appreciated what I had to sell…..me.

Around this time I begin to receive unwanted attention from an Asian lady I quietly nicknamed iron lady. About the same age as me, nil boyfriend nil husband nil kids' deadly combination. A colleague on the same scale she is hard to avoid, I am asked to let her shadow me for a two week orientation period. What is it with no, this desperate maternal clock ticking babe wouldn't leave me alone.

Feeling wicked and grateful I give in and bang her in the linen cupboard a one off on our last day together. Glad to get rid of her presence I return to my normal routine. The TV drama is making waves the tension between blacks families and cultures drawing in audience numbers unexpected, I continue to receive a nice retainer and walk the corridor of power regularly.

It's time to visit Nigeria, I have been away for 14 years; I will be staying in AIH Lawal Street in Jibowu as a base then shuttle back and forth from Epe. My parents meet me at the airport, they cannot understand why I will not make Epe my base; I appraise them with business opportunities in Lagos. Once settled at the hotel we head to Epe hoping the morning traffic between mile 12 and Ikorodu would have eased up, no such luck the drive down takes us 2 hours.

Chief Seriki's wood work is still there, the smell from fisheries hasn't change, the drive uphill past command school reminds me of my youth, I must have walked that hill a thousand times, there has been a lot of changes in Epe fine houses no doubt built by away abroad kids like me, but in between these beautiful structures is the real Epe, mud houses peeling paintwork, traditional healers and spoilers. Lots of newcomer Igbo boys practically trading on the road with their wares spread as far as the eyes can see and Ghanaian teacher easy to indentify by their facial markings and conservative dressing test books clutched to their side.

Tradition! Tradition! Tradition! first stop is the graves of my grandparents to pray and let them know I am back safe, asking them not to sleep in heaven but to keep an eye on me and my welfare always. You haven't lived until you eat the fat obokun fish cooked in palm oil with a nice side of ewedu and the lightest lafu available. I eat and rest, my mum sitting quietly in the room will I doze, my dad whispering to her to leave me alone.

We spent three days like this no visitors, I do not know our neighbors and have warned my parents I wish to rest, my presence is guarded like the crown jewels.

Day four my mother asks if I'm ready to meet the girl she has in mind. Yemisi is twenty five, graduate from the school of nursing and is practicing at the General Hospital, we agree I will meet her alone without the interference of any of the parents. We agree to meet on Saturday afternoon; I speak to her on her mobile and ask her to pack clothing for two days, when she begins to question me I cut the call.

Midday Saturday she walks in with an overnight bag, I put her bag in the boot and assure my shocked parent's we'll be back on Monday before her afternoon shift. We head to Lagos, we chat freely, she is no stranger to men's company neither is she forward. I like her quiet strength and determination and her recognition of her own strength and weakness.

I love her command of the English language without her trying to westernize herself. I am not bowled over neither am I disappointed. I ask about relationships, there has been one serious one, he left her married someone who lived in the States in a position to give him life with a green card. I laugh and she laughs with me. It's a good easy atmosphere.

That evening I took her to Lord's the place lived up to its name, she struggled with champagne and wine, I suggested a cocktail similar to today's Pina colada, she likes it and downs several not realizing the effect but loving the sweet refreshing coconut taste. Back at the hotel she's sick, I help her into her night wear and put her to bed.

I am woken by her distressed crying at 06.30 hours, she has disgraced herself, I am liking this woman, I gather her into my arm and say nothing, just nuzzled her on the cheek and curled myself around her.

She eventually falls asleep, I think back to the sort of women I've being exposed to the likes of Helen, the wealthy business women who see me as part of their trip to London, I look at Yemisi in the light of the dawn breathing softly and something moves in me. I wake her and ask if we can make love, how she feels about me.

Stated she fell in love with the person my mum described, I'm not a virgin she says and would be okay if you're okay.

    We make love gently at first and then I struggle to contain myself, starting and stopping telling my brain this is not an assignment she does not question me and simply holds me in her arms, caressing content to be with me. Our twin girls were conceived that morning, it was the only time we are intimate.

Chapter 22

Did I want to marry a girl straight from Epe, educated but with nil sophistication? I know I won't be able to live with her, too set in my ways, a prisoner of my shag me rich sentence and greed of how easy it is to get money out of rich folks.

I ask Yemisi if she can be a Lagos based wife, she asks if I have someone in the UK, I tell her no and explain for now my work, lifestyle, travel and building my business up does not give me the room needed to take a bride along. She agrees to my plans, whatever they are. I know this woman will be peaceful, it is okay for me.

We spend the next day shopping; I spend enough on her to back up my intention. On Allen Avenue I find a jeweler and buy a matching 24ct engagement and wedding ring, I put both on her hands.

We arrive back in Epe at 11.30 her shift starts at 1pm. Her parents are waiting with mine there is tension, I prostate to her parents and apologize, I tell them in our generation it is important to meet, have space to talk so there will be no misunderstanding, her father looks like he wants to cutlass me I call Yemisi over, she has been kneeling down during the whole exchange, I hold her hand and formally ask the two set of parents for their blessings.

The tension changes to celebration, I request an engagement ceremony before I leave in 6 six days' time. I give the money needed to make the necessary arrangements and head back to Lagos, I do not love this girl but I will be good to her, I will use giving her a happy life to appease God for my wrong doings. I will arrange for Yemisi and her mother to visit in a few months.

My father had found a property for me as instructed, it is a rundown, blocked off, abandoned family house on Onike road Yaba Lagos, my father is joining me tomorrow afternoon for the viewing even before seeing it I know I will buy it and build a home for Yemisi, relocate her to Lagos, set her up in a business of her choice. If she remains in Epe on her own she will become a laughing stock.

I am shocked at the size of the property; there is a story building at the front, a middle court yard with a well and another building at the back. It's in a good location and I don't want to lose out, I agree to the family asking price, it's a done deal, I now own a dilapidated chunk of Yaba.

My father uses his contact to assure me the basics of pulling the building own and fencing it off will be started as soon as the proper exchange of documents and filing has been done. To his horror I buy the property in Yemisi's name.

The engagement goes well; Oba Kassim gives us the official blessing. I take off for Lagos and fly back to my nemesis. I set an alert on my phone for 07.45hrs every morning and call Yemisi wherever I am. The money needed to build the property in Lagos is a joke and I quickly ensure Yemisi is in the thick of it, meeting with architects and putting her idea of a dream home into shape. She reminds me gently I have said she can visit with her Mum. I make the arrangements and book some leave.

Knowing I would have visitors spurred me on, I begin to realize that as much as I hate what I do I am addicted to it, I crave the women who need me, I loathe the men who want me, the sex parties the excesses each gathering trying to outdo the other, same faces different venues. I shag like it will be denied to me when Yemisi arrives. The five month gap between when I went home and she arrived I exhausted myself with providing my service to my various collections of sex addicts.

Chapter 23

Gatwick airport: their flight is due at 05.20am, I am there by 4am, having a coffee to keep me awake the incoming passages from US pour out, I am gob smacked to see one of my older ladies, older as in oldest, she smiles wickedly at me, she's flown in to see Pavarotti & co perform at the Royal Albert Hall.

The Nigerian cab drivers are watching me with interest, am I competition, the old bird does not realize she is openly shimmering at me and touches my hand a few times; this is the stuff of nightmares. Her chauffer arrives the same time a few of the Niaja drivers move closer. I welcome her once again and assure her I will see her this afternoon, she waltzes off in a cloud of Balenciaga.

She's what I refer to as old money, the original American whose forbearers made enough money which was then well managed by the other generations to date to ensure they move within the circle of those who run the USA.

Two of the Naija cab guys say hello and ask jokingly about the rich old woman, they don't mind oh if I want to connect then. I explain I work in a hotel and she is one of our guests, I pacify them with the information she is a big tipper.

Yemisi and her mother come through, dressed like they are going to the moon. I feel embarrassed acutely aware of our differences to my shame she curtseys and addresses me as eh....the way one address an elder. I feel I owe this young woman and pull her in for a hug which reduces her mother into a laughing ball. Is this how it is in London, you shameless people her mother hoots? I can tell she's delighted.

Yemisi feels thicker, solid I guess her standard of living is much better. She carries on smiling at me, squeezes my hand and shatters me with the words "can't you tell I'm pregnant", my world implodes, pregnant! for who me?

I look at her like she's spoken in German, her mother steps in chastising her, "I told you, you should have told your husband, surprise, I want to surprise him, why don't you children listen to your elders", I step in quickly as I see Yemisi begin to fall apart, we are in the middle of arrivals in Gatwick I want no drama, I hug her again and put all the effort I can into saying I'm pleased very pleased we head home.

As promised I pop in the hotel in the afternoon, my excitable American is waiting for me naked under the covers, all parts of her body shows years of plastic surgery whatever battle she wanted to win with nature she's lost big time. She has breasts that look ridiculous as everything else has gone downhill, her skin is milky white dotted with age spots, and the sun is to be avoided as it ages the skin. Pure white scanty pubic hair awaits me. Her knobbly hands reach hungrily for me, eager hands touching, tugging, undoing and pulling me in between her legs.

I have given up trying to understand if or when a woman's need for sex wanes. As usual I give the performance she looks forward to bring her to climax through clitoris stimulation, I watch detached as she trashed about for an old bird she can take a long time.

Her favorite thing and a must is for me to withdraw at the last moment and climax in her mouth, she then spends a quarter of an hour licking and enjoying the feel of me in her mouth and hand. This is the thing with money I tolerate all the quirks, I leave with £10,000 in cash. I divide this into two and give five 5,000 each to Yemisi and her mother.

I see my life through the eyes of Yemisi and her mum, to them I live like a king, my word is law, I am treated like a demi-god. I arrange for Yemisi to see my Harley Street doctor she needs iron tablets otherwise appears to be doing fine. I ask her a burning question, is the pregnancy mine, she says it is, I feel a desperation I've never felt before I want it to be true, I want to have made something beautiful.

I ask about getting married at the local registry, I want my child to be born in my name; she's booked in for her first scan two hours before we go to the registry. I pay for the special license needed and provide all documents requested. I tell Yemisi I want the baby to be born to married parents, my mother cries hopefully tears of Joy. I explain I have no friends this is why I have been able to make a success of life in London.

There will be the three of us, Yemisi has a friend from school of Nursing in Lagos who lives in London she invites her as a witness. I am feeling stifled and make an excuse to go out. Francois is free for a quick drink at his new apartment in Sloan Square. I walk in and pounce on him, I shag, shag, shag and shag, he asks no questions just lets me ride him. We chill for a while and I go home.

I settled them in they are no problem really, they are happy in the house delighting in constant flow of everything and the nonstop TV programs. Though I'm on leave I continue to pop into work whenever my phone demands I do. I took my new family to all the necessary places, Trafalgar Square, Buckingham Palace, Madame Tussauds, China Town the big name shops.

I watch their fascination with all things western, the underground excited and thrilled them, Petticoat Lane market was a nightmare, in the end I stayed at the salt beef cafe and told them to come and get me when ready. Julie walks in, she is one person I should have given the curtsey of keeping in touch properly, as we hug and hug Yemisi and her mother walk in.

I do the introductions; Yemisi asks Julie if she can hug her, she thanks Julie for all she's done in my life. Julie is touched. I promise to keep in touch better. It takes some explaining by Yemisi for her mother to understand that without the marriage to Julie I wouldn't have been able to remain in the country.

She is cross I didn't mention it, Yemisi begins to give her examples of people they know who have married various nationals to remain in their country. She wants to know if Julie and I have children. I tell her we never slept together; she offers prayers and blesses Julie.

I have a taste of my worst nightmare. People constantly in my space, however small they try and make themselves, I am aware of their presence. We head to Harley Street for the scan. While Yemisi's mum prays that no evil eye will do the scan we are thrown when the technician asks if there is a history of twins in the family, yes a third cousin removed! Well there is one placenta and two babies, same sex did we want to know, hell no actually yes.

I am in shock, twins two children what am I going to do with them, I am not father quality, with little time to brood on things we go to the registry and the deed is done. I am on auto pilot. Think think think, I suggest Yemisi returns to Nigeria as planned, I will begin the process of her coming to join her spouse Visa before she leaves.

She must return well before the babies arrive. We share a room yet I have not touched her and she hasn't tried to initiate intimacy I feel like shit, each time I go out to shag someone, I bring back a gift a watch perfume, dresses all the nonsense women like. I'm not coping; I really want these two gone.

I go and see Helen who comes up with a brilliant plan, get the property in Yaba built, set Yemisi up in business, something like textiles that would require only very brief visits to England, I insisted I want the children's education up to secondary school level in Nigeria then University in England. I'm not sure of the logistics of this but it's a plan.

Feeling more settled it enables me to take a closer look at Helen, she looks rough, her flat looks unkempt what I had mistaken for excitement at seeing me and problem solving I realize is some form of mania.

Helen begins to talk about the pilot, there is a party for his wife on Saturday she would like me to take her pretend I am her boyfriend so she can see the wife who is forcing the love of her life to host a dinner and dance at the Cumber field Hotel.

I try to reason with her no end. Something is wrong, Helen is totally obsessed with a married man, she's lost touch with reality and truly believes this guy who is probably screwing all left right and centre, is faithful to her plans to leave his marriage, wife and three kids to be with her. I left Helen with a feeling of foreboding.

We had just enjoyed my favorite dish of amala ewedu & Gbegriri when my phone goes it's Helen she screams and shouts and threatens, I can hear voices in the background and ask her to pass the phone to whoever is there, it's a police officer and the security staff at the Cumber field, Helen has tried to crash the party, the pilot himself had come out when summoned looked at her and stated she was not an invited guest.

She is really kicking off. The officer informs me they are using some holding power they have to transport her to a place of safety, I didn't realize she has lost it. I ask to be kept updated and also what could I do, the first suggestion is idiotic, can I come and get her and try and calm her down. I say no, London Police, in that case Helen will call me to let me know where she is and the line goes dead.

Helen is a friend a good friend, she has helped me and being there for me. The nearest hospital to her is Paddington I dress up and head there.

When I arrived she's been seen because of the threats she made to end her life she is placed on a Section of the Mental Health Act, place of safety! Mental Act, this is a whole new world,

Helen herself is so doped up she is incoherent and falls asleep trying to talk to me. I head home I will call to ask how she is and when I can visit. I hear words such as Mania, psychotic, reactive to stress, tested positive for opiates, cocaine and cannabis. Helen had clearly not stopped her descent into drugs.

Tonight in bed I draw Yemisi close, it's strange to have this woman with me, she falls asleep in my arms and I pray I don't do too much to hurt her, that she doesn't go over the edge like Helen because of her love for me. Her belly moves gently of its own accord, my daughters are in there. Surely that is hope for something. I doze off. I wake to the phone ringing; Helen is awake at the hospital and screaming blue murder for me. I explain as I get dressed, all that shit and nonsense about a friend in need.

Visits to the mental health acute care ward becomes a routine, Helen is an inpatient for a total of 10 months, her final diagnoses is Paranoid Schizophrenia, at some point she summons her mother over from Nigeria the poor soul is given a visa as a carer. I watch as Helen's life descends into a depth I am unable to fathom. She talks about witchcraft, conspiracy theories, the real meaning of life, acts of the Illuminati and it goes on and on pouring from her mouth like a tap, totally warped and out of touch.

Some days she recognizes me, others she asks for help to protect her from me. I continue to visit attending reviews all focused on what to do with Helen, when she is allowed out it always ends in disaster and it becomes quite clear she is cannot function independently.

A decision is made she will be sent to live in supported accommodation that will meet her needs in Bean Kent. The day I stop visiting her is still as clear in my mind as yesterday, it is another one of those reviews and I have being invited.

We sit in the circle I have become used to, Helen comes in she is excited and doesn't acknowledge me. The doctor is talking "you did a really brave thing today, I hear you are to be congratulated for saving someone who got into difficulties in the pool" she glows and laughs softly to herself.

The doctor asks if she wants to share anything with us these are her exact words "He was very wet to make sure he is dry I have hung him up to dry", all hell breaks loose, the young man was discovered hanging from the back door hinges in Helen's room, they were unable to revive him. I leave during the uproar; the Helen I know is long gone there is no one to visit.

Chapter 24

I read about the incident in the papers and feel sorry for a wasted life a life that at times mirrored mine. Helen will be locked up for a long time a danger to herself and others because of her illness. In a warped way it is a relief. Helen is one of the few people who knows me and my dirty secrets, she can pull off the fake facade I have put up. Oh well life sucks.

Remember the iron lady I orientate at work, email bounced in from her she's popping over for a meeting and wants to meet for coffee, I decline, her reply sounds threatening, "believe me you want to meet me for coffee". What now, as she is tight with top management I say I'll make the time.

We meet at Lucci's a few minutes' walk from the hotel, Naija man, what do I want with cafes. She walks in and I swear I soiled my-self; I lost a few drops of wee. She's pregnant very pregnant. I sit there looking at her the way one would a Cobra. Pulling my Naija wit around me I ignore her pregnant state, instead smile a hello I don't feel, following it with 'I need to run I'm quite busy.

She sits looking at me and finally speaks, "meet the linen cupboard liaison", I sit back and stretch my leg as if she's made a comment about the weather. I boldly ask how it concerns me, lots of things to do with unwanted pregnancy, her reply "on the contrary this is very much wanted, I want permission to use your name nothing else".

She calls a pretty lady over, this she introduces as her partner, they plan to have the boy she is carrying and felt they owed me that much, she needs me to go to the birth registry with you. Her girlfriend speaks up, I am astonished, and she is quietly very well spoken, polished and clearly educated to a high level. She apologies for the way we meet. This is very much a wanted child; my linen cupboard liaison is bi-sexual.

They would like to raise the child and need nil financial support from me but would appreciate contact if I feel I can be charitable enough to do so. I take her card and take my leave. I can't tell you how I got through the few remaining days of Yemisi and her mum's stay. What will happen, will I go from one hospital to another playing baby father. I felt such a fraud. Linen cupboard's partner is a black woman, no wonder she wanted to lay a dark skinned man. Well I'm a man and have to behave like one. A bastard is a child not acknowledge by its father. Wed or unwed if the father accepts that child as his it cannot be referred to as a bastard.

My home is mine again but there is a feeling of dread in my stomach, it's knowing Yemisi will be back and at some point more people, my parents, her parents. I call Francois and we have dinner and then watch the cabaret at Madame's in Soho, this stew pot of a place has rich pickings.

At 04.40am Francois has left with a fancy boy and I am in a Hyde Park Apartment with the man I met, Pierre is an Attaché to an embassy in Europe from a French speaking country, words are not needed. I am taken aback when he brings out gadgets I am unfamiliar with, I shake my head to make him understand this is not for me, he agrees, for me he gestures, it's for me to use on him.

He shows me how to tie him up the way he wants in a kneeling down manner, a short rope with a ball is tied round his head with the ball stuck in his mouth metal clamp goes on the base of his willy, he's shown me he wants hot candle wax dripped on top of his heel where he's kneeling, the rope tying his legs join the hands tied behind his back, wraps round his neck and snakes back. So many bloody instructions, one sentence he makes keeps me there "I am at your disposal".

When I leave at a few hours later with £15,000 in cash and 4 gold bars I know I have struck the jackpot. Gold Bullions, cash in any country.

It's not midday and he's called me, this man is seriously into rough sex, punishment sex that sends crazy messages to him, if he gets too excited and trashes there is the danger of strangulation, I watched his madness as I tried new things on him, I have to keep a close eye on his as several times his eyes rolled when I made a move to untie him and ease things, he moves his head in disapproval.

He tells me the bars are worth £5000 each then gives me an address in Hatton Gardens to ensure I get a good price. There is a party in Brussels on Friday night and a show in Paris on Saturday, we will be back in London on Sunday would I be his guest. I agree, to this day I don't know if I am party to hiding a criminal act.

We meet at Biggin Hill Kent, I have never flown in a private plane, it is surreal, there is luxury and there is luxury. The atmosphere is relaxed and well before take-off, the lines of Charlie is available discreetly at the back, I have never tried drugs but in the heat of the pleasures happening all around me I rub some speed on my gum. I experience why it's called speed standing in the isle in full view of the others I shag the attaché while someone caresses me and another pays attention to my nipples. I am pumping away and telling myself it's all for the money and connection, I laugh out loud all boundaries down, I am not gay I have three children on the way.

The rest of the weekend passes in a blur of faces legs party sex sleep and champagne, there was more champagne than water. At some point we must have shopped as I came back with a new suitcase stuffed with expensive designer goods. Monday morning when the haze lifted I knew something was bothering me; the young blond guy who had been cupping my balls had disappeared at some point. Last I saw of him was during a cruise on the Seine he was in the thick of arms and legs, I don't remember him disembarking.

I call Pierre to say thank you and mentioned the young lad, in his halting English he says no boy, forget. That statement still haunts me. I continue to party and meet up with Pierre and his crowd knowing my time with him and his lifestyle will be short. I must have a guardian angel that is wide awake. In the short weeks I have known Pierre I have been given cash close to £400.000 and clothing and presents worth another £70.000 I greedily want to make as much as I can. Pierre has invited me over, a few of us he says.

I am held up at work and running about 90 minutes late but still head over to see him, the parking is awful as there is a function at the Dorchester, I park in Marble Arch and enjoy the stroll down, as I approach I notice an ambulance and the Police, I slow down but carry on walking then join the small group of lookie lookie a man is brought out handcuffed and distressed, trying to explain to the police officers "the French man asked me to tighten it, I did as the Frenchman wanted", he shouts hysterically over and over as Pierre's body is carried out on a stretcher.

I waited and walked away the same time a group of tourists walked away. It is a cool night yet I am sweating, I can smell myself, my fear, if I hadn't been held up at work that would be me in handcuffs. I stay away from Madame's.

With renewed energy born out of fear I put effort into what I have begun to see as routine indulgence that yields money. I am also sharp and have picked up on several other managers like me and a few of the male staff who are obviously playing the same game. I change my game tactics and suggest an evening of fine dining at the Savoy, surprising each of my shag me real good ladies with my room booking. While they pay for dinner I cough up £259 for a standard room. I have hit the jackpot as each feels special and reward me for what they see as a one on one time. The bulk of my contacts are from the States and Canada.

One evening while in the lounge of the Savoy waiting for my lady to arrive I got talking to a Japanese lady she had mistaken my dinner jacket for a serving member of staff tried to order a drink and had apologized repeatedly. To put her at ease I strike up a conversation about her presence in London, she is here for an old school reunion is Sussex, we discuss the changes since her education and return home to Japan, she has all the politeness of the Japanese but the bolshiness of someone raised in the west.

On an impulse I ask if she would like to see the African scene in London when she returns at the weekend, she agreed instead to drinks at the bar at 6pm then we'll see.

Hito as she's known as, when we got together leaves me shocked and surprised. A tough no nonsense talking lady she gets straight to the point, she is curious about the black man's body is it as described. The boy who came to London with nothing is the one that responded. "Black men had dicks so long when they need to piss they put their foot on the toilet seat, then hold their trouser leg open that's how long the dick is no need to undo flies and pull trousers down", she laughed and laughed a good icebreaker.

After the drinks we head to Mama Calabar good reliable Naija joint. Hito is interesting, she takes picture after picture, what is it with Japanese people and pictures. Everything about her speaks of the clash of old culture versus west.

She stinks of money breaths money, her slow sure movements tells you this is money. I am on unknown grounds; she gives me no signal other than friendship and a free spirit. A merciless tease, I'm never quite sure where the conversation is heading. By 11pm we're back at the Savoy, as I walk her in she asks if I would like to accompany her to the races, Cheltenham meeting, I accept. First race is at 1pm I would need to be back at the Savoy at 11am to get to Heathrow for midday. Heathrow!

11.45am and we are sitting in a private helicopter, it feels like minutes later we are dropped at the edge of the field and walk across with the other privileged ones who arrived by chopper. Hito gives me an envelope a present from her, "today don't use your money", I feel patronized but I'm in it for the money. She explains form and encourages me to place bets.

I checked the envelope when I went to the loo, no way am I throwing £30.000.00 on horses, there is only six races my guess she's thinking 5 per race. I bet a £100 on each race and keep my ticket out of sight the whole time, I watch her loss a cool £120.000 and smile like it is pocket change.

In-between the races we small talk, people came up to say hi to her, lobster and champagne by the bucket, strawberries and cream and steak that melts in your mouth, these guys know good food. We are both merry by the time we head back to London, the lights of London from a helicopter is simply breath taking.

I do the unthinkable and invite Hito back to my place, the only word she spoke when we walked in was condom, sex with her was like being with a trapeze artist, strangest thing was the avoidance of pubic hair, girl was smooth all over and smelt good too, it's kinky having sex with someone knowing outside the chauffeur is waiting and knows what you're doing. I did the image of the black man proud that night and hoped the liaison might continue on other visits.

Chapter 25

Hito left promptly after a shower and I never hear from her again, I guess at some point she must have seen beyond the facade. This really is how my life passed in a blur of thighs and money, investments and popping in when permitted into the world of the rich.

Moses breaks off as the waiter comes to clear away our breakfast plates, Moses has spoken throughout the meal, I vie between fascination and irritation, what the hell is he expecting me to say, he had plans to get rich via his dick, he must have certainly succeeded judging by his wealth.

That it left a profound effect on him I have no doubt, but I am a friend not a therapist, coffee arrives and I'm looking for an opening to end this contact, why did I say we could spend the afternoon together, as if Moses could read my thoughts he touch's my arm and brings me back to his world, I've never shared this with another soul he says, what am I supposed to say, I say nothing I'm don't feel honored.

I didn't expect a blow by blow account of the last 30 years a summary would have done just fine, Wale and the others had better not be fucked up like this when I meet with them before the planned dinner at Federal Palace Hotel.

Moses is still talking, "you have no idea what a sense of relief it is to talk freely. I've forgotten who I am but reality will come knocking from time to time, I am about to become a father months apart. Do I believe linen-cupboard, who says she wants nothing from me, what if she turns up one day and demands weekly contact".

Yemisi and her mother return and my home becomes unrecognizable, do people really need all this junk for little humans, I call in someone to design the nursery all of a sudden Laura Ashley becomes our household name. I practice patience, I cannot afford to get upset but I feel unsettled in my home. What would Helen suggest if she was of sound mind, I hear her voice loud and clear, buy a small bolt hole.

That is exactly what I bought a flat in Lancaster gate, to my horror a Nigerian family lived on the third floor, I know because I could smell the lingering odour of fried fish & apon when I checked out each floor. Once the place is ready I move a few of my things in and begin to give the impression of working long days.

Najia women are awesome, despite all the concerns and gargets on standby for a caesarean, Yemisi gave birth easily and without complication, for a brief moment I wondered if she has given birth before. The girls were delivered screaming blue murder and ugly as sin. I thought babies were supposed to be beauty. They looked nothing like me or her with their screwed up angry faces.

I pleaded long working hours in the days that followed witnessing the chaos in the morning and hearing it during the night. I ensure I spent a few hours resting at my flat each day before heading home. Before the babies arrival Yemisi and I had started to attend the Methodist church on the corner of Kensington Church Street. To avoid a noisy Naija naming ceremony I have already approached the Reverend.

The naming will be a short special service at 7pm on the 7th day with dinner at a nearby restaurant. As long as people are not trooping to the house I don't care how many guest turn up. For someone who didn't have many friends in London they all certainly came out of the wood work, combined with few family and her mother's guests we had over 50 people turn up, 29 of them bought the girls a white leather bound Bible! as a naming gift.

Six weeks earlier I was visiting linen-cupboard at St Thomas's, my son is amazing and I fall in love there and then. I am treated with distain and suspicion by linen cupboard and her partner for the next 18 years. True to their words they took nothing from me but make me feel uncomfortable whenever I asked to visit, in this manner we tolerated each other but it made bonding with my son difficult.

I gave him the name Pelumi and put money aside for him each month. I visited him monthly even during his University years, he gave me the honor of being there to watch his convocation into the Forces at a US base, a child I couldn't declare I have, grew up went to University then Masters at Imperial College studying Statistics then off into the Military. I sure got my just deserts.

The twins on the other hand ripped my home and peace apart, they always seemed to be crying or frazzling about something. When my mother came over and Yemisi's mum left things seemed to ease off but Yemisi clearly preferred her mother around. I used this to brooch the subject of wanting the children raised in Nigeria, she wasn't happy but didn't have a choice, we agreed their return to Nigerian for the celebration of the children's 1st birthday.

My mother assured me she could cope with the twins so I sent Yemisi to Nigeria to ensure everything was in place for the return and birthday party, to lessen the sting I suggested Dubai shopping for herself on the way home and threw in £20.000 We have still only had sex once. I certainly don't want any more children well, not with her.

With my mother in the house things are calmer and I begin to get to know my daughters, they are actually funny little individuals. Anyway back to Nigeria we all trooped.

The birthday party took place at Shell Hall in Surelere, it is still talked about by Yemisi's friends and family as the most lavish party they ever attended. I head back to London as fast as I can. Back to the world I had created for myself, I have it all but have nothing.

In no time I make Junior Executive Director something that saved my sanity, the women wanting to get laid were beginning to dwindle, still fit and young I was no longer the flavor of the day, I hadn't even noticed my service was not so much in demand. I have had a good run but what now? I know I can't live with a woman; I'm not gay so I don't want a man. Helen who is as mad as a hatter is the closest thing to finding someone like myself.

For the second time in my life I'm diagnosed with depression. To me this is a western disease, like anorexia, you see food and you don't eat, it does not exist in Africa. I am started on Citalopram and remain on it till today I tick along nicely, my parents died ages ago, the twins are also graduates and married with wait for it, a set of twin boys each, Yemisi accepted that was all she was going to get from me and adjusted to her life, raising the children and launching a very successful chain of eatery the Yummy in your hand and tummy catchphrase, corny as hell. I also set up a transport business that pays for itself, I have coaches, taxi's and Okada's, believe it or not I have six family size caravans, in the west they are used for camping here I rent them out for events like weddings, it's used as a changing room during events. Oh yeah I also have freezer trucks strictly for parties and events for the drinks not for transporting goods. Yemisi is at the helm of all this in Naija she certainly has a good business head.

Ore, this is me in a nutshell. If I have talked too much abeg file me away. It's really is good to see you and you must let me support you with your Mum. I can get trained nurses and carer's. I have to say you haven't changed you are still the listener.

I thank Moses and make all the right noises, the time spent with him allowed me to know his weakness; you never know it may come in handy one day.

I quickly decline his offer that is the last thing I want. I came all this way because I want, I demand my time with my mother, the time and space she denied me when young, the writing me off as a no hoper, well my day has come my time has arrived, my mother will have a story to tell on her arrival in heaven or hell.

Chapter 26

I am going to control everything, no help no witness wanted not even Tayo's reluctant one if she volunteers it. I bid Moses goodbye I need to keep my appointment with Mum's consulting team, we hug and part, I turn round once and see he's joined by a young yellow lady, no doubt if Moses is getting laid he is the one doing the paying in Lagos. Christ what a holy mess.

But for the grace of God I think as I look at the driver jump up when he catches sight of me, if it had been up to my mother I'm sure I would have ended up serving cold drinks in the canteen at Kingsway or Leventis store. Such was her distain for me because I am not naturally academically gifted like Tayo.

She would call me and make me stand for hours just looking at me from time to time and sighing, "what can I do with you", her friends will also have the privilege of looking at me like I am filth, such intense dislike like I am a virus, I don't blame them, if your mother treats you like dog shit it's license to others to wrinkle their nose.

I bore these sessions with submissive silence but behind my mask I planned, I plan for the day when this wretched woman called a mother will experience what is called role reversal, I live for that day, I dream of that day, I ache for that time. I kept quiet; a quiet child is a deadly child. You never know what they are thinking. I start to laugh and catch the drivers alarmed look; I put my mask back in place.

The house is been readied for my mother's arrival, she will be in the contained room downstairs, I pop in and stare at the senco mattress waiting to be inflated, a must if you want to prevent pressure sores, I am getting in all the right equipment.

The movement aid is already in the corner a bulky contraption to aid getting up plus in and out of bed. I plan to teach her a send-off lesson before she departs she will get it and get it hard, I can see myself again standing still while she talks about me in the third person, what to do with this object what to do, she always spoke like I was sleeping with all the men in a ten mile radius but form mein my head I am a virgin I have never had consensual sex only what has been forced on me.

I am transported back; I'm in school living with yet another strange family, two sons, and two daughters. The older son age about 19 years, makes me sit on his lap, he gives me little food presents, sweets and fruit but always makes me sit on his hard bit and moves me around slowly.

I can't think of one happy time all moments tinged with someone touching me or making me touch them. The 19 year old didn't let me lock the bathroom door and would walk in and touch me, I used to be scared to wash my face in case he came in then, yet all of this was avoidable and totally preventable.

Even when there were visitors once and we all bunked down in the same room people sleeping where they could during the night he moved me on top of himself and made me lie there for ages. Within a few weeks the school ask to see my parents, guess who my mum sent to the school to represent her, the same guy, the teacher expressed concern that I was falling asleep in class and didn't seem to be learning anything.

The bastard gave feedback that I needed help with my studies, he will help me during the weekend to focus on my studies, the abuse then shifted from week nights to Fridays and Saturdays and still nobody noticed. I was a difficult child, I was a slow child, I was told I was a lot of things but nobody asked me 'WHAT IS THE MATTER' that's all it would take, that is all that it would have taken to rescue me from daily nightmares.

I feel a rage only the abused can feel my entire body is crawling with explosive energy I want to hurt something someone. I pick up the bottle of bleach and head to the toilet; I need release I need to feel pain. I sit and ease myself then rinse with the bleach, the fire is good the pain is good, I can feel something, I am alive, I am me, I have release.

I am burnt sore but that is okay it will heal. I head to bed walking that penguin walk of post-delivery mothers because of the rawness.

I'm meeting Wale mid-afternoon at Water-margin on Adeniran Ogunsanya, I hope I am not in for another shag money story. Wale is nothing like that from what I can remember of him.

Chapter 27

I was 14 when he caught up with me walking along Wensley Street, he stopped me said hello then asked if I would be his girlfriend, I told him off for having the nerve to ask me to be his girlfriend, "I'm not interested in a driver", I shot back at him.

His face practically collapses, "I am not a driver", he answers quietly, "yes you are", "no I'm not don't lie", "I don't lie. How come you drive Tokunbo's family around"? "Mr Tokunbo is my Uncle, my father his brother died and I was brought to live with them. I am not a driver". I apologize and say we can be friends but no boyfriend nonsense. We walk together to campus square. He is not in education but can read and write a bit. We become friend's two losers.

Wale is always in the background a member of the pack but not a member of the group, present but knows his place. A very silent friend, a recorder who listens, and rarely offers an opinion.

A few years after we became friends his girlfriend had a son for him and dumped him not long after for not having money or the means to support them, she got together with a local champion who had a barbering saloon. I remember his distress and acceptance of his plight.

When he had our bucket chat, Wale wanted to come to England simply to better himself, he had heard about early morning operation, keep London clean and wanted that avenue of money making, he simply wanted the funds to support his son. I am looking forward to seeing Wale I hope he's done well for himself.

WALE

If I charged for hugs Wale would owe me zillions, he hugs and holds me for a long time, patting my back holding me at arm's length then enveloping me in his arms again and again, I accept the love, in his hugs is the words he can't say. I love you and wish we had ended up together.

Wale adores me he can't hide it. I feel humbled and surrender to his embrace. It is the connection of two lost souls who found their way to a destination of some sort maybe not where they wanted but somewhere is home and it is enough.

He clears his throat and a man jumps forward with a bag and a small red case. He puts both into the arms of the waiter who jumped forward to accept the parcel on my behalf, we are shown to our seats, the restaurant is empty, then I notice the sign closed for a private party. Wale and I are private party.

We sit and I get a good chance to look at my friend as he lights up a hug Wilde Havana, Naija man, no may I smoke. Wale is dressed simple in white polished lace, casual slippers but there is something I can't put my finger on it.

Image of an older man crossing the street to greet Wale flashes, he bowed to Wale, a man young enough to be his grandson, that puzzled me as it should be the other way round, the owner of the restaurant now comes out same behavior as if Wale is doing him a big favor by his very presence.

I order a Chapman and tea; I will drink tea and coffee no matter how hot it is. Wale just watches me with a slow smile through the haze of his smoke, I love the smell of cigars, I get the message he has not forgotten my likes. We order and sit back.

"So" I said, "so" Wale replies and then for some insane reason we both start laughing and can't stop, he drags me to my feet and holds me, so tenderly something in me gives and I hug this old friend of my fiercely. It has been a long time. I open the red box and whistle, an emerald and diamond choker set seats nestles in cream satin, this is worth the price of a house somewhere, I remove what I am wearing and ask Wale to do me the honor, he jumps up like a cheeky school boy and puts the necklace on me, I walk over to a mirror and marvel at the clarity of the diamonds the volume of emeralds.

I am wearing a queens ransom then it hits me, when we were young I had said I preferred the green stones in rings when everyone was gaga about rubies. Wale had remembered, the set has paperwork for Mappin & Webb a yearly maintenance clean for the next 10 years and Insurance paperwork. Wale had insured my gift for 5 years they are worth a whooping £117,000 I peep in the bag and see several bundles of top class exquisite lace; I recognize good makes like HOH Filtex & Eddy of Austria. Wale better start talking as I need to understand, my first thoughts the boy has done good. A Chinese man comes out to talk me through a seven course meal, I am impressed stare long and hard at my childhood friend who clearly still holds a torch for me.

Wale talks:

After you left I tried and tried but couldn't get a visa, I presented so many different passports used so many different names it was like the British Embassy had my picture pinned up to recognize me. There was no one around to talk to my life dragged on being sent on errands, feed and watered but no life skills. A trader guy Mauruf in Agoro Street told me of an alternative route into London, overland West Africa cross to Europe then make the way overland to Paris finally cross into England. A well-used well tested route, that had not yet come under the full radar of those in Europe. I will work my way in each country doing menial jobs for transport and food and shelter. In Paris the contact there will put me in the back of a vegetable truck. My cousins promised me a roof until I find my footing.

Mauruf gave me 4 $100 bills the crossing will cost me $100 the rest was for emergencies. We went to Yaba bend and pick, he looked long and hard before buying a shirt he also bought me a pair of black trousers and two pairs of shoes one canvas. I watched as Mauruf's girlfriend a tailor unpicked the collard and neatly arranged the dollar bills then sowed the shirt back.

Keep the shirt and trousers as your entry clothes into UK, you must blend in. Mauruf said he knows I will make it and pay him back; his belief in me spurred me on. I had a son I don't see, my father's relatives treated me like a spare part I have nothing to lose. I told them I had been offered a job opportunity in Ofa and wanted to check it out. Their indifference motivated me no end.

I left Nigeria on the 1st of October there were three of us and a leader who had taken people as far as Paris several times.

West Africa is strange, you don't get the gist of the dividing of Africa until you move from country to country, English, French, Creole, Portuguese throw in the traditional language and the stew pot is beaming. First into Benin then Togo, Ghana, Ivory Coast, Guinea, Senegal, Mauritania Western Sahara, Rabat in Morocco. Africa accepted my Nigerian passport, stamping and stamping each country we came to they had no interest in us.

We worked in the motor parks, helping unload and load goods, in return for thousands of miles, some had us in the carriage others we stayed in the back with their goods whatever it was they were transporting. I changed my religion so many times, in Christian countries God Bless you in Muslim Countries Shukrah Allah, first lesson learnt is when people identified with you they relax.

I ate food names of which I can't pronounce, I washed in rivers and streams, and I slept under the stars and in designated accommodation of sympathetic people on this human railway. Strangers who wanted us to get to the land where the streets are paved with gold so we can make good and send aid back home.

It took us 9 weeks to reach Morocco, my change of clothing shirt and trousers never far from me. We had each paid our guide to Paris a whopping 1,200 naira a king's ransom all the money I had squirreled away. Before we left I stood at my father's grave and told him to guide my footsteps I also asked that he give me the strength to end my life if the guide duped us as I couldn't face coming back to my present bondage.

Moroccan's seem to be middle of the road unless you are a Muslim brother; I quickly reverted back to my religion, praying with the brothers in the area we were in, and waiting for the right conditions to cross from Rabat into Spain.

The crossing itself was uneventful. Nil prior notice we had eaten sat chatting quietly in our room when our guide knocked and said it was time to go, within two hours we were on the shores of Spain and in the back of a lorry heading to our next location.

In Spain we were kept indoors, moving from one location to the other during the rush hours when we didn't stand out. We stayed with some lovely African families and others who simply wanted the money our handler handed over.

From Spain we made our way into France uneventfully, we were delivered to our handler for the final crossing into England. I asked the lady of the house for needle and thread to mend my clothing, to this day I suspect her and her husband both indigenes of Warri knew I had money hidden in my clothing and wanted to retrieve it.

I locked myself in the bathroom and unpicked a few threads as shown, I took out a $100 bill to change to Francs as instructed, I need the money to call my cousins and to assure Mauruf his friend had done good.

The crossing was in 24 hours we would be going in a refrigerated truck of tomatoes so needed warm clothing minimum a padded coat. I can never trust Warri boys, this guy we were with Michael took me to change my money and spoke on my behalf. The conversation went on for a long time but as I didn't know French I had no idea when it started or finished.

On the way back he told me to wait while he popped into a shop, I waited patiently trying not to panic when he didn't reappear, 10 minutes later two police officers approached me, papers they demanded.

No papers, no French, no address, in my distress I wet myself and started to cry to curse my ancestors, my parents, my bad luck, Michael who had gone to the shop for such a long time. I cursed and cried as I was put in the back of the patrol car and taken to the police station.

An English speaking French female officer was called, the kindness she showed me I will never forget, I was honest and told her my journey, she asked if I wanted political asylum, I didn't know what it meant asylum back home is for the criminally insane. She explained Michael had probably set me up to possibly get his hands on my goods, I explained I didn't have any goods until I remembered my shirt.

$300 is a lot of money it's 1981. I am taken to the CRA Centre Retention Administrative, simply centers for those who do not have a valid resident permit or awaiting deportation for various reasons.

Chapter 28

I am to be deported back to Nigeria. My first attempt at suicide failed I tried to hang myself with the rope from my pyjamas, unsuccessful I ended up in their infirmary. Bastien was my nurse, a happy sort of man who told me not to be sad. Life is beautiful you go home to your country you no die. I thought of his words, you go home, going home means poverty but not death.

I looked at the cocky Italian in the next bed, we have been next to each other for over 72 hours yet not a nod, he just watches me. Its night time the nurses are watching a rerun of Dr Zhivago the Italian suddenly speaks, he knows English, I am surprised. He explained to me once physically fit I was to be put on Air France for the trip back home. Simple as that he asks would I like to do business, make money lots of money.

I wonder if the medication I have been given is making me hallucinate. He's talking he will give me numbers I must memorize, in Nigeria I am to go to an address in Ikeja, it is a night club, I am to ask for Luca the Italian his brother, I am to say Marco sent me.

Apparently I will need money at Muritala Mohammed Airport, I have to bribe my way out or they will take me through the formal process of getting back the funds for the plane ticket the Nigerian Government will be billed. This is all above my head; I am locked up in a detention centre when I should be in London. I am on my way back to Lagos and an Italian is offering me a job.

True to his words I am unceremoniously woken up and told to get dressed two nights later. Marco gives me an envelope stuffed with Lira's millions but as I had never come across the currency I had no idea how much I was given.

At the airport we were boarded first, all at the back with Police guards until the last minute. I will never forget the humiliation of

Nigerian's looking at me like I am a parasite, the money Marco gave me was not taken off me, I still have my francs but was fearful.

At Muritala we were the last off the plane and were processed like livestock. A lady called Ruth took me aside and offered to walk me out if I gave her what I could, I narrated my story and said I had the equivalent of $100 in francs, could we split it, no, she would take 80% leaving me enough to get transport home.

We walked out of the airport together; I had given a fake name so wasn't worried about being found. I didn't look affluent and I didn't have a suitcase so no one bothered me assuming I was someone working there sent on an errand.

I can't go home so I head to the night club in Ikeja. Luca is a Xerox copy of his brother; he is expecting me and addresses me as 'my friend'. He is flying out to Italy tonight for 3 days but wants me to stay and we will talk business when he is back. From poverty to a European detention centre to Lagos, then into the lap of luxury. Maybe the ancestors are not asleep after all.

Luca addresses me as "my brother my friend all your needs will be taken care of we are brothers, right, I'll send the tailor in and Usman my right hand man will pick up all other things you need". I am led to an apartment. This is the first time I will experience a hot and cold shower in Nigeria, I stand under the water for hours it feels like I'm scrubbing and scrubbing the months of misery away. Breakfast of Yam and eggs with a peppery sauce is waiting. I eat and fall asleep.

Those three days Luca was away I never left the flat, I could hear the world going on around me but stayed cocooned waiting for the re-birth this contact which the Italians must facilitate. I am still planning to kill myself than go back to Lagos Island with nothing.

I have a new wardrobe busting with everything needed both native and the finest Italian material called Lino, linen in English. Every morning a series of newspapers are delivered to my room rather than ignore them I practice reading sounding out words and reading the simple ones first to try and understand what the news is about.

I am revitalized and curious, I need money, I can dig my parents out of their grave if that is what it will take, I just want to survive.

Luca returns and smells like something you wrap up and put away for safe keeping. Luca popped in to say hello and hopes to see me soon. When he returns later in the day I dress under the watchful gaze of Luca, he makes suggestions, following a haircut, manicure and pedicure I barely recognize myself and that smell, a spray called Quorum, we hit his night club.

I am walking amongst the rich I mean rich, I recognize faces I have only ever seen in newspapers or on the news, everywhere is babes and rich powerful movers and shakers, some of them are clearly foreigners, one thing they have in common is their spending power. Remi Martin, Hennessy, red wine, white wine, none of the Gulder and Star larger I see on the island.

Luca is indeed treating me like a relative. We go into his office I am amazed, my first two way mirror, there are also black and white screens showing what is going on in different parts of the club. Luca pulls on headphones and listens for a while, he then gives them to me, I listen to the conversation open mouthed, and he points to a screen to show me which of the private rooms the conversation is coming from.

Top military brass is discussing a possible coup if the current government continues its weak rule.

I listen in on another conversation a well know road building firm is handing over $6000, weekly palm grease to an official. I begin to wonder what Luca wants me to do, spy-listen? Nah he says as if he can read my mind, I listen because sometimes it's good to know what the big wigs are up to, and no information is useless Wale just store it and use when the time is right.

Luca wants to know about me and the ties I have, I bring him up to scratch no one is looking for me. Luca takes me out again, towards the south end of the club there is a closed section that plays jazz, we push the door open, a few hours ago it had been near empty now it was heaving, the smell of Indian hemp is heavy in the air while on the tables are large round mirrors with thin lines of white powder.

20 Naira notes the highest denomination was rolled up and put at the end of the line, then the person took a big breath in sucking the white powder through the nose, I stood transfixed, Luca smiles lowered his voice and told me if I ever did that shit our association is

over. This is what we will be dealing in importing and exporting. I learn a new word Cocaine.

I don't know how it's made or the route into Nigeria but I am the route out of Lagos into Europe and USA starting with the UK. It is now a case of who should I send. Call me cold hearted but I know what I am doing. I contact my ex, I have job with the Italians, would she like to visit her sister in London with the boy for the holiday.

She asks if I am dreaming, I invite her to the club during the day and once convinced told Usman to drop her off. I give her the entire Lira I have to change into Naira then get a passports and tickets for the two of them. I tell Marco the person is ready. I ask my ex and the kid to spend the day, I will take them to the airport that night. I tell her I will give her an additional £1000 spending money it will be brought to her by my friend, as a gift she is to give six pairs of shoes to him for himself, wife and their daughter. I give her £900 to take with her.

Thus I send £30.000.00 worth of pure cocaine into London, there can be no detection unless the shoes are ex-rayed because they are made with the shoe from scratch; there is no suspicious opening, no gluing. My ex goes on to become my biggest courier and does not find out she's carrying drugs until she is detained at New York's JFK airport in 1992.

She is given 7 years imprisonment, by this time I am rich beyond my dreams, I have 17 women working for me and unwisely end up with four as wives at one point. Apart from the mother of my 1st child the others are a disaster, all have had several children for other men before I suspect deliberating getting pregnant for me.

Money was coming in at an alarming rate. I cannot fathom how much money the Italians made. I was constantly on the move having started an importation company to explain my prosperity to the Nigerian community. I listened to the good advice Marco and Luca gave.

I changed the route into UK and USA regularly, using countries such as South Africa, Gambia, Ghana, Sierra Leone, it was easy to recruit women and ask them to give a pair of shoes to a friend or my relative, I rarely lost a shipment.

The daft women I associated with eventually brought me to the attention of agencies who wanted to know where my money came from, these gutter girls who didn't think to better themselves now started competitions, throwing my name around, though I said not to use my name they would introduce themselves as my wife, I gave up in the end and used my importation company to cover my tracks, I started importing animal feeds, household electronics, power tools and investing in buildings and renting out properties.

But I had four sets of in-laws and a total of 16 children with only four belonging to me genetically. The women and their relatives spent my money like water trying to outdo each other.

When the military boys came into power our man on the inside gave me word the Drug Enforcement Agency were coming for me. Luca got me an Italian passport and saw me onto a flight to London. The London I couldn't get to, I was now heading into in Business Class of a BA flight all in the space of 9 years.

My second wife had by now settled in London, London was an eye opener, till today I have not forgiven her for the way she treated me like a visitor, I had no access to her flat, if I went out and she was out I had to wait for her to return, she refused to give me a key to her flat and had dumped my daughter somewhere in the countryside at a child minder she went to once a month to bring the child home at the weekend. I accompanied her to collect my daughter during a quiet business period.

From the train station we caught a bus, the child minder and her husband live in a terrace block, their house is the last right next to the park entrance, I like what I saw thinking my daughter would spend hours of fun in the park spoilt rotten by the English couple who were childless but looked after a couple of Nigerian children all by word of mouth from grateful parents in London many of who were supposed to be in the country to study and needed to hide the fact they had a child from their family back home.

With my wife in the lead we walked round the back, it would appear people in this part of the world are trusting as we walked in through the kitchen, on the floor was my daughter who's nappy was being changed the woman on her knees had her face down, I initially thought she was kissing my daughters belly, my brain asked for the sound we make when blowing noises on the belly, then it hit me while my wife was smiling and laughing with the woman.

I asked my wife in our language if she had seen the woman just kiss our daughter's private part, yes she said, you know these people they love children so much nothing about a child revolts them, I am rooted to the spot as the husband walks in with a naked child in a bath towel.

My instincts tell me something is wrong, I tell my wife in our language to tell them we are taking her back with us for the week can they pack a bag. My wife begins to ask me what I think I am doing, it is the only time I will threaten violence in my life.

Chapter 29

A news item I heard discussed at a Nigerian cab office on Oval Road in Camberwell came to my mind, a young Ghanaian girl with child minders outside London had complained of a sore throat when home with her parents, when there was no improvement with the second course of antibiotics a swab was done, she had the std virus in her throat, I asked what that meant and got the shock of my life when told an adult had put his sex organ in her mouth, no other way to explain how the virus got there, it turned out her child minder's boyfriend was messing with the little girl.

Why would a grownup woman be kissing a baby's private part and it's considered normal by the foolish women with me. That day we took my daughter home and never returned her to the minder.

I instructed my wife if she really is a mother and had an ounce of decency she will let the other women who have children know we've removed ours. I found a nursery for my daughter and happily paid the £375 a month, peanut money in the scheme of things.

Years later a lot of child abuse rings was exposed, some unregistered child minding couples who gave the impression of respectability, most of the victims you can guess, children of rats and rabbits like us who thought because they are white then white is better.

I lived quietly concentrated on being the receiver in London using the extensive network built up in areas like Peckham Rye, Hackney, Brixton, Dalston, West End and surprisingly the home country. We continued to make money; the Nigerian government took me off their radar, this time ladies were picking up shoes for me on their way back to London.

I was generous giving money, they were greedy to get their hands on not wondering why some much money, the fools just assumed I was flushed with money and fancied them. While living in Tulse Hill I put an advert in a newsagent's window for a retired teacher who could give 1:1 literacy lesson. I quietly learnt how to read and improved to the stage I didn't need to mouth or sound out words, I will never be able to write other than the basics but I can read documents such as landing card without needing help. I feel a great sense of achievement.

Let me tell you about my cousins the two fools who treated me like a paralyzed arm to be tolerated now constantly sang my praise, I bankrolled them, bought cars paid bills their school fees, they needed money I gave it and they needed money a lot. Not once did they attempt to talk about my treatment in Nigeria.

The foolish female cousin tried really hard for me to date her friends introducing one after the other until I lost count. To that end I did well I know it would have cost me dearly if I did, as she would escalate her demands. Neither one had a settled home and would treat my flat like a shop; going home with carrier bags of food stuff, clothing you name it.

They wore clothing and watches like Rado, Raymond Weil I didn't dare, not in England. They were like caterpillars eating and eating, I held my peace and took care of them much to the distain of my wives but trouble is brewing.

You noticed I said my flat, with the treatment from my second wife I put the word out I'm interested in acquiring a council flat, within months a lad who's met and married a Nigerian living in Maryland will hand over his flat for £5000, this includes his National Insurance Number if I wanted to work.

Thinking how generous he was I later found out it is to his advantage for me to work as all the taxes mean a healthy pension for him one day. The down side is nothing is in my name; all household bills remain in his name. A compact one-bedroom flat on the fourth floor in Meeting House Lane Peckham, a mecca for Nigerians in South East London.

I lived here peacefully until the Council decided on pulling down the buildings to build better houses; each tenant had to come in person with all documents including a valid British Passport to be eligible for re-housing. I contacted the guy in Maryland offering to buy the flight ticket and throw in £2000 he thanked me but turned me down flat.

The number of African's affected was staggering. I quickly found alternative accommodation in Short Path Herbert Road, Plumstead.

My second wife is having an affair, if you live in England you will know the country belongs to women, it is ruled by women and they can decide to fuck you up anytime.

There are also issues in Nigeria, a change of government, the bastards who used to come to the club at night and do business now want the place closed down, it is difficult times and trade drops drastically, with that I go from controlling goods and distribution of £15-20,000 a day to that amount a week.

I have nothing less than three couriers per flight, I have contact from the Embassy in Nigeria to airport staff, airline staff you name it I had oiled the wheel well, but you know white people are unable to keep low profile. I have a lad at the Embassy who is on a £50 grand annual retainer to process visa's I request without any hassle.

What does the idiot do, buys a top of the range sports car which soon attracts the attention of his superiors. Quietly investigated and confronted with the funds in his accounts he is shipped back to England, it's not long before I find another contact, as long as people are paid shitty money, they will always be vulnerable.

The bitter truth is I have four women in my life who are only interested in money, when the eldest wife was released from prison and deported back to Nigeria I gave her 50 million Naira, she wants nothing more to do with me but took the money, since her incarceration I have educated my son at a boarding school in England an exclusive boys school. She cannot see him as she is now an undesirable person on the international travel list UK will not give her a visa.

Business is slow and wife number two can hardly bear the sight of me, I keep a low profile and stay out of her way, as I said earlier I ask around and find someone is emigrating to the states to join their spouse, they want to sell their council flat in, I give them £5000 and they give me the keys to the property instead of handing it back to the Council, it is a popular trade amongst immigrants. I move in before I can catch my breath wife number four is kicking off about joining me.

Luca obtains the paperwork and sends her down via Italy where Luca gives her a bag of shoes she has no choice and brings the bag through successfully we are in business, 3 million pounds worth of cocaine brought in by one courier without any hassle. My domestic life though was about to start a downward spiral.

Chapter 30

Several things I didn't do in London, dress flashy, drive or do direct business with the receivers. I watched what people wore and stuck to grays and blacks from Burton's or Marks & Spencer, I never wore sportswear or trainers, always trousers and work wear men's shoes. I went on the buses; the police rarely took sniffer dogs onto the buses.

I moved around with my couriers without drawing attention to ourselves, there could be a quarter of a million worth of cocaine in the Safeway shopping bag stuck between frozen peas, washing powder, baked beans and what not to the naked eye, It was a man with the weekly shopping. I took great care of my distributors and their families.

My rules were simple; no flashy dressing no delivering using cars, under no circumstances, become familiar with the receivers or say you will grant them an audience with me.

Cocaine was moved around the housing estates in black rubbish bags loosely tied so you could see the leafy spinach poking through. I never carried or delivered but will be a distance away watching, casually strolling by. London A to Z became essential.

I would visit locations for delivery prior to doing business. I avoided speaking to the white man like the plague. I could never understand their accent, after a couple of pardon me, they usually gave up trying to talk to me. There was no period I thought this is it I need to get out.

Wife no 2 who had a British passport refused to marry me so every two years a college I never set foot in would forward my passport to the home office for another renewal at £2,500 it was chicken change.

One evening a delivery had taken place in Hearnville area while I waited in Safeway's on Balham High Street, as I did the usual pointless shopping a Nigerian lady working there asked if she could help me find any of the items I wanted, she spoke lovely English, fairly light skinned like my second wife but polished, she was well read.

I told her I was waiting for a friend, girlfriend she smiled, male friend I offered. This stranger smiled at me stating she likes the dignified way I carry myself...me dignified, I introduced myself; it was the early days of mobile phones, I had a phone and gave the details to her. She threatened to call me as soon as she finished thus Motunde entered my life...motun for short.

We met at Whitley's and ate at a lovely Chinese restaurant Poon's on the first floor. Motun insisted on paying for the meal. I have four women not one of them in the years I've known them every offered to pay for a meal. I fall hopelessly in love.

Motun is in her final year of a Master's in Business studies, she is assistant manager at the store, both her parents are Accountants based in Lagos. The mothers of my children do not know a third of what Motun knows, I have never disclosed anything about myself to anyone but I told her all about my rags and linen.

She listened never once interrupting me like the women I am used to. When we got up to leave she asked if she could hug me. No woman has ever held me like that. I walked her to her place in Pimlico and went home feverish. I told wife number 3 it was time for her to go back to Nigeria to keep an eye on her business.

Till today I don't know if Motun saw me as an assignment, she took me places, London Zoo in Regents Park, Museums, Trocadero, Chessington, Leeds Castle, Four Tenors in Hyde Park, and the show Five men called Mo. I lived the childhood I never had and saw London as a place other than a drug distribution station.

Making love was crazy she would sit on me, go down on me, swallow me, something none of my wives would tolerate or do, Motun was comfortable with me giving her oral sex, sex became a beautiful thing rather than a submission to your husband. I realized my wives really didn't like me the person rather they observed cultural guidelines of total submission.

It was her suggestion to get married so I could have a red passport, we do this and I am given my stay, in the next 5 years I receive a British passport. We quickly divorce, no third party is aware I have a British Passport. I am devastated when she has to return to Nigeria, planning to rent a flat in Ikoyi I hurriedly purchased a detached property for her on Boudillion Road and gave the paperwork to her a few months before she left.

I know I can never marry her but at least I have lived. She assured me she would always be a part of my life and keeps her words. Motun has one of the finest lace shops on Allen Avenue; every month without fail material is delivered to my tailor and is forwarded wherever I am.

Trouble comes in three's. Shortly after Motun left one of the few male couriers we use, an elderly man was stopped at JFK, he had ingested and became nervous while going through customs, and he immediately told officers what he had done when pulled aside. As soon as I was informed I got one of the lawyers I retain to go and see him on Island Penitentiary and assured him his family will be taken care of. He was given a 5 year sentence. I sent word to his wife that he will be remaining in the USA for a few years and made arrangements for a sum of 1 million naira to be given each year to cover cost and meet all household bills.

Thirdly I am under the looking glass of the Nigerian Drug enforcement agency again, they now work alongside their counterparts here, my guy at the college calls to tell me the police came to the college to ask for me. I need to leave London. I head to Belgium that very evening.

Motun advises I start to deal in vehicles or chemicals, scale down my drug operation to what I can manage from afar and start importing cars into Lagos; I quickly set this up, vehicle parts and cars from Belgium with paint from France, within 18 months I hear that NDLA are no longer interested in meeting with me.

I venture into London, business has dwindled, a few of my trusted workers have headed off to Ireland, where if you have a child there the child is entitled to an Irish Passport, which entitles you to all sorts and at some point an Irish passport yourself. I make do with a handful of old faithful and plough on.

Number 2 & 3 wives have gone off with other men when things were down for me. Number two is back sniffing now money is back, what is it with this yellow babe I can't resist. I think of Motun regularly cussing my luck and lack of good upbringing.

A friend of mine had gotten involved in Politics having become a Governor he insists I came back to Naija. I was awarded a 1 Billion Naira contract to construct houses. I frantically approach established constructors and second then to do the contract I am making silly money, electronics and farm machinery is piling in from China, Cars & Trucks from Belgium, paint from France and the Government contracts, following the big award the trick is to accept contracts under 17 million Naira every month, anything above 21 million belongs to the big boys like Senators and Commissioners.

I am offered oil contracts; crude oil that I will sell on as well as the option of dirty oil, I didn't know there was dirty oil a by-product of refining used for greasing joints in heavy machinery. I decline. Motun joins me from time to time, she is being hassled by her fiancé and parents to get married, I write her a cheque for 75 million Naira and I wish her well, I do not attend but buy the new gossip magazines that covered the event. I deliberately put distance between us.

My eldest son graduated in Aeronautic Engineering and joined the Aviation Industry as he's always used his mother's maiden name I was sure he wouldn't have any problems joining. He got married in England a few years ago, that was difficult, the girl's family didn't approve and didn't want the alliance. I had a private meeting with her parents and told them as much as I felt they needed to know with regards to my early childhood misfortune, I played heavily on the fact that I had done what I needed to survive.

My honesty appeared to make a difference but I was hurt to learn they insisted the wedding take place in England so that Yoruba society did not get to know their daughter married the son of a controversial figure. They have two sons and move round in various high society stations.

My dear that is me in a nutshell, I have money, good health, children, grandchildren, yet I when I move in society I know the tag of drug dealer remains attached and in all fairness I am not totally off the scene. Today we are more sophisticated importing, using frozen seafood via China and Indian, you'll be amazed how much cocaine you can stuff into a large Kingfisher. I have links with several frozen food outlets.

The cargo is always part of their order, behind the shop front the fish is defrosted enough to retrieve the packages, now it's almost like a game, they close one entrance I find another. I wish I was educated, I know I would have been something great. The Italians and I remain tight I am forever grateful to them.

Wale sat backing looking at me the way one would inspect their desert. I ask him about the other bucket guys, nil contact he smiles, you know how it is in London everyone is busy doing their own thing.

As we tuck into the final plates of lychee, slices orange and toffee banana mine washed down with saki, a rice wine, I thank Wale again for his generosity, all the time his phone has buzzed endlessly, he has ignored it, as it begins to vibrate again I nod at him to answer it, "you sure" Wale asks "it will ruin the atmosphere", "go on answer", no sooner does he say hello that a voice begins to bellow whine and whine at him, in response he looks at me raises an eyebrow and switches off his phone. Wife number 4.

I am delighted his has not been a shag me rich experience. Wale had made money alright but like the rest of us the demons money can't appease remain.

Wale's simple approach to life has kept him looking good, he's retained the same stature and approach to dressing, nothing about him is flashy or screams wealth but wealth he has both clean and dirty money.

I need to end the afternoon now and walk away before Wale expects to hear all about my years abroad as in saved by the bell the hospital calls to finalize arrangements.

I use this opportunity and make a move. After yet more hugs with a don't hesitate to ask me it will be a pleasure, I make it to the car and feel a sense of relief as the car moves away. I could so easily have ended up being Wale's wife, two no hopers, stuck on Lagos Island orAguda, not sure where the next meal will come from, I can't imagine my mother supporting the union except to get me out of her sight. I'm meeting Ayo tomorrow I hope he's done good too.

Chapter 31

Ayo
Ayo and I meet at our favorite food joint the White House in the road opposite Regan Girls High School; though we both dress down we stand out. The best food in the world is served straight up and unpretentious. We order lafu gbegiri ewedu and the famous fried stew. We are given spoons which made us dissolve into laughter. Ayo is what you will call tall dark and handsome with the round belly the sugar babes like to rub. Contact with Ayo is going to be short, he certainly is not as affluent as Moses and Wale, neither is he destitute. As we eat he talks.

My way into England was via a lady Sheri who spotted my photograph in a friend's album and said she was interested in meeting me. I gave her your phone number your mum didn't mind me coming to your house to receive calls, we talked for several months then she said she was coming to Nigeria for Christmas.

I was then based at the Ministry of Waters Broad Street as an admin clerk and readied myself to welcome London babe. Sheri arrived loaded with stuff for me from shirts to native wear, shoes and slippers I had seen my top bosses wearing was suddenly mine. Sheri made her feeling quite clear she wanted to marry me; I hesitated as she is 8 years older than me though looked much younger than me. She had been married but the marriage failed. She promised to take care of me and treat me well.

I had nothing to offer or to lose, we were married four months from the time we started chatting, so many people thought I was the luckiest man on earth I have a wife from England and will be joining her soon. My parents expressed concern about me marrying a girl from an unknown background, we kept her age to ourselves, I assured them all will be well.

I arrived in London via Heathrow on a foggy March afternoon, Sheri was at the airport to pick me up, I thought she was so amazing, successful driving a Honda Civic ESI special edition. Home is a flat in St Domingo House Dockyard in Woolwich. We relaxed a bit and I asked what I would be doing, job wise, conscious of those at home expecting me to make good money and send it back. Sheri said to relax she would do all the work for now.

After a meal I asked to shower, Sheri had taken some leave time to help me settle. I had a shower and headed to the bedroom, Sheri is laid on the bed naked with her legs spread apart like Carter bridge, I felt a bit taken aback but I will get used to how folks behave in London.

I got into bed next to her and reached for her, she moves out of my reach and tells me she hopes I like going down, I am confused, then it dawns on me she means oral sex, I have done oral sex before but not in this crude manner. Its early days so I do it, I do not enjoy the act one bit having never spent more than a few minutes giving pleasure that way.

I try to get into the spirit of things when she comes and makes such a racket and trashes about on the bed, I am really shocked what the hell is this, I know women enjoy sex but is Sheri normal. In my first twenty four hours in London I would have spent nothing less than a total of five times giving oral sex.

A man is a man and has to do what a man has to do. I alternate between flattery and reservation about Sheri's behavior she wants sex, long stretches of it, it is unfulfilling for me because my face is between her legs. What else can I do, this woman has made it possible for me to come to London. I wonder if this was a factor that contributed to her marriage dissolving, oh well rather late now.

By the end of the first week I find it hard to eat, my tongue is coated in furry white. I ask to see a GP. Sheri takes me to a nearby health centre, the nurse who does the first visit screening took a look at my tongue and asked if I had been having oral sex with multiple partners, I said no just with my wife, I have thrush a yeast infection that is easily treated, during treatment no oral sex. Sheri too needs treatment or we pass it back and forth.

When we got home Sheri remained in a foul snappy mood until the following week when we could resume sex. I felt a big sense of relief when she returned to work but that was short lived, as a housing officer in the same borough she frequently popped back home and that encounter involved bringing her to an orgasm through oral sex, I began to dread the sound of her key in the lock.

One weekend we went to a party I was introduced to people as this is him, here he is the one I told you about my husband. I wondered what it is that had been said about me by the multiple non-verbal communications but lots if varied facial expressions.

Maybe it's the alcohol that gave me courage or seeing Nigerians at a party gathering and witnessing that husbands were in control of their wives. Well something gave me the courage to say no to oral sex when we got in during the early hours, when she insisted I slapped her.

Big mistake, Sheri calls the police who arrive prompt, from the moment I slapped her I heard the story of my life the threats of returning me to Nigeria in disgrace, did I not realize I needed to fulfill her needs, who did I think I was, I was going to jail for hitting her and on and on she went assault and battery.

Interesting people the police in England, I wasn't scared, I guess because I had my papers. They listened to both of us; she kept saying it was a domestic and that we had resolved it. The police soon lost interest and left. No sooner did they leave she stated she hadn't told the police I hit her to protect me as with a police record I wouldn't be able to get a good job.

That day I had my first good sleep since arriving without the taste of Sheri in my mouth. I feel out my dept. We quickly settle into a routine, she goes to work I keep house, light cooking cleaning and then wait for her to return.

If there are prizes for daytime television viewing I would win it hands down, there was nothing to do. I am a prisoner in London a good liar to my family and friends back home.

I wondered if Sheri has done to others what she was putting me through, how can a woman want to spend her life her sex life oral sex and more oral sex, the sight the feel of her labia minor put me off eating, the bulge and prickly feel of her pubic hair, not nice occasionally she would shave but that just showed me discolorations, bumps and old boil scars.

I think about running away frequently but run to who run where. I am not in a good place, during the day anything sets me off, loading the machine handling her underwear would have me weeping with sadness for my plight.

Any mention or discussion about me getting a job is met with not yet, relax enjoy, one thing she gave me was money, to appreciate money you need to have access to the shops to spend it, some days she would give me as much as £500.

I start to venture out into my neighborhood. Walking to and from Woolwich in a relaxed manner, taking in my surroundings. I enjoyed watching the ferry coming and going. Woolwich is a vibrant shopping centre, British Home Stores, Zale, Rumberlows, Currys, Ratners, Marks and Spencer's, Richards, Burton, Argos, Bridal boutique, Dorothy Perkins and a Co-op that gave me hours of delight just looking around. There was a big Bingo place and a Cinema. I felt I was in London as there were only a handful of black people around and most were Asians. I shop for myself but buying new clothing and sitting around in the house soon lost its sparkle.

I had been in London 9 months when I lost my temper again and struck Sheri, this time I gave her a good beating, same scenario give me oral sex it's the only thing I like, by now I recognize I am an object of ridicule, the fellow husbands treat me with pity the women see me as Johnny just brought over and me I feel like if I could kill this woman if I could get away with it.

Again she calls the police and threatens me. Same as last time the police came and went if you didn't say you had been assaulted then there was little they could do it's very different now. I got the impression they really couldn't care less if we broke each other's neck just don't call them. The following day going out for walk I am so deep in thought I do not acknowledge the greeting of the Nigerian lady in the lift.

Several Nigerian families live in the same block, she taps me "Bros if front no fit, carry go back". I laughed, the irony of it me stuck, here nil progress in Nigeria so I can't return; I am at a standstill here.

I say hello and we walk into Woolwich together, she is on her way to clean she informs me the headquarters of a Building Society in new Woolwich Road, we chat as we go, it is painfully obvious that though I've been here for a while I am in no way savvy of the ways here. She tells me about herself and asks about me, apart from saying I am married and my wife works I have nothing else to share.

She tells me they are looking for another cleaner would I be interested as I have no work restrictions, I explain I have no National Insurance number yet. If I'm not busy I should come with her. She opens the door to her work place I am shocked, she explains this is what is meant by a key job, you do the cleaning between the hours of 17.00-09.00 when staff are not in the building.

I watch and follow her as she skillfully empties bins without stopping, swiping cups up on the way and duping them in hot soapy water with a bit of bleach. Out comes a feather duster, she skims over the desks without disturbing any documents, then the Hoover. Back in the kitchen she makes me a cup of tea while she washes and puts things to drain; she has done all her work in 23 minutes flat and gets paid £35 a week for the two departments she covers.

She takes me up to the top most floors and to my surprise makes a call and talks in Yoruba for ages. She tells me she uses this to make International calls but only to Europe and the USA. Perks of the job she laughs. This stranger who introduced herself as Titi, lives with her mum, unmarried but mature beyond her age. I decide to take a gamble and tell her my story leaving out the sordid bits.

Chapter 32

As we head back to Woolwich Dockyard she tells me a plan. She will show me what to do in applying for an NI card, it will be in my name, I will also open a Woolwich Building Society account with a stipulation no account paperwork is to be sent to my house, all my dealings will be in-house.

True to her word Titi was waiting for me at the Woolwich Library, by the afternoon both actions had been carried out. She told me to be vigilant for when the card will arrive in about a fortnight; I prayed it would arrive during the week and not on a Saturday. I took to waiting for Titi and accompanying her to work, I gave her a hand, one day the entire work took us 12 minutes to complete, and an idea began to form.

I asked Titi if it would be okay for me to try and get a cleaning job in the building, to my surprise she informed me she has already spoken to the manager who hired her to say she had someone who will be able to start soon. I don't know how to say thank you.

All I know is I cannot continue with this wretched life. I am decorative something to be displayed on the arm at the appointed time. Every weekend we are out partying and I mean every weekend, lace, gold, shoes & bag, endless parade of head-ties and me stuck there sitting like a mannequin until it's time to go home.

Sheri's friends are a loud bunch most divorced or on their third husband, their language is crude and they think nothing of discussing their sex life with each other. Talking of changing a man like one would change a dress. It dawned on me I was picked from a photo album for that purpose, there was and is no love, Sheri and her friends had burnt up all the rubber in England and now look back home to Nigeria for desperados like me to sneer and bring over.

I am a tongue before I am a man. I eat well, dress well, clean house, go shopping and give oral sex, there is currently nothing to add to my CV, I still have the 5 O'levels I left Nigeria with over a year ago, nil college nil work nil structure. Titi is a blessed distraction. Thames Water sometimes looks an attractive way to end my woe.

My NI card arrives on a Tuesday morning, it is the first mail I have received in England that had nothing to do with Sheri, I memorize the number and reel it off to Titi when we met. I also ask her to take care of it for me, today I find out she lives on the 7th floor. The following week I start work at the same place but on the ground and 1st floor cleaning. All forms completed and Woolwich Building Society Account given for payments.

When I mentioned to Titi I was not registered with a GP she took me to a practice in Eglinton Hill, St Marks Medical Center an Egyptian doctor called Nabil Raphael and got me registered. As the practice nurse did what they jokingly call an MOT a physical I thank God for sending Titi to me. Again when my National Health Card drops through the door I memorize my National Health Service Number and give the card to Titi for safe keeping.

My wonder woman Sheri who finishes work at 5pm is rarely home before 9pm this gives me ample time to do my cleaning job and be home and in bed. When she rolls in I have to get up and listen to her tell me how good I have it, a wife that works all day and gives me all I need. She may or may not eat and when done leaves the dishes in the sink. It occurs to me Sheri is behaving like a man our home is a complete role reversal. She is about to teach me a lesson.

When we retire to bed the usual using her foot to tap me to meet her needs start some days, I ignore her tonight she is doing the foot thing, I am tired and no longer find this woman attractive an erection is impossible even with me thinking of blue movie images, she is in a foul mood.

When Sheri snakes her way down my belly I was under the false illusion she was going to give me my first blow job, something a sixth sense screamed a warning at me I moved just in time to stop her from biting down on my you know, in fury she sinks her teeth into my thigh. Then my belly all the time trying to bit my manhood, she is strong real strong for a woman. When I fling her away from me there is blood in the bite sites.

I get dressed and leave the flat to the chorus of her screams and cusses of how useless I am and what regrets she has. "You have nowhere to go no one", she yells as I close the door behind me. If anyone harbors' me they will die a cursed death. What sort of demented woman had I allowed to bring me here for the sake of a better life. I am a big man at 6'1 if I was to use half my strength to punch her just once she would need intensive care.

I call the lift and press the ground floor then make my way up the stairs to the 7th floor. I explain my situation to Titi declining her offer of sleeping on the settee. I tell her I am going to sleep at the Building Society building and will leave before staff arrive. Titi offers to come and wake me at 07.30 to make sure I leave the building on time. She rolls up a duvet and puts it in a black bag, thus became my pattern of sleeping in the store cupboard housing the boiler and the warmest room on each floor after a fight.

I learnt that brick and mortar have their language, initially I used to be scared stiff to be in that building alone, then I gradually go used to the noise the building makes, it's as if it shifts it's position slightly from time to time like we all do.

I washed using jay cloth standing on a towel, those were harsh times in the winter, I struggled to sleep from the cold and discomfort, in the summer I was unable to sleep from the stifling heat but dare not open a window because of the alarms. If I slept in the main offices that had fans, human smell will not go unnoticed.

I now had bite marks on my torso, legs and back but nothing above the cloth line. I guess you can say I am 1st generation domestic violence man. Sheri is really mad because I am no longer in her control. I leave evidence around that I am looking for and applying for jobs or to attend Thames Polytechnic in Woolwich.

My life is pathetic really, it's a vicious circle of me giving oral sex getting feed up, followed by her anger and frustration which eventually erupts into violence from her and me becoming a broom cupboard occupier for a while. I once threatened to report her to the leader at her mosque she laughed in my face and said he is her ex! so that was that, I still hadn't told my family she is a different faith.

On my own I admit to crying the hardest thing for a man to face is a total removal of his identity, Sheri didn't want a man she wanted a man servant a yes person, a licky licky. To this day I find it hard to enjoy oral sex. We continued in this destructive manner for the next 10 months. She would demand sex, not only did I not want it my you know what lay placid floppy like a summer hat.

On the occasions she tried the friendly approach I still couldn't get an erection. Sexual frustration is a thing to behold in a woman. She informed me one evening an Ann Summer's rep is coming to see her. The name Ann Summer means nothing until the woman begins to unpack penis of different size, material and shapes.

A large demonstration one had a suction attachment, she stuck this on the TV screen. My fascination outweighed my disgust, Sheri laughed with excitement and tried to draw me into the conversation as the white woman demonstrated speed and rotations.

Sheri loudly tells the woman I will be using the vibrator on her. This promised to be interesting, by now the very sight of her nakedness repulsed me, She bought three vibrators, a slim sliver one, a thick latex one which moved up and down with a rotating head and a small one the size and fitting looked like a ladies lipstick, this one is for discreet use when out, she's bought nipple creams, edible knickers and an array of junk.

No sooner had the woman left that this shameless female Sheri got two AA batteries fired up the latex one and asked me to use it on her. I have final confirmation I am with a woman who has lost the plot. I am shortly to take back my disgust of vibrators and see them as my savior. I switch it on and touch her clitoris with it, following her instructions what took me hours to achieve was done by the vibrator in 2 minutes. Three times that evening I used them on her for the first time in a year I sleep easy.

I took the vibrator to bed and just before 6 am fired it up and open up her legs myself, from that morning an uneasy peace settled in that flat, why she couldn't poke herself with the vibrator escapes me, but then it's all about her being in control of the husband she brought from Lagos.

Chapter 33

I go with her to the parties but now talk to others, I engage the men in conversation or simply say hello and stand and listen to what is going on, by and by reading between the lines I understand most of the brought over men from Nigeria are having a rough time with the women who married them and gave them access to live here.

As they discuss the problem they also look at possible solutions. The secret accounts, sending money home to the Naija account every month, buy buy buy land, start building. I listen and apply all that I hear and feel suit my situation.

I continue to keep important documents with Titi and see my GP as needed. At Titi's suggestion we take on a few more cleaning jobs in and around Woolwich, flexi home cleaning, usually home bound elderly people, we had no business with them just said hello and got on with the cleaning, in a week I find myself earning £300.00 after tax deduction.

I begin to buy and send small essentials home to my people, freezers, upright and chest to make ice to sell. Titi encourages me to buy land at 37 thousand Naira a plot in Aguda she urges me to get a move on. Through Titi I purchase several plots over the course of two years.

Around this time I notice a distinct change in Titi she is dating a guy from Peckham, a so called big boy who picks her up from work. Occasionally he comes in and uses the phones while she is working, one day I come across him rifling through the directors desk another occasion he sits practicing signatures.

I see him put an office stamp in his pocket and leave. I warn Titi and express my good wishes for a better person for her.

Titi continues to treat me like an annoying big brother, when I try to express my concern she laughs and says cleaning is not a job or a way of life, she wants to go places this guy is her ticket to a better place.

In the April of 1993 Titi was arrested at work an accomplice to £75,000 cheque written and cashed stolen here from the Director's office, there were smaller charges of abuse and unlawful use of equipment. Her Bolaji boyfriend was nowhere to be found, she was given a 6 year jail term at Holloway Prison and a recommendation for deportation after her sentence.

I went up to see Titi's Mum, I had tried every day since Titi's arrest, I had a heavy feeling in my stomach but understood it was a difficult time for her, each visit I left word. Today a young man I had never seen opened the door and told me he was the new tenant, he must have been alarmed by my reaction or expression because he invited me in.

I told him my circumstances and explained Titi had looked after all my documents for over two years. The man let me have a look at the paper junk left behind there was nothing for me. My passport and all other documents I kept with her was gone, no forwarding address for her mother.

The gleam of the Thames is calling me to jump in end it all, was I cursed before I left Nigeria. A grown up man like me, cleaning during the day and using a vibrator on a woman at night, what kind of wretched life is this. I look around me Woolwich Dockyard has become my hell on earth. Where do I start, I am once again at the mercy of Sheri, the lack of passport scares me. I sink into a state of misery.

My saving grace is I have been asked to clean the whole building, if I can cope my salary is increased to £100 a week for the whole building. I accept, yet what used to be fun now weighs heavily, I arrive at work on the dot of 5 and manage to finish for 9pm. I am careful not to touch the phones and stay clear of documents and draws. 9 months later I am given notice the building is closing down my work will be finishing.

The morning after this news Sheri had barely left for work when the phone rang, it is the Immigration Service at Heathrow terminal 3, could I confirm who I was, I did, they asked if I was prepared to come to the airport they had someone in custody who had just flown in on my passport. They will cover my travel expenses, I call a cab for a return journey and head to the airport with my marriage certificate and album.

I left Heathrow midday with my passport, making out I didn't know it was missing thanking which ever God had worked a miracle. The guy who tried to use my passport said it was for sale under Eko bridge, he had paid £2000 as it was genuine, this desperate fool looked nothing like me. I am home without Sheri even knowing I left the area.

I see a course for Care Assistants advertised it's in New Cross a one bus trip on the 53, I enroll. The entire 42 students are Nigerians and Ghanaians'. 10 weeks later I have a certificate that means I can feed you, move you, wash you, take your blood pressure, temperature, pulse, support nursing staff with whatever it is qualified staff want you to do.

We are encouraged to apply for jobs at Greenwich District Hospital and Kings College Hospital they are recruiting. Sheri and I have an uneasy truce, I simply tell her I am looking for a job, she says nothing lately she seems preoccupied but as she tells me nothing except to say who's party we are attending at the weekend. We have very little communication going without the wiz of a vibrator.

Even that curiously is not every night. It briefly crosses my mind she might have found another man to give her head, if she has good luck to them both, better him than me.

I start work at Greenwich Hospital in the autumn, I walk there not because I have to but I want to, the feel of the breeze the cars people makes me feel a part of the community. Sheri is indifferent to me and makes no response when I say I'm starting work.

I quickly find my way round the hospital, the frequent destination being Path lab to drop off blood samples that couldn't wait for the porter to come. Coming out of path lab one day I see Sheri, wonder what she's doing at the hospital but caution myself to mind my business.

When I get home she informs me she is taking some leave time. I expect her to travel but she's at home, mainly resting and talking on the phone. I sense something is wrong but she says she is fine.

A letter came addressed to her I saw the word McMillan Nurses, when I asked what it meant and why they were coming to see her at home, plus the statement about moving into a hospice she said it was work related. Sheri died 3 weeks after I saw that letter she had ovarian cancer late stage.

I cannot tell you how difficult the next few months were, the God honest truth was I was in conflict half of me felt a sense of relief and the other felt sorry that a human being had died.

The visitors her friends their husbands, her relatives I didn't know came to pay their condolences, the wailing the lamenting on and on it went. Finally they moved on with their life, there was work to do and parties to be attended mourning period had to be realistic.

The housing officer came to see me a routine visit, I mentioned a two bedroom flat was too much for me I would like to down size if they have a one bed in the Greenwich area.

Within a few months I move to a flat in the heart of Greenwich Haddo Place, the Cutty Sark and I become neighbors. I make enquires about Thames Polytechnic and find it is in the process of being made a University; I can do an access course. A letter arrives from an Insurance Company, Sheri had a £47,000 life cover, as her next of kin and identified beneficiary the attached cheque is mine. I am saddened, in death she is giving me an avenue her behavior didn't alive.

Chapter 34

For the first time in my life I know peace, I wake up and go to sleep without any tension, I do a 60 hour week my choice, I am on top of my bills and keep my expenses down. I lose count of the Nigerian women who try and strike up conversation when I'm buying food stuff, 'Uncle shall I come and help you cook all that' spoken light heartedly but all I need to do is say yes.

I begin to wake up with an early morning erection, it is a good sign I am healing from my abuse, I view my marriage as a walk of tightrope fire, Sheri is dead and I can thankfully move on. I do not mourn her at all. I am in England, I have my papers, I am legit but it had cost me dearly.

Me who couldn't study in Nigeria am now going to University in London Devil don hammer. I do Business studies, I didn't want to become a nurse social worker or work in IT like the Nigerians like me were opting for. Surprisingly I find I enjoy studying, I make a few friends but avoid the party and drug scene.

I am attracted to a lady called Sheridan on my course, her English is different from what I hear around me when she speaks if I close my eyes it sounds like a member of the royal family. Because she suggested it I went along to the Frog and Radiator pub with a group of them one evening. It was a Friday night and the place was heaving, smoke made it difficult to see so after my third drink I was ready to leave and walk back to Greenwich, Sheridan left with me we walked without speaking for a while when I asked where she was heading she simply stated your place and linked hands with mine.

I opened a bottle of Concorde wine the cheap students plunk, we drank and chatted, she made the first move, nestling into me. That night I had sex, sex like I hadn't had since I left the shores of Nigeria , Sheridan urged me on, there was no lengthy oral sex just good raw sex that left both of us sore.

She spent the night and left after another dose of sex that left me aching. I felt good really good. I am at University and keeping up, I'm working money is coming in; I don't need big things and find I am content.

That evening I decide to stroll into Deptford and eat at Tommy's kitchen, I am craving Togolese beans, as I order the food I heard an almighty shriek and my name when I turn Titi flung herself into my arms, I am so shocked I just stand there staring at her.

She is babbling trying to tell me everything at once. I was right he was bad, good behavior early release, no one at address mother moved as was frighten, all your documents are safe, that is all that registers 'all your documents are safe' I missed you I'm sorry I didn't listen please forgive, on and on it pour, all I hear is the magic words all my documents are safe.

I ask if she wants to eat, we buy and head to her place; they live in Deptford a room in a shared house. As if to prove her point she hands me a folder indeed all my documents are safe except my passport, I get the feeling she knows nothing about that issue and makes a decision to say nothing. After eating I insist she comes to know my place.

Something has melted my heart towards Titi a long combination of the helping hand she gave me and the documents in my hand. She is not a bad person and realized in prison she had being targeted. That evening we talked and talked her fear of the future, the stigma of going to prison, her early release due to good behavior and nothing said further about deportation but this was her fear every day, on the spur of the moment I told her we will continue the conversation tomorrow morning lets go and sleep.

For the third time in less than 24 hours I have good sex, the sort where when you get up from the bed and feel like a King. Titi never really leaves after that. The prison services put her on a re-integration into the community program somewhere along the line the instruction to deport her had got lost.

As there is funding available for education I tell her to ask to train as an HCA, what better way to give something back to society. In a short while she does the HCA course and begins work at the Day treatment Centre in Greenwich Hospital. We were married a few months later, the 1st of or our three boys was born on our second anniversary.

Very unusual but following graduation I decided to start a small business, one thing I know will sell is lace, having spent time with Sheri's crowd. I collect all the information I need and book a flight to Zurich from there I take a train to St Margareta's changing at St Gallens, by the last leg of the train ride the Naija's outnumber the Swiss and Austrians, I am the only man and attract gentle teasing, such as why can't madam come and do the buying, I explain she is a nursing mother and would appreciate if I can tag along with them.

This is how I began the 2 monthly trip to buy lace material, we kept the cost down and rarely sold any above £120, making a tidy profit of £50-60 on each sale. Around this time I decided to venture into the New York buying and selling, the package for a three night stay with hotel and flights was £299 this suited me just fine.

On my first trip I thought long and hard about what to sell, which market to target what was missing in London, as I walked through customs the answered stared me in the face, fatty fatty sizes. I made my way to Delancey and Essex and also Flatbush, from the Chinese I bought 100% linen suits, dress trousers, two pieces, three pieces, all were the same wholesale price $18. Children's linen outfits I found for $9. Loaded with two suitcases I headed home. My dear I remember those 1st trips because on the dresses that cost $18 we sold each piece for £75 and the children's dresses went for £25 each. This is how I turned things round for Titi & I. We are not rich but very comfortable. The 47 grand sat in a post office account earning good interest. Titi went on to train as a nurse, I am happy with my buying and selling and working alongside the nurses and doctor.

The New York route suffered a setback when customs stopped me and charged me £500 with a fine of £350 for walking through the nothing to declare zone so I shut down that business, it's no point working hard saving the money paying tax only to have to pay the tax again.

When the Euro Countries took off I ensured I limited my business to those countries. Today we have 2 shops in Peckham, two shared shops in Ikorodu selling cloths from Primark a low cost shop in London. The investments we made as cleaners have offered us the best we could ever hope for.

The land we bought in the early days are now retailing for millions and millions, so if we are ever in need of raw cash there is something to fall back on. Titi is into cosmetics and regularly flies out to Lagos, she has a small training project/school in which makeup artist are trained, that is located Ojuelegba, that venture is also doing well.

The important thing for me is we have been able to raise our children ourselves without needing child minders and the such, I didn't want my children to suffer abuse and criticism the way I suffered when I was young.

I have no real friends other than you four, it sounds strange but I've never showed my real self again to anyone the way I showed you guys. I never did make it big but I made something of myself.

So tell me how are you and things in the States. I smile and make all the right noises. I think of the four of us and fruit salad comes to mind, we have all turned out so different so far each journey has been rough. I wonder what Pitan will have to say when I meet him tomorrow. The rest of the meal is spent in a comfortable zone, the sort two people who have nothing to hid or prove share.

Chapter 35

Pitan
"My dear sweetest pea' Pitan says as soon as we take our seats at Crown Restaurant Maryland not far from me the following day. He doesn't beat about the bush after enquiring about my welfare launches straight into his catch-up spill.

I came to London for one reason and one reason alone oh, to marry a white woman have half-caste children sorry mixed race, they say caste is insulting oh, whatever I never want to return to Itafaji. In those days I thought of my parents as irresponsible, how can you live in one room with a wife and four children.

My childhood can only be describes by one word Stock Fish, how I hate the smell of that fish, it was stored in the same room we lived in everything in that room had the underlying smell of stock fish, that shit was so expensive we never actually ate it, life was spent making sure the customers did not steal it, it did not get wet it did not rot it did not a lot of things. I hated the way we were all crammed into that one room at night and took to sleeping under the fruit tree in my teens.

I had been awake too many times when my dad had quietly told my mum the children are asleep let's do it, when you get to a certain age listening to your old man rumbling your mum doesn't cut it. My father sold newspapers running alongside cars to quickly hand over the paper while keeping a grip until he got his money. Regular falls and tumbles were a norm.

I come from a low class background and grew up with an intense dislike of those who do not try and improve their lot. I was embarrassed by the state of my family and had as little as possible to do with them.

I bet you didn't know I sold newspapers in Tinubu Square before heading to school in the morning, and then sat at my mum's stall by the roadside in Itafaji in the afternoon after school. Did you ever notice I wore the same Starskey and Hutch tee shirt whenever we met?

Man those were hard times, I didn't want to be me, I envied all you rich folks so much, I dreamt and pretended there had been a mistake at the hospital and my real parents, people like your mum and dad would one day turn up to collect me. Apart from my school uniform I probably had less than 7 items of clothing to my name and two foot wears. Gloriously second hand.

I remember our bucket evenings well, it was the only time I ate and drank like the rich. You people had so much food and yet you were never hunger picking at food that's all you ever did. Your servants eat better than me, I loved and hated you at the same time but gave up fighting my feelings towards you as you were just you, no malice no me rich you poor.

You seemed grateful for our company; meanwhile I suspect we were your friends for the guaranteed food, free soft drinks and chocolates you gave away so freely. We used to talk about you giving us your money saying take it, I wondered if you were a 'mumu', years later I understood you gave out of pure simple friendship.

I loved your house, your family, your cars, your food, clothes, even the smell of your house was glamorous, that furniture polish the wooden floor and the granite tiles so cold and refreshing to walk on, who lives there now?

I smile and watch Pitan, the envy he's always tried to hide surfacing no holds barred. Today is not about me, giving him my best smile I steer him away from me. "Tell me about Obodo our slang for abroad". Pitan takes a deep breath I'm not sure what is coming but let's have it.

Pitan talks:

I stole slow and steadily from the stock fish money, each sale I made I added a few naira to and kept the difference, you guys had said a return ticket on Nigerian Airways cost 210 naira so I had a target, it took me months and months to save up that amount and the additional 500 naira I changed into £499.20p. I told my parents I was going to Ahmadu Bello University to sit an exam for the Faculty of Arts, they gave me 130 naira to cover travel and other costs believing me when I said I would be gone a fortnight.

I arrived in London and was given 6 months visa at Gatwick, just like that. 6 months keh...me I'm not going back except in a body bag and even then immigration will have to catch the dead body first.

White men are bastards, don't interrupt me to protest, I learnt my lesson the first day, from Gatwick I made the connections and arrived at Bermondsey station, my friend I was staying with lives in Abbey Road said it's less than a five minute walk, with a small suitcase I was ready to walk to save the 40p bus fare.

I made one big mistake I asked a white man just to be sure I was heading in the right direction, he told me to continue walking along the A200 turn right at the end walk across the bridge and ask again, thus I took an unnecessary walk across Tower Bridge, till today if I am unsure I will ask anyone but a white person for directions.

What a welcome, it must have been so obvious I had just stepped off a banana boat as I learnt they say. The first English words I learnt were mind the gap, tickets please and alright love. Dele my friend had warned me about winter but until you experience it you don't get it.

Dele came from a trading background like me, his uneducated mother was here buying whatever it was she was bought to bring back to sell to rich folks, when she went into labor and gave birth here entitling Dele to stroll back into the UK as a British citizen years later. Dele had no idea of his rights until we told him, once he presented his birth certificate to the Embassy at the age of 16, they paid all costs as he is classed as a minor and child in need, based on the stories we told him to tell and the beating scars on his body. Leaving care he was given his own place, money to furnish it and left to his own devise, Dele takes people in for £10 a week until they find their feet the only condition you are not to put his address down at point of entry.

When I used 10p to call him Dele laughed apparently that is the norm with some young people, white or black all meant in fun, no harm done. Dele came to meet me part of the way, I told him of my plan and looked at every white girl we passed as a potential wife.

You need to see Dele's flat on the 13th floor of a high rise the view takes your breath away, dose of reality kicks in when the lift breaks down which it regularly did. The one instruction I am given is do not answer the door it could be TV license, fine for not having a license is £200.

A license to watch TV... in Naija you buy TV and plug it in adjust the Ariel and watch. I need work please as quickly as today, but my friend has changed this is his territory, first we sort out NI then we sort out your passport then we start work. How long will all this take, a few weeks he says with all the confidence in the world.

That afternoon we go to the local cemetery I am alarmed, while Dele picks up flowers from someone's grave and makes me walk around looking for anyone born in 1962, we find a couple of girls then find a young man called Steve Barr, Dele takes the details and makes a call from the local phone box the person does some checks and gives him the go ahead. Next day we go to St Catherine's house to obtain a copy of Mr Barr's birth certificate we pay the cost and walk out in 27 minutes an NI application is submitted in that name. I give Dele £400 and hang on to my £90.

We go to Camden Town station and wait for a guy who takes my passport and £40, he returns 30 minutes later and I have a stamp extending my stay to 2 years nil restrictions from the date the 6 month visa expires. Before we go home we drop in at the post office and apply for another NI number in my real name.

We visit a Nigerian lady that afternoon, middle-aged but jovial, she is head cook at a nearby College, I will start work as a kitchen porter, the deal is she's recently widowed and wants someone to accompany her to functions. I will accompany her to funerals if that's what rocks her boat, just give me a job and let me start earning.

It's walking distance, six hours a day split into two shifts lunch and evening mealtimes. I am free to find something to do in the morning. Dele suggests a cleaning job at the local train station, for a guy who doesn't work he sure knows where the vacancies are. I look back now and see that at any one time there is nothing less than 5 other guys living at Dele's, because we work all sorts of shifts we are rarely home at the same time. On top of his benefits he has £50 a week top-up, not bad for a Sandgross boy who didn't know he had British citizen rights until a few years ago.

I start work as soon as the NI arrives, I use my proper name for the kitchen post and Barr for cleaning Bermondsey train station. In no time I have two salaries coming in. I ask Dele if I can stay for a while to find my way around no problem, I up the money I give him to £80 a month, effectively working to pay him one week each month but I have plans. Rarely do I miss the chance to say hello to white females, at the station, in the streets, in the lift you name it, I smile a 'hello alright love' as I've heard them address each other.

Mixed response some smile some say yes love and others look down on me, one responded, love who? I gradually began to work out the class factor based on their appearance within a few weeks, I knew the alright love, the educated ones the office workers that look right through me the one parent mums looking for a dad for their child or just some fun for themselves.

I look, I say hello but have no courage to ask anyone out, but my mission is my mission nothing will make me compromise it. All white people are not British some are Welsh some Scottish and then you have the Irish, the Irish are Nigerians born in a white skin, what a lovely bunch, they are quick to like and share and some can drink you under the table but with such a good heart.

The women are rounded like Naija women, they laugh and flirt with their eyes and can talk all day. Dele tells me the key is politeness and presentation. With money coming in I treat myself to the 3 for £10 shirts in Roman Road market a couple of trousers with the shop brand cut off and nice shoes from Barrett's. Dele suggested I buy aftershave, I stick to Brut it's the cheapest in the shop and smells fine to me.

I am not having much luck with the white women but know it's just a matter of time once I've ironed out my kinks I'll find one. Madam kitchen matron has a function she would like my help with, an engagement party in Stoke Newington. Thank God of my ancestors I went, there were white women there wall to wall, the bride to be is a nursery nurse white girl from somewhere nearby called Kent.

I said hello I chatted mindful not to upset my kitchen boss, all the ladies were friendly, one went as far as to say she has fun with black boys but won't be taking one home to introduce to her parents. It's all okay I'm learning my accent is also improving. Lisa a cousin to the bride gives me her phone number do I want to come clubbing in Woolwich Flamingos Nightclub.

That nightclub is the best thing that ever happened to me, there is one word to describe the place...meat market. From my first visit with Lisa I went there every Friday unfailingly.

Chapter 36

Wall to wall ladies most looking for good time, if you didn't look too closely you won't notice their tired worn and desperate looks, as for me I felt I had arrived surely I will find a woman here and I quickly do. She's called Dolly after Dolly Parton, she has a flat in Cherry Orchard estate in Charlton. Dolly is two years older than me works as a legal secretary and liked me.

We met a couple of times at the club then she invites me for a Chinese meal, I am only familiar with special fried rice or spring rolls so I ask Dele for advice, I needn't have bothered. Dolly does the ordering and I like everything we eat particularly duck Cantonese style, what I would have given to chew the bones.

When I thought it was goodnight she asks me back for coffee, we walk from the little Chinese restaurant tucked into the corner of Spray Street in Woolwich to Charlton, talking and laughing not feeling the October cold.

I have sex, sex with a white woman is different they like to touch and caress for a long time, kissing and rubbing and kissing and rubbing, when she offers me a condom I say I am not seeing anyone is she, she says no, I have rehearsed this so many times it just rolls off my tongue, let us be boyfriend and girlfriend we won't sleep with anyone else so we are okay.

I gain entry this is what I came to UK for to make babies with white women; I take my time and manage three rounds before we fall asleep. I wake up in the early hours of dawn to see a ghost lying next to me, I start to pray in a labored voice calling out to Jesus trembling that there is a ghost this is a bad sign when you see a ghost in Nigeria death has surely come, I don't recognize where I am but the ghost is moving, it switched on the bedside light I sit there drenched in sweat babbling to Dolly I have never been with a white woman.

She comforts me. I am scared senseless, all my plans of coming to UK marry a white woman; I just woke up next to one and panicked. Can I do this.

Dolly offers to make me soup I say yes Oxtail is fine thinking I will enjoy chewing the bone, that will surely revitalize me. She gives me a bowl there is no meat or bone to chew just a thick brown gruel. I try a few mouthfuls; this is not the oxtail soup I know she sees me struggling and takes it away. I am happy with a cup of tea. Before I leave we have sex again, I hope she gets pregnant soon.

The white man says all things come in threes, that Monday Sue joined the kitchen crew a feisty divorced mother of three she picked on me as soon as the shift started, how would I like her to bend over the huge pot we were emptying of spuds, a pat on the backside a wink when no one was looking.

A mature woman who knew what she wanted she told me she would have me before the week was out. Have me she did before work on the third day, she lived two streets from me and all three kids were in full time school. A nice three bedroom house, me being used to flats and the one room I came from I thought her thru lounge a mini palace, we didn't make it up to the bedroom, got as far as the stairs and took her from behind with her kneeling on the stairs.

She's stick thin for a mother of three, small cute peach bottom pert small breast that didn't require gathering just cupped beautifully and she's tight, also has this clenching thing going on that makes me feel she's going to squeeze me permanently and keep me in her, she is a delight.

I remember the first time a female swallowed me in Nigeria it left me so unsettled I spoke to an elderly uncle who assured me the girl must like me a lot so nil reason to worry, I am so superstitious. Long after I climax Sue continues to gently nuzzle me, in the end I have to ask to sit down. As we walked to work she assures me I can drain myself in her anytime as long as her kids are out of the house. I ask about her ex, he's moved to Spain wanted for some benefit money irregularities.

On Friday a woman who I later came to know as Carol passed a bit of paper to me in the lift of our apartment block and left with a smile. I pocketed it and read the short note later, she is direct and to the point, she has been watching me for the past few months likes what she sees would like to get to know me better if I am free and single. Well! what I went to Sokoto to get is right under my nose in Shokoto.

What is with white people and tea, would I like to come up for tea, no I would like to come up and get you pregnant. I say yes please and buy a small box of black magic chocolate, white women like gifts like that.

She is harder to break, works at the local library and lives on her own after moving to London from a small village called Ledbury near Worcester. She seems nice like for a good home doesn't use words like alright love or innit.

Between working escorting madam kitchen to a function seeing my ladies I am pretty busy, at our flat people come and go I check my continuing stay with Dele from time to time he says we are kool. I guess the fact he could still be rotting in Sandgross if I hadn't given him information he didn't know is what keeps me special to him. He thinks my plan is hilarious.

Carol cried the first time we had sex she called it love making, if I had known she was a virgin I would have run a mile, it wasn't until after I saw the blood and realized the tightness was not from nil sex for a long time but nil sex full stop. I don't like virgins in Nigeria once you sleep with them you are done for, they will threaten to use that virgin head you took to curse you if you step out of line.

I had been in England for 6 months, no one was pregnant yet but I'm servicing three women no condom, I begin to suspect they may be using tablets like Dr Bonjel a contraceptive pill we have back home. In May Carol asks if I would like to move in as there are six of us in the flat, I ask if I can spend the nights at her place, thus starts a pattern, I go upstairs to Carol's just after 9pm.

The Saturday morning she drank tea and threw up I knew she was pregnant, it had happened to one of our co-tenants in Nigeria, I heard her tell my mom 'if I drink tea and vomit I don catch' I said nothing when her period is late she tells me. I ask her what she would like and promise to respect her wishes, I'm meeting Dolly in two hours so keep it brief.

My sperms must have received turbo boost as Dolly shows me a stick, it means nothing to me until she says the lines mean positive for pregnancy, I repeat off heart what I had just told Carol, Dolly is clear, I want this child and I want you to be a part of its life, I want the child to have your name and know you but I won't insist on marriage unless it's what you want. How pregnant is she....not sure periods have been a bit light and she's put on weight recently, she will have a scan, a new imaging thing used to see how far along you are and check all is well with the baby.

As I returned home to Carol freshly showered after sex I begin to sweat, surly three women won't all be pregnant yeap....all three are pregnant but no one is clamoring for marriage. If I had to choose and I need to ensure I can stay in the country I will choose Carol, she is manageable not too much trouble compared to the other two.

Chapter 37

Dolly is 21 weeks pregnant !!! her cervix has not closed fully hence the light periods, Carol is 6 weeks and Sue is 11 weeks. I haven't met Sue's kids but know from the photos they have a black dad, I have never asked to meet nor have I been asked to meet them. I am surprised by my calmness it's what I want, I came to England to impregnate as many white women as allow me.

Well three are pregnant. Dele laughs and laughs but I have a more pressing issue, I had recently bought a metro, small neat car paying £40 in a North London pub, Dele took me to for the purchase of a Nigerian International Driver's license. Today the police are doing a routine stop and check and advised I take the British driving test asap.

Dele says no sweat he will do the test for me we send off for a provisional license, sometimes I wonder if Dele is a saint or a crook, he knows what to do where to go and puts me through in no time.

To all things there is a limit, Dele saw the flowers I bought for Carol and told me to stop wasting money, fresh flowers the best is available at the local cemetery every day. Steal flowers from the dead I don't think so bad enough I stole one's identity.

Life carries on in pretty much the same way the women make their plans, if kitchen madam is disappointment with me she doesn't show it just muttered something about baby father.

Two weeks before Carol gave birth I asked her to marry me, I had already paid £40 in North London for a Nigerian Birth Certificate, I asked her to let our child be born into a married home she agreed, with my birth certificate and a passport that had a visa still valid for a year we married quietly at Southwark registry 34 Peckham Road, pulling two students from the Art college across the road as witnesses.

The three deliveries take place in different hospitals Greenwich District, Kings College and St Thomas's. All three are boys. We register Dolly's son at Greenwich Council in Woolwich. Carol and Sue will be more tricky, as it's the same borough. When we registered Sue's son I make sure I am detached and matter of fact, she actually said she was confused by me in there when we left.

To my relief it was a different person that attended to us when Carol and & I went to register Alani, a name I choose carefully so it fits in with the English life style without being difficult to pronounce. I have been away from Nigeria for 19 months and I have three children.

Dele helped me to send someone to speak to my parents they were supported to receive my call from a call centre in Massey Street both seemed overjoyed but sad that I felt I had to lie, I pointed out the principalities at work and me wanting to make it over safely, knowing their reasoning they quickly agreed. I send them a £100 every month to help with the expenses. I have told them not to expect me home for a long time as I need to establish myself properly.

With the arrival of baby Alani we are given a two bedroom terraced house towards the Greenwich end where Southwark begins, it's a lovely place in a quiet road, and my name is also on the tenancy book. Two years in London two jobs three babies and the standard going rate for any document is £40.

Carol seems happy we get on great apart from food, she tried so hard to get her head around how to cook Naija food, I took over and we have two different meals in our house with her marveling how I can eat rice in the morning. The other women are not asking for child care or any form of contribution.

Sue is clearly an expert regarding the benefit system, she is better off not working and has told any official asking questions we have lost touch. Sue is given a 4 bedroom house in Cold Harbour Lane and spends her time drinking coffee gossiping with her friends and watching daytime programs.

I pop in to see the two boys once a week, with Sue I always ask prior to visiting, with Dolly I visit on Thursdays. Dolly is the first I disclose my marriage to she guessed because of the tell-tale pale ring when I take MY ring off. She took it well, if she was annoyed or disappointed she didn't show it and confused me when she made sexual overtures. Dolly and I were back having sex when our son was 6 weeks old. Like Sue Dolly was re-housed in a two bedroom house in Dursley Road Blackheath. It would seem in England have babies and they throw houses and benefits at you.

Now I begin to think about what I am bringing to the table, I have always been interested in mechanics. Not the filthy stuff I see on Lagos Island but the nice blue uniformed type that I see at Fix-it Tires. I apply for an apprentice post, as a mature applicant with a low income family I don't have to pay in fact I am paid a salary of £608 a month after tax.

I pack in the station cleaning Dele gives the details to someone else as I start work at the Deptford Branch of Fix-it. I am quick to learn but not great with the written work or the various customers accents but they are clearly pleased with me and I eventually pass plus I am offered a full time position take home after tax will be £1,200, it's a 37.5 hours a week job with alternative weekends off. With Carol's £900 a month we are okay; she is also pregnant again and has finally gotten in touch with her parents.

A surprise is waiting for me at home Carol's parent have written to her they would like to meet their grandchild and me. Carol is tense beyond words I don't get it, we arrange to meet at Butlins in Minehead they wouldn't have to do too much travelling.

I am now driving a Nissan Sherry I bought from an accident auction and did up myself. We book a Monday to Friday half board stay and her parents do the same. I thought only Nigerians have family tension, there is something not right with Carol and her Dad, her mum on the other hand is a gem, she spends the five days cuddling and kissing Alani who loved all the attention.

I get on alright with her dad as long as we are talking cars. I am surprised we are not invited to Ledbury, whatever his thoughts are that his daughter married a black man he didn't show them. If I had known the storm that awaited me I wouldn't have bothered with the idea of the break.

On the way back Carol is quiet, when I ask what is wrong she quietly tells me she once had an older sister, Karen who claimed their father had been abusing her, Karen and Carol were removed and put in foster care, Karen went on to self-harm, take drugs, neglect herself put herself at risk at every opportunity successfully killing herself at the age of 16.

Carol had stopped speaking to their mum because she chose to remain with her husband. Because we had a son Carol felt she would be able to tolerate his presence. I make a decision no more contact with her parents.

I try hard to think of examples where fathers have sexually interfered with their daughters in Lagos, I can't recall any because the girl only has to say and the father will be given the necklace treatment.... car tire round his body petrol to ensure it burned well and a match. Nope justice is swift on Lagos Island.

Carol and I go on to have three boys and finally a daughter, I keep a low profile staying under police radar, work, home, visit my other sons, home. I have never found the right time to tell Carol about the other two boys.

I have been in England for twelve years when Immigration did a dawn raid. As the family had grown, the Council had re-housed us, we now lived in a four bedroom, semi-detached house in New Cross. I hear the knock on the door at 06.00hrs I can't think who it is and go down to answer the door, there are three men, two of them look like wrestlers the small man with them is the immigration officer and behind in the street is a police car and a police van.

I know I'm not going anywhere but have to address these men properly, I have no doubt they are specially chosen for their job. They look at me like I'm shit; they give Carol the same look when she comes down.

They insist my two yearly renewed visa is fake and for the past 11+ years I have been an Illegal Immigrant, I know that but I insisted I sent it to the Home Office when I arrived and decided to stay longer, I quote the Commonwealth Law that states if you are from a Commonwealth Country you can go to another Commonwealth Country to live for two years without any restrictions after two years you must declare an intent.

They ask if I am a lawyer I say no and act like a 'mumu'. They check my marriage certificate, as they check documents the older children come downstairs that seemed to shift things. Regularize your stay I'm told and off they went. In the spirit of the shock that day I tell Carol of the two other boys ...big mistake.

It's strange to see a white woman lose it, the skin color disappears and she's like any Shukura or Sikira you'll come across at Idumota bus stop. Carol reverted to the primate we all are, she yelled, she howled, she hollered, she broke plates after plate after plate, she cried she threatened to leave me she wanted me to leave she wanted me to stay.

Our marriage is over, no it's not you're going, you're not going anywhere, you are a fraud a cheat double life and it went on and on, I did not say a word just stood there looking at her, if this daft woman thinks she will come between me and my stay she has lost all plots. As long as she wouldn't listen I won't give an explanation. We fall into an uneasy truce.

As I left for work that afternoon my neighbor Iqbal a hello alright Asian came over and asked if I was okay, first the police then fighting he states. He doesn't give me a chance to say much before launching into how a man must control his home, you see me my wife she do as I say, or I tell her you back to Gujarat .

Let me tell you something odd I learnt about Asians, where black people are concerned they see themselves as white. Looking down and totally suspicious, with an intense dislike that's hard to hide. In response the black man pokes fun at a dark-skinned race who think they are the white race after the western white man.

We laugh at their accent which the 1st generation has no hope of losing, we laugh at their aggressive attempts to integrate which only makes the westerns look down on them more. We laugh at the fact there is no courtship with both parties, knowing each other from pictures then marriage, just like that. We Africans dislike the lack of respect when we shop from their stores, it still hasn't occurred to the many Asian shops and butchers if Africans boycott them for a week many businesses will crash.

In this uneasy unspoken truce we live, circling and avoiding each other, neither trusting each other, and instructing the next generation to be wary. The only thing in common is academic focus and top achievements in education of our children.

So here we are Iqbal with his awful English, which believe me he totally is convinced he is speaking the Queen's English. We've got on ok-ish and would often chat on a Saturday while I'm working on my car, today he shows me the newspaper he's carry, front page is a bunch of Nigerians done for fraud, pointing to the headline he states "Nigerians don't know how to do fraud, not like us Indians you are too flashy you make small fraud for £20,000 you make big show always cars and fancy clothes small time police attention because neighbor unemployed jealous tells police.

We Asians better much better we do pharmaceutical fraud, you understand medicines we bring in not bring in collect large money for medicine not coming then collect VAT.

The money hundreds of thousands for VAT and for medicine not coming Millions. You not find the money brother, you see, no keep here. I make deal I get £900.000 I go Tooting, Southall, Wembley, Green Street, I buy three sets of jewellery pure gold diamonds, good stones you understand, maybe buy 2 bangles, to white man all stones yes.

I make journey home when airport say where Gold from we are saying in the family for years taking gold home for wedding, Indian wedding all the time always travel with wife for cover. In India make gold and diamonds into cash, then buy land buy things build in village buy high rise flat in city make money disappear. If police come here to my house me nothing, me say poor English, me no English. English no goodie.

To do this business good English always my brothers and nephews do the English talking all working in business. You know my brother we laugh you for many reason we Asians when we come England we put age up, so for passport we say age 32 for age 25, you Africans you put age down in passport you say age 17 for 28 years, so we work like you but retire quick quick you work for long years unnecessary.

I tell you my brother", my brother he calls me, "the woman of house keep business away from her, you want make business come talk me. I make good business with you but no women you tell they make fight". He finally takes a breath and asks if police found my money I assure him they didn't. I tell him I will think about it and come and see him.

As I drive to work I digest the information he's given me on the Asian 419 versus the Nigerian 419 trade he is right the few pounds Nigerians make is spent making others take notice, whereas as my neighbor points out the huge amounts of money they make is taken out of the country under the very nose of the British by travelling in family groups and using alternative airports for weddings, something no immigration can question.

Chapter 38

I marvel at the simple yet effective way their pharmaceutical fraud is executed. What does he mean make good business with me I'm a car and tyre man. A call from Dolly interrupts me the boy is not feeling very well and she also needs to see me can I pop in briefly.

It doesn't rain it pours, my son has tonsillitis, not a problem but Dolly is pregnant again and again she is alright with us not being together yak yak yak, in no time she begins to swell like bread dropped in water she's carrying twins and is ecstatic.

Work is going well, at home the cold war is on and will not be thawing for a while as we are not on normal terms, I don't waste my time telling Carol about the new pregnancy.

A few weeks after my neighbors conversation he comes over while I'm washing the car, have I thought about his business offer, "what do you have in mind", I ask. "African women like gold, we sell gold you and me make money, we buy and sell to Africans you know plenty", he asks.

I think of my main contact madam kitchen supervisor, she knows half of South London women, it's the 90's and 24ct is coming into its own, people are recognizing the investment worth of Indian Gold. I tell him I'm interested, there and then he pulls a couple of red pouches out of his pocket. "I give you each set £250 anything you make you keep, you give me money end next month. We make deal, have a deal".

I stop what I'm doing and call madam kitchen supervisor, she is delighted to hear from me and invites me over. I can hear lots of noise in the back ground must be the usual no husband all single Saturday at her house thing. When I arrive there are 8 women there, they sure are interested in me I feel like I am dinner with a couple going as far as making breast feeding jokes.

After dodo and ewa I tell them my mission. I have found a contact in Green Street Jewelers, gold worth £1,200 is available for £500 cash paid twice. I bring out the six pouches, all six are sold and I have two grumbling female to pacify.

I stress it must be cash sales and each person they introduce to me gets them £50 off their next purchase. My dear this was the start of Alani trading.

Madam kitchen supervisor ran a tight ship, I made £200 profit per item giving her £50 per sale through her, once a year I also gave my old supervisor a set to keep her sweet and ensure people pay on time. I never once queried my neighbor's source; I started to make basket load of money every month.

I couldn't let it appear in my account so took out a £10,000 loan opened a Building Society Account and used that to run my cash in hand gold business. Within two years I had people selling for me, I targeted the illegal immigrant Nigerians and gave them goods to sell, and they were awesome in selling and delivering money on time always spurred on by the £50 per item sold.

Eventually things thawed out at home, when you are conditioned to sex every night and you stop getting it you go cranky, in bed one dawn Carol simply got on top of me, my umm stiff as a pole with the early morning pee did not complain, the cold war was over.

Do not be fooled I have not lost sight of my goals, I am now working in a recognized profession, I am making money selling gold and about to become a father again to a set of twins. I am sending money home regularly, enough for my parents to move into a two bedroom place in Campbell Street, walking distance for both to get to their trade which they refused to stop doing and retire.

The twins are born on a cold winter morning with snow falling softly. I arrive a few moments before they entered the world, a normal delivery all the staff are jubilant, I wait quietly in the background. Dolly is fine, the babies identical boys are doing well. We register the birth.

Within four months with Dolly kicking off at the housing office regularly, they are re-housed in a three bedroom semi-detached house in Westmount Road the Well hall end.

Life generally goes on uninterrupted this way. I regularize my stay, go through the process of Nationalization and having sworn allegiance to the Queen apply for and receive a red British passport.

Carol wants us to go on holiday and chooses Benidorm in Spain; I go along for the peace keeping appearance. While they are eating ice cream and jumping in the sea, I look to see what business is available, I discover Gomez Rivas shoes and bag, I like what I see the currency rate in Pesetas is very okay.

I buy and ship 6 dozen all large female sizes 7,8 & 9. I find a classy make called Magrit, I don't think South East babes are ready to pay big bucks. I give the shoes to my various selling ladies the asking price is £150 per set, each pair they sell earns them £20 per sale. I am cleaning up with each set costing me £38 in sterling.

With the summer comes higher demands and I'm too-ing and fro-ing from Spain at least three times a month. Buy bag up ship. Between '91 & 97 I outsell the Liverpool Street shoe shops.

I have 8 children four of which I behave like a responsible father to and four I don't, fleeting in and out of their lives when we argue Carol calls me a postcode Dad, the truth is that is what I am.

Chapter 39

Things are about to get even more complicated. I meet Funke at the car garage of all places, she brought her car in for an emergency exhaust, when you say eyes that speak, hers truly spoke, naturally light skinned we were laughing and joking by the time she had paid up.

She asked me to come for something to eat all the time smiling those eyes of hers twinkling at me, as I had finished work I said yes, we went to Saigon Restaurant in Greenwich. She didn't ask but I told her my wife is white thus making my availability known.

Funke has that kind of backside that a driver will crash looking at; she walked slowly and deliberately rolls her ass cheeks as she walks. I bought her story that she had noticed me several times when driving past, she asked for a statement of intent; I was lost, so she said she would make one.

"I want to spend time with you, here or abroad, I want a physical relationship I want to explore my fantasies with you, I want to try all the things I've wanted to but couldn't", by now my hard on is so tight I feel uncomfortable, Funke smiles at me and slides her foot up my leg and into my crotch, looking me in the eyes she states "I want you to be my sexual soul mate", all reasoning went out the window.

Funke lives in Sandy Hill Road in Plumstead, we make it there in no time, instead of heading to her room having sex she takes me out in her garden and there we have sex like the survival of the universe depended on it, I have had sex, there is sex and there is sex this is different.

I have never had sex outside and it blows my mind. The feel of the breeze, the way the grass gives way and you sink slightly, feel of the grass on your skin and the thrill you might be spotted, my mind has stopped working all senses heightened.

The slight coolness of the breeze on your nakedness while you are hot and sweating, the smell and feel of the grass under you, the way you dig your feet in the earth and it gives, if academic rewards are given for sex Funke had a Professorship for fresh ideas, till today I cannot even think of her without getting a hard on.

Funke is great I tell her I am all for what she wants. Driving back so she can pick up her car she spends the short drive fondling me just before we arrived she lifted up her blouse so I could drive while caressing her breast. Why don't wives do exciting shit like this.

Funke is all sex, she is comfortable with her body and wants to try anything and everything within reason, me with a vision of having as many half caste children as possible is now screwing a home girl like a crack addict.

Funke is also business minded our first trip away was to New York, we stayed at the Hemsley Palace Hotel, we had a ball, sex, sleep, shows, I am not westernized but enjoyed myself, while there we met a group of Nigerian ladies heading to the fashion district, wholesalers they said, we tagged along, returning to London with 5 suitcases stuffed with children's clothing all 100% linen each costing $10 at an exchange rate of 1.8 to the pound we were not complaining. I gave the clothes to my sellers at a wholesale price of £22 and was delighted to find they were reselling for between £35-45, we are all making money. We decide to specialize in the metal Swarovski crystal evening purses, buying them for as little as $30 and selling for £120. It was good business.

Home life is now stale, I pay the bills, give sex when the overture is made, attend all the parents evening but Carol bores me. I can't wait to get away to be with Funke. Carol and I tolerate each other. As money has rolled in we've moved to better areas starting with buying our council house and renting it out.

We now live in Court Road in Eltham, a better Borough and environment for the children with the older ones enrolled at a private fee paying school in Kent, I dare not leave Carol as she will clean me out.

I put in an application to buy a franchise in Fix-it and continue to go to New York with Funke every six weeks for stock. As we all know all good things come to an end. More Nigerians are now doing the NY selling route, and very quickly the market is saturated and profits drop.

Funke who has never showed any inkling for commitment drops a bomb she is pregnant, like the others she's going to go ahead with the pregnancy insists on one thing only that my folks formerly ask for her as a daughter. Carol has shown no interest in ever coming to

Nigeria secure in the knowledge she will never find out I give instructions to my parents to make arrangements.

Funke is to tell her parents we will be there for the traditional ceremony. Funke provides contact details for an event planner that uses Shell Club in Surulere. I pay up and enjoy a short day trip to Austria with Funke to buy what the immediate family will wear.

I don't need to make up a story for Carol to visit home, it's my first visit and to cover my tracks I ask if she wants to come with the children, she declines perhaps next time. I change £50 notes in bulk and spread them into clothing pockets I'm taking, thus walking pass customs here and in Lagos with £175 grand without having to explain my money or give bribe.

Coming out of the airport is another business, I am mobbed by guys asking for money welcoming me home just begging for any assistance I can give. I remember those days when I had nothing and give the three most persistent guys £100 to change and share apologizing that I wish I could do more.

We stay at the Sheraton Hotel in Ikeja, I leave Funke to rest while I charter a taxi for the day. Going back to the island and Itafaji is a revelation. I cannot describe the feelings of fear that I will wake up and see that I dreamt the London dream the freedom from wretched poverty, parents who think living in a two bedroom house is the height of luxury and siblings who are happy hustling in the ministries in clerical posts.

None of you guys are available so I have no guests at the ceremony, just family, so many of them, any excuse for free food and booze they pour out of the woodwork. I am not in love but feel something special for Funke and it shows, no expense spared, her friends are jealous her siblings make jokes about finding someone just like me, her parents keep thanking me.

Everyone knows I have a white wife, I don't correct them when they say they understand it's for me to obtain my papers, we have a fun day, speeches and the fun demands before I can see Funke, food and drinks flowed, a good time is had by all. Before I leave I buy Funke three plots of land in Ote-Osa local government a place for her to call home.

Do you remember my younger brother Nuraini, I brought him on board with land acquisitions and building properties. He secured a lot of land for me in Ikorodu not too far from Dangota's cement factory. It felt good to be reaching out to close family.

I officially have super charged sperm, Funke's pregnant with triplets !!! all identical boys when they are born. This time I am more mature and know the system, Funke is dually housed in a three bedroom Council house and moves in just before the boys are born, we find an agency for Eastern Europeans au pairs and hire a live-in Latvian who wants to improve her English, all food and board Saturday afternoon and Sunday off for £80 a week.

Funke is a natural and settles into mother hood, never making any demand but remaining supportive, sexy always a welcome home smile on her lips.

The first time I spend the night there is by accident. I help with the children and fall asleep in a rocking chair I wake up at 06.10hrs and let myself out, when I got home I expected the row of the century but just get a cool welcome. I made the mistake of thinking it is the start of a brother sister existence and head to have a shower, as I emerged from the shower all hell breaks loose, kicks bites screaming shouting cursing I thought a mad woman had again taken the place of a normally placid Carol.

I didn't offer any explanation just stood there and took it, in all situations my conscience will not let me act. When she got to that hiccupping state that women get to when they are all talked out, I took her in my arms laid her on the bed and made love sex with her, rather strange that is what I choose to do but it worked.

Once bitten twice shy, Funke and the boys are not coming to Carol's attention ever, best to keep them separate, how wrong I was. Two years later I am on a plane to Nigeria to bury my father. Carol and the kids are with me, Funke left with the boys to be with my mum as soon as the news broke.

I lodge all of us at the Sheraton, Carol and the children marveled they were in Nigeria and all the creature comfort of the West is available, I don't tell her our suite is costing just over £200 a night. We give all the arrangements to the big shot funeral director Ebony in Kakawa Street on Lagos Island.

All goes well until dust to dust, I am on one side with Carol and the children, Funke stays with the crowd on the other side, when the three small boys who draw looks everywhere they go are supported to pour dust into my father's grave Carol asks me who they are. I simply stated family, she gave me that strange look I have seen on two previous danger laden occasions.

The fun and games start back at the hotel, someone had told her that is her husband's children, this time is very different, I walk in and she clubs me on the back of the head with a coca cola bottle. Blood splatters everywhere, I need four stitches. I could kill this woman here and now but remember as I always do the access she gave me to a better life in the west.

I say nothing before leaving for England, I purchase a hectare of land in Ilori , pay 50,000 naira to the architect who puts together my dream home, For the next two years I focus on my business in a different way making money becomes an obsession as I build.

My Fix-it outlet is in Brownhill Road Catford and is doing great, it is the best risk decision I ever make. I ensure I get the staff balance right not too many of any nationality and having monthly incentives that rewarded whoever brought in the most business.

An accountant takes care of the taxes and gives me peace of mind where her Majesty's tax is concerned, once I learnt that is one thing that they will jail the riches person for I make sure I am paid up, submitting everything from petrol receipts to major purchases linked with my business.

I send money home every 2 months and I'm kept up to date with pictures and vhs video recordings of how things are shaping by Nuraini, so I'm able to see the progress made every few months. I beg my mum until she agrees to retire from selling panla (stockfish) every month I give her money to live on and tell her we will be moving back to Ilori in the future.

When the Ilorin house is ready I send Funke back with the boys to move in the same time as my mother. I take a sabbatical from work. I have good staff and transparency; it will be hard for any of them to defraud the company.

I tell Carol we are going to Nigeria for the summer holiday, initially she resists when I tell her the children and I will go without her she quickly changes her mind. We arrive in Lagos at dawn, I have hired a people carrier to convey us to Ilori, Carol looks worried when we hit the express she is expecting lounging around the pool at the Sheraton Hotel.

Everyone is tired and cranky when we arrive several hours later. The gate man and security open the gate we drive to the main building.

Let me describe the property. You drive in and there is the gate house to the right. Drive on and you come to a bungalow on the left, drive up to the main house which is massive and actually contains a total of nine bedrooms, with a four bedroom part of the house independent of the main house if you wished.

You can park fifteen cars side by side comfortably. There is plenty of ground, freshly planted flowers a barbeque and pool bar beside the glistening pool on the right, we pull up at the front of the house with the sound of the ornamental fountain gushing water in our ears.

Previously tired children come awake, desperate to jump in the pool. My mother comes out holding a tray, she prays and blesses each of us and sprinkles us with water as we pile into the house. The car is unloaded and I head to the shop, I need to get additional stock of fresh food in.

When I return Carol is standing in the same spot I left her, I can hear the children shrieking in the distance, I spot Funke in the background sitting quietly with my Mum. We are on Nigerian soil, my word is law and it's possible it's dawned on Carol. I calmly tell her I want all my children under one roof, there is no bastard child, the only child that is a bastard is the one rejected by its birth father, and I have not rejected any of my children.

A film drops down over Carol's face, I feel sad, she looks like someone who realizes they are trapped. I ask her to let me show her around the house, I hold her hand and she lets me, we walk round the house including Funke and her children's side of the house, in our bedroom I step into the shower with Carol fully clothed and put the water on, I slowly undress her and make love to her, then for the first time I apologize and I truly meant it.

Carol tells me she will try, I don't know what that means but I thank her. It's day one, there is a lot more to come, I recognize if I flood Carol with all I have in mind she will freak out on me so in this manner I begin to educate her in a teasing manner that here in Nigeria there is God then husband. I ask her to please exercise patience with our unusual setup. I suggest a cookout in the evening as we fall asleep.

It is a surreal atmosphere my mother and I with seven of my children by two women. I have another four children in England, I have shared this with my mother. The older children are soon playing with their younger half siblings, Funke stays close to my mum while Carol is friendly but detached, my mum knows three bits of English, hello, good-du-bye, you wante milike?

We all focus on the children and thus get through the first week without any incidents. Funke is polite and strong, she accepts love making is off the cards for now but has and hides well that smugness a home girl has when on home grounds.

Let me tell you if I had known the horror that awaited me and my family the second week I would not have set foot in Naija.

I spent the first week chasing my brother on the cell phone, I told him to head to Ilorin we will then go and view the properties in Lagos, do an inventory of what is needed to complete and make arrangements for funds. I would like to let the properties out as soon as they are completed with the agreement he can live in one of the two bedroom flats free while keeping an eye on the other properties. Like me he ended up in a dead end clerical post at one of the general hospitals.

By the middle of the second week I am pissed off with his behavior and tell him so, he promises to head to Ilorin Friday afternoon.

It was just after 03.00hrs when I am roughly prodded awake, in my sleep addled mind I think it's one of the children it then registered none of the kids would be shining a torch in my face, I am instantly awake, I make out the shadow of four men, I am looking down the barrel of a gun I sit up as I'm told to, Carol wakes up and lets out a cry, she is clubbed on the side of the head and falls slumped on the bed with a thin line of blood oozing from her hairline, all the time the torch is beamed in my face, the lead man warns me not to make any noise.

He shows me a picture of myself and asks me to confirm it's me, I do so, begging for leniency, explaining my mother was recently widowed, I have not hurt anyone nor have enemies, if it's money they want I have some I will give it to them, the lead guy's answer is that they have been paid to execute me, but nobody knows me I have been away for 16 years I explain.

There is a whispered conference between them, I pray Carol doesn't wake up and start screaming. The lead guy asks me did I fly into the International airport in Lagos last week, I confirm I did and then to my shame defecated I am going to die, these bastards are going to kill me, they have a photo of me.

I am in too much of a state to make sense of what he's saying but I hear loud and clear when he says, you gave some guys money when you arrived, that act of kindness my friend saves you, you are lucky, this guy here recognized you as the one who dashed us 2 £50 note at the airport.

We were given a contract to take you out, whenever we take a job we take a picture of the person ordering the job without their knowledge, a little bit of security for us you understand.

Right we will leave in a moment but first tell us who this person is and with that I am shown a picture of my brother on a mobile phone....my brother Nuraini wants me dead, fear grips me and I am unable to control my bladder.

Carol stirs beside me, the instructions from my assassins is clear we are leaving do not make any noise or raise alarm and with that the torch is switched off and they melt into the darkness.

A groggy Carol is waking up I hold her close and tell her not to make any noise, she understands and we stay in that position, with the smell of my loose bowel choking us, at first light I get up and check on the rest of the house, no one has been harmed and nothing taken.

I secure the back door used to gain entrance, just as the gate man comes to tell me Nuraini arrived very late last night and is asleep in the gate house. I tell Carol to start packing I go and wake my Mum up to explain what took place during the night.

I wake Funke up and tell her to get packing we are heading for Lagos by 08.00hrs. I don't realize my mother is missing until I go looking for her, I am reluctant to leave the house and worry she may have gone to confront Nuraini.

My mother comes in just as I'm thinking of taking the car to go and find her, she has 16 men with her I am shocked that that many people can move around without making any noise, it is still 05.10hrs, all appear to be in their 20's to late 30's.

The woman in front of me cannot be my mother, her eyes are wild, and her body has swelled to twice the normal size her voice is hard, her instructions are simply, they are to get my brother from the gate house, stuff a cloth in his mouth, bind his hands and legs and bring him to the main house.

I tell Carol to stay in our room she is more than happy to oblige. Within 5 minutes my brother is dragged into the living room, his eyes bulging in terror when he sees me, he is thrown on the floor like a bag of dirt. My mum sends one of the men off to the motor park to book two people carrier vans to arrive at 08.00.

She pulls the rag out of my brother's mouth and asks him why he sent people to kill me, me who is providing and supplementing them all. He has no answer, he is asked what has happened to the money buildings and various transactions I entrusted to him, his reply is flat and instant, there is no land there are no buildings there is no money.

He has been taking pictures and short film clips of nearby developments, the money I sent he has used for himself, funding a lifestyle totally out of his league, this man speaking cannot be my brother, he sounds evil, hard, capable of anything, he says why should I be struggling when you have so much, that last word is hardly out of his mouth that our mother attacks him.

I am in shock and sit there watching what has become a horror movie; her kick catches him in the neck though I think she was aiming for his head.

My mother rained blows on my brother, stumping on him and kicking and hitting him at one point she was biting him all the time cursing and cursing him, I just sat there like a statue, not a word not a movement.

My mum ordered the men to take Nuraini away and do what they need to do to a bastard like him. I am rooted to the same position as a couple of the men hoist my brother up and all depart with him. By 08.00hrs the house is locked up and we are on our way to Lagos.

Carol has let Funke support and attend to her, washing the small gash on her head with salt water and recommending pain killers and what not. I check my family into the Sheraton Hotel and head to

Victoria Island to bring our departure date forward to next week as well as make arrangements for my mother to join us in England.

My mother arrived in Lagos two days after us to this day she will not tell me what happened to my brother, I have no idea if he is alive or dead, it is a no go area and I have given up asking. In my heart I know he is dead, justice is swift in Nigeria.

Carol to date has not set foot in Nigeria again and I do not blame her, I am grateful she was knocked unconscious as she thinks it was an armed robbery, the house in Ilorin was sold to an Ilorin/American buyer.

The only business I have kept going in Nigeria is our Printing, Video and Photographic event one based at the events centre I built in Banjo Street near Tejuosho.

You will be amazed at how much money that brings in per annum, it always shows a profit, this keeps Funke and I popping back to Lagos from time to time, no family member of ours is employed there.

My mother has never recovered from that incident; she aged overnight, white hair like Mrs Santa Clause. She lives with Funke and the triplets but regularly spends time with Carol and our children. I have introduced her to her other grand-children. She is not happy in England and has just one instruction, take me home and bury me next to your dad.

The irony is that I am responsible for Nurani's four children's education and send money every month to his wife. My other siblings I continue to help but keep them at arm's length, all are puzzled by Nuraini's disappearance.

These days when I fly into Lagos you'll think I am Father Christmas the way I dash money at the airport, always £100 put aside for that purpose. The small amount of dash money that let me live.

I flew in because I wanted to see you and the bucket crew, I am wary of everyone, it makes me sound like a spineless man but if my own blood can say do away with him what can't a stranger do. It's good to see you I can't wait to see those three clowns.

I take a deep breath, I feel like I have been holding my breath for hours, what a life. Finishing our food he offers me the familiar "you must let me help with your mother". We say our good-byes and I head home totally drained. What a crock, life can suck so much.

Chapter 40

Mum
I start the day off at Ebony's in Kakawa Street, I want Mum buried within 72hrs of her death, no ice pack no returning to the states and coming back for a funeral, I am charged 450,000 naira for a Platinum Package.

I go and see the vicar at Hoare Memorial Methodist church where she's worshipped since the 60's. The vicar is taken aback but accepts my tearful explanation as I don't live in the Country.

I just have time to pop into Shell Club to make arrangements and agree they will do all the catering for the reception at a cool 5million naira, all I need now is a body to bury.

Mother's home coming is today everything is in place, the room is set all the special furniture and equipment all waiting to receive the patient only thing is they are all for show. I arrive back home early waiting tingling and running a temperature I check my eyes they are my main give away the way they glass over when I'm losing control.

I look in the mirror several times and see the child stare back at me, the abused, abandoned, rejected isolated, unloved, ridiculed and disgraced at every opportunity child, I pull my lips back in a snare, that action that always comes before the beast in me lashes out, there is no room for the beast today, the private ambulance bringing my mum will be arriving any minute, to ensure I make the right impression. I have asked that two of the nurses stay until 7pm to help her settle in then I take over.

I am shaken from my thoughts by the opening of the gate; it is 15.30 and mum has arrived. I wait on the porch as they unload her. I look at the woman that has made my life miserable, her left side is useless from the stroke, with that side of her face showing evidence of the cerebral vascular accident that took place on the right sideof the brain, I listen to the grunting guttery noises she makes as she tries to communicate, and of course nothing audible comes out having been robbed of her power of speech.

All her hair is grey and has been plaited into two braids; she's wearing a loose blue dress with flowers. I watch closely I need to measure the strength she has in the right side of her body, she is quite weak and her movements really languid. The four members of staff who have done the transfer unload my mother, they treat her like a precious cargo, yet that nasty woman is trying to use her good hand to swipe them away, she certainly can't function on her own but even now in her twilight years she is still mean.

I move forward mechanically and welcome my mother home all the time ensuring I had people witness my kindness and loving behavior, in response my mother pinched my arm, as one of the nurses scolded her for hurting me "mama is old" I say but she reads me, the old witch can somehow sense she's not safe and trashes around as they lift her down to wheel her up the temporary ramps quickly made for her arrival.

When they bring her in the room they all agree if they were in the end zone of life they would want to be nursed in a room like this with the soft lighting and pastel color deco. Because of her agitation she is given some sedative with a cup of warm Milo, within 20 minutes of her arrival she is installed in the bedroom sleeping off 0.5mg of Lorazepam. The two nurses sit quietly in the room with her, they marvel at the things I bought from the states to help care for my mum, nappy rash cream, special comfort cushion for the sacrum, I could hear them say how lucky my mum was.

I sent them packing at 19.00hrs, they were not keen to leave and wasted time saying how much they will miss my mother, at some point each had asked if I wanted them to move in while mama is settling in, I decline.

I pull up a chair and sit to watch my mum as she slept twitching and jerking from time to time. I think of the word helpless and laugh, I laugh hard and long then get up and shake her good side, I shake her in a rocking back and forth motion, she wakes up and looks mad at me even today there is no let up.

She looks at me the way home helps are looked at, something to be tolerated because they are there, my mum looks beyond me, I know that look it's a get out of my view where is your sister. I unpick her two plaits, I ease the head part on the bed down, I have already placed a bowl under the bed, my mum is making those guttery noises, and it sounds like she's saying Abu-dabi.

I put a towel on my mother's face and pour water on her face its called water boarding. Her right side comes alive but can't reach to pull the towel off, before starting I had tucked her arms in then tucked the sheets tightly under the bed, she can't move nor free her good hand, she is drowning, coughing and spluttering, each time I stopped the process when she quits struggling, I lifted the towel off and raised her head to drain her mouth and nose. I think she gets the message loud and clear she is at my mercy for the next 72 hrs until Tayo's return.

I pat dry her wet hair deliberating leaving it damp then turn up the Air Conditioning and leave the room returning with a steaming cup of tea, I sit near her head and begin to talk.

My Conversation

"You will listen because you don't have a choice, you cannot call yourself a mother when the word mother is mentioned you have no right to think of yourself as one, you failed miserably as a mother. Me an object, the earliest memories I have are those of abuse, 95% of a sexual nature.

You ignored all the signs, instead choosing to ruin my childhood, it was like you were possessed by evil spirits that forbid you to ever let me get away with being happy, if I smiled that smile had to be wiped off my face. If something made me happy I would scuttle off to bed before you could spoil that feeling even then you gave me no peace, if you found out I was in bed the questions would begin.

Later when I was having several abortions a year you deliberately looked the other way, yet I know you knew. You are my mother but I hate you, you have no idea how much, for the next 72 hours you will listen for all the years you should have listened and didn't, you will listen. Between the age of 0-10 this is what I remember, this is what I experienced when you should have being doing your protective duty and didn't.

Older men middle aged men touching me for sexual gratification, home help, drivers, gate man, washer man, one way or the other they had inappropriate contact with me. Some will hold me close, some rubbed me against them others touched my little pipi while doing things to bring themselves sexual release all knew the magic words, your mother won't believe you, don't tell anyone if you do they will beat you and send you away.

Being told you had to put up with funny smells and thick slimy goo was frightening, yet as young as I was I tried to tell you, refusing to go near certain people, running away from them, all explained by you as I am a difficult child. Even your bedroom was not safe, if I go in there thinking no one would come in they will watch and the minute you step out of the house whoever needed to used me came to get me.

I am small I'm trying to wash myself in the bathroom like I see others do, as I wash my face I feel a hand thrust itself between my legs, I am so frightened I wee, all it draws is amused laughter, the hand fondles me briefly then goes, I have been too frightened to wash my face to see who was abusing me, all under your very nose. You see but you are blind, you hear but you are deaf, you feel nothing nor care to see nothing if you feel it does not concerns me.

I get a brief respite when I start school, I loved school, children like me all happy chatting learning. I watch to see if anyone is sad as they head home at the end of school they all seem happy they must like being touched and their body rubbed. I don't like it so I am not happy going home.

The driver is another bastard who makes me sit in the front seat, curses me and touches me then makes me hop in the back seat when we are a few streets from home. He never once made my sister sit in the front seat.

Are you listening to me mother don't you dare fall asleep. She responds by sneezing, I bring out the masking tape and cut two thin strips off, pulling her eyelids up; I use each tape to stick her eyelids up, it is now impossible for her to close her eyes and ignore me.

By the time I'm 10 years old daily abuse is like my bread and butter. From the local Imam to the useless young guys who were supposed to be serving the Lord all were doing their own level of touchie touchie don't tell anyone you are my special friend, I love you what I do with you people will be jealous if you tell them and so on and so forth.

I developed a smell that I later recognize as fear, fear smells, it stings through your skin, erupts in the armpits and between your legs starting in your breast bone. You never sent my sister on the useless errands you sent me on that only put me more at risk and ensured my abusers had easy access to me.

The driver will take me and I will give the letter or message to Mr so and so, the driver abused me to and from the trip and the Mr so and so would have a good fondle while I was at their house or office. You knew I was soiled so you let it carry on, the people you associated with meant more to you than your daughter, me".

The phone ringing interrupts my train of thoughts it's Tayo the apple of her mother's eyes. I tell Tayo to get a move on, I don't think Mum is going to last more than a few more days if we are lucky, Tayo gives an anguished cry, she is leaving Kerala for Delhi on the first leg of her return journey, it will take under 72 hours to get home because of the times and flight connections. I have less than 72 hrs; mother's deterioration must be slow so as not to rouse suspicion.

Chapter 41

I look at my mother she is shivering and sneezing but look at her eyes they are murderous, if she could get off that bed I know I won't last but a few minutes. I savior how I felt when I was water boarding her, it felt great, victorious, liberating, empowering, me in control. Complete and total role reversal.

I look at the room and wonder if I should do another session, I want to ensure she has a small amount of water in her lungs so she has that drowning feeling for longer, I can hear a slight rattle it will have to do for now. She is struggling to stay awake and is doing her dawn hardest to close her eyes which she can't, a torrent of unrecognizable words gush from her.

I get my phone I have downloaded hard core metal music for today, I put my earphones in mum's ears and blast up the volume, her good side practically lifts off the bed in alarm, it's so loud I can hear the racket clearly, I turn down the lights and walk out, the battery will last for three hours I will return then.

I stand looking at myself in the mirror for a long time, society is so two faced, I hate my mother with all my heart and soul yet cannot say so, if I was allowed to express that there may be no need for the current state of affairs.

What do I see when I look in the mirror, soiled goods, abused child, disadvantaged youth, confused adult or a psychopathic human created by experience. I don't know anymore.

I storm back in my mum's room with the big plastic bowl used for washing up, I place it over her head, nothing wrong with a dose of claustrophobia which she will soon get if all she sees is the plastic container a few inches from her eyes. Try that for taste.

I walk in at 12.03 just as the battery to my phone begins to weaken, I take the ear phones out of mother's ears and leave the plastic in place for now. Crushing 2 Senna tablets I mix it with Milo, the nurses are returning at 07.00hrs I need to give them work to do.

I put this into the special cup with the spout I brought over, removing the plastic I stare deep into my mum's eyes then pulling her head up not too gently I put the cup to her mouth, she tried to avoid drinking, letting her head fall back slightly I pinch her nostrils close, each time she opens her mouth for air, I pour the drink down her throat, she quickly gets the message and drinks the Milo, it should kick in early morning. I have her attention again.

"Listen very carefully to me mother, the first time I got pregnant I was 13, it was the youth corper you hired to teach me, while sending Tayo to an after school learning club you decided I needed 1:1, I learn nothing except the experience of the searing pain as I tore when the man forced himself on me. I cried and begged for mercy as he slammed himself in me, holding me in a vice grip with one hand while bending my head back until I thought my neck would snap and you...you paid him to do this to me, never checking on the progress of teaching just anything goes as long as I remain out of your sight.

5 days a week I was subjected to this brutal abuse, I felt sore and raw down below, so swollen I couldn't wash myself properly, walking past you one day you called me back, sniffed at me and told me I smelt, get some deodorant.

When my period stopped I told the youth corper, he took me to a clinic at Costain where the young doctor who performed the abortion first had sex me to his heart's content. Piece of meat, piece of meat, take a bite take a piece have a share, grab a taste piece of meat piece of steal, all you flesh thieves steal a piece.

By the age of 16 I had nine abortions each time the culprit told me to take pills or took me for a termination the worst being the nurse who opens your legs and uses what looked like a knitting pin pushed it in and out until the blood started to flow and the foetus aborted".

I look at my mum as I talk trying to measure her thoughts, get a feel of sorts but nothing she's all there but there is no one at home, even in her wretched manner she still makes me feel small, I feel the anger boil in me, I must not get angry if I do I will make mistakes and mistakes lead to being caught.

I boil the kettle again. I get the crude feeding tube substitute I had bought, in reality the rubber bit of a douch pulled out, pinning her head down I inset the tube down into mum's stomach, I love the funnel I jammed in at the top, I will only use 100ml of boiling water, nil surface proof but the insides should be scaled raw just how I wish. I pour the small amount of water down the funnel, mother jerks, her eyes roll back and she passes out, I am elated, finally she is reacting.

I gently pull the tube out, it is bloodied at the end, I prop mum up and surround her with additional pillows, nil blood from her mouth that is good, I watch her head sagging on her chin and wedge it up with a rolled up cloth, my mother's eyes are blank, that is not what I want, she is trying to retreat somewhere from me, I am not going to let her not for a nano second. Her stomach rumbles and moans a mixture of boiling hot water and laxatives.

I adjust the bed covers never expecting what happened next, as I walked past my mother uses her good hand to grab me, she gets a hand full of my stomach and pulls hard, I am so shocked for a moment I am frozen, this woman is supposed to be weak, vulnerable, I try to pull her hand off, when that doesn't work, I head butt her only then does she let go.

I am mad, mad as hell; I hurry to my room returning to the kitchen with the microwave gel heater, I heat it for the recommended two minutes then an additional minute. I approach my mum from her left side rolling her to her right side I stick the hot water bottle in the small of her back and roll her over.

Then I sit and watch her, the old crow is so angry she makes guttery noises, whoever said speech impaired people cannot communicate is lying. She's communicating fine and will get up and kill me on the spot if she could.

"Do you get it now mother bad things happen to people, lots of bad things happened to me here on my home turf because of you and I am not a bad person. This place where I should have felt safe under your watch, I feel safe in another Country a good 19 hours flight from you, that's where I found safety.

You have to pay you really have to pay for treating me like shit, like dirt, what did I ever do to you to deserve the shitty way you treated me all my life. You worshipped Tayo, hah! At the mention of Tayo's name you come alive, if I were you I will calm down", and with that I grab my mother's good arm, wrap the masking tape round it and extending it up I tape that arm to the drip stand.

"She how you like that, you have to feel pain, pain pain pain, like I've felt all my life, when the muscle begins to ache think of the teacher you hired to teach me, who used to extend my neck until I thought it would break. It's now 03.00hrs I'm going to have a nap", I set my watch for 06.30hrs and leave the room.

I wake up before the alarm and make a cup of Milo crushing in another laxative, I walk into my mum's room and remove her arm from the drip stand and tuck it in under the sheet tucking the sheets in at the edge the arm now weighs a tone she should experience another set of pain as circulation returns and pins and needles set in.

I force feed her the Milo and remove the thin strips of tapes from her eye lids, they are dry and blood shot just how I want them to be. I check the gel bottle in her sacrum; it's cooled to her body temperature. Her hair is slightly damp and her nose is runny. I blow dry her hair and plait it into two, the way it was last night. I listen to her breathing; she has retained fluid in her lungs, not a lot but enough to give her a mimic of the death rattle. I get a flannel and scrub mum's face then I put almond oil on her eyelids.

The nurses arrive the same time the first dose of senna kicks in, as they say good morning and comment on how tired I look the smell of shit envelopes the room. They set to work cleaning, I instruct the gate man to arrange for his daughter to go and buy food locally for the two nurses.

Having arranged for their three meals for the day and showed them the cans and cartons of Ensure, a meal supplement for mum I head to bed. Conscious of the fact I have less than 48 hours to kill my mum, I pop the six packs of freeze blocks in the freezer ready for tonight.

Her passing away must seem normal, it must be natural slow and steady and not detectable, my last thoughts as I fall into a dreamless sleep.

Chapter 42

I feel good for the first time in 32 years I sleep for 10 hours straight. Whoever says talking therapy does not work is wrong; it works alright my way, this way, talk action pain, talk action pain. I feel nothing for the woman downstairs but hatred, so bad so dark if negative thoughts could kill she would have died a long time ago.

Denied a childhood denied my right to, as they say in the west, normal developmental mile stones. Well in the next 15 hours my mother will die, with this delicious thought in mind I am rejuvenated even more. I bounce off the bed and head to the bathroom.

I am living on adrenalin. I eat a snack bar as I get dressed in a simple kaftan, very carefully I remove a tiny amount of white pepper dividing it into two I put a few grains in each eye, they immediately redden and the tears flow, I repeat this process several times, looking at me with red swollen bloodshot eyes I want you to think poor soul about to lose her mother, that is what must be feedback about me.

Going downstairs I am met with gasps and comforting words from the two nurses, who fussed and wanted me to allow them to stay, I of course declined soothing them with the words "it's what mum would have wanted, end of days, end of life care from the hands of her children".

Using the Yoruba culture against them as needed, as expected they agreed marveling that one who had lived abroad for so long could be so observant of culture, they bless me. Asking how mum's day has been I am informed they gave her Imodium at 14.00hrs the stools have stopped.

Despite the air conditioning the room smells foul and in spite of their 12 hour shift it takes a while to get rid of them again I am over generous, in between crying I give them $100 bill each and thank them for taking good care of my mother I will see them in the morning.

I listen to their extended departure and the various clangs and clung as the gate man locks up. I pull a chair up and watch my mum. All women are hens or ducks, gathering their young ones under their wings or on their back, not this one, madam as long as I'm alright! What possessed her to have children.

I pull the reading light closer and position it to shine into her face, she twitches and makes low guttery noises. I wander to the freezer to check the state of my ice packs they are ready, double checking the doors are locked the countdown session begins.

It would be much easier to suffocate the old crow but that will leave tell-tale signs that can easily be picked up if foul play is suspected, nah tonight we start with more boiled water in conjunction with the ice packs. I put the kettle on and laugh at the set up, the same water that's going to make me coffee is going to strip and burn my mother's stomach.

I make a large cup of coffee, extra coffee mate and a dollop of honey; I take this over to my mother's room and go back for the tube and small measuring jug. Coffee is one of her favorite drinks the aroma must have woken her coupled with the light and heat in her face from the lamp, as I walk in my mother's look of sheer horror is befitting, she struggles and trashes around with her good side.

I ignore her and move to her head, as I did earlier I immobilized her head and insert the tube....then I sat down and stared at her.

My mother is an iron lady, she eyeballs me back, and I can hear the rattle better now she is struggling with the tube at the back of her throat. "Mum" I ask, "have you ever felt dirty, so dirty that no bath or scrubbing will shift it. That's how I feel, soiled always dirty because I've known nothing else. You made me use my body to get the things you should have provided.

When father died you became even wealthier than ever, he left you everything, what he had achieved and the stuff his parents and grandparents left him. I heard the word millionaire associated with you after the funeral at the age of 8 I understood this meant a lot of money.

I couldn't understand why Tayo got treated like a Princess and I like a second class citizen. You would buy us similar items but not let me wear mine; by the time you gave me mine they were too small you then cursed me for wasting your money, your money!

You made sure I was standing there when you gave the items away the words were always the same, look at her how much taller is she going to get everything you buy gets wasted! how big will I get, don't you get it a previously thin child starts eating nonstop anything will do eat and eat all day the weight is pilling on, I tell you why, I don't want to be slim and attractive, I don't want men or boys to notice me, I want to feel safe I want to stop hurting, I want to stop the smell, they makes me gag don't you get it"? I look at mother and she's closed her eyes, "don't you dare, open your eyes if you close them again I will tape them".... the roaring lioness is now toothless, my mother obeys she opens her eyes but will not look at me staring at a point just above my head. Even in her sorry state contempt for me is glaring.

I watch as her chest labors to rise and fall. I pump the bed down and climb on next to my mother, half lying on her I curl up in the foetal position and stay there, a position and warmth I have not known, a contact I have not had, a flesh that was denied me. I laugh and jump up, "I was crushing you, death would come too quick if I carry on" I take another sip of my coffee.

"Your cousin Uncle Yele died of poisoning did you know that, nah, bet you didn't think back to the last time I was here, he died three days after I left, the bastard, not even a blood relative the strays and down and outs you pick up and make into family. He used to touch me his fingers so rough.

You left me in his care again and again not once did you ask on your return how are you, are you okay. I bought the rat poison I used on Carter Bridge in the Iddo traffic making sure I was in a public taxi, getting off at the petrol station I bought some bits and pieces in the shop then asked to use the loo, there I took only the little potion I needed and left the rest in the corner making it look like they had put it there.

I booked a room at the Solitude Hotel, I knew the bastard would come, I lured him with the promise of the lace, shoes and money I had for him making sure he came the day before I left. A greedy soul through and through I ordered food with all the trimmings, feed him well downstairs, making sure he was slightly drunk I ordered a bottle of red wine orange juice and ginger ale to make Sangria while ensuring he had a small scotch in his hand as we went upstairs. The piece of crap tried to grope me as we went upstairs telling me I've always been special in his heart.

Once in the room I set to work, telling him of my wealth in the USA, asking if he would like to visit making out I had no recollection of the abuse I suffered at his hands, I put the poison in his glass then added the sugar, I then poured his Sangria in making sure I had done mine first, the greedy sod downed the glass in one pull, I am delighted and while pretending to refill his glass broke it, calling room service to clear it up I gave him money and asked he be escorted down and a cab called promising to see him tomorrow.

The fool forgot about lace and shoes when he saw a large bundle of Naira, blessing me and singing my praise that was the last I saw of him 72 hrs later he was dead. Nice and clean if I may say so myself. Where is this all going, don't worry mother I'm not going to waste rat poison on you, you are going to die tonight from the pain I will inflict".

In response my mother begins to shake, is she fitting? Do I care, I wait for the tremor to stop and boil the kettle. I carefully measure out 100ml of water and pour it down the feeding tube, the moving side of mothers body arches beautifully, her eyes roll and she actually passes out.

I get the six ice packs from the freezer and arrange them underneath her body on the good side, the coldness of the temperature brings her round, she appears disorientated as she tried to take in a burning stomach and freezing flesh, I ease the tube out, fresh blood and little particles of flesh cling to the tube, I have an idea and roughly push the tube back down her throat, she arches again and passes out.

What is wrong with people who are so mean, why are they so weak when they experience a little bit of meanness their pain threshold so low. I pull the tube out again this time I can see evidence that inside her is raw, bingo just what I wanted. Her labored breathing fills the air.

Do I feel anything for her, no well yes rage, rage that she will actually die and that will have to be it, rage that I can't keep this going longer, rage that she is my mother, rage just rage. But I have conditioned myself. I have waited over 40 years so I savor this moment.

She coughs up blood, not a lot but blood is blood, I begin the bed game I pump it back up first, I tilt the head down then tilt the legs up, hopeful whatever is going on inside her will be assisted this woman must be taking her final breath at dawn.

I will deny her and her precious Tayo a goodbye that will have to do me as a consolation prize. Shit I forgot to strap her down and she nearly flies out of the bed head first. Even in this state she manages to make me feel small, and look stupid, inadequate.

I restore the bed back in the right position, I hear mother well for the first time, and her breathing is labored, hard and harsh to listen to. I poke her and continue to do so until she opens her eyes, she is looking for release but I won't give it, I tell her to hang on Tayo is on her way, I knew it, I knew it would work and it does, she wants to see the apple of her eyes before she dies, well if I have timed everything well mother should give up the ghost a few minutes before Tayo arrives I want her body to be warm.

I gently sit on her chest she almost folds into two on her good side with the pressure on her chest, I get up poke her until she opens her eyes and then sit on her again and again her death rattle increases, she is laboring to breath, "I bet you want to hang on to see Tayo, well no such luck, I will suffocate you if she arrives early that I promise".

You see that pressure on your chest mother it is the pressure and incapability to move that the men who abused me, subjected me to, they pin me down, can't move, can't escape, can't breathe, dead weight pinning me down.

Do you know why I got married so late mother, it's because I couldn't bear the thought of a man having access to my body, even today I cannot lie still and have a man on top of me, think, try and think what that did to my marriage. How I got pregnant is known only to God.

I did everything you didn't, I spoke to my child and protected her, and no day passes without physical contact, abundant hugs smiles, unlimited, male relatives kept at bay. I enrolled her in Jujitsu at the age of 4, I equipped her so she might be able to take care of herself, and in short I raised her the opposite way you did things.

She turned out lovely unsoiled like me. On the morning of her wedding I got the biggest reward ever, both her and her husband shared with me they are both virgins, clean that meant to me, clean! I did what you couldn't do, I kept her safe gave her a normal childhood, protected her from unwanted undeserved attention and cursed you ever single day.

People talk about God, I didn't think about God you are the 1st 2nd and last thing on my mind every waking moment. My strength lay in knowing one day my turn will come to give you your just deserts and treat you to a world of fear, pain not knowing who will hurt you next when or why but pain and violation".

I am so enraged at the increase of her death rattle, she is now breathing intermittently, and do I feel release? Hell no, mum is slipping further and further away from me, but I have one last ace, I know just what to say to bring her back.

"If you die before I say so, I will hurt Tayo", her eyes fly open she tries without success to make sense but communication is communication in whatever form, I hear mum loud and clear, if anything happens to Tayo by my hands she will come back and blah blah blah, she struggles to continue her rant depriving herself of much needed oxygen in her determination to make herself understood.

What I have being hoping will happen did, the old crow suffers a heart attack, clutching her chest with her good hand she falls back against the pillow 100% dead. Damn I am good.

Chapter 43

Mother is dead, it's 05.47hrs, I immediately call her physician, what do I do, I cry down the phone, wailing and wailing making sure I don't make sense or answer his questions, tired of telling me to pull myself together he confirms he will be on his way at first light.

Great! Tayo will be arriving any minute now, I know her she will head here straight from the airport her flight arrived at 04.30hrs, with baggage reclaim and a 10 minute drive at most at this time of the morning she should be arriving soon.

Going back to the room I remove the ice packs and boil the kettle pouring it on the towel, I wring it out and begin the process of tidying mother up, I pay attention to her back by rolling the towel up and applying the heat to the areas that had the ice packs, I give her a superficial wipe just as I hear the car draw up at the gate, I just have enough time to roll up cotton wool and stuff it deep down mum's throat I don't want any blood dripping out, before heading to the door my eyes nicely red and swollen from the fresh application of ground white pepper.

Tayo takes one look at me and collapses on the floor, stupid cow as if throwing herself down will bring her mother back...please! I walk her in the room and watch as she throws herself across mother's body delighted I had time to stuff her throat my concern being any compression on the stomach and chest would result in blood regurgitating.

The wailing and mourning starts, mentally I am tidying affairs of burial up, it's Wednesday today, wake keeping service will be Friday evening here at my house and burial will be on Saturday at Ebutte Metta cemetery. I stand there crying making all the right noises, I do a brilliant collapse when the doctor arrives, the two nurses join in when they arrive closely followed by my sisters family, yuck and yuck again, bloody nuisance all getting on my nerves but steady does the job, this is the last leg and then I'm out of here.

It's funny the nonsense people say, we expected her death but not this quick, how quick then I wanted to ask, this being from the two greedy nurses who have just seen their $ chances fly out the window.

Once the doctor departed and I had given the nurses $100 to share by the time they depart it's mid-morning, I call the nearest Yummy Yummy shop and speak to the manager regarding bulk order home delivery for the next 72 hours he assures me they can accommodate me the store is five minutes away, I am impressed he offers to come round to see the set up and get an idea of what will be appropriate to serve.

Naija customer service not bad, but really its money talking. Tayo is distraught, I watch silently as her husband comforts her and she sits in his embrace, it makes me want to shake mum awake and tell her another normality she's denied me.

"Tayo", I begin trying to sound like the loving older sister mindful that not once have I touched or held her to me to comfort her. "Tayo while you were away I made as many arrangements as I could, as it was clear mum was deteriorating every day. I know this is a very difficult time for us all but we must make sure Mum is giving what is befitting, this is what I've booked", and I talk her through.

"So soon" she asks alarmed, "I would like to spend some time with her body", I keep my look sympathetic but would really like to say take her home put her in your bed and when the maggots get too much then consider a burial! "It is important we do things in a dignified manner, also remember most of mum's group and age mates are quite frail".

I watch Tayo's husband as I speak I can read this dude's brain and it goes like this....damn how much is all this going to cost me. I focus on Tayo, "I have paid for all that's in that file, what is outstanding is bussing people in from Ekiti and Ilaro and providing a coach to bus church member to the cemetery and reception". I round up with the phase "I had to keep busy it was a distressing time", and nicely dissolve into floods of tears.

Tayo looks stunned she gets up and puts her arms round me, I keep my eyes closed and concentrate on my crying, Tayo thanks God for my forgiving spirit, she tells God to make her like me and bless her with a forgiving spirit as she knows in lots of ways Mum and I hadn't seen eye to eye. I take deep measured breaths to convince her that the soothing words are taking effect.

"Tayo" I say, "we need to start making calls, I will sort out the rest of the transportation, you need to sort out the Lagos people, the catering will be for 1500 people so please make sure no one is left out". "Thank you" Tayo and her husband say in unison just as the manager from 'Yummy yummy' arrives.

I tell him to take a seat and call the Pastor at Hoare Memorial informing him of Mum's demise, I ask for the wake keeping service to start at 6pm a short 45 minute service followed by a short reception to allow folks to get home at a decent hours. I also ask him to think of what the family could do that would be useful for the church to honor mum's memory.

I call Moses and tell him the transport needs; he will send one of the managers within the hour. I call Wale and tell him I need lace materials today that must be made and ready for Friday, he assure me he will send Motun in person in the next hour, now that is what I call a hold over someone. Informing Pitan my mum had passed away I ask if his wife can provide the full package of make-up gele and what not. He will call her and ask her to send someone over in the next hour. Ayo's multi-media outfit will take care of printing the program and recording the event again one of the managers will be with me within the hours.

I encourage Tayo to pop home to pack a small suitcase of things she will need and to bring back enough pictures of mum ranging over the years to be used, I gently remind her we have 72 hours to make mum proud, that galvanizes her into moving, stupid spoilt brat.

Going into the kitchen I make myself a black coffee and add a liberal amount of vodka, nil colour not smell. The warmth cruises through my veins, Mum is dead how do I feel.....surprisingly calm on the outside yet boiling mad on the inside. I can't put my finger on it but things feel uncompleted.

I wander into the room she's laid in, I brought along enough Yankee candles to light up a highway. Piling them in small number around the room I have lit most of them, the beautiful smells of peach, vanilla and strawberry drift around enveloping yet not overpowering. If not for the stiff lying on the bed it would pass as a therapeutic environment. I stand looking at my mum for a long time, just studying her face, not an unattractive woman for her age even with one side of her face slightly frozen.

The opening and closing of the gate brings me back to the present. Grabbing my phone I speak to my bank manager, I will need 3 million Naira in thousand naira notes and in 10,000 bundles, each member of the family travelling down from the various villages will be given an envelope with 10.000 naira 'owo omo oloku' money from the departed's child.

Crazy the things I do ahead. In my case I have 500 envelopes with my work shield. That little useless child has made good and is going to subtly ram it down everyone's throat. Transport manager arrives first, I am assured the coaches will sleep over on Friday night and depart for Lagos at dawn ensuring arrival for the pm burial.

Motun walks in and takes my breath away, if Wale had married this woman it would have been the making of him, I watch her walk towards me and feeling stirring I have not felt in a long time, I feel envious and awe at the same time.

Motun is dressed in a long dress that hugs her at the top to her waist then flows out, her breasts are full and well controlled, I can't stand women jigging. She envelopes my senses in a cloud of Chanel as she knees to greet me, this blows my mind, I pull her up and embrace her, this is how I want to be. If there is reincarnation I want to come back as this woman.

I accept her greeting and offer coffee; we make our way to the kitchen and small chat during the short period it takes for Tayo and her family to return.

Several cases are brought in, we agree white lace with wine accessories for the burial and pink lace with grey accessories for the wake keeping on Friday, the Taylor appears like magic takes measurements and disappears promising to deliver Friday's clothing tomorrow morning and Saturday's later the same evening.

I walk Motun out holding hands I thank her for being a part of Wale's life, I use goodbye as another opportunity to admire and compliment her. She seems happy with life, an inner contentment shines through.

Walking back in Tayo has spread what seems like too many photographs on the dining table. I join her and the communications man, I look at pictures of me with my sister in our youth, am I the only one that can see only one child is ever smiling. I say nothing but feel I will explode; I need relief, sex self-harm, or both. All pick up on my tension and ask if I'm okay, I say I am just tired.

I realize now why I am not triumphant, showing mother what it's like not to be liked, loved, treated with compassion is not going to settle the rage in me, I look at the table and realize my mistake, to hurt my mum to get to her the one thing that mattered I did not do. Realization hits me hard and I cry bitter hot tears harsh loud sobs, the fools in the room think I am over whelmed by the death of my mother, Tayo is the key to hurting Mum and I missed the opportunity.

That's who I should have taken care of Tayo's death would have crushed my Mum's spirit, now that would have been the ultimate, why oh why did I not think about that, I have spent years focused on dealing with mother I didn't once think take Tayo away from her and that will kill her. What to do. Ironic when Tayo herself suggests I go and try to get some sleep. I don't resist but once in bed sleep won't come.

I am that little girl again unsure if I am getting it right, what do I do, with this ruminating round and round I fall asleep. I dream of Motun, Motun rejecting me, Sadly I realize my attraction to Motun it is the normality she has that I do not that attracts me. Un-spoilt describes her, something I would like to be.

I wake up several hours later sweating despite the air conditioning, I am mad as hell, mad I missed the point of what it would take to hurt mum, mad at Tayo an annoying undeserving spoilt little shit who is gently knocking on the door, I pop a few grains of white pepper in my eyes before opening the door to a sister who flings herself into my arms and starts wailing.

I force myself to hold her and make all the right noises, 72 hours that's all I just need to keep my irritation in check. Tayo detangles herself and returns shortly with a cup of coffee. I thank her and leave it on my bedside table, bitch may be trying to poison me .Well I'd love to poison her.

Damn if I try it now it will raise suspicion, how the hell did I miss a chance to really hurt my mum, I'm heading to that dark place and feel myself tumbling and tumbling I need to cut I have to cut this is not good. I pick up one of the Vanilla incense sticks, lighting it I head to the toilet, I hitch up my dress and hold it to the hollow between my torso and hip small burn but the release is helpful, better than erupting. I empty the coffee and wander out.

My home is buzzing, we do a head count and order food in from the lovely manager in charge of chops on Friday night. Death or no death people will eat, the Reverend arrives just as we finish, it's interesting the few days I had her home no one came to visit but since her death the stream had been steady.

I am informed by a new arrival that her women's group are coming to pay their respect tomorrow evening 7pm; we are to have no other visitors except immediate family. This sounds rather cult like.

Mum's doctor returns with the death certificate and suggests less candles and more air conditioning so she doesn't begin to deteriorate, fucking idiot I want her to deteriorate I want her to begin to smell, I want her precious Tayo to avoid her body because of the stench.

I want her to find her precious mother revolting. Interfering little shit. He informs us the two nurses will be returning to sit with mum tonight and tomorrow night 21.00-07.00 hrs ......whatever.

I have to say I am a good events planner; we get through Thursday without any major needs to be met. Mum's rag and tail collection of friends arrived as planned, combine age nearing 2000 years. They go in the room where she is laid out and sing and speak to her, I hear a voice ask her if anyone had a hand in her death she should let them know, I nearly burst out laughing, how is this going to work my dead mother is going to sit up and say "yeah I was murdered", tradition and culture, too complex and sometimes daft in action for me to make sense of.

I have arranged take away packs following their noisy bye-bye they depart with bags of food. We batten down the hatch for the night tomorrow is songs of praise a wake keeping service, this practice came about years ago when people were accidentally buried because a pulse was not detected as they were in a deep coma...ironic or what.

The laying in state and songs of praise was a chance to ensure you really are burying a corpse, the Christians used the opportunity to sing Christian songs, I guess if you're not dead the racket should irritate you enough for you to show signs of life.

Chapter 44

Friday morning and I take the car out, I head to Federal Palace Hotel in Victoria Island and have a lazy breakfast I need to get away from Tayo, whose very presence is beginning to nauseate me.

Federal Place is a joy to behold; someone with a vision has beautifully refurbished it. I have breakfast sitting overlooking the beach as a treat I opt for a club sandwich. I am dressed smart casual and know I am attracting attention from the wealthy business men and leaders in the room.

A sharply dressed man comes up and asks if he can have the pleasuring of sharing my table, I nod in agreement, he explains it's his favorite view when he stays here. He introduces himself and offers his hand in a handshake, I touch palm that has clearly never handled any rough object in its life time, and it makes my hand seem rough in comparison. He orders then reads the financial paper of some sort while waiting.

By ignoring me he intrigues me. He looks clean and smells divine, he must be about 6'3 legs long enough to stretch out giving me a view of a pair of Churchill brogues, he formally introduces himself as Bashorun Tunde Solonge 'TeeA' his friends call him.

The usual checking out conversation begins, I can see he needs to eliminate me as a working lady who may be looking for early morning business, he noticed my slight American drawl once we start speaking.

I tell him I am in town to bury my mother tomorrow morning and needed to get away from everyone to catch my breath for a few moments, with memories of the club sandwich as a kid I drove down here. We chat easily and continuing eating and topping up our coffee until the waiter asks if we would like to have our drinks in the lounge, it is 11.30am and we haven't noticed.

We laugh and head there neither of us wanting to break the relaxed spell of talking freely to a stranger we may never see again. I liked the spontaneity of his idea when he suggested we go for a walk on the beach he just needed to change his shoes. I agreed at our age in your 50's what is a 50/60 year old man going to do to me in full glare of the public in Nigeria, not a lot.

He disappears and bounces back in loafers and two panama hats handing me one and giving the waiter instructions to keep our table free for lunch in two hours, we walk the short distance to the beach and head off on a slow walk, the sand is pristine white the Atlantic Ocean is roaring it's presence with each crash of the waves, rolling his trousers up we walk in the ankle surf. I don't know when I began to laugh or remember when or how we walked for over an hour in this manner, talking and laughing about everything and nothing. I tell Tee-A about my life in the USA keeping my dirty laundry to myself. Crazy experience trying to talk when the breeze takes away every few words, occasionally we will sit on the hot sand just looking out to sea.

He makes no move to hide his wedding ring, neither do I. When he begins to talk about his family I listen very attentively.

Tee-A

5 children by two wives, a Ghanaian and a Nigerian. The Ghanaian had made it possible for him to acquire British status describing her as a large black woman with low self-esteem, he had been grateful for the opportunity she made possible never experiencing anything deeper than mild affection, he found it easy to live with her, she quickly had 3 children in the space of 5 years.

What she lacks in beauty she makes up for with hard work, networking and total devotion to me and the children. Her Uncle, who was a high ranking government official in Ghana, gave us our first break with Cashew nuts! He rang up one day and asked if I wanted to supply cashew nuts! Both raw and roasted. I said yes and set about getting the funds together.

I hit the ground running, heading straight for the Asian and Chinese trade who use a lot of Cashew in their products. I registered our company and plunged into the world of 'fit for human consumption' by European standards.

While waiting for the harvest I found traders who wanted to take containers off me wholesale and others who just wanted as little as 250kilos. The entire venture back in 1980 cost £21,000, I couldn't sleep from worry but from the 1st shipment we were in profit. My wife and I took it in turns to go back and forth from Ghana, within 3 years we were supplying the bulk of Cashew nut coming into United Kingdom, business had started coming in from Europe.

In 1985 we won the contract to supply major players in the UK finding small packets of cashew nuts in the shops on airlines or on train buffet cars with product of Ghana gave me such a thrill. I bought a two bedroom flat in an area known as little Venice in central London as an investment and moved my family's main home to Blackheath, a detached house bang in the middle of the heath, hardly any neighbors and surrounded by greenery in all directions.

In 1989 I was offered dirty oil. I had no idea what it meant but said yes and flew back to Nigeria to find out more. Well dirty oil is the by product from the refinement, this oil is used to lubricate machinery and car parts, using a simple but easy name I set up Lub-oil, importing the oil to other African Countries for sale not in bulky containers but in reinforced sealed heavy duty polystyrene bags.

When the nut allergy no nuts to be served on flights started we lost a notable contract but in its heels was an offer from chocolate companies in France so all in all we've been lucky. From the first profit made I have invested in stocks and shares, I pay an expert firm and have lost nil to date even the crash of the early 90's did not affect me as it ruined some people.

I married a young Nigerian widow an old school love who gave me two children. As I said I have been lucky everything I have touched has turned to gold. Over the years I have dabbled short time in chemicals, Gold and Diamond investments. With that we head back for lunch.

As we relax with chapman laced with Dubonnet I switch my phone on briefly Tayo has called me 15 times I switch it off again a plan is forming. I look at Tee-A then deliberately start to cry, he is all over me like a rash with comforting words.

I murmur over and over how will I get through the funeral, as I hoped this total stranger is pledging his time and support for me in the next 72 hours. I accept and thank him for his friendship, he promises to be a good friend, nil sexual moves yet but I know that will come, dick in their brain, brain in their boxers.

I have five guests of my own for my mother's funeral. We have a lazy lunch, conversation flowed freely, I tell him about my childhood friends, he offers to host the meet-up with the Chinese caterers but on an island he owes nearby in Badagry he has a boat moored at the prestigious Lagos Motor Boating Club.

Tonight he will be at the wake keeping service, I give him the details thank him from the bottom of my heart; I really don't think I have one and head home. The selfish bastard of my sister has not once asked where Tunde my husband is, it's all about her grief well a man by my side at the funeral is no longer an issue.

I hadn't even remembered to tell Tunde and most certainly will not be disturbing my daughter. A grandma she knew only by name.

And so I make my 5th friend less than 72 hours after crushing the light out of my mum, way to go. I am making friends with Tee-A because he's wealthy, rich beyond my dreams. I can sniff money out, stick me in a room with a bunch folks I will pick out the wealthiest for you in 5 minutes flat, it's always the same money does not need to shout or broadcast itself.

In any gathering money simply commands attention by a look or a gentle clearing of the throat. Old money does not even bother introducing itself it new money that shouts its vulgar presence from the roof tops.

I decided to encourage and accept Tee-A's friendship for one reason only he mentioned a home on a nearby island as he spoke I realized it may be the perfect solution for my sister a watery grave away from prying eyes, nil body to autopsy, I will find a way to make it doable. His generous offer to host my friends and I will not be wasted for them an afternoon of leisure for me a recon run.

I take my leave and switch my phone on as I descended the bridge into Yaba, my hysterical sister had rung 28 times. It's 5.35pm I can understand her anxiety, just before I turn into my street I put a minute amount of white pepper in each eye, stinging and making me weep but not enough to blind me that I can't see to drive the last 200 meters to my gate.

With tears streaming down my cheeks I am in awe of the transformation to my house. Money is good; chairs with white covering and burgundy sash are neatly arranged, catering staff moving around quietly offering drinks to these who have obviously left work early to avoid traffic.

A quick hello to people I wouldn't waste my time remembering their names. All the clothing for tonight and tomorrow neatly ironed and stacked. My sister flings herself into my arms, I don't need a scene and take her to my room with me once I calm the irritating sod down I encourage her to go and get ready.

I quickly shower and apply a light make-up accentuating my eyes, one of the bastards convinced me I was special always told me I had beautiful eyes, beautiful eyes and then sex, I wonder where he is now, nothing would make my day than to run into more of my abusers.

I clear my thoughts and head downstairs after a generous dousing of Vintage Soul Curve. I am ready let's get this show on the road. Tee-A arrives just ahead of my four buddies, they cause quite a stir, I leave the four to catch up while we are waiting to take our seats. Tee-A sticks with me, squeezes my hand briefly.

The service is short as I wanted it, some will say it is sweet for me it is short, nothing too long it's going to be a long day tomorrow. Tonight I make my mind up to close the house after the funeral and spend the remaining time at Federal Place.

Moses, Wale, Pitan and Ayo are rolling back the years, I watch them from afar and remember some of the gut wrenching times each has lived through yet they've survived and made the best of each situation they were faced with. I am amused by their protective sense of responsibility towards me, these guys don't know the real me, best we keep it that way.

The last of the guests left at 10.00pm, most of those who were here tonight will be with us tomorrow, I shower again and crawl into bed tomorrow is going to be a nightmare.

Chapter 45

We are off to an early start, all is well with those been bused in, they are on track to arrive with enough time to eat and then head to the church, it is important for those who wish to have a final word with my mum to have a chance to speak to her corpse. And so it begins, the excellent catering took care of food and drinks clearing up as they went; the makeup artist et el has us looking like we had stepped off a magazine cover. The funeral director arrived like clockwork. Tee-A called and asked if I would like to ride with him to the church I gratefully accepted anything to get away from Tayo. I hide my pleasure at the sight of his Cadillac. I watched as my mom's coffin was loaded and all cars took off for Yaba at a sedate pace.

Once on the move Tee-A closed the shutter and separated us from his driver. He quickly poured me a shot of Peach Schnapps; dude had been listening when I spoke about my favorite things. My new friend wants to please me.

Christ almighty give me strength, If only I could ask for all the crap to be cut out, service went well it all deteriorated once the coffin came out the church then the dancing started, the lulling this way and that with the coffin, ye saints, I just want it put in the ground and that's that. For the short trip to the cemetery Tee-A gave me a glass of Champagne and a petite beef and mustard sandwich he had asked the hotel to make, ironic isn't it the golden apple of my mother's eyes was crying fit to make herself ill, maybe she could just cry her way into an early grave that again would do me just fine.

Dust to dust, I stared hard at the coffin and tried my best not to laugh as I remembered a joke in which a man had taken his family to Jerusalem and the mother in law had accompanied them. While there the old woman had passed away, when enquires were made it would cost $700 to bury her there or $7,000 to ship her body back to the States, the man choose to have the body shipped back, his explanation, a man once dies here and after three days rose from the dead, well this one is staying dead he says I don't want any shock after 3 days.

The sound of Tayo's distress brings me back to the present she is near collapse when they begin to shove dirt into the grave, she is helped away by her husband as we head for Shell Club.

As per the instructions I gave the catering team all those who arrive are to be served food and drinks immediately and the fuji maestro was to start playing once guests arrived. I felt like I was attending someone else's party. I sit briefly with my paddies and thank them for their support, Tee-A is happy to chew bone with them I get up and begin to do my round of the folks from the home town.

I sit with the most senior and give her an envelope first, she gets the equivalent of $200 she beacons each to come forward and greet me, we exchange greeting and I give each an envelope for 10,000 naira about $50, with all their take away food packed and handed over they are on their way by 5pm, they should all be home by 8pm with their departure my duty is done, I dance briefly then leave the floor to Tayo and sundry.

At my table are the five men plus Motun, Yemisi, Funke & Titi. I am touched that the men have asked their women to be present; I feel them watching me looking at me trying to figure out if I had had a relationship with any of the men. Over the noise of the music we did our best to talk.

Each lady around the table is exactly as described by their man, Motun is sitting at an angle where I can't see her but that's cool, and there is too much going on around me. I am regularly interrupted by fools who wish to tell me I have done well my mother would have been proud. I don't think so.

Finally it's over Lagos people are no longer into all night parties and by 10.30pm I'm home, I've encouraged Tayo to go home, we'll speak in the morning. My house is quiet, I undress and make a coffee and wander into the room that became a chamber of horror for my mum. The Spenco bed is deflated and all machines long gone, either back to rental or donated by me to St Nicholas Hospital, I stand in that empty room staring and staring could I have done things differently could my life have been different would I have felt different..... if only she had shown me some affection and then I begin to cry, huge great big sobs, I cry and cry for a long time, have I got release no! am I happy no!

I feel the dark clouds coming, I need release, and the pain is too much, I am over whelmed; I can't cut, not the way I want to. I go in the kitchen and get a scotch bonnet pepper out I liquidize this, returning to the room my mum had been nursed I put mackintosh on the floor and spread newspapers over it.

I undress and find the feeding tube to the top I re-attach the funnel, lying down on the newspaper I insert the tube into my back passage and pour the liquidized mixture into the tube, the nearest pain to cutting to the bone is a pepper enema. The pain hits me and I curl into a ball, I will stay like this for a long as possible.

I am on fire inside and begin to cry again. I am the little girl who just wanted to belong, to feel safe, and to have a mother who smiled at her and is pleased to see her who gave her food like she wanted to feed her not chuck a plate at her.

I am the damaged child who couldn't ask for help, who didn't ask for help, who when she asked for help wasn't believed.

I manage to last for 12 minutes and then I emptied my bowel and lay in the mess coming out of me. This is me the real me a piece of shit lying in shit. My inside raw and on fire my ass swollen by the shock. I lay like this until I am able to get up and walk, my legs give way the first couple times I tired.

I take the newspaper and empty the content in the toilet, it is painful and hard to walk, I still don't understand how the pain helps me feel a sense of relief other than the theory of the only thing I can control after a childhood experience like mine is my body.

I take a shower and get into bed. I cry because I have lost, I thought I would feel good, better, victorious instead I feel the shitty way I've always been made to feel by my mum. Even in her death she is able to distress and torment me. I cry and cry as I have been crying all my life.

Chapter 46

Well in her death I will not let her rest Tayo her precious child is so going to get it. It's 1am the early hours of the morning when I reach a decision. Tayo must be sent to join mother. With this I feel a sense of release of sort and purpose. How Tayo will die.... the logistics of that I will work out later but die she must before I leave Nigeria. Finally at last sleep comes.

By midday I am in one of the Snr executive suites at Federal Palace Hotel. I call the men to let them know we have a change of venue, each confirm Saturday is fine, we meet up at noon returning at 7pm, to my horror Tee-A insists on including Tayo when we met for a quick bite at lunch.

I pray the bitch will say no but no such luck, she accepts gushing she needs to spend as much time with me as possible before I fly back to the States. With that nonsense ringing in my ears I call the Protea Hotel in Wuse Abuja and book 4 nights, another quick call and I book Virgin Nigeria.

In 1980 when Abuja did not exist as Capital City I bought some seriously large amount of land in the region, at 200 Naira a plot a hefty amount at the time I had poured money given to me by my abusers to keep me quiet, into land I had never seen, time to check things out.

Tee-A offers to accompany me I decline, he insists on arranging transport to and from the airport at both ends. I fly out to Abuja Monday morning. Seated next to me is a Hausa man in flowing robes, we are in conversation before the plane takes off, he is direct and tells me he likes me, he is impressed with my American accent! and wishes to get to know me better then the pierce de-résistance he works for the Mint!

Okay this would clearly impress Naija babes but what am I going to do with goro-mouth from the mint. Not realizing he is annoying me he asks when I am returning to the States I say next week, he has the affront to tell me I won't be going back then, apparently we will be spending time together and he will take care of all my bills here and in the States.

I remember someone mentioning babes fly back and forth between Lagos and Abuja in the hope they meet loaded men who want to spend their money. I do what I haven't done for a while, I stick my headphones in my ears and listen to the Boss Bruce Springsteen, dancing in the dark drowns out goro-mouth and he gets the message.

Things have certainly changed. Within a few minutes of landing I am impressed by what I see around me, the maintenance is first class but then this is the main International Airport, apparently the Branson dude refused to use the local terminal. There is a uniformed man standing holding a card with my name on it, within 30 minutes I am in my room at Protea a stone throw from Legislative Quarters in Apo.

Protea Hotel has its resident drivers and I head to the Town Planning office. I am again impressed by the orderliness, in no time at all I am given all the information I need and confirmed as the rightful owner of major prime land.

Nigerians will be Nigerians, within the short period I am there one of these buggers must have called an Estate firm who probably gives them a retainer because of people who own prime land but are not contactable like me, anyway this man comes in and introduces himself to me, he's a real estate who can get me top money on my land if I want to sell.

When he states my land is the size of a small estate, all areas around it are already built up, I can command between 75-90 million Naira per plot, I am staggered. I thank him and accept his business card.

I head to the American Embassy, I have heard good things about their roof top restaurant and I'm quickly shown to a table, lunch is fab and I find myself relaxing, not too much though just enough to enjoy my surrounds and people watch. It's interesting how quickly you can spot what you are looking for in a crowd.

There are white men with their young black male lovers, if you're not looking for it you will miss it but it's there, subtle in the unnecessary closeness and the way the men smile at the black boys they are with, well all consenting adults or is it. After a leisured lunch I hit Wuse market. As you drive in the first block to your left holds a small jewelers outlet a friend mentioned to me.

Outside the front another mallam sells guinea brocade. I treat myself to four bangles 24ct gold and load up on materials to take back to the States. While speaking to the mallam I quietly ask if he can recommend an agumu (word for local medicine) for poor sleep, in no time at all I have a small packet of greenish powder, a pinch in my drink and I will sleep like baby. I store this away quietly an idea forming and call Tayo, I ask if she's a good swimmer and suggest she packs a swim suit for Saturday, she eagerly agrees. It's time to settle old scores.

I politely seek the audience of a policeman who once he has a good look at me can't wait to help. I explained I have been out of the country and would like to track down an old childhood friend, I ask if we have detective agencies, he says no but that the detectives already working for the Nigerian Police Force are capable, he will speak to his oga and get back to me.

Just for taking his time I dash him some money and tell him I will be back in 20 minutes. I go back into the market and purchase a cheap Nokia phone and sim getting it activated immediately. Going back to the entrance to the market the police officer is waiting I give him my phone to call his oga who agrees to meet me at my hotel at 18.00hrs.

I give him the details and call Tee-A, I tell him I am missing him and want to head back to Lagos tomorrow afternoon if it's okay with him, I am suddenly his dear, my darling I have missed you more he says, would I like him to fly out and return together tomorrow, I decline but push home the fact I have missed his company and am looking forward to seeing him, I ask if we can have a wander out to the island for me to get a feel of how things will be on Saturday Tee-A agrees eagerly. Damn I am good.

At 6pm prompt I am waiting in the lounge, dressed smart casual and modestly, Mr Umo Akpan arrives with a colleague he introduces as Organ-Bassey. I ask them to join me for dinner. While we are waiting to be served I give them my sob story of wanting to reconnect with a childhood friend and not knowing where to start, gently pointing out that if it's the states any detective agency will find that person in a matter of days.

Mr Akpan confidently asks me to give them a chance we are just as good as the Americans he declares. I give him worm-man's name, last known location which is Lagos and bits and pieces I can remember such as surname, school and Uni details. Again he confidently says if he is here in Nigeria we will have that detail for you by Friday. I thank both men after the meal and give an envelope with 100,000.00

Mr Akpan has my details, I assure him I will be delighted if they find worm-man, otherwise I am just a sentimental old friend and for their trouble in meeting with me they should accept my small token. Promising to send a text if he is unable to reach me I double check he has the nokia number. We say our byes and I'm in bed by 8pm, the excitement bubbling up inside me.

I head back to Lagos to meet a very smiley Tee-A at the airport, if this daft man thinks I'm going to sleep with him, think on, not a problem thinking, it costs nothing, if I need to I certainly will, how difficult can it be. In baggage reclaim the nokia rings, it's Akpan, worm -man is alive and well, working in media and in local terms is a big man. I thank Mr Akpan and ask him to forward the details to me. Just like that I have the information I need about a dark bastard who took away my ability to trust in friendship.

Tee-A is waiting with his driver, I say a warm welcome, smiling a lot I'm getting plenty of smiles back from him. At Federal Palace he lingers downstairs, I'm game to sharing a bottle of red wine followed by freshly made sushi and saki. I tell you even before I get up I am slightly pissed.

It's late afternoon when we make our way to my room, once in the room I exaggerate the extent of my drunkenness, hugging and touching Tee-A playfully, my gamble is he'll put me to bed and clear off, I am taking a huge risk if this guy listens to his dick I am fucked. Good breeding is hard to ignore, he laughingly helps me into bed tucks me in and lets himself out.

I lie there quietly for a while then get up lock my door and jump in the shower. Taking a pinch of the herbal sleep aid with a glass of water, I get into bed, the next time I open my eyes it's 10.00hrs in the morning. That shit really works.

I reach for the phone and call Mr Da'Silva a well-known architect company on the mainland, for a sum of 70,000 naira someone will be sent over this afternoon to take details and draw up the bungalow I want to build, I tell them the location of the land, Ikorodu near college area, I am told they are well aware of that area. I ask if it's possible for them to provide me with all the experts needed to get the project off the ground quickly, I am assured this is the norm nowadays.

I call Tee-A's room, nil reply but he's left a message in-house, great he is away until this evening. I have a lazy breakfast in my room, I call Tayo and check on how she's doing, big mistake why does this woman get on my nerves so much, she's not coping she can't bear the loss of her mother she can't bare me heading back to the States next week, in short 'she can't' as if I give a 4x, still I keep my voice calm soothing and talk love and caring talk, my dislike for my sister is fast catching up with the intensity of my dislike for mother.

She brings forth feelings and memories that I thought were buried, the little shit would stand and watch mother ignore me while basking in the glory of her words and hugs the attention that was never ending whilst I was a treated like a piece of useless furniture.

Chapter 47

I listen to her while I pace the room like a caged animal, with each whine she puts a nail in her own coffin, I say all the right things, make all the right noises, Tayo is so used to her needs being the main focus she doesn't once ask how I am, the little shit !!!

When Nigerians get things right they sure get it right, the young architect arrives without any fanfare and gets to work, I show him the layout of the land I want to develop, I want the bungalow built in the far end behind which is a valley, if he is surprised he doesn't show it, I say this bungalow will eventually house my domestic staff, he nods along.

So we draw up a 3d computer image there and then, he asks why the 3rd bedroom will have no face level window, I explain it away as a dry storage room for things like suitcases and non-everyday essentials. It's a long three hours and I'm glad when he gets up to go but in that consultation, I know once the final estimate is in and funds are made available the building can be ready in 3-4months of focused work at the equivalent of $30-35,000 max, I'm good.

That room will have earthworm man as its first resident; no one who enters that room is coming out except hopefully as food for the valley. A thought crosses my mind and I log on to my face book page, I enter earthworm man's name and up he pops, I send him a friend request, I then begin to enter the other names I remember, each entry is a hit.

The oldest alive, and with a face book page-62. I send requests to each with the same short message, remember me 'Amuda', instant replies but I will ignore the messages for now. I have confirmation four of these guys are alive, remember me and are available, that is good enough. The completion of the house will start the ball rolling.

Tee-A calls from his suite, I agree tonight we dine by the pool there is a South African troupe entertaining, it should give me the distraction I need. I dress carefully, I want Tee-A to be smitten, I choose a pale blue embellished ASOS maxi dress with transparent sleeves and match the dress with silver Swarovski Dune slides finishing it off with a navy wrap, I don't carry a purse. I spend time doing my makeup and get the effect I want walking into the dining room.

Tee-A stands while the waiter seats me, we are the focal point for all diners, the men watching me hungrily the women wanting to be in my shoes, I smile as Moet and Chandon is popped and our glasses are filled. Tee-A gives me all the compliments I want to hear but it has it no effect.

Instead I smile at him and ask if my eyes are puffy, can he tell? His mood changes straight away, have I been crying, is it about my mum, has something else cropped up can he help, the sizzling sexual undertone is gone, that's my aim achieved. He remembers I lost my mum.

I keep the atmosphere thus, not moody or overly happy; this guy is like putty in my hand. I ask if we can go over to the Island in the morning Tee-A is more than happy to oblige. We walks me to my suite around midnight and he kisses my hand, I lean against him briefly, just enough for an exchange of body heat and step back thanking him for being there for me and confirming I will be ready after an early breakfast, could we have lunch on the island, my yes man says what I expect to hear, yes of course.

As I undress I caress my body, I have a nice body, breasts are still firm, I have seen other women's nipples over the years and know mine are the most beautiful, the contrast to the lighter area and the size, just right, I haven't been laid in a while, I walk over to the bed and lay on the cool crisp sheets, I weigh up my options what do I have to lose if I sleep with Tee-A, zilch, if I did or didn't it is clear he wants to be a part of my world.

I pick up the phone and call Tee-A, he answers on the 3rd ring. I say hello then keep quiet, he is flustered, am I okay, do I need something, should he come over, he is concerned and the alarm in his voice is audible. In a small voice I ask if I can come to his room, stay there he says I'm coming to get you. I jump of the bed and pull a kaftan on over my nakedness a few moments later he is at the door.

I step out and hold his hand as he leads the way back to his suite, I keep my head down and make no eye contact, in his suite, I stand in the middle of the room doing my best to look lost, he pours me a shot of Remi Martins and holds it to my lips ensuring I drink the lot, he then leads me to his bed, if you can call it a bed, 8 of us can sleep in it comfortably.

I slide in and he pulls the covers over me reassuring me he will sleep in the other room in his suite, I reach for his hand and hold on, I finally speak "please don't leave me", "I won't" he assures me. He moves quickly round the room and returns from the bathroom in his pj's and slides into the bed, before he can adjust himself I curl myself into him, he had left the bathroom light on with the door slightly ajar.

I smile in the darkness. Damn I am good. Tee-A gathers me in his arms murmuring reassuring nonsense words, I deliberately fall asleep, knowing what I will do in the next few hours.

I open my eyes three hours later, Tee-A is sleeping peacefully next to me, I slowly begin to caress him and though still half asleep I am rewarded with a rock solid erection, the size and girth as I touch takes my breath away, I was not expecting Tee-A to be well hung so this is a bonus, as he begins to wake up he is confused just as I wanted.

I slide down and take him in my mouth, the fool is trying to talk and check if I am okay with what I am doing while straining and jerking his hips to the rhythm of my tongue and mouth, I cup his balls and slowly gently tug and roll, Tee-A is in that place folks talk gibberish, I climb on his facing away from him, Tee-A jerks and trashes, he says words I can't hear what I can hear sound like profanity.

I close my eye, all the tension of the past weeks easing from me, I am multi-orgasmic, Tee-A is completely off his head, I pace myself, I want to give this man an experience he will want to repeat, as he begins to build I concentrate on my pleasure, releasing myself from control I feel my climax build and hold on as Tee-A begins to climax I join him, growling convulsing and breathless, I gasp over and over and talk the nonsense a man loves to hear.

As I roll off Tee-A, the entire time I have been on top of Tee-A, now I can no longer feel my legs, then he shocks me, Tee-A parts my legs and begins to give me head, I am shocked senseless, I certainly did not expect this, it is not sexual, not trying to turn me on, I get it, he simply wanted to taste me. It feels nice, gentle tongue probing and like that he stops, somehow knowing not to prolong what he was doing.

The heat we are giving off makes it impossible to continue skin to skin contact. Tee-A gets up and pours us iced cold water, he wanders into the bathroom, in a jiffy I have my kaftan on and tell him I need to go, no man can stop in the middle of taking a leak, banking on that I let myself out as he calls out no please wait.

The phone is ringing when I get to my suite, he sounds distressed, I keep my voice quiet and gentle, I am embarrassed by my behavior I explain as expected he says all the right things to reassure me, do I want him to come to my suite, I decline, I will see him at breakfast. This is almost too easy.

For breakfast the following morning I dress in a loose white linen dress with a matching short sleeve jacket, twin set pearls and Cartier Jackie O sunglasses finish off my look, with a casual pair of Stuart Weitzman sandals. I use my Oleg Cassin generously; I make sure I am running 5 minutes late.

Tee-A looks like a man who hasn't had much sleep, I can read him and he is unsure where to start with me, I smile at him the sort I give to Board members in meetings, I order breakfast without looking at him, I can feel his eyes on me, he tells the waiter to bring the same for him. As the waiter walks away I speak first, it's important I speak first, I look directly at Tee-A, keeping my voice low I apologize for my behavior stated hope I haven't spoilt our friendship. Tee-A looks at me really perplexed, he is so transparent this man. He simply replies, "sometime between last night and this morning I went to heaven".

I smile at him and continue to do so, I show excitement about visiting his island and we are back on safe grounds in no time. Breakfast is pleasant, the short drive to the Yacht club is uneventful. I ensure there is no sexual tension between us telling him lame jokes and generally having both of us laughing at life.

The crossing is a pleasure once we leave the busy Apapa waterways, Nigeria is truly a beautiful place, if it was located in the USA it would make Billions per annum from tourism. The Niger Delta conflict, Boko Haram et el have put paid to anyone heading here without justifiable reasons. I ask questions and study the layout as we approach.

Tee-A points out the calm in coves and areas where the current is rough and dangerous, I ask how he knows these things, the few locals he allows to reside there know the water well.

I pay close attention as we walk, I ask if we can do a quick walk round the island, it's not quite noon and the temperature because of the breeze is bearable. As we walk I ask loads of questions, all relevant except for the one that mattered. I ask Tee-A about swimming, he points out the areas not to swim in because of the swift undercurrent, there is a total of three such points on the island, the nearest to the house is less than 20 meters from the back garden wall, this is great.

In discussing the barbeque I choose a point about a 30 meters from the house, pure white sand and glistening water with a brook bubbling nearby, I am looking forward to bringing Tayo here, I promise myself she will not leave this island the way she arrived.

Chapter 48

Buoyed by this thought I give my full attention to Tee-A who is looking at me like he wants to scoop me into his mouth like ice cream. Tee-A shows me the well stocked cellar, as he reaches for a bottle his hand brushes my chest, I catch my breath as my nipples instantly react through the thin material, they stand erect like knobs.

Tee-A stands there frozen his gaze on my chest, I take the forgotten bottle from him and return it to the shelf, I pull him into my arms and start laughing, he holds me tight for a long moment and then joins in the laughter. I have slept with this guy and feel the need to do so again, only because it is available, uncomplicated and bloody good.

I move back from Tee-A and step out of my pants, he is already panting while the bulge is threatening to break his zip, I free him from his cage then turn my back on him and bend over holding on to the shelf in front of me. Tee-A raises my right leg and eases himself into me, thank god for common sense, his strokes are slow and hard, drawing a sharp breath from me each time, this guy is reaching all the right parts.

I shudder and shiver with the pleasure of it not expecting what I feel, and still the slow hard sex, now fast now slow, then he stays inside me simply rotating himself inside me without thrusting, orgasms yes, multiple climax no, but then it begins to build, Tee-a has reached round to cup both my breasts.

I can feel him trying to control himself, for some insane reason I look at my watch, he has been doing me for 45 minutes, I decide to bring things to an end and begin to wiggle and twist my ass, what I didn't expect was another climax, it hits me catching me unaware and reducing me to a feverish mass of flesh. As my legs begin to feel they will give way Tee-A climax. I have had sex with him twice and managed to keep the self harm scars hidden. I need to be careful; I don't want him asking questions. I slip my pants on and ask if we can make a move, the cellar reeks of sex.

I freshen up in one of the rooms and enjoy a leisured lunch with a man who cannot work me out but is happy to be with me. He finally speaks, am I okay with him, totally I say. I quietly remind him I'm married and apologize if I have caused him any distress. Tee-A comes over and pulls me into his arms, he looks at me for a long time and says what I know is coming next, "whatever you decide please don't walk away from me".

I hug him tight, this man has no idea how useful he is going to be in the next 72hrs, walk away hell no, I do something I don't do often, I kissed him and he kissed me right back, not a bad kisser either. We go for a short walk then head back having left final instruction for the barbeque. Tonight I will not sleep with Tee-A even if he came to my door and barks like a dog.

Back at Federal Palace I excuse myself with the need to make contact with my office and do a tele-conference. I'm actually not feeling that great, the second orgasm made me feel feverish and gave me a slight headache. I stand in the shower for a long time, I am struggling with what lies ahead, do I need to carry it through? Images of my mother fussing over Tayo while I always looked in like an outsider flood me.

Tayo is not blameless, though a child I remember moments when she showed off and would make a point of basking in the glow of our mother, knowing full well I couldn't even go and hug the old cow or sit and pass time away the way they did. Tayo has to pay for her sins and her contribution towards my distress, with my mind made up I decide to sleep with Tee-A tomorrow night.

I need his mind and judgment to be clouded so that self blame will play on his mind and nil suspicion towards me. Like a spot you think has cleared up but returns each time my phone is ringing it's yours truly Tayo, the same mushy conversation, when will the pain of losing her mother ease. I make all the right noises then invite her over for dinner.

Tayo arrives just as I woke from my nap, my head is clear and the feverish feeling has gone, I speak briefly to Tee-A to let him know I am spending the evening with a distressed Tayo who is on her way over. Tee-A tries to keep the disappointment from his voice and reminds me he is at my disposal if needed; I thank him and ring off.

We order a seafood platter and sit on the floor in my suite, the huge lobsters you'll pay top dollar for in the States is just local chop here and treated as nothing but a giant prawn. For a mourner her appetite is intact, greedy little so and so. I look closely at my sister, she had aged, the skin under her eyes are puffy and dark, this silly woman really misses her mother, well not for long, I will soon send her on her way to join her.

I am off to the States in a few days and can't wait to distant myself from everything for a while, it's been full-on the past weeks, I play back in my head and hope I haven't made any mistakes. I promise Tayo I will be back soon to see her and I mean it but not in the way she thinks. At the very least tomorrow I have to make sure she is maimed if death is not possible. Tayo departs at 8pm I remind her to pack a swimsuit. I call my friends and remind them of the meeting time at the yacht club; conversation with them is always easy and flows well. Tomorrow is set, 20 meters from the back entrance, a total of 50 meters from where the barbeque crowd is, the distance between life, death or damage, Tayo shall see.

Chapter 49

What a glorious morning the weather is amazing but look closely and the tip of the horizon a few dark clouds roll, it's 07.10am I know Tee-A is up and go up to his suite, I wear another kaftan with nothing underneath, he answers the door on my third knock and is surprised to see me, expecting room service with his coffee, which arrives hot on my heels, we sit sipping coffee on the balcony with our legs propped up on the railing.

I let me kaftan ride down showing legs and the tip of pubic, Tee-A drinks coffee without tasting it, I smile at him and take his gaze to his bulge, putting my coffee cup down I slide off my chair, I don't want this lasting more than 5 minutes, he soon collapses back in the chair and mutters "ye gods" over and over again.

I drop a kiss on his head and tell him to get ready; he laughs and says "when he can walk he'll attempt that". I have him where I want nicely, sexed up, his senses will be dulled to any of my actions.

Tayo is waiting downstairs and rides with us, nil need for any introduction, Wale has everyone in stitches by insisting we all wear a life jacket which we comply with. The drinks is flowing before we cast off, I am impressed by the orderliness, as we walk towards the mooring, I hear a voice I have not heard in 40 years a voice that will wake me up if I was in a coma, it is worm man, I remember he used to boast they have yachts here.

I locate and watch his from the safety of my dark glasses as I spiral into that place where I need to hurt whatever, whoever. Worm man is giving instructions, he has filled out over the years, but repulsive to me same as he was day one. He looks fit and strong, I realize seeing him today is a bonus, it gives me leeward to plan forward properly for what I have in mind for him.

He is a big guy, I'm going to need proper restraints and tranquilizers to control him when the time comes, at 6'3 and big boned he won't be easy to stuff into a car. Well I have time to figure out how I will get him to the house in Ikorodu, probably the thought of getting sex will get him there. I watch him closely, arrogant bastard gives instruction while others run around, he must be doing well as its money that calls the shots in this part of the world. I now know where to leave a note for the ass wipe if that's my chosen contact method.

I pull myself back to the present, it is hard, the horror of worm man pretending to be a friend and then seeing him in his dressing gown. I don't know why I didn't scream such is my horror of worms that I would have stuck my hand in a coal fire to get away from contact with worms.

I'm talking and smiling responding to my friends but moving and changing position to keep that bastard in full view until we round the corner. What I really want to do right now is get worm man in a room, get a toothpick and shove it in his urethra, that should make his eyes water. My skin prickles I shiver and it's mistaken for chills, I've got chills alright but not in the way you all think.

I split my mind into two, taking part in conversations and going over the fine details in my mind of Tayo's hopeful demise. I watch my sister, standing close to Tee-A, looking vulnerable and for the first time I wonder if my shitty life is this pathetic creature's fault as I've always thought, it's ironic how you are thinking something along the line of compassion and an action or omission puts the murderous plans back on the playing field.

My sister has a look on her face, I can see her reflection in a small glass panel, bitch doesn't realize I can see her, she's looking at me like I'm dirt, I check this out a couple of times but face to face she gives me a warm smile. Am I underestimating Tayo? Does she feel about me the way I feel about her. This could be an interesting turn of events.

All doubts are briefly dispelled when she pulls my arm and tells me she's always been jealous of the way I am strong and independent, the way I have stayed strong after mum passed away and she has fallen apart. I pull her close and give her a hug; bitch is giving me all the alibi I need for all witness to say we have a close relationship. It's not all sad to the observer.

It's a chatty loud champagne filled crowd that came off the boat, heading first to the house we attended to our toiletry, a quick tour of the house and we hurried to the smell of roasts and good aromas. A mixed staff of Chinese and Nigerians are in attendance, Cantonese duck straight off the spit served with a light cabbage salad. We were crunching bone and laughing our heads off in no time, ribs the size of a small paddle, crispy seaweed, a variety of dim sum followed, an array of drinks was passed round by the cocktail staff, we just sat back and enjoyed, talking and remembering growing up, school, expectations and reality.

The women are an easy going bunch, if they didn't like me they masked it well based on the relationship and position I hold in their partner's life. Our host Tee-A is charming and gives nothing away of the intimacy we share, I think of him as a fuck buddy, he clearly sees me through rose tinted glasses, oh well never mind.

I'm pitching things well and slowly turn the conversation to business talk, I encourage the men to network and point out the fact though in England none had crossed paths, I suggested ways in which each had a business the other could link in with that will be beneficial to each party. I kept this brief knowing football will follow next and knowing the women will soon tire of money and football talk. We gradually move into the two groups, I want the women slightly apart from the men. The ability of women to make the best of any situation they find themselves in is astonishing. We quickly cover a crazy and wide variety of topics, laughing and jolly away the next hours before we regroup for the main meal of the cookout.

All dishes were cooked in small portions but what a meal, sticky rice with an undertone of coconut, spicy crispy chicken, lobster flesh in ginger and spring onion sauce, mixed seafood in black bean sauce and sizzling steak platter. Steamed sea bass with lemon grass and garlic mussels, a vegetable stir fry of delicious Chinese mushroom, mango tout a few slices of bean curd a hand full of carrots and baby sweet corn.

All that stuff and nonsense about food being too much, we polished off the lot, nothing was wasted which was great. Chinese food always has a flat ending desert I expect will be the usual fruit platter, caramelized apple/ banana or lycee and ice cream or so I thought.

We were served delicious fried ice cream that blew our mind and had us cursing foreigners under our breath, leading to the usual what did the white man do when he came to Africa jokes, my favorite, the white man arrived with the bible, we had the land he had the bible, he said close your eyes let us pray when we opened our eyes we had the bible and he had our land.

We laughed at the china man and his hurried walk and fast conversation, we laughed at ourselves and our belief we went to England to take back from the white man what he took from our fathers, we laughed and laughed and all the time I am waiting, waiting for the men to drink just that bit more, waiting for a few more of the ladies to need a toilet break, pretending to rummage in my bag, I slide the catch on my amber ring as shown, pick up my sisters glass, she is drinking a fruit cocktail with a dash of Dubonnet , it's slight bitter after taste will mask any taste of the power, I walk over to the guy mixing the drink and dropped the few specks into the bottom of the glass to melt while he's distracted with my orders, I ask for a fresh drink, a tall glass, when ready I poured most into my sisters glass then walked back sipping from the tall glass giving the impression I had drank half my glass.

Tayo took her drink and sits back, I watch her like a hawk, at some point conversation about coral came up, with Tayo and Yetunde showing an interest Tee-A asked them to the house to see a few he kept there. I watched the three of them walk to the house as I've shown no interest in the subject I remain back.

Giving them a 3 minute start I head to the house, using the side entrance, I hear lowered voices from the dining room, it's Tayo and Tee-A, he's apologizing "I'm sorry darling how was I to know she is your sister, baby hang in there, she will be gone in a few days and life will be back to normal, she doesn't suspect I know you and it's too late to say so now", Tayo snaps back "I don't trust her mum said not to ever trust her". Tee-A offers reassurance and suggests she asks herself why I would mean her any ill. This appeared to pacify Tayo.

So the venomous looks on the boat was not my imagination, I walk back quickly; this is one hell of a development. My butter won't melt in the mouth Tayo has a lover of all the men on the Island I end up with him, shit and double shit, I get another drink and make my way back to the house, nosily this time calling out and asking for a view of the Coral. Yetunde emerges from the toilet apologizing for being gone too long.

Tee-A and Tayo resume their charade, I'm not sure what I'm feeling there will be time for that late. Jesus this can only happen to me, how that cow mother of mine must be laughing her head off wherever she is.

Before I could gather my thoughts properly Tee-A picks up the cocktail Tayo had left on the side board and downed the lot, wiping his mouth he asks no one in particular why ladies like such sweet drinks. My brain and mind collide trying to make sense of what just happened, the puffer fish poison meant for Tayo has just been swallowed by Tee-A, slow acting he should go into a coma in 72hrs with nil pulse detectable within another 24hrs of that.

Chapter 50

My head is about to explode, I am confused and all thoughts of luring Tayo to swim goes out of my mind, Tee-A is going to be buried alive. It's what I want for Tayo yes, not this man. Apart from not telling me he knew my sister once he realized who I was, I have nothing against him. What a holy mess.

Then the unthinkable creeps into my mind, what if all this time the two had set me up good and proper, Tayo encouraging Tee-A to keep me close so she can keep tabs on me, but is that possible I ask myself, are folks in Nigeria that clued up.

I am on auto pilot, mask on laughing, talking, socializing paying good attention to all, you would never guess what is going on behind the facade presented. Tee-A is going to die, Tayo and Tee-A are lovers. Bloody Nora!

We are back with the main group, I listen to the men chat and all marvel that in all the years in England they lived within a ten mile radius of each other but never met. Listening to them helps me get a grip. I smile, what I hope is warmly at my friends and their partners who from the sound of things are planning to pull all resources and expertise and become movers and shakers.

Inside me a rage is building, I try, oh I try and keep it at bay, I want to take Tayo lead her to the water edge and throw her in the strong undercurrent Tee-A warned about. Today is my only chance to kill my sister, anywhere else any other occasion and questions will be asked. It dawns on me and I have to instantly accept Tayo is not going to die on this trip, I am back in 6 months time so full stop for now.

The reason I remain under the radar and I'm not on America's most wanted is this.... I know when to stop. I want my sister dead; it's not going to happen on this occasion. Lock up the feeling another opportunity will come in the future, why loose all I have, incarceration in Nigeria is not on my agenda.

For the demons raging in me, I demand music, the get together is not complete without music, Tee-A gives instructions and 70's soul music floods the place, volume just right, thus begins another round of boogie gists. It is the servants that alert us it's time to head back. I remain on auto, saying the right things, only Wale notices something is wrong when he asks to cover my tracks, I clear my throat and address everyone.

Telling them how much I appreciate them for today and asking to be forgiven if I haven't always seemed to be on the ball, sighting it's early days since mum's demise but thanking them for their friendship and love we depart the island, well fed and top tanked. The crossing back to Victoria Island is pleasant. The day by all standards has been a smashing success, excellent food and wines, relaxed and a great way to reconnect even if I had murder on my mind. The little girl in me who refuses to grow up un-avenged says you have 48hrs before heading to the States, anything can happen, I smile, I still have a minute silver of the powder left in my ring as well as the paper infusion.

I'm coming alive again, returning to Federal Palace I want to know what it's like to sleep with a dead man even if he doesn't know he is dying.

I suggest a night cap on his balcony as we ride up in the lift after the others depart. If Tayo is planning to double back this should put pay to that, his usual debonair self we agree I come up in a few moments.

Getting to my suite I call Kirk Stapleton, he answers immediately. In floods of tears and hiccups I thank him for taking my call, he reassures me he's being on standby with the welfare of an American Citizen the highest on his mind round the clock. I tell him I thought I was coping okay but now feel completely over whelmed, I don't know how I'm going to cope in the next 72 hours, "I don't think I can cope" I say dissolving into another round of tears.

Kirk is in Abuja, he promises to be on the flight out to Lagos tomorrow. Am I safe, will I be okay till he arrives, he has an attaché he can send over. I decline saying I can hold it together and will remain here at Federal Palace as I can't bear to be at home on my own. We agree to meet at the Embassy at 13.00hrs

I put the phone down laugh and laugh some more.

A quick shower and I head upstairs, Tee-A looks well, I am looking for a sign of depression in normal functioning, none. Tee-A is waffling on "wow lady you blew in and now blowing out, two consenting adults as you say in the West. So my dear can I expect contact after this visit"? While he's talking I've moved behind him and now have my arms round him.

Resting my head on his back I let my hands do the talking, sliding his belt loose, I undo his flies and gain access to him I don't free him just caress, he stands still groaning, I increase the pressure, noting he's watching his pleasure in the mirror I rotate him slightly to the left, I don't want him to catch a look at me as I talk to him soothingly, "it's a shame I have to go, you've made this trip bearable, you are God sent, I didn't think at my age sex would be on the agenda or that I would experience this' you've made possible, the pierce de résistance, if I could choose a husband I would choose you, you have rocked my world" and with that I take my hands out of his boxers and head to the bathroom.

Tee-A is slummed in the chair with a dressing gown round him, taking the champagne flute from him I take a sip and take him in my mouth, the contrast of warmth and cool send him into excitement that threatens to split his skin, I begin to tease him, while using the back of my hand, no knowing how much puffer fish poison is in semen.

This time when I emerge from the bathroom with a wet face flannel to clean him I find Tee-A deep in thought, he says nothing as I refresh his private parts.

Thinking of my sister, this guys deceit I feel the old stirring "you want sex, I will give it to you", taking a small palm full of almond oil I begin to massage him, shoulder, back, chest then torso, when I get to his waist I add more oil and begin a slow massage of his private, he mumbles and groans a "nooo", he sounds desperately tired but is reacting, with each stroke, "you're killing me he says" the irony of it all.

I start a breast massage, I am on a mission, I want this man exhausted enough to have a lie-in tomorrow, giving me time to pop out first thing and also for my meeting with Kirk, and so I rock him to yet another climax, this time he groans as he bucks, I note the look on his face, that of an exhausted man that borders on irritation or is it panic that he will not be left alone.

I clean my chest and hand him a bottle of water from the fridge, taking a deep pull he pats his side and motions for me to join him, I decline putting on my worried look. He is instantly alert "what is the matter my dear" I stall then share "I have over spent the dollars I brought with me"; I get the exert reaction I expect. "My dear is that all give me a moment", getting up he goes to the toilet for the longest wee of the century.

Returning he brings his brief case to the coffee table where he drops heavily into the chair, I ensure I am sitting in an untidy manner, with enough flesh showing but nil tackiness. Opening the brief case he brings out six bundles of $100 bills each one has the seal intact and states $20,000. Take it my dear, you're good for it, what are friends for.

I burst into fresh tears just for the occasion, adding hiccups to it for max effect, I drop down beside him and rest my head in his lap, as he says soothing words and asked that I do not embarrass him, "this is left over change I do not boast, the money I have I cannot finish spending this life time so please let me reimburse you for your outgoing in picking up the tab for your mum's funeral".

I cry long and hard, I cry for myself, I cry for this fool who is going to be dead in a few days. I cry for the fact he betrayed me and could easily have told me in the early days we met he knew my sister. I cry because Tayo has this extremely wealthy man as a lover and must have lived a life I can only imagine. I cry because the wrong person is on death pathway, but even as I cry my calculating mind is looking for a way any avenue to snuff my sister out. Between hiccups I ask if he will be kind and keep in touch with Tayo, as my friend please look out for my sister, keep her close and I will be able to relax knowing she has you as I'm so far away. "Of course my dear I give you my word" he replies.

Tee-A continues to say soothing words to me but now they are not so intense, the man is flagging he wants to sleep or either get into bed or I go. Dropping the money into the envelope he offered me I kiss him good night, tucking the envelope into my dressing gown I head out to my room. For the first time I think about cctv camera's, is Nigeria as big brother mad as the west, while waiting for the lift I look round but see nothing obvious. Perhaps Federal Palace Hotel is happy with the security agents that patrol each floor.

Chapter 51

I call Wale and apologise for the late hour, I explain I need to leave $9,000 with him to be changed to Naira if needed or I will collect it on my return in 6 months. I also ask for a lift to the airport when I depart. He will send his driver over for 10.00am and personally take me to the airport on Tuesday morning. Thanking him I get busy, I have a lot to do in the morning; I pack my roll-on case and set the alarm on my phone for 06.30am.

I am up and in the hotel reception by 07.00hrs, I eat a quick breakfast and head out dressed in a tie-dye abaya hair covered in a stylish tie of the same material, unless you look closely I blend in well with the crowd. I get one of the hotel taxi's to take me first to Tejuosho market where I purchase a nokia and a sim card which was activated there and then, I put a 1,000 credit on it knowing I will only use it once. I also bought small slim line two storage tins with screw on lids that are airtight.

I ask the driver to take me to Excellence Hotel in Ogba Ikeja, I pay for a suite for two nights and leave my cabin bag in the room. I ask the driver to come back for me midday. From Ogba I head to Ikorodu chartering a local taxi for a return ride. Near college and the location of my property to be built I find what I am looking for pay and put the receipt away making a note of all I need. I walk round briefly to familiarize myself with the immediate and relevant lay out of the area for when I return in 6 months time. I return to Ogba in time for the drivers pickup to head home to Ilupeju.

Going into my room, I take each bundle of money and roll it into a tight wad then rubber band it, each tin takes three comfortably, I then roll the tins up in a thin throw material, tying a knot at one end. Unscrewing the metal head stand at the end of the bed nearest to the wall I stuff this down the hollow cavity. The cloth acts as a cushion if in any event my bed is moved there will be no curious rattling noise I super glue a piece of the cloth to the side for easy retrieval.

Wale's driver arrives promptly and takes the envelope containing the $9,000. I also sent a thank-you card with a personal message to the others via Wale knowing the men will keep in touch. Tayo's call interrupts my thoughts, she wants to come over, I ask that we meet in the evening.

By 1pm I am at the embassy, dressed in a pant suit, building appears closed but as the driver drew up we are asked who we are and promptly passed through once the car was given the once over. Kirk certainly deserves his name, his parents I have no doubt are fans of Kirk Douglas, this Kirk spotted the cleft Douglas made famous. He welcomes me in a warm but professional clinical manner.

His kind, you can describe as the Ivy league type, everything in the order generations before him did, all necessary trappings in place, the breath taking homes, from apartments in the city to holiday home in Martha's Vineyard. A wife and 2.5 kids as needed for show. But one thing I can tell, this man has a red blooded hot Nigerian babe draining his juices every night, when you see a man getting seriously laid and satisfied there is an aura they carry a bit cat who got the cream twice stance. Plus he are too comfortable around the natives.

As we walk through I am shocked by the amount of people around and the buzz of activities going on, clearly America is fighting against something every day so no time off. The room we go into is like a conservatory, light and airy with the air conditioning just the right temperature after the heat outside. Iced tea and choc chip cookies is laid out on the coffee table.

Sitting opposite me Kirk asks me to feel free to begin to talk when I'm ready. I ask how much he knows of my circumstances, Kirk replies he has been briefed I may need support, nil in-depth information and nothing in writing he assures me. While he's taking I have been gauging him, he's sharp.

I tell him little about myself, key points as they say, making sure I keep to the sort of information needed for a decision making process. I share my last Psychology session and the reasons for asking to see him which is I simply became overcome with the loss and my sister needing me and me returning to the States in less than 48hrs, no one to talk to and the feeling of stress that comes from giving support to all and now feeling drained. At this point I take my sunglasses off, the dry pepper have done the job again, red bloodshot nicely swollen eyes.

Kirk asks me how I feel, any unusual thoughts or experience. How is my sleep, am I eating well, any self harm, what about excessive use of alcohol, have I used non prescription or illicit drugs. I have been in this position before and can tell you what you want to hear and make it sound like you and only you have been able to reach me. I switch to this mode now.

I feel drained with the death, nil unusual thoughts or experience, sleep is good though broken, eating well, some alcohol, nil drugs nil self-harm. I lay it on thick, crying softly I tell Kirk I needed a release valve and he has provided that, I thank him for giving me the space to talk, he makes all the right noises.

I am surprised when he tells me should I need it the embassy can host me for the remaining hours, they have buildings within the compound, I appear indecisive then decline ensuring I say all the right things and thus ended a two hour meeting. Kirk offers to see me on Monday and even at the airport before my early morning flight. I thank him and ask how much notice I need to give if I want to see him, he is available 24/7 by phone and will make face to face contact asap, It's my job to do so he says smiling. He assures me should I like need any intervention to call him, on this note I get up and he follows suit.

As he walks me to the car I wish it was Tayo who was dying, I would certainly accept the offer of accommodation, it would be the perfect alibi, well now I know that fact for when I return in 6 months' time when as mum stipulated her will was to be read.

Arriving at Federal Palace I check to see if I have any messages, nil, I phone Tee-A's room no response.

I check out and head to Ikeja telling Tayo to meet me there and pack a bag if she wishes to stay. I need to keep her with me so she has no access to Tee-A to raise alarm that he's not well. Nigeria is not backward when it comes to medicine and poisoning is something that will be considered when triaged on arrival at any medical facility.

Ye God's Tayo arrives with her youngest in tow, maybe it's a good thing as it provided a distraction for me and my murderous thoughts. I go into my good listener mode, I have less than 48 hours and know by hosting Tayo and listening may very well help me find ways to hurt her, I shall let her identify her weak points, starting with her husband's business that's not doing that great.

Tayo has shares in anything that has shares for sale in Nigeria, I listen to this little shit and think not once did she ever call me and ask if I was interested in acquiring any land, built property or shares yet here she is giving me an a-z rundown of what she has. It is so true that the enemy cannot know how to get you if you don't tell them.

I look at my sister and think how I would love to wipe the smile off her little face, it is a good job I threw the ring away, as I am so tempted right now to feed her rat poison the most easily available. I am raging inside, one thing is clear she doesn't like me either and thinks she's making a good job of not showing it. Sunday night is spent gisting and dinning in the hotels luxury surrounding. As usual we draw admiring glances from the people around.

I had never heard of eating disorder, self harm and other habits I developed, the argument remains nurture environment or learnt, if I had been well nurtured will I have turned out well, where did I learn the responses I have from, when did the West influence me and how did I not notice or is it in all of us, we just need the right buttons pressed.

Maybe mother was right when she said "You are sick in the head" wander what she meant....sick in the head. Is that what Kirk was told, she's sick in the head if she calls prioritize seeing her. Was my meeting with Kirk support contact for an American citizen or was I just reviewed for levels of dangerousness.

Tayo's pitch has changes, something has excited her, Tayo is only excited when she sees money or is given money, I listen to her and make all the right noises as she tells me about the ladies who have just arrived, all diamond dealers all flogging the Dubai route and all spreading their legs for top officials in the corridor of power.

Tayo's real persona is really bang on, greedy, vain desperate to fit in and be acknowledged by those she sees as making waves. Looking at Tayo I know it's going to be a pleasure to watch her die or leave knowing she's dying. I try to keep the disgust from my face as my niece orders food she can't finish but greed won't let her stick to what she can.

I fringe migraine and retire to the smaller bedroom in the suite leaving the master room for Tayo and her side kick. I do something the makes me chuckle, I lock my bedroom door. The hunter relaxes not in the vicinity of the prey.

Monday is spent spending my money, I am dragged to the in places, we have lunch, manicure and pedicures at ridiculous prices, the only visit that saved my sanity and kept me focused is the National Museum on Lagos Island, the little restaurant there is to die for, the two ladies who run it kept me in stitches with their antics over the years about men, they also produced good wholesome Nigerian food which of course was not what the two idiots with me wanted.

I have had no contact from Tee-A, I am reluctant to call him and feel thankful when Tayo brings him up, clearing my face I ask her to call him, it rings and goes to voicemail, we both leave a message thanking him for his support and hosting us. If my Haitian friends are spot on he should begin to slow down about now with nil pulse detectable by around 17.20hrs which is when he drank Tayo's cocktail.

Returning to the hotel Tayo's husband shows up with two friends in tow, men in their mid-50's dressed down in jeans and tee shirts, they looked an odd sight but to the young girls looking for sponsorship it must be the pulling look anyway out comes the Remi Martins with Tayo and I opting for red wine.

The company is loud and easy going, I am shocked when I realized I am actually enjoying myself, these guys are the biggest gossip on the planet, in this manner we pass a few good hours, with our group growing as people they know or who are of the same social class joined us. Finger food dun-dun, do-do, scotch-egg , suya, massa and the never ending order for goat meat pepper soup.

As is the norm business cards are exchanged or given to you whether you show an interest or not. We head to our suite when the circle break up at dawn. No one drives around at night anymore, if you are out past midnight you stay where you are and head home at first light.

Heading to the suite I stop in reception to enquire about the bill for the night, calculating in dollar terms it's a bargain, we've eaten and drank the best quality stuff and it cost me about a grand, not bad, not bad at all.

I remind my sister Wale will be arriving at 7 to get me to the airport on time. We shower and meet back in the lounge. I give my sister some money she doesn't need it but her nature will not allow her to say no thank you. We doze lightly with CNN in the background telling us all the latest bombing and crashes.

I settle my bill while Wale's driver loads up, Tayo and her daughter leave at the same time both urging me to call when I get to LA. I watch as they drive away and ask how I could be related to such a wretched person. Not once did she try to open conversation on our upbringing she was okay so what is there to talk about I guess. Besides she once had the cheek when I tried years ago to say how I struggled and is still struggling with how mother treated me to say just forget it!!! forget it, forget that which shaped my life and turned me into a raging ball of anger.

It !!! that has never let me enjoy the joys of sex except when I pay for it or I'm humiliating or manipulating someone. Forget it, it that made me such a clingy over caring mother that my only child felt suffocated and moved to live where I have to get on a flight to visit. It that totally fucked me up cannot be forgotten, I will get you for that statement.

Driving to the airport conversation with Wale is comfortable and relaxing, my thoughts turn to Tee-A, I know he is dead, lying in the suite on his own that saddens me, that act of drinking Tayo's cocktail is his fault, it also confirmed his relationship with my sister, Naija men don't pick up drinks and down it unless you have a connection. I touch the cheap Noika phone in my jacket pocket. I will make the call in the gap while my cases are being unloaded before we walk into the airport.

Luck is not my side, no sooner do we pull up that Wale is surrounded by friends, I mouth that I'm going to the hausa sellers trading in kilishi, as I walk away I switch the phone on, before I could dial the driver is beside me sent by Wale to do my bidding. I sent him to buy 5 packets of Kilishi and head back to Wale and his entourage.

Checking in is something else, the chaos the noise the lack of clarity regarding systems, first the check-in guy asked if I had anything for him, when I played dumb he gave me my London-LA boarding card and told me to come back after security has cleared my cases, I get unto another line for that, again the same request while asking me what food stuff I am taking out of the country, I declare the 5 packets of Kilishi and let them know I am happy to chuck them in the bin. I am sent to yet another lot who then tag my bag, I give up and give them a $10 pathetic really, and back to check-in and what do you have for us. I see Wale laughing his head off at my dilemma and I lose my cool.

Seeing two white men standing nearby I walk up to them and ask if they are Senior officials for the airline I'm using, yes they confirm, I'm travelling 1st class and do not wish to give money to your member of staff checking me in, I rant while pointing to the man.

Quickly realizing what I had done he hurries out from behind the desk and hands me my boarding pass, saying madam you forgot this, I snapped at him I hadn't turning to the two men I repeated he had refused to hand them over if I didn't give him a dash as it's called, with this I stomped off.

I have a 999 call to make and don't have time for this nonsense. Hugging Wale warmly I remind him I'm back for the reading of the will in 6 months time, as I step back worm man comes into my line of vision, I shut and open my eyes to make sure he's real, he's real alright and is travelling, I start a nonsense conversation with Wale about all that is wrong with our Airport, worm man is not travelling but the woman his with who is clearly his wife is. There are two flights I hope she's on mine either way I have a bit of time to make friends, I will find a way to start conversation.

Worm man turns round and stares right at me, his eyes rests on me for a while, he does not recognize me, this is the trouble with perpetrators they don't keep a victim photo page. Worm man is interested in me he stands at an angle where he can keep an eye on his wife's check-in progress and check me out. She is travelling economy while I'm in 1st, she can't come to 1st but I can sit in economy.

I turn my attention to Wale and tell him it's okay to leave, happy I'm okay he takes his leave. I buy a coffee and use the entertainment of the check-in to relax; Worm man is keeping me in view but has not made a move other than a smile which I didn't return. His wife does not hang around and bidding him bye she heads into the Immigration control area.

Worm man heads straight to me, it's 08.35hrs, is there a time during 24hrs that men do not chat up women. I look at him coolly, he says good morning and asks if he can buy me a coffee when I say no thank you the bastard addresses me by my name, I have been mistaken all along that this wile creature did not remember me.... I think of the property being built in Ikorodu as we speak and smile at him. This huge man who I need to lure to Ikorodu.

I keep an eye on the time as I have to make the call in the next half hour away from the constant announcement in the departure lounge. Worm man bombards me with questions do I live in Naija, no oh okay, You're in LA, okay, when are you back, 6 months that's great, can we meet up, this time it's me "that will be great" he gives me the customary card, I don't offer him mine, I'll give you a call when I return, satisfied with this he takes his leave, I order a large coffee to take away but tell the girl not to fill it to the top, do not make the mistake of blinking, when I turn round to pick up the business card it's gone, taken no doubt by one of the ladies who will ring him and try their luck to convince him he gave it to them when they met, oh well, taking the coffee I head out towards the Hausa sellers.

Ensuring no one is near me I dial 999 and keep it brief if the call is recorded the experts cannot identify it as mine. Producing the perfect local girl Ibadan accent I tell the operator there is a man dead in a room on the 5th floor at Federal Palace hotel "I think they killed him for the contract money lots of dollars in suitcase" I said and hang up.

Putting the phone back in my bag I dismantle it chucking the battery in the bin as I walk past, I then turn my attention to the sim card which popped out easily, this went in the next waste bin wrapped in a tissue I pretended to blow my nose with topped with a few drops of coffee to make the tissue look vile.

Taking the lid off the new cup of coffee I purchased I pop the phone back in my pocket and use the handkerchief to clean it for prints as best as I could lowering the cup to my bag I put the phone in the cup of coffee and put the lid back on, again making out I'm blowing my nose, I place a thick wad of tissues in the coffee cup, pop the lid back on and throw it in the back of the filthy rubbish van that just pulled up, smiling at the man working I give him a 1,000 naira bill and bless him for his honest work. There has not been an announcement.

I buy a few touristy things for my immediate staff and head back into the airport. Immigration and customs ask for no bribe and show nil interest in me. I find worm man's wife in the lounge smiling sweetly at her I order coffee introduce myself and complement her on her beauty. Once sure I am a childhood friend to worm-man and not a threat she relaxes. We chat until our flight is called, she is heading to London for a family wedding, I invite her to dinner Thursday night as I head back to the states on Friday morning, she accepts, this delightful woman who has no idea what her husband is capable of is going to give me the access I need to lure him to the kill.

I decide not to sit with her, once on board I request the duty free book and purchased gifts worth $1,000 to be delivered to worm man's spouse when duty free opens, not only is she my way in she will give him to me on a plate, the insight I will gain from her over dinner will form the foundation of getting worm man to Ikorodu to deal with him.

I order champagne and kick off my shoes, we are flying at an altitude of the captains voice begins I don't hear him as I stretch and smiled, I can celebrate, I am celebrating as the gassiness of champagne hits the back of my throat, I have just got away with not one but two murders, bring on Worm man.

Chapter 52

Worm Man

I'm feeling great, accomplished even and a little smug. Stretching my legs out I make myself more comfortable in my seat, champagne and strawberries always a nice touch. My thought wanders to worm man's wife Kike, ironic her name, as it means to cherish, worm man can abuse one and cherish another. His stance at the airport had me worried I need to do my homework on worm man, his non-verbal had a threatening I'm superior undertone, and the bastard clearly thinks he is dealing with the helpless little girl who will not be believed.

I wonder if that's why he chose me, had he studied me from afar? after all we went to the same venues, Ikoyi Club, met abroad as our parents dragged us to the same countries and enrolled us in the same foolish activities, remembering one summer the entire 6 weeks spent in Abidjan brushing up on our French. It wouldn't be hard for anyone looking for cracks to see mine making me perfect food for the hungry abuser.

I call one of the air hostess over and explain I have a friend in Economy may I pay the difference and bring her over to 1st class, I ask for the cost of including her return journey, $980 a doddle, I make my way over to Economy with the hostess in tow, machine in hand, it's sad really the tiny little bags of pretzels and miniature drinks they give economy passengers. The busybodies watch curious as to what I may or may not have done.

I find Kike and ask if she would kindly join me while gushing it will be my pleasure to treat the wife of a childhood friend, the lady sitting next to her urges her to go and offers to come with me if she refuses. Refuse she does until those around her urged her to accept the love. I left her collecting her overhead baggage and headed back where she joined me a few minutes later.

"I don't know what she say" she starts, I cut her off and tell her both her and her husband I am sure would invite me to join if they were up in 1st class, she hesitated, that tiny nano bit gave me the answer I needed. They are not loaded, wealthy by Nigerian standards but not enough to burn up money willy- nilly. Good to know.

Once settled she accepts the glass of champagne offered and sits grinning at me, a sister tease follows in the context of this is how you rich folks enjoy yourself, I give back the same "your husband can afford this, sing his praises and see him cough up", at this we both dissolve into laughter. I tell her I wish her husband had introduced us formally, I hadn't seen him until she went through departure, but expressed delight at getting to know her, throwing out the line "I have been away from home for a long time and now looking to gradually relocate back home I need to reconnect with childhood friends", I put an emphasis on childhood stating I feel safer with those I knew before we all became professionals in our various fields.

She agrees with me totally, disclosing she knows a lot of people but has only a handful of friends, I asked how she manages that. Kike explains her husband belongs to various groups and the wives are expected to linkup hence knows lots of people but friends! "I worry about the usual women palaver, she said he said, and then she said", it must be the champagne as we both dissolve into fresh laughter. I am glad I changed my mind about contact with her on the flight.

We women are a strange bunch, if the rapport is right we are like long lost friends but nil common ground and the same women can remain in an enclosed environment for days and not exchange a word. Kike has thanked me several times for my generosity and kindness, I play my sympathy card of work, loneliness and a husband who is pleasure focused always chasing tail, husband in name only.

I tell Kike a bit about my life, work and recent visit home, in turn she tells me she is a Pediatrician, happily married to worm-man nil kids, husband has been understanding nil pressures making do with a full manger of nieces, nephews and God-children. I reached out and held her hand for a moment, nil words needed. Kike and worm-man had been introduced by their parents the relationship encouraged and marriage commitment expected by both parents who had spent lavishly to achieve their goals.

Kike describes worm-man as caring, the best of the crop. If single she would choose him again. Quite a compliment! In this manner we eat drink and chat the flight time away. I have my motive for having Kike nearby; it pays off and goes beautifully. Once through immigration and waiting in baggage reclaim I switch my phone on, it takes less than 30 seconds for it to ring, it's Tayo, crying uncontrollably, Tee-A found dead in his hotel room he had been dead for a few days!!! I totally deserve an Oscar, bursting into tears, I then fold over in a faint, Kike was quickly joined by airport officials who summoned first aid, all I wanted was for Kike to talk to Tayo and of course she picked up my phone and spoke to the person on the other end to say I had become so distressed I had fainted and was been attended to.

Let me tell you smelling salt sucks, they need to ban it. It stings your sense back into you no end. Shaking my head from side to side I moan over and over again, like one wounded. Kike has dispatched Tayo and taken over from the crisis respond team. We are in a side room our luggage with us. I ask if she will be kind and stay with me just until I am at my hotel, I promise her the driver will drop her home. No problem she promises. Home for her and worm-man in London is a flat in Chelsea, a wedding gift from the in-laws and not too far from my hotel of choice.

I can tell she's impressed by the opulence of the Savoy once we are in my suite. I order a hot seafood meal for us, it's 5.20pm I ask when she needs to leave, and she assures me she doesn't feel right leaving yet. I thank her and call Nigeria. I listen as Tayo tells me her story, I say her story as it's a loss she cannot acknowledge, she refers to Tee-A as my friend and states what a shock it was when she found out. How did you find out, she mumbled something about the news. I wish she had been caught there, something hadn't gone smoothly, the hotel and police had not acted as swiftly as I expected after my anonymous call.

Not to worry her lover is dead, I am safely out of the country, I have done one and got one free, I am not complaining. I make all the right noises about how precious life is and thanked my stars for his brief support and friendship. Tayo talks about various theories as to the possible cause of death the most popular and acceptable is a multi-million naira deal gone bad and Tee-A possibly suffering a heart attack because of the stress of it all, after all he already had high blood pressure, when I asked how she knew about his BP again the newspapers had mentioned it, at this point Tayo took her leave possibly realizing the more she talked the more she might give away.

I thank Kike for her support while waiting for food I look online at the hotel gift page selecting a white gold Mappin and Webb watch at £12,700, I ask for it to be gift wrapped and delivered with the meal. Kike is over whelmed by my generosity, she's never met a female like me, and I listen to her while we eat. I am grooming her nicely.

Worm-man is away often by the nature of his job; she works long hours because there is nothing to hurry home to. When home worm-man has a set routine, I listen carefully. Walking Kike to the car for her ride home I remind her of dinner tomorrow evening, she is surprised thinking the seafood meal tonight is it. We agree she'll come to the Savoy and we'll leave from here.

Chapter 53

In the bedroom I lie watching the ceiling.....playing back the important screen shots of the past weeks. Mum, Tee-A, hearing Tee-A and Tayo on the island, lovers, poison, dollars, anonymous call and finally worm-man. What I could have done different, kill Tayo before mum died and tell Mum to her face, which would have been good, I groan as I think again of missed opportunity. Tell Tayo I heard her and Tee-A and know they are lovers, nah, no way; I would be the first suspect if I had disclosed that. What then I feel I have overlooked something, maybe I have maybe I haven't, when you get away with two killings this must be the 'what did I miss or fail to do stage'.

I pick up the house phone mindful of Moses' antics I ask for a female masseuse to be sent up in 10 minutes, I jump in the shower and lay in bed waiting. I learnt a long time ago there are things rich people don't need to do, if you don't want to open the door you don't have to the hotel staff can jolly well open it themselves, when they knock you simply answer come in and wait, once they realize you're not coming to the door they let themselves in.

Right on cue comes the knock, I answer come in and rollover, face down on the bed. Within a minute she's in, I cannot describe her as I didn't see her face. I point to the $50 tip on the bedside and remain laying facedown. I ask for a deep tissue massage. At some point I fall asleep waking up at 04.00hrs I ring for coffee and continental rolls. I put CNN on for company and login to my emails.

When coffee arrived I am answering emails from the boys, all shocked at the news of Tee-A's death. I express the same shock horror and leave things that way. I am restless, the massage has taken the edge off last night but I am bubbling just underneath the surface, I need release, I have underestimated how much missing the opportunity to kill Tayo affected me.

I rummage in the draw and sure enough there it sits to be found in every good hotel room round the world a sewing kit. I take out the needle thread it and walk into the bathroom, holding my middle left finger steady I push the needle under the nail and keep pushing, I can see its progress and register the pain straight away, I slide down the wall and sit on the cold marble floor, there is no blood yet that appears after I pull the needle out, worm-man is certainly going to get a taste of this. Getting up I use the thread to pull the needle out, with it the blood tickles out, small blood, big pain, my finger throbs, I could have waited until I got home but know myself, if I don't get release quickly I become a ticking time bomb.

It's nearly 06.00hrs when I get back into bed, I sleep until 07.30hrs. Awake I order a full English breakfast and requesting for the masseuse I ask for an intra-muscular massage. I down my food before the lady arrives and 30minutes after her arrival we are done, I feel loose, no tightness no tautness.

Another call to the Concierge asking him to book a table for two at The Wolseley 160 Piccadilly, tonight I want to impress with fine dining, nil patience for have you got a table telephone call when the hotel concierges can make things happen, he calls back to confirm I have a table for 7pm peak time. I thank him and just for the fun of it called The Wolseley to try and book a table, they have availability in a fortnight, laughing I say thanks and put the phone down. I'm expecting Kike for 18.30hrs; I intend to be down in the lobby crowd watching by 18.15.

Ladies:

After years of living in the states and like lots of black women who believed for a long time we did not look complete without the perms, colors, weave-on, I came to my senses in my 40's sick to death of the pillow smell of grease, stains and the other products used to achieve our synthetic look, I grew my perm out and went for locs, today I spot quite a crown on my head, a fortune to maintain but beautiful in the various intricate designs the hair dresser thinks up, the down side of having long locs is a visit to the hairdresser, it is a few hours affair popping in is not possible with my mane despite the fact they are super thin.

Exiting the Savoy I jump on the District Line, changing to the over ground at Whitechapel. I arrive at Locs Unique in New Cross at 09.20hrs expecting to be one of the first customers of the day, no such luck there are three loud Nigeria women already there, the first insult of the day is delivered as soon as I walk into the shop, in Yoruba they warn each other to be alert as Ireke (a slang for Afro-Caribbean's) are fast at lifting bags! Keep your bag with you don't take your eyes of it they caution each other. I ignore them and speak to Sharon the owner to identify myself as the person who spoke to her two weeks ago.

Assigned someone to take out the current plaits I sit back relaxed as the young man gets to work, listening to the loud useless gossip of the three women whose name I knew within a few moments of sitting down, folks let me introduce Ann, Labi & Sara. Loud colorful hair, scary long talons for nails, tight colorful trousers and tops all with possible fake designer Fendi Chanel wraps and equally matching designer shoes, slips and wedges, tired old and hardened, Ann is covered in tattoos like some form of art work gone wrong, she spots a nearly faded back to normal skin tone large intricate AL on her neck.

I listen to their talk all man focused who is pocking who, who is taking care of whom and ignoring their responsibilities at home. I said a silent prayer; this crazy bunch will be here for hours so time can fly with the entertainment they provide. I hear the words abused they've moved on from the superficial conversation and my ears prick up, this bunch of over the hill, gone way beyond their sell by date have something serious to said.

Chapter 54

Ann talks:

My aunty came home from England I guess my age was about 7; I was so impressed I was related to someone from the land of white people that we see in magazines and TV. She dressed nice, smelt nice and smiled at me a lot, she constantly asked if I wanted to come and live with her in England, I said yes and felt special when she asked me to sleep on the bed with her, she bought me clothes and told my mum to release me into her care, as she had no children of her own.

I prayed she would take me with her, I knew my life would be like that of the white children, I'll have nice things and speak the words of English we hear on TV shows. My mother cried a lot, I thought she was such a bad person, crying and crying I secretly cursed her thinking she would spoil the plans, I wondered if she was jealous I had been chosen. I knew I would be going when I heard my father say to my aunty take her along if you will treat her like she is your flesh, educate her so she can be useful for herself and the family, when I heard my Aunt's plans for me I thought I would die with happiness, not only will she educate she will make sure I acquire others skills.

The year is 1992 and for the next few days I am coached over and over when asked "where is your mummy" to point to my Aunt, I also started hugging and smiling at her a lot, she returns the affection. The story is she had me and left me behind with my grand-parents which is not uncommon in our culture, she has now come back to get me. It was as if she had one purpose only to leave Nigeria with me, leave with me she did.

It was a night flight on a Tuesday, apart from my mother who cried uncontrollable everyone was happy; my siblings were only interested in reminding me not to forget them and send them nice things. I simply held on to my Aunts hand and followed her, no one challenged us.

At Heathrow Airport Child Protection and Safe Guarding had not gathered pace, my aunt showed two green small books, the white man looked at me and the book, stamped something on it and gave them back to my aunt he didn't speak to me which disappointed me as I had practiced so much.

I later find out there is a lucrative business in people going to Nigeria to bring other people's children into England for a fee using passports with the old youthful black and white photos, I guess all black children must look the same to the uninterested people manning the border. Today it will be impossible.

I will never forget my first sight of escalators, I cried and clung unto my aunt, for this I got my first clip round the ear and was told to get on or she would leave me, I was so stunned, I obediently held on to her hand and stepped on to what looked like killer metals coming out of a hole. The train journey was just as traumatic for me, sometimes you could see the sky other times you were underground and sometimes you were nowhere, the train stopped with walls either side. Home when we finally arrive is in North London, the street is Harvist Road Kensal Rise.

As we walked towards the house I marvel at the quiet, none of the cars are pressing their horn like is the norm in Akure where I lived with my family. The streets are clean, there are no gutters, people have small spaces outside their houses, and you can see everyone's front door and their curtains are pristine white. London smells nice I like the red buses. I haven't said a word since the clip round the ear at the airport as we approach a front door I ask my aunt if the school I'll be attending is near here and would I be in primary 2 like I was back home.

I get no reply, she opens the door stands aside to let me in, shuts the door and then decks me one, with that first slap I hear my full family history, in-between curses and threats. I better get my head out of the clouds, school what school, did my parents go to school, I better not give her any problem or she will send me back home, I stand there crying and shivering sure the devil had changed my sweet dream to a nightmare and I would wake up soon. No such luck.

Within a short period I am given a plate of eba and egusi soup told to eat quickly, I eat fast not because I am hungry but to keep safe from another assault. As I shove the food in my mouth I try to think when we've eaten eba in the morning at home and can't. I finish and take the plate to the kitchen, seeing my aunty has finished I ask if I can take her plates, she replies "you better" one word I didn't understand but none the less understood fully.

I washed the plates and left them to dry, taking me upstairs, my aunt showed me to a small bedroom and told me "go to sleep" within a minute I hear the front door slam, I toyed with the idea of getting up to explore my surrounding but thought better of it in case it's a test and she's lurking somewhere downstairs waiting for me. Despite my fear that I've been left alone I fall asleep waking up several hours later to the sound of talking downstairs, not sure what to do I stay put. I am busting to go to the loo but stay on that bed like my life depends on it. Finally my Aunt shouts up the stairs, I jump up and use the loo quickly then hurry downstairs.

She introduces me to an older man, this she says is her dear, the lovely man who bought her this house outright and opened a restaurant for her, all of this meant nothing to me but like a good girl I went and knelt in front of him to greet him, he gave me some paper money which my aunt thanked him for. I returned upstairs and waited in the box room that will become my prison on bad days and my sanctuary on good days.

It's getting dark and I'm hungry, I lie in the dark my rumbling tummy a constant reminder of emptiness, when I couldn't bare it anymore and it became obvious I wouldn't be feed I went to the toilet and drank as much water as my belly could hold then settled down to sleep. Getting up twice to wee during the night, I could hear my aunt and her dear talking but from the bedroom. I'm seven years old and want the cozy relationship we had in Akure I go over events of the few hours I have been in London, have I become a bad girl. I vow to be a really good girl so she likes me again and goes back to the loving warm fun person she was when I meet her.

In the morning I am woken with a sharp slap on the thigh, given various toiletries and instruction never to touch any other item in the bathroom, I'm shown how to run the bucket bath and told to learn to use only one bucket for my bath always, no running more water into the bucket. I thank my aunt nonstop; ignoring me she instructs "come downstairs after bathing and cleaning your teeth" I don't waste time and present myself pretty sharp. I am given a small plate of fried eggs and 6 slices of bread with a massive cup of tea. I eat quickly already feeling weak from one meal yesterday; again I pack the utensils up and wash them.

Calling me upstairs my aunt shows me round the house and begins my induction. I will be cleaning daily; when she switched the Hoover on I screamed and ran away. My aunt comes to get me all the time laughing and telling me the machine won't bite me, I ask if I can use a broom instead but they don't sell our home type call igba-le here. When she puts the Hoover on again I pluck up courage and move near it when it keeps the same noise up I touch it I can sense my aunts impatience building and quickly follow her action pushing the growling monster back and forward as shown.

Downstairs and in her bedroom there is a small black item, now it begins to ring, my aunt picks it up and begins to speak, I stand there open mouthed, she tells me it's a phone and puts it to my ear, I can hear her dear clearly and kneel down to greet him, my aunt laughs and tells me he can hear me but not see me kneeling down. When she's out later in the day and the black box begins to make the ringing sound I call out to the box over and over from a safe distance that she's not in but the black box ignores me and rings for a long time.

Next the cleaning of the bathroom, toilet, kitchen and the massive through lounge sitting room. I listen and learn, making a mental note to ensure I complete tasks in a timely manner so I am not late for whatever it is my aunt has in store for me which is not attending school. Having shown me my aunt asks me to go and begin. Thus I spend my first full day in England cleaning a three bedroom end of terrace house, quickly learning if I mix Vim and bleach together the fumes make me dizzy and hurt my throat.

Mid-afternoon my aunt took me out and bought me lots of clothes from a red and white shop called Red Cross, for years I thought it was a classy shop until I understood the currency Pounds and Pence and began to wonder how a dress would cost 50p. When we returned home an Indian man knocked on the door, my aunt spoke to him at the door after looking at the papers he brought she gave him what appeared to be a lot of money, he apparently is something called a supplier, turning to me she said let's go.

We got into a car; I was impressed to see a woman drive and watched admiringly. We arrive shortly at our destination, a restaurant where my aunt was greeted warmly and referred to as madam, lots of people said they had missed her, we went to the back where there was a small office, my aunt told me to sit on a box and left. It's a busy place with rich aroma of food filling the air, it's been a long time since I ate, I spied the toilet and go in after easing myself I drank long and hard.

I must have fallen asleep because my aunt is shaking me awake, it's quiet, the music has stopped, the busy buzz is gone replaced by a lot of clanging that goes with cleaning up, go and join them I am told, making my way to the back I am told to scrap any uneaten food into a bowl and left to pile after pile of plates.

I begin to scrap, left to my device I soon learn to keep an eye out while popping food in my mouth eating and swallowing quickly. Scrap, pile, scrap, pile I have six piles of plates when the grownups returns, we then begin washing, soaking the plate in one big sink, washing and rinsing in another then putting them in a stand upside down so they dried. When we finish my back aches so bad, one of the adults pats me on the head and shows me where to dry my hands.

I dry my hands and follow her to my aunt; I am shocked to see day is breaking when we walk out. In that instant I realize my Aunty brought me here for this restaurant. I don't understand any more but feel proud of her, I'm sure I would have thought different if my belly was empty and rumbling.

Thus begins a routine, I clean the house get given a meal in the morning and feed on the scraps and leftover's at the restaurant. Several years pass this way, at the restaurant I work behind the scene, cleaning, chopping, arranging goods, helping to prep, the general dog's body. Those who worked for my aunt assumed I was in education and often made comments about not falling asleep in the classroom. My aunt had warned me not to talk to anyone so I remain tight lipped about all that happened to me.

When my aunt is happy my life is relatively okay, if things are not going as she wants then I get it, the slaps and curses. She also started to lend me out, if her friend or close acquaintance had a child I would be dispatched to go and help for several weeks. During those times I was feed three times a day and treated quite well by most of them, though I worked hard and suffered sleep deprivation, as while the family slept I was left holding the babies during the night.

In this manner I lived in England, cooking, cleaning, working at the restaurant, given out as free labor.

The day that changed my life is clear in my mind, it was midday we were asleep having got in just after 08.00hrs from the restaurant when there was banging on the door, when we didn't answer you could hear a loud announcement over and over again, this my aunt responded to shouting at me to get some cloths on we both poured out of the house into a wall of police gas and fire brigade personnel.

I have no idea what my aunt told the police when they asked which school I went to and why I wasn't at school, I had been in England for over 7 years and couldn't speak the language, the people I came in contact with spoke Yoruba. The suspected gas leak exposed the fact my aunt was not living alone, me no English.... but I understood perfectly well when the next door neighbor's wife kept saying to her husband "I told you" all the time looking at me, I smiled back at her, thank God my aunt was so preoccupied with how tired she was she didn't notice.

At 08.20hrs the following morning we are woken up again, my aunt goes down cursing under her breath, then I hear the alarm in her voice, she calls me down. In the front room are two policemen the size of a mountain in build and three other female. They are talking to my aunt and looking at me, when they try to speak to me, I can only manage a few broken words of English. One of the women brings out a mobile phone and calls a number we all wait tense, the woman speaks into the phone and gives it to me, a nice Yoruba voice says good morning to me and asks one question only "is the woman I am with my mother", she cautions me to only answer yes or no in Yoruba, I answer "no" she tells me to give the phone back to the woman and I do.

The only two silent are the policemen. My aunt begins to cry and make a protest about something I don't know what, the Yoruba speaking person is talking to me again, she explains I am to go with the white people they are there to help me because someone called to complain I am been kept in the house and treated badly. In that instant I review almost 8 years in England, nothing to show for it but cleaning and cooking skills that is not certificated. I have nil to my name whenever anyone gave me money my aunt took it off me, in that moment I walked over to the police men, I am 14 years old and maybe getting it wrong but can it be worse than this. I can't read or write apart from my name and basics. I am ready to go now, the women sense this and gives a lot of paper they have been writing to my aunt and we leave, I am treated like some sort of precious cargo by the white women.

Chapter 55

The drive is short and we arrive at some offices, going in I am surprised to see my white neighbor who had smiled at me yesterday, she comes to me and hugs me murmuring soothing words I don't need English to understand, I kneel to thank her as the Yoruba speaking woman comes in closely followed by someone with food. I eat and drink while they carried on talking, I stay close to the white woman from next door, her name is Dorothy.

We are in Wembley Central an area that will become home. I have left my aunt with nothing but these people must have a lot of money because I am given four bags of brand new cloths and £65, the interpreter explains that will be my pocket money weekly, mine to do with what I wish, finally I am told I will be going to live with a family, black but not African, they work with Social Services and will be looking after me from today.

I am driven to my new home in Caledonia Road. I have a bath and change into my new St Michael's night wear, my room is big, real big compared to the box room at my Aunts. Not once have I thought of my aunt, as I nod off my last thought is I am glad she brought me here but that is all. I have achieved nothing and thinking of the way I ate restaurant leftover food made me feel sad and angry. I later realized my aunt knew that was where my second meal of the day came from and turned a blind eye. Such wickedness.

I wake up in a panic thinking I had been dreaming this morning then coming fully awake not recognizing where I am. What do I do can I go downstairs or do I wait until I am summoned, I need the loo, getting up to see if I can get a top from the cupboard I open what I thought was a cupboard door and found I had an en-suite bath and toilet, the flush must have alerted them, as soon there is a gentle knock on the door. It's the woman called foster parent her name is Josie, she offers me a cup of hot chocolate and festival, I recognize festival as buns which is what it's called in Nigeria.

She sits watching me and smiles while I eat, I am presented with a mobile phone, I have seen them but never used one, the phone rings and it's the interpreter, back and forth we passed it for an hour, the gist is this....over the next week I have lots of appointments, first one is tomorrow for a physical well-being check with the doctor, then education assessment to see where my deficits are and so on and so on.

The result of which the GP gave me a clean bill of health and I start home tutoring, I needed to start from scratch, re-learning and trying to make sense of the alphabets, I picked up quickly, there was nothing to disturb me, I spent all my free times practicing and practicing. Every week a lady called Iris my social worker came and gave me £65 and a weekly bus pass, plus shop vouchers every three months for essentially cloths shopping. They had made me something called a ward of court, it means no one can take me out of the country, remembering how they tried to smuggle Umaru Dikko in a crate may have woken the British government up that nothing is impossible with Nigerians when they are determined. As my Aunt has insisted my passport was lost or stolen, the people looking after me also applied for leave to remain for me.

Dorothy a constant companion, encouraging me, willing me to improve myself, not blessed with children I think she decided she had definitely found the missing child she never had. For three years I lived like this, nil contact from my Aunt but I understood the Nigerian Embassy are trying to contact my family in Akure, the embassy also issued me a new passport using the 1st of January for my birthday as I didn't know the day or month.

My aunt had received a caution, she got away with any serious offence other than denying me something called my right to education as the clever so and so had drawn up a document and made my parents put their thumb print witnessed that they were happy to give me to her to take abroad to keep house and other domestic chores. One good came out of this, with my case alerting the border services and agencies of the scam of bringing children in unlawfully.

I am 17 years old with the literacy skills of a 10 year old, I have had my stay regularized, I am now in the system whatever that means, I cannot catch up with education so ask to learn to cook and learn properly. I am enrolled in college, my set is a sorry looking bunch of folks with special needs of some sort or command of English is so bad instructions from the teachers takes ages to make sense of, each block that should take a year took me two years, by now I realized no one was judging me or going to throw me out of college because I wasn't achieving at the set rate.

Food technology involves placements; my first was in a local pizza shop. The pervert Turkish man who presented himself as respectable and responsible when his wife is around used every opportunity in the book to brush past me; he would purposely reach across me brushing my breast rather than ask me to hand him a utensil. I didn't have the courage to tell anyone, even when the hot pizza utensils meant I ended up with small burns most days, at some point I recognized I could use the situation to my advantage so I started smiling at him instead of frowning. His excitement knew no bounds.

I got the best shifts, the best feedback and my paperwork was completed in a timely manner, all for boob and ass touching. By now he had graduated to holding me close when no one was around, if his wife suspected anything she kept mum. This man did not restrict his behavior to me, a lot of the young local girls came to buy his regular special offers, I watched as he would take money and hold on to the hand just a tad longer than needed, if the girls didn't have the correct amount he let it go telling them to pay later. Every day was the same group after group of giggling idiotic girls whose parents believed they are whiter than snow in good behavior.

This man had forgotten not everyone likes foreigners , one Saturday evening a few minutes after his wife left an angry English man descended on the shop threatening to kill, break, burn everything down, his daughter had told him how the man touches hand, smiles and asks them out. Realizing I had struck gold I threatened to call the Police, sticking up for Usman and telling the Dad he should come and see how the girls behave when their parents are out of sight, I shouted so much it stopped the man in his tracks and turning on his daughter he forbid her to come to the pizza outlet again, a difficult order as it's a hangout for the teenagers.

Before Usman could thank me, I told him coldly, that will be a £1000 tomorrow afternoon or I tell the college and find the parent to tell them you had threatened me that's why I lied. You need to see the face of a perpetrator humbled, swear words I neither understood nor cared about poured forth, as it was my last week I wasn't bothered one bit.

The next day I am a £1000 richer, let me tell you how it works, in the shop there are two tills, the trick is to ring 99p to £3 items on one, large orders on the other, so the tax man gets to inspect if he so wishes till receipts giving the impression the shop is just surviving. Usman has a total of six shops. Not realizing I could hear him on the phone he once boasted to someone "if I say I am low on cash it means I have less than £100 thousand in the house". Asking for my book which he signed he told me not to come back, I didn't.

I kept that money in an envelope under the carpet in my room I knew what I wanted to do it with. At college I had made friends with some of the rat tail lot on my course. The constant tread of conversation was buying land, shipping things home and sending money to their overseas account. I have no idea how to contact my parents, the authorities were still trying to find them, I was too young when I left to remember any information that would help trace my parents. It turned out the lady I called Aunty is not a blood relative, the address she gave the authorities was of no use yet she insisted that is the last known address for my parents. So now I don't know if my parents are alive or dead.

My £1000 went towards the purchase of land in an area called Abule meaning village. This plot of land is actually in Obanikoro a well-developed area with a stubborn community living the simple life and refusing to bulge for property developers, when the plot became available the elderly man and his wife wanted to move back to their village and stipulated they didn't want to sell to anyone in Lagos, I got lucky the guys were discussing it, none of them could raise the amount required, I begged to be given the opportunity to buy and they agreed and supported me, the young girl as I was referred to. So ass and boob touching Usman paid for my first land acquisition.

Things are about to go pear shaped , I am nearing 18, there is talk of getting me my own flat, I speak to Josie my worker saying I am not ready to live on my own, she talks about support from the leaving care team up to the age of 21, possible to extend to age 25 as needed.

While this was going on my foster mother needed to go to her country of Origin for a funeral, leaving me at home with her daughter and husband. I haven't said much about them because they simply did their job I was welcome in their home, they got paid for it, made sure my needs were met, I was never given the false impression I was family.

Two days after she left I was watching TV and fell asleep on the settee, I woke up to the pressure of someone perching on the edge of the settee, when I tried to sit up my foster dad had his arm across the back of the settee and was leaning across asking me if I was okay.

If I had been able to just sit up, I think I would have been fine but because sitting up would mean coming into physical contact with him I answered I was okay and stayed put. That man did not touch me but he might as well have. I never felt comfortable again with him and asked to try semi-independent living, I moved out eight months after that incident and never went back to visit, feeling no real connection with them.

I met Alfred who is the father of my two children on my first day in the new accommodation. It is a 10 bedsit building with 24hours single staffing in Camden town. You had your freedom but you also had help on standby if needed. Al as everyone called him is mixed race, nil knowledge of his parents as he was taken into care at birth. To me he is sophisticated and streetwise, handsome and very likeable. We met in the communal area downstairs with him joking asking if I can cook, offering me £50 a week for 5 evening meals. Al shows me the ropes and the local area, I tell him a little about myself.

Whereas I am at college Al drifts between college and vocation courses, regularly walks out of apprentice placements. He tells me he is known to the police because he's been naughty in the past. I like him apart from him smoking cannabis I have no concerns and look forward to seeing him in the evenings. I encourage him to try and find something he likes to do then make it into a job.

I'm young he's young and we begin to hangout, I have no role models, no one to caution me. He holds my hand when we are out and it feels good, it was nice to have human touch, the first time he kissed me I couldn't breathe as I wasn't sure what to do. Al took things real slow looking back he was grooming me. We began to move to intimacy after a few months, I tell him upfront I am a virgin. We get free condoms from the local clinic promoting sexual wellbeing.

We had sex just before my 19th birthday, it was neither here nor there as I didn't know what to expect, at one point I felt a sensation that left me breathless as it made me vibrate below but also gave me the urgent feeling I needed to get up and move about a strange feeling like restlessness, Al explained I didn't need to get up, that I had experienced a climax and to enjoy more to come. Al taught me all he knew and encouraged me to feel comfortable with sex, he also made it clear sex was only to be with him.

Al began to introduce me to the night club scene, he had a preference for Ragga and we would regularly head into Hackney or Brixton, I wasn't one for drinking so nursed a glass of wine for ages, Al was popular and always seem to be in discussion with one person or the other.

My world came crashing down soon after that. While we were on our way to the shops Al asked me to hold his packet of cigarettes and box of matches, it was towards midnight. On the high street we stopped at the cash point, taking the box of matches from me Al opened it, nil matches but cards, 8 credit cards, looking at the time he took £200 out from each card and gave the money to me, this brought us to midnight, he then went through the process again leaving the cash point with a total of £3,200 in the short space of half an hour max.

I trembled all the way back home, once in my room I gave him the money and told him to leave, I did not see the slap coming, Al laid into me with punches, all the time telling me not to dare make a noise, he was careful to avoid exposed areas, he then throttled me until I guess I passed out for a few moments. When I came to I thought I had been dreaming until I tried to move and the pain ripped through me. Glaring at me Al spate at me and told me it was my fault I had made him assault me, he then sat at my table cutting the cards up following which he flushed them away, muttering to himself they are only good for one withdrawal either side of 12 midnight, with this he let himself out of my bedsit.

What do I do, I got up and had a shower then went to bed, the shock the pain and fear Al will be back kept me awake. Thank God it's Saturday. Al knocked several times during the day. I ignored his calls. To my horror the support worker on call comes to my door and calls out that Al is worried about me, she will use her key to gain entrance to do a welfare check. I get up and open the door, give the excuse I am not feeling well, Al stands there crying saying he is so happy I'm okay glad I'm not seriously sick, he then takes me into his arms, on this note the support worker returns to the office.

Pushing me backward into my room Al is a changed man, "don't you ever ignore me and never ever lock me out of your room" he hisses "next time I'll tear the door down, now get dressed, we are going out". What is happening to me, I dare not disobey. It doesn't rain it pours. We have something to eat in one of the many dotted restaurants in Kings Cross, we are joined by some of Al's friends, and I sense a tension but can't make sense of anything anymore. What has just happened to me, I am so numb.

I am an accomplice in credit card fraud, if the police had stopped us, the card would have been found on me at 19 I would have been sent to jail. At the table I am one of three females, the other two are just as quiet as me. Al is talking to me but my mind has wandered off and he has to nudge me, I am to go with Del, he will bring me back. I follow as in a dream, thinking I am going on another errand to defraud the cash point machines again. Al's instruction is do what Del says.

Del drives across town to Kennington, I couldn't describe Del as I didn't once look at him just followed him. Arriving at a block of flats he takes me to one on the 5th floor, it's obvious no one lives there, furniture was a settee in the living room and a king size bed in the bedroom, telling me to go ahead and get undressed I look at the man like he is mad, he tells me to get a move on, I go in and undress slowly, I don't know where I am, this man could kill me here and nobody will know.

Del comes into the room and I ask what I've done, I look at him now he couldn't be more than 23, Caucasian not bad looking but hard eyes. He tells me, "Al hasn't got money he owes me so he's paying the debt through you, did he not tell you" "no" I shook my head side to side. "Never mind I'll not hurt you". For the next hours until early morning this man does what he wants with me, it is my first sight of an uncircumcised penis loose skin at the end when he pulled his foreskin back, I wanted to run away at the sight of the pink albino looking head exposed, Del does not physically hurt me but I died that day, the innocence went never to return.

As we left Del gave me a small brown paper bag to give to Al, I sat quietly for the journey home. Letting myself in I head to my bedsit Al is up and waiting, Del must have alerted him, coming into my room with me he takes the package from me and putting it on my coffee table tells me I've done well and to take a shower. I do so like a robot, coming out of the shower Al is sitting on the settee with a small gun in his hand, I begin to pee myself with fright and quickly step back in the shower .

I came out when I could sum up the courage, as I toweled myself dry Al came up and touched me with the cold metal, if you ever disobey me I will kill you and get rid of your body, all I could is nod that I understood. Putting the gun back in the paper bag, Al takes me to bed and has sex, not even an hour ago I was having sex with his business guy, I feel dead and disgusted, I lay there while he pumps away at some point he barks at me to stop lying there and to romance him. I automatically begin to run my hands on his back and make murmur noises, but I am far very far away from the act going on.

Chapter 56

Over the next two years I transport it all, moving around London like a black cab driver. Drugs stuffed in my private part, money strapped to my thighs, weapons shoved down my backside hidden by coats, and girls, moving girls around, sitting with them until they are needed I thought until I caught on they are sold on. Where these unfortunate girls came from I have no idea but name the color they were all represented, most spoke even poorer English than me, I guess that is why though we were many we were so isolated by language we couldn't help each other.

I learnt not to ask questions and to study Al's mood while trying to second guess his next move. To the observers he is the most loving attentive partner. My social services care team thought I was going through a difficult stage but I stopped attending college not because I wanted to but because Al put a stop to it. I lost count of the sexual favor repayment when things didn't go well. Al stashed his goodies as he called them in my bedsit.

Beatings followed by lovemaking and tears are daily regular tonics. I don't know what to do about this boy who will not leave me alone or let me live. He informed me to pack for the weekend we are going to Bognor Regis with a group of other friends, we set off in two cars, sprites is high amongst the men as they discuss riches to be picked and money to be made.

I don't know the names of drugs but know the two packets in my suitcase is not for headaches, one is white with M stamped on it, there must be anything up to 2,000 tablets, the other package looks like poor Disney copy stamps, why stamp will sell for £5 each is beyond me. I wonder how the stamp is used; again there must be anything up to 3,000 tiny stamps all perforated and ready. Are we doing a drug run I wonder but the conversation is about the crowd, music and fun to be had.

I understand better when we get to our digs, it's a themed weekend 70's 80's disco, 15,000 capacity, and we have come to sell drugs. From Friday evening the four of us girls taken along did not sleep but catnapped, we sold and sold, the smallest sale been £5 to larger orders of £500 to those who had the money and couldn't be bothered to go back and forth for supply. We blend in well and experience no disturbance, every hour the boys took the money off us and topped up the supply, we were simply dispensers.

Sunday afternoon we head back to London, we girls so exhausted we slept most of the way, if we had been stopped by the police it would be explained away as a weekend of hard partying. I slept straight from Sunday until early hours of Tuesday, when I woke up I felt different, heavy, full breast like when the period is due except when I calculated it was four months since my last period, I had been so abused and battered periods coming or not coming never crossed my mind.

Though Al has made it clear I am not to step out without him, I wash dress and have several cups of tea while waiting for morning. When my local chemist opened at 9am, I am the first customer. Purchasing a double pack of the pregnancy test kit, cheaper at £5.99, I head back and have a positive result within 1 minute. Going against orders I call Al, his phone is answered by a female, when he comes on the line he barks at me and cuts off the call. I don't know what to say so I call my leaving care team support worker Rosie and tell her. She drops what she's doing and comes over to see me.

We see the GP at 11.30, questions too many to answer, is it planned, was sex consensual!!! I don't even understand what half the English means, do I want to keep it, as I nod yes I wonder dare I say I don't. I am sent for urine and blood test and taken to the hospital for something called a booking-in appointment. Rosie produces housing forms and tells me I have priority as I'm deemed vulnerable, we complete the form and application for all sorts of grants to top up the current ones I am eligible for. Rosie leaves me feeling hopeful.

Al rolls in at 8pm and first beats the shit out of me for calling him; I curl into a ball and take the beating telling him over and over I am pregnant, speaking low as I am not allowed to make noise when he's hurting me. At some point he heard me. Pulling me up he squashes my face with his and tells me I better not be thinking of getting rid of it, I nod obediently, does anyone know, I tell him Rosie, that earns me a box on the ear.

Like the disturbed person he is he suddenly starts to cry, holding me tenderly he tells me he'll change and look after the kid and I will have everything we need and be a real family, it's now gone 9pm he insists we go and get something to eat, not sure what part of town he dragged me to but there was a late barbers shop that had a tattooist at the back, he drags me in and pays for his Initials to be put on my neck, the guy must have recognized this was not someone to mess with because he simply asked if I was 18 and proceeded. I was duly tagged and labeled like a piece of luggage.

Chapter 57

You would think being pregnant meant I was let off, you thought wrong. I carried drug and money packages back and forth all over London in Mothercare and Boots carrier bags; you wouldn't give me a pregnant girl a second glance. On one occasion I was given a parcel that weighed heavily and clanged when I accidentally dropped it. I delivered it to the Turkish guy in Finsbury Park and asked to use the loo, when I emerged he had opened the parcel, on the table laid gold like I had never seen before a king's ransom, I left as quietly as I came.

Al is making money, serious money; do you think I saw any of it? Nil, not a penny. As my due date approached with me going to the anti-natal classes on my own, my weight, swollen ankle and shooting blood pressure slowed me down. When I was hospitalized at 36 weeks gestation Al visited me to tell me I was slowing his business down. Al left telling me to call him when labour starts. I did as I was told, Al showed up a few hours after my call, when shown into the room and the nurse left for a moment he told me not to make any noise as he needed to catch up on his sleep.

The midwives thought his presence was a calming influence, I dare not tell them the real reason I was as quiet as a mouse. My son was born at 7.15 in the morning with Al not supporting me but standing behind the midwife staring at the baby being delivered and shaking his head as he saw my rectum stretch, his only comment was "it can never be the same again down there", everyone laughed except me. From the hospital I made sure staff had concerns about my ability to care for my son who Al named Jerome, I need to delay being alone with Al, I was sent to a mother and baby unit where I stayed, with Al visiting frustrated I couldn't do any work for him as I had to adhere to the timetable set by staff at the unit.

Jr as Al called him was 22 weeks old when it was deemed I was able to look after him independently, with Rosie's help we moved into a two bedroom 1st floor maisonette in Wood Green. I told Rosie it was important to me to have a place of my own and not to encourage Al to come and live with us, not that he had shown an interest "good girl", she said. We met the young man Joel Browne of Afro-Caribbean decent living downstairs on our moving in date, he said hello looked me over like one would merchandise came to a conclusion of sort, bid me a polite welcome and walked away saying he didn't want to be late for lectures.

Al showed up in the evening with a Chicco pushchair showing the modification made to it, he instructed me I was always to use that pushchair when I ran errands for him, tonight he wanted me to drop some money off for him in Seven Sisters, for that I used the baby carrier strapping the money to my chest, when I should have been resting I was making my way to the train station, I returned just before 11pm to find Al lying in the same spot waiting for his dinner.

Not sure what to do after feeding him I waited, I didn't have long to wait, Al wanted sex, that night I conceived my second child another son. I didn't know I was pregnant until I was six months as I was breastfeeding, I just thought I couldn't get pregnant. This pregnancy annoyed Al more than the first and he put me to work transporting, delivering, moving drugs receiving drugs, money, weapons and the things stored at my flat. I saw gold, diamonds, watches and cheques, bank drafts, money transfers & Bureau de Change paperwork.

Al continued to beat me regularly, if Joel heard he said nothing, one was so bad I lost 60% hearing in my left ear, Joel avoided me like a plague, I suspect he read Al and I well and wanted nothing to do with the likes of us. Al and Rosie were my only visitors, I tried to join local mother and baby groups but attendance was sporadic as Al would tell me to leave what I'm doing and go here or there.

When I was a few weeks from arrival of the second child, Al got angry beating my head against the wall was not enough he unceremoniously used his foot to push me down the stairs where I was lay dizzy from the beating, as I rolled down the short flight of stairs into the kitchen area something snapped, the flat was on two levels I could hear Jr crying and the hiss of Al pulling the tab of a can of larger, rolling over I used the drawer handles to pull myself up, in front of me sat the knife block, taking the sharpest, I walked to the sitting room and knelt beside Al where he was lying on the settee, he patted me absentmindedly with his right hand holding the larger with his left, putting my arm on his forehead I drew the knife across his throat in one smooth action before he could react, I knew I got him good when the blood shot out like a fountain hitting the wall opposite. I shut the living room door and dropped the knife in the hallway, going into my room I picked Jr up and went downstairs to Joel.

Knocking on his door I asked him to call the police to say there is a dead man in my flat, I then used my mobile to call Social Services duty desk, I was only 20 years old. Well the rest is history, detention at Holloway Prison, gave birth shortly after my arrival in Prison, one arm was handcuffed to the bed while I was in hospital, standard procedure then, followed by trial at the Old Bailey. Joel who had never spoken to me came forward to speak on my behalf, telling the court the incidents of abuse he heard through the ceiling, the helplessness in helping as he knew Al was a gang member plus a fact unknown to me, the first day I moved in Al had shown Joel a gun in the evening, he came purposely ringing Joel's bell and warning him he would get the bullet if he as much as looked at me.

Dorothy who I hadn't bothered to keep in touch with came to Court every day, in the course of the trial rather than have my boys in long-term foster care Social Services approved my suggestion of Dorothy and her husband been their official carer. When I heard my sentence of 25 years which took in my suffering at the hand of Al, I felt nothing; after all I have already been reduced to nothing.

Holloway prison becomes home, Dorothy and the boys visit me monthly so they know who I am. I received a letter from Joel saying sorry he had felt helpless to help and wished me well. I was given respect in Holloway because I had killed my abuser. I quickly settled into the prison routine. Life begins after lights out, have you ever had sex with a woman. Girl you need to try it, who knows a woman's body better than another woman. We used sex to pass time and provide intimacy many missed. Don't think it's all rosy, women also rape women and treat them like shit with beatings and burning with hot water being the norm.

I acquired more tattoos, in prison you use a pin and rub in hair dye power in black brown or auburn. Years melted away, the one thing I did do was to try and study learn new skills. I learnt English and struggled with Maths. I learnt to type and gain computers skills,

I enjoyed pastry work and produced cakes and pastries that had great reviews.

In my 10th year in prison I was pulled up for a rehabilitation program for good behavior and having a support system waiting on the outside. The downside of the program is re-location; I agree and hope it's not too far from London. Meetings followed meetings; we had meetings about meetings and having meetings. They increased my contact with my sons to fortnightly and then weekly, I also started escorted outings. There was none to protest about my early release; Al had no relatives I knew about so things went smoothly.

I moved to unescorted leave and ventured further away from the Holloway area. When told I was to be relocated to somewhere called Medway, I used one of my all day outings to visit the place. A 45 minutes to an hour by train from London, the place is real country, dead if you know what I mean, I saw the odd black person, quite a few Asians but nothing and no one for me to identify with.

When some people love you they really love you. Dorothy offered to come and live with the boys and I during the transition period. We were given a four bedroom semi because of Dorothy living with us during the week. I am forever grateful to that woman, first year of my release she spent shuffling back and from London. Not once did she worry about my ability as a mother, she encouraged me and acknowledges all my efforts with a hearty "well done you".

Helping through the difficulty of attending parents evening, we told the boys their dad had died in an accident. When Dorothy's husband dropped dead of a heart attack she never really returned home, I begged her to move in with us and she agreed, selling her house she put the money in something she explained is a trust fund for the boys, they will get the money when age 30 & 29 when they will be mature enough to use it well.

We are a strange bunch when out two black boys happily calling a Caucasian woman grandma, and Dorothy ever smiling content to be with her boys as she calls them. We had a household where two cuisines are cooked simultaneously, English and Naija food. I caught the train once a month to stock up on Naija food, coming here to Deptford, it was on one such visit I met Bolaji fondly called Aji by his friends. Aji was here studying computing at some East London college he never attends but pays to send his papers for renewal at the Home office, while working as a conductor on the 53 bus route under a different name. We exchanged numbers and started talking regularly.

I tell Dorothy about him, she smiles and says she knows I will choose right. My probation period is a two year one because of the gravity of my offence, I have four months left and spend that four talking and flirting with Aji, he is Yoruba from the Awori tribe, pleasant and nice to be with. I tell him my partner died in an accident and I am raising two children on my own. When he asks to visit I decline stating the children would need to get used to the idea first.

I found work at the local library as an assistant 16 hours a week, money is coming in supporting the amount I get in benefits. I tell Aji we have a white grandmother living with us explaining her as my adopted mother, I let Aji know I was brought here really young have nil contact with Naija and want a quiet life. I finally let him visit four months after Probation ends. He gets on well with everyone and doesn't over do things leaving at the right time and asking if he can come and visit again. The boys take to him and Dorothy states she can't see anything to be cautious about.

Chapter 58

I like Aji and know he likes me but I still have not told him anything about the real me. In this manner we continue seeing each other on his days off, no intimacy, thinking there might be a problem explaining away my various tattoos, even in the summer I wear light turtle neck and always long sleeve shirts. I contact the leaving Prison service and ask if they can help. I am told I am eligible for laser removal for the one on my neck as it was done under duress and without my consent, it's seen as a tag and qualifies me for funding.

From Prison to Harley Street, I can only describe the clinic as posh. I am shocked by how quickly the Al on my neck fades away, the skin is lighter in the area but requires no scarf or cover ups. My boobs arms and legs do not qualify as they were done post Al. Things have reached the stage where Aji has proposed marriage. We had family discussion after family discussion and agreed everyone was comfortable with moving things on.

We were married using his real name at Greenwich Registry in Woolwich as he lived in a shared house in Ripon Road nearby. Because of his work he will stay in London and come to Medway Friday evenings. Dorothy said we had to honeymoon and packed us off to the Isle of Wright for a week. We had sex, it was okay, there was no gushing love between us but the atmosphere was cordial Aji being fun and easy to be it. If he was surprised at my tattoos all he said in a teasing manner was wild cat. Every month he gave me £300 housekeeping funds. I still hadn't told him my secret.

When we returned from our honeymoon he submitted papers to the Home Office asking to be allowed to remain in the country now he is married to a British citizen and has a young family. The day the paperwork arrived is etched on my mind in fire. The official letter arrived on a Wednesday and was kept on the mantel piece, by then we had been married 18 months. Aji walked in and I shouted a hello, he mumbled something back, it was late and everyone had gone to sleep I was waiting to serve his dinner and headed into the kitchen as soon as his car drew up.

When I came out with the tray he was standing reading the letter, I smiled congratulations at him and set the table, still no reply, when I turned round he was standing behind me so close I had no choice but to bend back over the way I was before.... this is what he said to me word for word "murderer did you really think any man in their right mind would want to be with you after what you did, you must think me a fool that I will not try and find out about the person I am dating. Look here let me tell you I married you to get my leave to remain, I now have it in this paper I am holding. From now on this is what will happen, I will continue to give you housekeeping, I will come here at the weekend you will not discuss this with anyone and neither will I. If you do I will go to the Sun and News of the World and tip them off where you are. I mean you no harm but I can't be with a murderer, what if I upset you? will you cut my jugular. I have to be with you another year and half to qualify for Naturalization and a red passport, once I get that we go our separate ways" and with that he heads to the bedroom.

Strange my first thought is relief that he knows, I don't mind being used, what use is British Nationality to me anyway, I am in my mid 30's and lost in transit. I had hoped Aji will be my passport back into the Nigerian community but this is not to be. I sit at the table for a while and am surprised when he comes out and thanks me for the food and asks me to join in saying no hard feelings. I wash my hands and we eat together, it is surreal, I look at him and can't get angry, then I ask him will we still be intimate, of course he replies but only with condom no babies.

In the following months we have the best friendship ever, the atmosphere is light and easy going, the sex is good but mostly we are like a brother and sister, if Dorothy noticed she didn't say anything. On the 4th of October Aji is involved in a car crash on the A2 on his way home, pronounced dead at the scene. London Transport really does look after their workers, financial support and counseling is offered. A few months after Aji's death an Insurance Company write to say he had a policy that pays out £150,000 accidental death, as his widow the cheque was sent a few days after the letter. I approached the council to exercise my right to buy and paid £47.000 for my four bedroom house. I paid £2000 for the four of us to visit Florida for a fortnight and banked £75.000 in an investment account, leaving me

£25,000 to do as I wish, in the mist of this all my prison record secret is safe.

As I talk to you my boys are unaware of my prison record and early life, I encouraged them to marry foreigners and have two daughter in-laws one Argentinean and the other from Cape Verde, they all live in Canada, Dorothy died a few months after my younger son married, a true mother I think she hung on to see the boys settled, the instructions she left was recently carried out each of my sons receiving just under £600,000 from the trust set up.

I haven't been to Nigeria since I left, no idea where my living relatives may be. I guess at some point we stopped looking for each other

Today I see who I want, sex when I want, travel when I want, spend how I want and live how I want. With that the other two whoop and they high five each other all the time keeping an eye on their precious bags.

Chapter 59

Labake aka Labi

Labi takes up the gist, ore she says meaning friend, my experience of the West, nah wah. I left Nigeria for Italy with my new husband, I was 20 years old, before Kola left for Italy three years earlier, and we had done our traditional introduction so I had the status of his wife before he left. Anyway later he came back we wed and left on the visa he had secured for me before his return. Come and see bush girl I was so excited the most technology I had seen is picture in picture TV. My new husband Kola smiled at me and my reactions, on the plane he helped me and I simply followed his guidance. We arrived in Milan and head home to Italian names I can't pronounce. The property is a four bedroom flat I am introduced to the other three couples all Edo indigenes we have an en-suite room each. The welcome is warm and friendly.

Kola is an attentive and caring man and in my first week shows me what sex and caring is about. We go out for the occasional walk around the neighborhood but it would seem each time we returned by a different route so I couldn't say let me go to the shops I can find my way back. He does all the shopping and I cook and keep our area clean, the other ladies are kept away from me which I think is unusual but as we are different tribes it makes little impact. Kola has taken a total of three weeks off to come to Nigeria marry me bring me over and help me to settle in.

At the beginning of the second week of my arrival he tells me we are starting work tonight, I am excited and ask what, where, how I should dress to be comfortable and presentable. Kola laughs and tells me I will need no clothing for the work I will be doing, I laugh and called him a pervert, when he boxes me in the ribs I am unable to catch my breath for several minutes, slamming me unto the bed he sits astride me and asks what job I think the other married women of the flat do, I squeak I don't know. Kola climbs off me and gives me the low down. I will be sleeping with men he brings back, taking my passport from the closet he walks over to the bathroom and flushes it away.

I lie there shivering I am in the grip of a nightmare. I am not even 21 years old, until last week a virgin and now expected to have sex with strangers. I don't understand this Kola is here to study and work I am expected to work while he is studying once he graduates and starts working then I will start studying or did I dream that conversation between the two families back in Lagos.

Kola walks back in and lifts me off the bed putting his arm round me he explains if I step out of the flat I will be detained by the Italian police and deported back to Nigeria as an undesirable criminal in this country seeing as I have no passport ID to prove otherwise, "please my darling" he says "help me this is between us nobody will know as I don't move with Nigerians and it is only until we are both on our feet, do this for me my love", when I don't respond he starts to shake me, it feels like my head will come off my neck, "okay, okay" I say and like one talking to a two year old child he tells me he needs to trim my pubic hair down following that I am to have a shower and wear the small piece of cloth he just took out of a bag and wait in the room. "I will always be nearby" he says "always be here to protect you".

As I shower he calls out instructions for me to pay attention to my genitalia "wash it well" he says, I dry myself and step out Kola hands me cotton wool soaked in something I ask what to do, he says "wrap the cotton wool round your middle finger and insert as far up your private part as possible" telling me to place one leg on the bed for better access. I did as I'm told then ask what it is... alum placed in water the theory is it will dry out virginal fluid and make you tight, I wonder if it will also give me an illness, as back home we use alum to clean slimy food such as snails.

He gives me nice scented oil to rub on all over and then opens small bottles of various things he rubs some on my nipples, when I ask what it is he puts his finger out for me to lick, it tastes nice sweet without being sickly. A different one is rubbed on my vulva, I watch Kola as he works, this is a man who I have known for four years from school who kept his word to come back and marry me to take me abroad with him, making me the envy of all my friends and family. If they could see me now.

I put on the transparent outfit that covered nothing and watched Kola as he remakes the bed telling me to pay close attention as this is how I need to make it after every few customers. I start to tremble how many men will I be expected to sleep with at night. At 7pm the first client arrives following lots of phone calls from Kola. I have seen white men in Lagos but this one is not white he is a shade of something, rapid conversation in Italian follows the man hands me a bundle of money and Kola leaves the room. I speak secondary school English and know no Italian.

In broken English he beckons me forward like a virgin's first time you never forget the first client if you are prostituting his name is Mathis. I don't know if it's the fact he paid for sex but he used me, getting his money's worth and did not tolerate me just lying there, do love he urged and urged, it lasted an hour and as soon as he left I was ordered to have a shower repeat the previous process and be ready and waiting. That first night I slept with a total of 13 men, some paid for an hour others just to have quick release and the Lira piled up in the drawer Kola shoved it. The last man left at 06.15 in the morning.

I shower while Kola counts the takings, he splits it into three giving me the smallest pile, he explains the two remaining piles, one is to pay off people who must look in the opposite direction and ignore what the house is been used for, the other is for him to pay fees and household bills. I asked if I had done well money wise, Kola snaps at me "let this be the last time you ask me that sort of question" I apologize and crawl into bed, too tired to change the sheets I laid a wrapper over the sheet and slept, I heard Kola moving around the room for a while and then nothing.

Waking up at 2pm my back screamed out a testimony of last light, every bone it seemed ached, walking I felt sore when I got a hand mirror and looked at my private part the lips were swollen like I had been in a boxing match. I have learnt to use the Bidet and sit on it running very warm water to sooth the soreness. Walking out to the shared kitchen the 3 Edo women fall silent when I walk in, I burst into tears feeling shame wondering if they know what I have done all night, all three jump up telling me not to cry as I would get a beating, closing the kitchen door they sooth me and tell me they are in the same boat. I ask them where in Italy we are none of them can tell me, even the one who has been here for a year has no idea where we are as she is escorted out and back on the few occasions she goes out.

One of them pops to her room and comes back with shea butter, rub it in she says doing the same, the other two take a bit and rub it into their private parts, I look at us four young women in a kitchen massaging shea butter in their private part, you must always keep it soft and oiled or you will be sore at night. We cook quickly saying little but laying hands on each other a lot and drawing strength. I want to tell them I am newlywed and innocent, I suspect they are in the same boat best to wait until someone starts that dialogue I don't want Kola beating me for disclosing information about myself. None of the men are around.

By 4pm they advise me to go back in the room and sleep as I'll be up all night....all night, it hasn't occurred to me I have to sleep with men every night. Going back in the room I rub Vaseline into my throbbing lips moisturizing as advised. I fell asleep just before 5pm. Kola's arrival had me leaping off the bed in a panic, relax he says lazily and I'm lured into a false sense of hope that I needed to sleep with men once a week. How wrong and deluded can one be, I worked every single day and on the days money was the minimum amount Kola wanted I felt his wrath. He never left a mark on my body just throttled me with the pillow until I passed out.

Time stood still each day the same, I had no idea how long I had been in Italy, nil sense of time or what was going on in the outside world. I had no idea what street or house number I lived in. Thankfully the clients who came appeared to be the same give or take a hundred guys with a few new faces every week. As is human nature, a relationship of sorts develops when you are clean and not a trouble maker. That first customer Belgian man started to come initially once a week, then three times a week, I know he's Belgian because he told me Belgic, pointing to himself when he said Mathis on our first encounter. He paid me in front of Kola but always gave me a large denomination note once Kola is out of the room. I fail to see the point of having money I can't spend freely, I can't send home to my family to help the household.

The Belgian man becomes gentle, though he paid for sex he put emotions into what he was doing, I watched him completely detached from my body. In halting broken English he asked me you good, happy. I shook my head to say no. Pointing to himself he says Mathis again, I am too frightened to tell him my name and he doesn't push. Days, weeks months after that first conversation he asks if I want to go with him "come Belgic I finish work Italy, I engineer go Belgium 6 weeks" Is this white man the answer to my prayer, I will die if I stay here, some days I am so sore I can't touch myself yet at night a non-ending line of men will be waiting on the other end of the phone to come and have sex with me when told I am free. When I nod yes he brings me off the bed motioning me to put a blouse on and takes me to the bathroom, with my hair combed he points a camera at me, "I get for you passport as my wife, you write name and birthday". While we've been talking I noticed a loose tile behind the space in the cistern, we quickly return to the room and he leaves after his hour is up, I sit there wondering dare I hope.

By now I know Kola's routine, once he counts the money he disappears for the day returning between 5-6pm. The other ladies and I are talking more mainly to lament there is nothing we can do. It is clear we were married and brought over for working purpose, Kola has not come near me sexually since the night I started working for him. I wonder if he has other women working for him. By now I have a thick pile of money, I don't know what they are worth and Kola leaves it with me knowing I have nowhere to go and spend it, even my clothes are bought by him, I am truly enslaved the year is 1991.

Chapter 60

Mathis comes back regularly and in broken English tries to communicate warning me not to tell anyone of his help. Today he tells me Passport almost ready and brings out a small square and ink pad, tells me to do my thumb print on the paper this done he gives me a small bottle of fluid to use to get rid of the tell-tale blue ink. If Mathis is a test by Kola I will fail as I am so desperate to get away from what I am doing.

My body and soul are sore, I walk like an old woman and have lost count of the amount of men I have slept with, the worst time was when I started in the evening as usual and men were still coming at 10.00am in the morning. That was the first time I thought of either killing myself or just taking a chance and running out in the street naked screaming my head off for help. I lost count of the last time I menstruated; Kola gives me a tablet every evening to make sure that never happens.

Mathis came last night and asked what time Kola comes back home before telling me today he will come for me be ready to run out when you hear alarm, he makes a ringing sound which made me laugh the first time in a long time. It is 11am and I go back to the room, locking the door I go in the bathroom and ease out the loose tile, nestled there in the hallow is my passport, Kola's passport and bundle after bundle of money, the space reaches quite far back.

I pull out everything one by one and carefully replace the tile taking care to clean the floor for any grain of dirt I might have disturbed. I packed this and my money with a few items of clothing, warm clothing not the rubbish I have been wearing for customers and waited.

At 12.30 the loudest noise I have ever heard goes off its ringing and ringing and won't stop, we hear a lot of commotion outside and people banging on the door and clanging the gates, all four of us pour out of the rooms the same time high tail it down the stairs out the door and into the streets, as soon as I hit the street my eyes are searching for Mathis, I spot him waiting quietly in a car, in the chaos no one saw me get in the car, I laid across the back seat as Mathis drove away keeping normal speed, within a minute a fire engine blasts past us. Over and over he says "it's okay it's okay".

I clutch the pillowcase bag I have with me I have some serious shit money in it Kola's passport and some paper documents I have not had time to look at. Mathis drives for what feels like an hour, in time he stops, when he steps out and beckons me out I see we are in a closed in parking of some sort like a basement, getting out we ride to the first floor and into his apartment, my first thought money is good. Mathis makes me coffee, milky sweet coffee that tasted divine and leads me unto the balcony, the first time I will look at the Italian skyline freely with no fear. I am clearly in an affluent area. Mathis smiles at me and hands me a passport, in it is my face date of birth the passport picture taken in the toilet my first name and I assume Mathis surname Maes. I put my arms round him and thank him, he smiles and holds me close, leading me to the room he points to a cabin bag, tells me to choose one pack my things ready, going to the wardrobe Mathis pulls out trouser suit and loafers, I will be travelling in those clothes. As if he can read my mind he drops a padlock and key for me to secure the case.

Within the hour we are at the local airport and on a small commercial flight about 70 passengers in all, while we were driving to the airport I was able to get a good look at Mathis, I put his age in late 40's, average looks clean and very well groomed which makes me wonder what he's doing with black prostitutes. In his broken English he tells me he was once married to a black woman, he did everything for her and she left him for a younger boyfriend who he had thought was her brother, helped him to secure a visa to join them in Belgium from the Gambia. He had told the Belgian embassy I am that wife and here in Italy my passport was missing no need to worry his ex-wife is on holiday in Gambia so now I relax.

We land in Deurne Airport in Antwerp on Belgium soil an hour and 40 minutes later, it is a short 30 minutes' drive to Mathis house an impressive gated property. This man has money, he leads me into the sitting room and who is sitting there but Kola drinking wine and leaping up to greet Mathis he ignores me. I am rooted to the spot and begin to hyperventilate, Mathis pats me and tells me no worries everything's fine. I just stand there one thing I know for sure, I will kill myself if I am expected to continue with selling myself.

Mathis asks for my bag and the key I hand both over, Kola takes it to the sofa and opening it takes out his passport, his money and the paper documents, in that time Mathis has come over to hold my hand, whatever is happening Mathis clearly has no control over. Kola then rips the lining along the sides of the carryon open, to reveal yet more money and four clear plastic bags of white powder like flour. In Yoruba Kola gives me my passport and tells me he will inform my people I met someone else and dumped him. He points out the marriage ceremony in Nigeria was a sham as he is already married.

Crossing over to where we are standing he hands Mathis a cd and walks out, his parting shot to me it's all business and hustle, don't be naive. Is Mathis my savior or a new tormentor, have I been sold to him, what is the connection with Kola, will Kola be back what is to become of me, Mathis has moved away from and inserted the cd in the player it is the sound of sex that snaps me out of my quandary, I watch open mouthed as Mathis and I have sex, Kola has video it and used it as a hold over the man threatening to send it to the media in Belgium if he doesn't play ball. I burst into tears and fling myself at Mathis, a few moments later there is a knock on the door, as I cower behind Mathis a police man leads Kola in handcuffs and hands me the bag he had with him telling me take your things, Mathis points me toward a room with the bag, going in I take all the money and paper documents out plus the passports including Kola's leaving the flour packages I hand it back to Mathis. Kola was nowhere to be seen, I think taken back to the police car while I was out of the room. Mathis tells me after the officer left, he will be charged with Cocaine you understand drug smuggling, jail and sent back to Nigeria after plenty years. For the 1st time I ask Mathis the date and what year we are in, he is looks at me not understanding when he works out what I want I break down, I have spent over two years in sexual captivity it is April 1994. I cry uncontrollable while Mathis strokes my hair and murmurs comforting words to me. He lets me cry myself out before leading me upstairs to a bedroom.

Chapter 61

I have never seen a corner bath, which he ran while pouring various little amounts of liquid from an array of bottles, holding up a white robe he motions me to get undressed and in the bath, he comes over and suggests I take my plaits out, I understand without him saying anything, this is a new beginning wash the old out. He leaves and returns with a tray none of the food I recognize but I am so hungry I try all washed down with my very first glass of wine. I enjoy the chicken bites but Mathis is trying hard to tell me it's not chicken, when he begins to hop round the room I understand rabbit.

I ask him to join me and he does so pronto, lying side by side in the massive bath we float quietly, he fiddles with something and I realize he had set a temperature so when the water falls below that some is let out and fresh hot water gushed in. Clever people. I try conversing but Mathis English is a struggle, asked if he has family he says yes, you see. Exiting the bath we dry ourselves and he beckons me again to follow him. I had not noticed but there is a second floor to the house.

Going up the stairs he shows me each room until we are back in the massive sitting room, going out the double doors at the back I stare at what looks like a field with a cluster of houses at the edge, Mathis points and says servants, help for house, my tour over we head to the kitchen, the house is wonderfully warm, we go down the stairs to a basement it is full of equipment gym Mathis points out in the corner is a small wooden box, sauna, steam good he says and so on and so forth he tried to acquaint me with my surroundings.

Opening the double door fridge I stand there, I have never seen such stock not even in the Lagos supermarkets, I look at Mathis ask what I can try, everything he says everything moving to the wall he picks up the phone and speaks into it, I hear Sole Meuniere, Stoemp, Moules Frites,Hutsepot, Flamiche, Vol au vent, Asparagus and start laughing they sound like medical conditions, dinner he says smiling and hold out his hand, walking hand in hand we head upstairs.

We lie on the huge bed, I feel and know Mathis does not want to touch me giving me a break between being used and participating willingly. He shows me how to work the control and find English speaking channels, I come across an Indian film and start to watch Mathis shows me how to put English subtitles on, I lay back and watch Shakti Amitabh Bachchan do his hero thing. An hour later the phone on the wall buzzes, Mathis asks if I want to eat downstairs or in the room, room I say, thus I have my first Belgian meal in the bedroom of a stately house of a man who rescued me from sex camp and is obviously wealthy beyond my comprehension, I enjoyed everything except the asparagus, they are funny limp white things with some sauce poured across. Apparently white asparagus is a delicacy. No thank you.

I asked Mathis if he likes African cooking, he has not tried it, my ex-wife he explained "eat restaurant everyday she like out out all times" from dinner I know he likes fish meats and vegetables, I will show this man gratitude through my cooking. That night I sleep and dream dreams aplenty, some peaceful some showing me back in Italy waiting for the next customer sore and voiceless living in fear.

I wake in a tangle of sheets Mathis is asleep with one arm on me protectively, I move and he stares, we say good morning at the same time and start to laugh. "How you feel, I feel great thank you, thank you again for coming into my life" I say. Opening the drawer next to him he pulls out the Belgian passport and asks me in his stop start English, "we make marriage for real or you want for to leave", I say "no I want to stay and we make marriage for real" all the time thinking, where will I go what will I do.

There is a discreet knock on the door, coffee and an assortment of glazed pastry is wheeled in and left in the outer part of the bedroom. Mathis pours the first cup I stop him and do the second cup, he nods his approval, I also serve the patiseries using the tong the way he showed me, I am 23 in a few weeks and ready to learn the ways of the west. We shower and I put my trouser suit on.

10.30am and we are heading into town, the name is Antwerp, with Mathis dressed casually in jeans and polo neck we move round unnoticed and shop until I say no more, stopping for lunch we have spaghetti and meatballs, I miss pepper and Mathis laughs. We arrive somewhere called the mile and Mathis buys me a ring, I don't know if the set is fake stones or not but soon know when I am given the Diamond Certificate separately. I cling to Mathis like something was coming to tear me away, throughout the morning he's been quietly taking calls and tells me we stop on the way home say marriage again, that's what we did and I was more than happy to do so as the Registrar handed the marriage certificate to me in an envelope.

We've been out all day and I am beginning to flag, one more stop Mathis says as we pull up in front of a building, once inside I smile a lot for the first time in over two years I hear English language spoken, I grin and grin like a little child, it is not lost on Mathis, I am introduced to Mani, he will be teaching me Flemish as this is what over 60% speak but there is also a mixture of French German & Dutch spoken. While teaching me Mani will work with Mathis twice a week on his English but for now I will spend 6 days a week learning. I understand Mathis needs me to learn to communicate fast.

Heading home, home I don't even know my own address or phone number but for now I am content, I feel no fear but affection growing each moment I spend with Mathis. Getting home I expect Mathis to open the boot for me to carry my shopping in, smiling he tells me it's already in the house, the shops had delivered it home. I believe him but still went upstairs to check everything was in one side of the walk in closet, clothes hanging up shoes neatly displayed and underwear folded neatly in drawers. For some unknown reason I burst into tears and run to Mathis, he holds me for a long time and gently rocks me. Tonight we eat dinner and retire upstairs to our bedroom, Mathis automatically puts the Indian channel on for me and opened his laptop to do some work.

I realized I don't know all what he does for a living apart from the Engineering he mentioned, he laughs and points at my ring, you sell rings no no, I am also diamond dealer, buyer, supplier. Diamond best money in the world, always buy Diamonds he tells me, any country it's money, curling up next to him I watch my movie while he works. Tomorrow morning he tells me "you see Doctor here or go there", "here I say, man woman doctor"? "Woman" he says, "no worries good doctor". I begin to understand the no sex, Mathis wants to make sure I am okay and disease free, that I can understand despite using condoms I would be glad to hear I am healthy down below. I haven't had sex in 72 hours and feel fabulous and relaxed down there. I go into the bathroom, while changing attempt to look at my private part in the mirror, Mathis comes in and hands me a hand held mirror I look and see loose flesh thin and loose from the constant assaults of the trade, surely a young person's private part should not be all flabby like mine oh well what can I do.

Another pleasant night passed, we have breakfast on the terrace and watch as a car comes up the drive it is the doctor, Mathis has done well selecting an older woman sparing me future gossip. She is gentle as she takes swabs and shines a torch once she opened me up with a plastic instrument. Results in two days she says and ask if I can shave so she can examine the tissue and side area, she hands me a can of Sally Hansen spray-on rinse off and I head to the bathroom, emerging 8 minutes later with a totally smooth private part that I have kept shaven since that day, she examines me again and gives me a cream Canesten to use rub not inside but between the hollows and the surrounding area, all the way to the rectum and up between the butt cheeks. I nod obediently as she smiles and says no problem just to be sure.

The following morning my lesson started on the dot of 10am and ended at 3pm, it helped to have been educated to college level and I pick up quickly for the first 6 weeks I am allowed the English translation I actually make more progress without been able to refer to it. Life with Mathis is great, he tells me when going out and calls me regularly on the mobile phone he bought for me. I learnt a valuable lesson in life never marry someone you are in love with, marry someone who loves you and you will learn to love and appreciate them, love will grow as you are shown unconditional love. Mathis loves me it is enough.

When the smear results come back clear Mathis gathers me in his arms and makes love to me, no peels of thunder, no lightening, no earth shattering moment just a feeling of release, released to love, to feel, to experience, to respond to, not pretend, a feeling of freedom. Never ever again taking my freedom of choice for granted.

Chapter 62

6 months after I arrived in Belgium I do not recognize the young woman speaking fluent Flemish and now learning to speak Italian, when I protest Mathis says I must learn so I am never again afraid when I am in that environment. Mathis gently explains his job involves a lot of travelling we will go to Italy he wants me to be able to understand the conversations around me, I see the sense in it and apply myself. To settle my nerves he tells me Kola was given a 15 year sentence with recommendation for deportation at the end of serving his sentence. Knowing he is locked away I totally relax.

Mathis is Roman Catholic and wishes to have a church blessing, a quiet affair that needed me to accept the faith and be put through my paces. On the 1st anniversary of my arrival in Belgium a small service is held 25 guests in total, I have two guests, the doctor and Mani. As I repeat my vows I thank God for giving me this man, old enough to be my father he has shown me nothing but love, I have never seen him cross or irritable with me, I think of this and begin to weep, he joins in and our guests all tear up. It is a good point in my life.

Mathis begins to take me with him all over Europe and further afield, I know nothing about Diamonds but sure know a good jewellery design when I see it, I begin to volunteer comments and to my delight Mathis encourages me, returning from Milan one afternoon he asks me to draw a complete jewellery set, necklace earrings, ring and bracelet and to show what stone should be set in each, not taking him too serious I draw what I would like to see, the usual bogus the bigger the better. Looking at it he asks me to draw a smaller version that could be worn with a suit, he then asks me to draw a middle range of the same collection, taking the papers from me he puts them in his suitcase.

After breakfast we have two visitors. Mathis calls me down, in front of the three of them are my sketches from yesterday, they open what looks like laptops and begin to duplicate my drawing digitally, you need to see my drawing come to life, the large bogus one Mathis tells me is for the African market in the USA, the mid-size is for the

European market like London, small version will end up in outlets all over the world. The small version will be the most expensive, all stones will be diamonds.

Ore (friends) this is how my career in jewel design started, Mathis sent me to learn the trade properly. I learnt quickly and remained humble and polite, despite the fact that by virtue of my marriage I was richer than all of the people I came in contact with.

At the age of 25 I had our first set of twins, two years later I have another set at which point we learn that I have something called a split womb, reality translates each pregnancy will probably result in twins. Mathis is smitten. At my request he agrees his elderly parents move closer, I tell him I want the children to have their grandparents close, it also dawns on me I have to put my fears aside and go back to Nigeria, go and see my family explain what happened and move on.

When the younger twins were 6 months old and weaned I flew out to Lagos, I had been gone exactly 10 years, the Eko Holiday Inn sent a car for me as requested. I kept in touch with Mathis nonstop. Once checked in I have breakfast and wait for the morning traffic to die down.

At 10.30 I set out for my parents' house in the Costain area, when I walked in my mum was just crossing the yard, she took one look at me and screamed it is a ghost, in the pandemonium that followed my mum was so over whelmed she raced to the toilet with diarrhoea. I looked at our two bedroom ground floor flat and knew my first project will be to sort out better living accommodation for my family. In the process someone had run down the road to call Kola's parents who hurried over.

Thanking the other tenants I tell them I will come and see them before I leave and close the door to our flat, leaving me and the two sets of parents. I ask not to be interrupted until I finish my story and promise to answer any questions at the end. I talked and told it as it was. Both parents cried, Kola's parents asked for forgiveness, I told them there was nothing to forgive, giving them an envelope stuffed full with Naira I had changed at the hotel I know it is the most money they have even seen in their life, I caution them not to tell anyone Kola is in Prison but to hold some money aside for him so he has something to fall back on when he is released. They leave shaking their heads.

My father feels awkward, I go to him and kneel down in front of him taking his hands I tell him how I thought about suicide every day and prayed for death, at the mention of suicide he burst into tears again and standing up drags me up and envelopes me, it is not easy for him a staunch Christian to listen to what I just told them. I bring out my wedding & blessing album and show them photos of the two sets of twins and point out family members.

I warn them I am home for a week only and that time was to secure passports and visas for them to visit us in 3 months' time when the weather temperature climbs up into the summer zone. Calling the hotel I book a suite and ask my parents to pack for a few days. We send the home help to my Uncle round the corner. I give each neighbor 25,000 naira, there are three other flats in the building, the sum makes my mum's eyes water, and I show her some of the jewels I have designed that are selling well in the industry.

Arriving at the Hotel I abandon my room and stay with my parents, for me my life in the west started on the day I arrived in Belgium and that is where our conversation started. We ate and laughed a lot and spoke to the family back in Belgium it was a happy chaotic call that ended with the two sets of twins crying for moeder the Flemish word for mother. That night I slept between both my parents and felt the safest I have ever felt away from Mathis.

We spend the next day's acquiring the passports and attending the interview at the Belgian Embassy, the mention of my husband's name brings the Ambassador out to say hello, we sit in his office drinking coffee while the passports are stamped and brought to us. I purchase two first class return tickets with an open return date, Mathis has said if my parents like Belgium they should come and live with us, I do not relay this to my parents.

I pay 5 million naira into my parents account as instructed by Mathis a sum that made them both declare they feel unsafe, I asked how neighbors will know if they didn't tell. I gave then more money for my uncle and various other relatives, both my parents are retired primary school teachers modest and God fearing in their dealings with others, it is this I feel made God send Mathis my way. To be safe I gave my parents 150,000 naira and teased if anyone has alerted the local armed robbers they should hand the whole lot over.

Parting at the airport was difficult but twelve weeks was not that long. Ladies today, I fly into London City to come and get my hair done. I take nothing for granted, both sets of twins are graduates married and working in their field of expertise, all four are Accountants which puzzled me but I guess they take after their brainy father. Mathis my Mathis was 69 last month, still fit and healthy, we lost his parents a few years ago, because of that he insists my parents spend every summer with us going home when the cold weather kicks in. Memories of my sex slave days are never far away it is the reason I set up Pathway (No questions asked) in collaboration with the Nigerian Italian and other European agencies to respond quickly to those wanting to escape sex trade no questions asked, so illegal presence in any country does not stop them from seeking help. We leave laminated printed cards in female bathrooms all over Europe especially in public phone booths, night clubs and GP surgeries.

Some years ago I went to Nigeria and popped in to see my Uncle, sitting on the pavement with his cronies was Kola, in his 50's like me, although he looked 70. I stared at him long and hard enough for him to get up and walk away. Useless fellow. I continue to design more for fun than anything else, my most famous creation is the Russian Butterfly range, it just sells and sells.

Ore it started out a horror story but see me so, each year on the anniversary of Mathis taking me out of Italy I go to Mass and light a candle, a higher order than me was watching out for me that much I know.

At this she moves her slim slight frame and calls over to Sharon to please ask the Nigerian food seller to come over. I study her as she looks at her friends with affection a common bond called horror binds this three together, I hope Sara is going to share her story before my hair is done, I don't have long to wait.

Chapter 63

Sara

I couldn't get a visa for England so went for the next best thing, Ireland with one thing in mind to use the crossing, yet undetected by the British Border Agencies very kindly provided by the fisher men who are sympathetic of the Africans, then take the train down to one of the main London train stations, as if I had been on holiday in Scotland.

Plan is avoiding the coast guards as we cross from North Antrim Coast using the Narrow sea as it's called to get to Scotland, the fishermen generally take you across in batches of 10 with the handlers on the other side waiting they then split you up into twos to travel down on the train into London with your friend or family members whose agreed to come and collect you.

If you don't have a sponsor on the British end they will not help you, mine is Abbey my cousin, he comes home regularly and told me about this route, I have a good job so have funds but want to come to the West to try my luck like just like everyone else. I promised to pay for the train tickets and agreed when he said we should spend a few days like tourists visiting both Scotland and Wales. I sent him the £1000 which he assured me will cover all costs, with the crossing costing £300 pounds we had adequate funds to visit surrounding areas.

I arrived in Ireland without ceremony and made my way straight to the address given in North Antrim; I am expected and speak to Abbey who assures me he is heading to the train station after we end the conversation. I am crossing tonight, thinking I will be staying in hotel, while waiting I am told I will be staying with the others at a farm house near the coast. I am taken there and meet 8 others mixture of Nigerians and Ghanaians waiting.

At 7pm we are taken to the boat sat amongst an endless line of nets and fishing paraphernalia and told to stay down. Incredibly the journey takes what seems like minutes, as we are lead off the boat and into a van we are reminded to stay quiet. Arriving at the prearranged place the back of a large pub people quickly step up to claim their arrivals within three minutes the place is clear with only me standing there.

The lad with me offers me his phone but is clearly impatient to leave, when he hears me crying as I tried to call Abbey who's phone was switched off he offers to take me to someone who lets those who haven't been collected stay a night or two, it will cost me a £10 a night with breakfast thrown it. I thank him and get back in the van.

God Bless the Irish, Mary who took me in is quite a character, I can barely understand her accent, she shows me into a room returns with a cup of tea and a thickly buttered slice of bread told me to get some sleep. I eat and try to sleep but I'm constantly woken by a giggling Mary who is either watching a comedy all night or I am staying in a knocking shop.

Breakfast is a hearty meal of eggs gammon baked beans and as much bread as you could eat. Going back to my room after giving Mary £30 pound which I decided I will not ask if Abbey showed up today. I wrap the rest of my money up leaving out £50 pounds.

I have a bank draft plus £5000 in £50 notes and roll this up tight rubber band it using a small nylon bag I found and washed, I wrap my money in this and insert it like a tampon, if anyone wants to steal my money they would need to take my vagina with them, tucking all but a £5 note in my bra, I go and ask Mary for change to make a phone call, she offers me the use of the house phone if I make it quick.

I called Abbey a total of 37 times that day, on day three I decide to ask Mary's advice as it was clear my only contact in London will not be showing up. Stay here and get a job she says, I can get you a job on the farms no one will trouble you until you know what you want to do, £70 a week cash in hand. I thank her and say yes not realizing the path that lay ahead.

Its November cold grey and damp, I can't imagine what work will be available on the farm I hope most of it is indoors. Lending me a thick jumper we walk quickly to the charity shop on the high street and buy clothes that Mary pointed out was a must as well as boots one leather one wellingtons. I couldn't understand why I bought two coats, one a size 16 and the other a size 18 I am a size 14. Same thing with gloves one pair that was normal and another, so thick I ask myself again what I was getting into, several thick leggings followed by hats and scarf's thick chunky knits.

I am starting tomorrow Saturday, a van will pick me up at 6.30am, I will return at 7pm in the evening. It sounded like a rather long day but as I still couldn't get hold of Abbey I had no choice I had briefly considered crossing back into Ireland and going home but thought I should give things a try.

Mary wakes me with a gentle tap and advices me not to have a bath as I will be cold. I wipe myself down and dress bundled up as she advised. She shoves a sandwich in my hand and says eat washed down with a warm cup of tea so I could drink quickly she advises me to take another leak before I leave. The ride is short but very bumpy, there are about a dozen other people squashed up in the van, we are all black. We arrive in a large shed open to the elements on one side but with a door you could roll over to keep the cold out. We are split into two groups, I am in the first group that will be harvesting cabbage and something I don't recognize called Brussels sprouts they must be left on the branches. I am grateful for the double doubles I am wearing.

It is 7.15 am when we start, two more van load of people are dropped off to join us, dark coats bent over in the fields moving slowing back and forth like ants. First tea break is at 10.15; you drink tea use the toilet and get back to what you are doing in ten minutes. Next is lunch at 1.30pm rows of steaming pot noodles flavor you want is irrelevant you take one and eat, that break is 15 minutes including toilet break at 4.30 there is a 15 minute tea and biscuit break following which the loading and tidying up commences, I am told the goods are heading to London, in that moment I understood why Mary had told me to bundle up it was to understand how cold the refrigerated trucks get and adjust my clothing accordingly to when I decide to make a move clever girl.

At the end of the second week I tell Mary I am going to make a move she asks that I don't tell her which day writes down an address in Welling DA8 and tells me to go there, she calls a number and tells the person she spoke to, to take good care of me, I am to ask for Lucy if I can make my way there.

I made the decision to head to London as I had narrowly escaped been raped on the farm by one of the other workers, I'm not even sure his nationality but he was one of a handful of whites who now worked with us. It was dark and I was making my way back to the shed, this man walks up, pushes me over onto all fours his willy out ready, while he was trying to get under my coat I picked up a rock and smashed him in the head with it and ran.

I don't know if he picked me or it was a random act but I can't hang around here any longer picking vegetables wallowing in worms mud and rotten vegetation and loading vans, a few weeks ago I was assistant bank manager at one of the top banks on Lagos Island, today I am in a field somewhere in Scotland cutting cabbage, trimming and boxing it ready for the journey down south. Totally surreal herded around like cattle every day eating pot noodle meals that had expired.

I leave my money tucked in my fanny as Mary called it and money earned on the farm I leave in my pocket at the end of loading I simply stay in the truck and say a silent prayer as it moves off gathering speed once on the motorway. I initially thought I imagined the muffled noise and then call out gently to be answered back equally quietly by five other voices, we stayed quiet after that, several hours in minus zero conditions, its pitch dark inside but I knew I dare not sleep, so I imagine all the opportunities waiting in London and what I will do when I see Abbey.

We begin to slow down slow enough to know we are in town and frequent traffic lights are in play, I slowly make my way to the back of the van, ensuring I stay in the second row of boxes offering me a hiding place from immediate exposure, as soon as the doors are open and the man walks round the corner I jump down stiff I fall over twice as I made my way away from the truck.

I take in my surroundings, I am in a large vegetable market and wonder if I am hallucinating when I hear Yoruba being spoken, I walk towards the voices, it is a couple, I approach them and say good morning I have to take a chance and immediately tell them I have just come out of the back of a lorry and need to find my way to an area called Welling, they look at each other, the wife grabs my hand and tells her husband "Baba Deola lets go we have to help this woman we'll come back and buy supply another day" she talks as she walks me towards their car.

As we drive off along the road I will later come to recognize as the A2 Walthamstow I look from the flyover and see the line of trucks waiting to deliver vegetables, there is a massive commotion around one no doubt the one I jumped from,

I say a silent prayer the others make it out undetected. I ask the time, its 3 am. I quickly tell the couple my story, they apologize they cannot do more but will take me to my Welling address, what they did was to write their number down and give it to me the Idowu's. When we arrived in Welling I hardly knocked before Lucy opened the door and pulled me in for the 1st time in almost 18 hours I feel warm I am inside a super warm building.

Lucy gives me chicken soup a thick slice of bread and a cup of tea. She shows me upstairs to what seems a room in the roof, beggars can't be chooser, now safe I am wide awake, I lay there thinking how long I can stay her before I need to move on. At least I have documents and there are no restrictions. I can work if I want with that thought I fall asleep.

Lucy wakes me up at lunch time with a cup of coffee and some clothing for me. I had washed my underwear and hung them to dry in the early hours when I couldn't sleep. Lucy is about my build a very attractive blond woman about 5'7 like me but with breasts that belonged on a milk maid. She shows me the shower/toilet tucked in a corner, I hadn't noticed earlier and I settled down for a good scrub under the shower still with my money where it was kept, every day I took it out washed the nylon and carefully dried it reinserted it, today I hope I am taking it out for one of the last times.

Food is a salad with grilled chicken breast and vegetables. I am not a fan of vegetable and feel sick at the lack of pepper in my diet. Lucy asks as were are eating I understand you are interested in working for me as a house keeper, I nod with a mouthful of bland chicken, 6 days a week with Mondays off live-in with all food, £70 take it or leave it.

Lucy outlines what is expected of me as she shows me round the house, three double bedrooms each with its own shower and toilet on the first floor with a fourth single room that housed a white leather massage bed and numerous bottles and scented candles placed there. Downstairs is a through lounge all furniture is heavy white and gold mixture of leather and metal the Italians like so much, the kitchen area is down five steps, you can tell very little cooking goes on here, everything is pristine, off the kitchen is yet another room used for laundry in the far corner of this is a small toilet and wash basin. Lucy asks if I can read and write, I confirm I can.

I ask if she can point me in the direction of the shops as I need to get suitable clothing and shoes, she'll do better than that as she's heading into Lewisham which has plenty of shops I am welcome to go along. Its Monday today so nil rush. As Lucy drives she points out areas of interest, Shooters Hill Blackheath then Blackheath Hill left at the bottom will bring you into Lewisham roundabout straight across to the car park, escalators down and you are bang in the middle of the shopping centre.

I shopped quickly looking at the sale racks only, I quickly acquire three sets of clothing two pairs of jeans, several tops, underwear, pair of trainers and one pair of black low heeled shoes from Ravel, walking to the far end I discover a market and buy ground scot-bonny pepper as well as bottled chilli oil, I know I will become ill if pepper is not re-introduced to my diet, buying a medium size suitcase, padlock and I'm done. I head back to the lift and notice a Mercury 121 phone shop, going in I sign up and buy a Motorola phone it will cost £15 a month all landline calls are free after 7 pm and all weekend. I give Lucy's address using my real name. Returning to Welling I notice a branch of Barclays Bank on the corner, I tell Lucy I need to open an account, nil problem, she will take me there, and its only round the corner from the house.

Taking my shopping to the room, I retrieve the money hidden on my person and take £1000 and my passport follow Lucy to the bank. Account was open and done within 20 minutes flat, nil restrictions you have money you can bank it, next to the bank is a Superdrug store, going in I buy Vagasil feminine cleanser, I need to do something after almost three weeks of carrying money round in my private part. I stock up on sanitary towels as that is also due any day soon.

Returning to the house Lucy explains what I can expect assuring me it is rare for her to have to call the Police, Police what Police!!! She refers to her business as massage, beauty and relaxation provider. The men and women come here for good time, some of them just want a Brazilian wax, Brazilian wax what!! Lucy laughs at me, its total removal of pubic hair she explains oh okay, I know Muslim girls back home who are baldies as we tease them.

Lucy has five girls working on a rotation there is always four in the building with one standby if things get very busy Lucy herself attends to clients. She gives me two sets of keys, one for the external doors the other for internal locks and cupboards. All bottles are clearly labeled and simply need topping up, if the door is closed I am not to enter the room but to provide what is requested and leave it outside the door. Lucy does not have a drinks license so restricts things to a welcome glass of white or red wine per customer. Without me asking her Lucy tells me she is unable to keep house keeper for long as the rich dudes take them away to a life the girls can only dream about.

Work starts at 6pm with the girls arriving at 5.45pm ready to attend to guests by the time they walk in. I can do what I like with the rest of today. Lucy suggests I walk round the high street and area for a bit to get my bearing, left will take me to Bexleyheath Shopping centre or Danson Park, a 40p bus ride or 15 minute stroll, popping upstairs to retrieve the new phone I had left charging, I walk left toward Bexleyheath knowing I will come to the park 1st. It is indeed a park worth a visit, beautiful with a lake and lots of open ground, people dotted around gave the feeling of having company without them being too close. Sitting on the grass with my back to the lake where I could observe anyone approaching me I make my first call to the 07956123... number I had spent weeks and months memorizing.

Chapter 64

Adjara picks up on the third ring and growls 'who is this' no hello.... I identify myself and remind him of our conversation when in Nigeria confirming I am in London and have the bank draft for £40,000. I asked if he is still able to take it to Europe clear the money and if his cut is still £5,000, he agrees the terms are still the same. He will speak to his friends in Belgium and get back to me in a week, I tell him not to worry I will call him on Monday.

There is a lot I haven't told you, working as assistant bank manager I saw money not money on a small scale but money big time, my then boyfriend Dehinde who also worked in a bank told me of his plans to divert money to himself via bank draft, making sure it's enough funds to enable him to settle in England, to cover his tracks he will apply for two years sabbatical leave, all had gone well and he made it to England 4 months ago where he quickly married someone he had been corresponding with nicely supported by the £65,000 draft he brought with him.

When I asked why the bank wasn't looking for him he explained what he took is chicken feed compared to what the bosses have access to. So here I am young single headed to the West with a total sum of £40,000. I should be able to put a deposit on a house or buy it outright then pay someone to marry me and settle here. I hadn't bargained for Abbey, or working on a farm narrowly escaping rape, a ride in the back of a refrigerated truck, living and working in a boudoir but hey bring it on, what do I have to lose. What did I leave behind in Lagos.

Not a lot, the youngest of a four children I had read business at Unilag (University of Lagos) and ensured my quick progress to the post of Assistant Manager by sleeping with all the right people, we lived in Obalenda not the nice end either, if you come to my house and don't watch out your clothes will be torn, caught by the aluminum roof sheets we used as wall paneling. We lived in a face me, I face you situation you could see and hear everything that went on in the room across you and hear what went on in the rooms either side of you.

At Unilag I singled out the rich girls and made friends with them feeding off their leftovers learning and mirroring their language and mannerisms, all the time planning how to leave my ghetto behind. I met Dehinde on one of the Banking seminars during the period he took one of the workshops we both could smell each other's poverty and ended up making friends laughing at what we have to put up with to be part of the in-crowd, Dehinde told me of his plans before we parted company and promised me one phone call if all goes well. His call to me at the bank a few months ago to say all is well with him in England spurred me on so here I am. I will make it in England give it whatever it takes.

Returning to the house Lucy is nowhere to be found, I look in the rooms each has a nice supply of condoms, wet wipes, water jug, mini towels, moisturizers and at least two boxes of tissues. The rooms are tastefully furnished with everything nicely coordinated. I check the stores and familiarize myself with the layout of the stock taking note of the ticking off system used when an item has been removed from stock, I understand the colored lights that represent each room, if a light comes on I check outside the door for what is needed and leave it outside tapping gently on the door to alert it's outside ready to be picked up. Of all that is expected of me I do not look forward to ironing.

Feeling hungry I pick up my bottle of pepper and head to KFC, for £1.99 I get two pieces of chicken a portion of chips a small coke or a tub of baked beans, I opt for the coke. Taking my food to a window seat, I eat taking spoonful of pepper sauce to add to the chicken, I watch as people walk past on the way to their various things.

Coming out of KFC an angry looking thick set white man with no hair growls at me, excuse me I said and he erupts "wog, coon, monkey, go back to where you come from we don't want you here, white people rule, slaves, slaves, slaves, wog, wog, wog, then BNP,BNP,BNP" I stare at this baboon of a man in total astonishment and walk away, no one around has said a word or intervened, what his gripe is I can't get my head round, I look around and hurry away then astonishingly he begins to laugh, great big belly body shaking rumbles and peel after peel of laughter followed until I could hear his "see that I scared that wog good" I come to the conclusion I have met the local madman finding out much later the BNP office is a stone's throw away.

Lucy is still not back, the nicest thing about the house is the warmth, I go to my room and strip the bed checking the mattress I find the weakness I'm looking for, using a pin I unpick a few threads, removing the money from my private part I ease it into the cavity, turning the mattress round I remake the bed, I will be sleeping on my money, Wednesday morning I will pay most of it into my account, I hadn't wanted to show such money in front of Lucy.

Taking the phone I call the Idowu's the wife answers the phone with praises to Jesus, sharing they had returned to the Walthamstow market early hours of today asking about the incident yesterday they were told four people had been found froze to death in the back of a truck only one had survived and is in police custody. I again thank them for being God sent and promised to keep in touch.

I turn in and sleep until midday, making my way to the kitchen I make Lucy a cup of tea and find her in the sitting room, it finally dawns on me that Lucy does not live on the premises. I wash and put on the black and white apron as shown joining Lucy downstairs, on queue at 5.45pm in walks four breathtakingly beautiful women, each petite and wafer thin, beauty fully made up and smelling expensive, introductions are done.

I wonder what their age is, in Nigeria you are considered an adult at the age of 21. They are polite but more interested in checking their appearance and finding out what room they are in and who does what. Once told they disappear upstairs. We are expecting four guests at five minute intervals between 6 and 6.20pm, leaving the building is also done at 5 minute intervals so there is no chance of bumping into someone you know.

And so it began walking around the house when guests are there making sure all that is needed is at hand and everyone behaves themselves, if they are surprised to see me working there they hid it well.

Chapter 65

On Friday night I have my first laughter, at about 1am two elderly very drunk men ring the bell and are ushered in, once in the front room Lucy instructs me to draw the partitioning door of the sitting room and open up the bed settee, dropping her voice she tells me to put one of the blow up dolls on the bed, as it was a warm night I was told to leave the two side windows open.

This done I joined Lucy to hear one of the men explain it is his friends 72nd birthday, they had spent the evening at the Shrewsbury Pub leaving to go home he had asked his friend if there was anything he would like to do to finish the day off, his friend has disclosed he hadn't had sex since his wife died 10 years ago, he would like to have sex if it can be arranged and so here they were nudge nudge wink wink. I didn't understand the nudge wink but Lucy had pointed the pub out on the way to Lewisham, it had taken this two an hour to walk down the road that is what I call really drunk.

Informing the birthday boy the room is ready I take him in and leave. We keep his friend company while I keep an ear out for birthday boy. When I hear him fumbling with the door I go to the rescue and lead him back to the sitting room swaying nonstop and in danger of falling over.

"Stanley" he says "there is a joke about sleeping with witches, I just sleep with a really gassy witch, I was giving it this and giving it that as my Lil used to like, I thought I'd give her a bite on the neck like my Lil used to like, just a little nip like, well I bite her on the neck and still farting she flew out the window, it was good though" and with that they headed out the door arms round each other singing a song only they knew the words to.

How I did not collapse with laughter when I went in the garden to retrieve the punctured blow up doll is beyond me. I put the room back to how it was, do a check upstairs and return to join Lucy, who smiled at me and simply stated "I don't waste the girls on them, they are so plastered they probably won't remember they got laid in the morning".

Come Saturday morning a couple turn up and begin an intensive clean of each room, by midday the man is doing the ironing and arranging things back in the linen cupboard in order. For this I am grateful I cannot keep unsocial hours and get up to wash clean and iron.

For this house in Welling there is no quiet nights, guest arrive steadily every hour and leave an hour later quietly, if the neighbors know they are clearly turning a blind eye. I later learn Lucy has cleverly employed them in one way on the other, cash in hand to provide maintenance; no one it seems will rat on her trade in flesh.

On Monday I phone Ajara, he is all set, I will meet him in Burger King in Lewisham he will be in Belgium for two weeks and let me know once he has the funds, he leaves on Wednesday. Adjara is everything I find repulsive in a man, a real local boy who would be referred to as an area boy, petty criminal and a menace on society, cocky and sure of himself, arriving in England he quickly marries a British passport holder beginning his reign of criminal activities always below the police radar, his nickname is 'library' you want to know he knows someone who has done it and for a cut he will link you up.

He addresses me in the casual manner these guys use, I hand him the check and stay polite, he asks if I'm expecting other checks, I say yes based on the outcome of this, reassuring me he is the man as others will take my money and run, on this note I thank him and we part company.

When I hadn't heard from him four weeks later I knew I had been 419. It is a lot of money, the Bank cannot trace it to me so I am safe if I decide to go back to Nigeria, I had hoped to use the money to set myself up, to help me cope I reminded myself I had never physically had the money so had not suffered a loss as such. I have £3,500 in my Barclays account at the rate of paying in £200 a month, with nil overhead I should be okay.

I met Bosun tall and handsome at the Barclays Bank in Lewisham in the queue, we got talking initially in English and then throwing caution to the wind gisted in Yoruba, he asked me to accompany him across the road to the Army and Navy Shop. He bought me several items and was direct and straight to the point, I like you and want to date you, I will take care of you and spoil you. Heading back into the main shopping centre Bosun asks me to wait outside Zales, he buys me a Raymond Weil watch, wouldn't let me see the price.

We go for lunch in Deptford here Tommy's kitchen had just opened I was not familiar with Deptford and appreciated him bringing me here, I stuffed myself happy to be eating authentic Nigerian cuisine. Bosun is attentive and honest, he goes to college, has a part time job but his main income comes from credit card fraud. Am I shocked I say no, we all have to survive somehow and looking back on the way he spent money on me today I want more much more of that .

I tell him I work as a house keeper and can only see him on Mondays, no problem as long as he can call me and speak with me regularly. He gives me a hug when he drops me off, I wonder if he has British status and can marry me. He smelt nice when I asked what aftershave he used he said Jazz YSL and his shoes, brown suede brogues from Russell and Bromley. Definitely worth hanging out with.

I work and see Bosun on Mondays, I begin to acquire designer clothing, he shops for me at Chloe in Blackheath, takes me to Selfridges, Petticoat Lane's Ozzie Silk, gold, lace all the usual stuff Nigerian women like in their wardrobe. He makes no demand on me and talks freely about the illegal things he's involved in, at the moment he sponsors drug deals, he puts up the money, say 5 grand towards importation of drugs if it's a successful run for a two week investment he could earn over 3 grand in profit.

Another angle is stolen cars top class cars, they are abandoned for a few weeks in side streets in Thamesmead marsh lands. If fitted with a tracker it will be recovered quickly by the authorities otherwise plates are changed, paperwork created chassis numbers filed and changed to head to Tilbury where insider shippers quickly load aboard waiting ships, stolen to order to be delivered where wanted. I look at this intelligent lazy guy who is rolling in money, he is telling me how he has a team of women working for him opening accounts at Building Society which he then manipulates and gets money he has not paid in out before the building society catch on. Accounts are opened in names to insult (Oyinbo Gor) meaning Westerns are gullible.

I tell him I would like to acquire the council flat everyone talks about, no problem he has someone in Genesta Road in the next Borough, I should begin to use the address so I have proof I live there, to get the ball rolling he takes me to Currys and buys me a portable cassette cd player and gives the Genesta address for the extended guarantee. He takes me to register with a Greenwich GP. Bosun should be running the crime branch for MI5, he will clean up England as he knows how to commit most of these crimes.

It's the height of summer, I am unsure where Bosun lives as he takes me to so many different locations letting himself in with his own key, he invites me to the Notting Hill carnival, there is a Nigerian corner where the music is great. I ask Lucy and she agrees, seeing I have made no requests nor run away with any of the clients she jokes. We get on just fine Lucy and I. I suspect she has a perfectly respectable life somewhere else were no one would dare to think she is a madam, but that is what she is living off the proceeds of women giving their body for pleasure to strangers.

We get on the train at Elephant and Castle, it would seem the world and its cousins are heading to Notting Hill. The atmosphere on the train is great everyone is in dance mode. Bosun knows exactly where he's going and in no time at all we are a part of the crowd where various Nigerian artists are doing short sets, I don't pay much attention as the colors and energy around carries me along but in everything in life are certain cue words that will bring you back and command your attention whatever you are doing, mine is the word Adjara on Wasiu the musician's lips.

Wasiu is on stage and Adjara is dancing in front of him spraying money like its snow while people admire him and women hang on his every grin. I stand staring so much that Bosun asks if I know him, I tell him I met him once, to my delight Bosun says they are firm friends and Adjara will come over once he tires of dancing.

Sure enough 40 minutes later he appears at our circle, if he was shocked to see me he hides it well, but there and then in front of Bosun he tells me he didn't call as things didn't go well, he is lucky not to have been caught in Belgium. I smile back like a dumb ass what else could I do. Turning his attention to Bosun there in the middle of a thronging crowd they discuss a trip to Belgium where

Adjara will load his car with cocaine that has arrived from Nigeria to be transported to England. I listen very attentively.

I had a damn good time, on the way back, I took a chance and told Bosun my contact with Adjara, to my horror he confirms what I suspect, Adjara did get the money. Bosun and others have been wondering where his sudden money and lavish spending came from but he remained tight lipped when asked. Bosun advised me to move on and offered to sort any additional cheque I may have himself, in that same breath he asked if I could open a building society account for him and gives me a name and address he had written down with £250. It is the only time Bosun involved me in his activities.

By now we are lovers; I know what he does on the side and enjoy the lavish way he spends on me. The presents, I've kept the money ranging from £500 to £2000 I have banked at the moment my Barclays account shows a healthy total of £21,000, me a live-in house keeper earning £70 a week. Naira is currently 70-1, in a couple of months I hope to have enough money to buy a 3 bedroom property in Festac Town outright. Bosun has promised to get me a council flat so I don't need to buy a property.

True to his words he asks me to meet him in Woolwich outside Marks and Spencer's, it's strange to see him so early in the morning, we go into McDonalds and join an elderly lady with two children under the age of 4. I am the main applicant the elderly lady is my mother and the two young boys are my sons, giving me all documents needed showing the children were related to me and the grandma's document, we set off to HPU (homeless persons unit), the story we have been thrown out of a friends property, my partner deserted us and my mum has health issues.

It was too easy, we were put in a bed and breakfast for the night and given keys to a three bedroom 1st floor flat on the Barnfield estate midday the following day. With Bosun's support and the councils decoration grant the place was soon ready for occupancy. I rented out the property to four men, using the sitting room as a bedroom, all four worked nights and slept during the day they paid their rent on time and when joined by their girlfriends and needed to move on they recommended someone else.

From that moment on I went from Borough to Borough with the same grandma and children who were now used to seeing me and behaved very well. I put tenants in the properties; they gave me no problem as most were illegal immigrants. With Bosun's help I married a Nigerian guy who I met for the first time on the steps of the registry when we went to make the booking, in no time at all I had permission to remain in the country, I wasted no time in apply for citizenship.

I also started to exercise my right to buy, Bosun had lawyers and financial adviser who drew up all the papers as needed so the banks approved the mortgages, in short today I have 21 properties all over London in some Boroughs I have up to four, as all I needed to do is play with my name using my middle name or last name first. The main win of that era was that the computer systems were not communicating with each other or cross border. Today you cannot live in one borough and try to be housed in another it won't work. Now I have built what all describe as a mansion in Lagos, to do that I sold one of the properties leaving me with 21 as I said earlier.

Chapter 66

Going back to Adjara, don't think I forgot his swindle of me. I got pretty close to Bosun, even when he got married we remained as tight as ever. I listened carefully to the stuff he shared with me and on the Monday he expressed concern about trusting Adjara to bring goods back from Belgium this Sunday afternoon when there will be the weekend rush of people returning. I soothed Bosun with the comment as long as it's not money you can't afford to lose, he has invested £5,000 a small amount as the total amount funding the deal raised is £80,000 with resale expected to fetch £400,000 everyone will do well.

I am ready and have been for a while. Getting back home I pull out the local News Shopper paper and write down the number I need. Strolling down the road, I use the phone box near Welling football ground. Calling the crime line I pass on the information spelling Adjara's name carefully and making sure they repeated the information back, he will be driving a dark blue Mercedes arriving back during Sunday rush hour and is loaded with a shipment of cocaine. The person assures me they will pass the information on to the relevant authorities and then does a curious thing, asks me to take down a number and to consider calling that number if I ever have any other useful information in the future.

It's another two years before I call that number a meeting is arranged would I like to work for the crime division, passing on useful information I pick up in the Naija circle. I do so for over 5 years passing on names and locations of those who are throwing cash round at parties, drug deals and stolen car movements. They were so easy for the police to pick up, most live in council properties and go from living modestly to driving top of the range cars overnight. I also did a few stints at the airport, Heathrow terminal three, hidden behind two way mirrors I identified those I knew were couriers or had contact with them including airline staff. If the Police knew I was living in a knocking shop they turned a blind eye.

Oh what a delight to hear from Bosun on our usual Monday meet up that Adjara had been caught and is now in detention, it's not looking good for him, jail is a certainty with the guys outside demanding their money saying they had warned him to send several couriers to bring the drugs in, split up amongst them that way there is guarantee some will arrive. Bosun is pleased he has not suffered a big loss.

By now I had been in England a few good years, dating Bosun for a mixture of money and lavish gifts he gives me, and not sure of what I want to do with myself I continue to house keep for Lucy and her brood. One evening we were short of two girls, this had never happened. Lucy asks if I will do the Dom session as I don't go in the rooms I don't see what goes on. She assures me nil sex involved I just need to tell the man what to do; he is a big high earning city executive and comes by once a week to de-stress.

At 6.15pm I am in one of the rooms waiting and feeling a tad foolish, Lucy shows the man in, I have never fancied a white man but this one, jezs, groomed to perfection, his suit Austin reed, shirt Hugo Boss, watch Ebel, shoes Churchill, personalized cuff links screamed money but with taste and class. I stand in the middle of the room and wait, if he is surprised to see me he says nothing. Shutting the door, he bows to me puts his briefcase down, takes all his clothing off folding them neatly on the chair, he then waits by the chair.

Not sure I tell him to crawl towards me, slowly I command slowly, he does so, getting to me I point him in the direction of the en-suite and tell him to clean it, crawling in I watch as he cleans the bath sink and toilet. I move the chair into the middle of the room and sit, when he had finished he remained just inside the en-suite, calling him out I pointed to the space beside the chair, he crawls there and remains obedient. I switch the tv on keeping the volume low, I run my hand through his hair, this is the closest I have been to a white man, I tell him to stand up in front of me, I look at his body, not bad at all, am I allowed to touch, oh well I find out as I'm sure he'll protest if I do something I'm not allowed.

I cup his balls, nice and heavy not hanging like Bosuns, I notice he's eyes are closed, I tell him to open them and stare straight ahead, he obeys, I like this new game. as I hold him, he begins to grow, no I say, no excitement, if you get hard I will punish you, his body trembles with the effort to deny himself an erection. I touch him again, caressing his chest, age wise I'll say early forties but what a body. Touch my breast I command and he does, still looking straight ahead, I am turned on more turned on than I've ever been sexually.

I tell him to stop and he does, releasing him for a moment I give him permission to hold himself.

This man knows what he is doing, I am not sure what to tell him to do next. I tell him "today I give you permission to touch yourself, next time I do the touching" he nods to confirm, the music in the room comes on softly a sign there is 10 minutes left, I really don't want this to end yet, I feel like pulling him up and stuffing him inside me, instead I tell him he can bring himself to a climax, don't dare stop until I tell you to.

I watch as his excitement mounts, his breathing is harsh as he climbs I waited a full minute then tell him to stop and get cleaned up, crawl I reminded him. I put the chair back while he's in the bathroom and wait in the middle of the room. Emerging from the bathroom he crawls to me, I offer him my hand which he kisses and then crawls over to his clothes gets dressed, removing an envelope from his briefcase, he opens the envelope and adds money from his pocket, leaves it on the chair and exits the room without a word.

I stand there feeling like running after him to drag him back into the room and satisfy myself. Instead I look at the bathroom to see if I need to do anything other than a change of towel. I do this and wonder what else to do when Lucy pocks her head in, "he's really happy with the service he wants to see you on Friday, oh any tip you're given you keep" she said closing the door. I go over to the envelop and up to today as I talk to you it is beyond me why he gave me £800 for what I see as humiliation but apparently it's called domination.

From house keeper I graduated to seeing four clients who like being told what to do, as 90% is booked in advance we are able to work round their needs, I did some crazy things, I remember a man that liked me to open my bowels, hard to believe or image yet he came every other month and that was all I had to do, nil sex, just sit on the toilet and defecate at the moment he orgasms. I also had a man who liked to be caned, not hard but enough to leave his backside a delicious pink as he requested. The strangest by far I have seen is the man I had to dress up and one of the ladies breastfed, a grown up fully bearded man, that took some getting used to, the nicest thing was because they felt their request was well met they tipped generously. A slight tension developed with the other girls. I am taking money away from them.

Bosun continues to be my main sexual partner, I use Mr moneybag as I refer to him, my first client for Dom-sex, sometimes I'm brutal with him enjoying myself without a thought for his comfort, I would make him ride me like a horse even when I could tell he was exhausted I wouldn't allow a climax until I was sated, then I will permit release.

Chapter 67

By now I had lived with Lucy for over ten years, dated Bosun for that amount of time in which he got married had three children and continued to see me several times a week unfailingly. Lucy and I parted company when I got pregnant, it wasn't planned but at 32 I knew it was my only chance of motherhood and took it. Bosun delighted me by putting the deposit down for a three bedroom house in Hargood Road ironically an ex-council semi but with a good SE3 postcode, when Princess was born I thought it would be a quiet affair but the house was packed full of his friends and relatives.

With the arrival of Princess the British government must have decided it had had enough of the bank, housing, benefit fraud and what not because all of a sudden all the guys who for 15 years lived like Kings suddenly started to complain, that is those who were out of prison and able to complain. Barely a month passed without someone been arrested and remanded. The gayness went out of the parties the excesses were curbed, it became easy to see those who had always had steady jobs as their standard of living didn't change.

When Princess was 5 years old Bosun relocated his family to Lagos, he had used the bulk of his ill gotten money to build properties, schools, hotels and several shopping complexes. Bosun paid off the mortgage of £57,000 on my house before he left, disclosing all the years he had been in England he had not used his real name, so with plans to settle the family then apply for a visa, using his real identity he will return to spend time with us. He was killed in a motor accident three weeks after he arrived in Lagos.

Because I had so much money stashed away and money was coming in from my properties, I decided to approach an estate agent and did an apprenticeship, with that I opened my own outfit Princess Letting, focusing on rentals, I haven't looked back. My main tenant the local authorities, who having run out of properties are putting tenants in private let, ironic isn't it that I took their properties and now get paid by them for the same properties. Like my work I have short term boyfriends, based on the occasions I've overheard potential spouse say once we are married they will enjoy my money.

I am so engrossed in the women's conversation it takes Sharon touching my shoulder to remind me the dryer session is complete and my hair is ready. It has been an interesting 6 hours, paying Sharon and giving a decent tip. I check my appearance in the mirror, as I do so Ann repeats the bag alert, picking up my bag I faced all three speaking perfect Yoruba told them "none of you have anything worth stealing" and walked out as all three started to shriek as one, shock and embarrassment kicking in.

On the train I think of the women, Ann has been the luckiest of the three, some early hardship, apart from the attempted rape, her sexual experience has been consensual, I had wanted to hear more of her role as a dominatrix's not able to visualize a Nigerian woman ordering a man to crawl and maul her to her satisfaction. The scale of her fraudulent activities is staggering, 21 properties, quite a portfolio.

Entering the hotel I head to the beauty parlor and have the works, manicure pedicure, full body massage, and facial scrub, mask and eyebrows tidied, I book for someone to come up and do my make-up at 5.15pm. At 6.15 I am in the lobby crowd watching as I please. I draw admiring glances but no one approaches me. I'm wearing a lime dress with a black bolero jacket courtesy of Balenciaga, my accessories shoes and bag are Balenciaga, why waste money buying Gucci, Chanel, Burberry when half the room will sport the same items. I wear a simple emerald 18ct set trimmed with a set of emerald and diamond rings. I scream money success without opening my mouth.

Tonight is full friendship attack and fact finding mission, I hold the small bag of Rumba a Balenciaga perfume ready to give to Kike, I know she will say she loves my perfume, hers is Fendi, nice but easily recognizable. Well here is to a good evening, I need to know as much as possible about worm-man before I return to Lagos in 6 months time.

Chapter 68

Kike's arrival, hellos are said during the short ride, taking our seats at the restaurant is a non-event. As soon as we are in the car she gushes about my perfume, I hand her the gift and she gives me one, it's a Ferragamo scarf nice. She is clearly delighted by my choice of restaurant. As we eat I am like a tape recorder whenever she speaks about her husband worm-man. Filing away information to be retrieved when needed. Naturally she told worm-man of our meeting plus my generosity he apparently confirmed I am a childhood friend.

I am friendly but want to send a message to worm-man, Kike leaves the ordering to me, I achieved my aim of impressing ordering the Lobster Bisque with cognac soup followed by Scallops with Pea puree. Mains were fillet steak for me and Lemon Sole St Germain for Kike. I ordered a variety of deserts for us to have or pick at if we didn't like. Caramelised lemon tart, Apple strudel, Petit-pot au chocolate, chocolate Liegeois, ice cream coupe all rounded off by coffee accompanied with cheese from the Pyrenees, served garnished. I noticed she mirrored me when I ordered drinks sticking to one glass of red wine, fresh orange juice and sparkling water.

Thus we spend a pleasant few hours, I gave her my phone contacts cell and home number I do not want my business card found on her in the future and with the usual promise to keep in touch we and part company. I instruct the cab sent by the hotel to take her home and jump in a black cab for my ride back.

Kike has spoken enough about worm-man's likes and dislikes for me to get a better picture of the mature man's displayed habits, during dinner she mentioned he is mildly allergic to bitter leaf, a vegetable cooked in homes everyday in Nigeria, he reacts with a rash and itching that responds well to anti-histamine, he dislikes snails in any form it's cooked and was once physically sick when overwhelmed by the smell of palm wine. A cleanness freak who likes things kept just how he likes it.

I've kept my phone off during dinner, switching it on I listen to the messages, all from the building crew, the ground has been cleared, they break ground for the foundation of my bungalow tomorrow morning and expect all to be ready on schedule. I eagerly await departure for the long 13 hours flight back to LA in the morning, I have lost interest in my surrounding and call each of the four men for a quick chat, the conversation is repetitive the importance of living life to the full and taking good care of health. I ask them to watch out for Tayo, sounds compassionate right, no, I want to keep tabs on my sister, I'm still going to get the shitty little so and so.

I call it a night and arrive at Heathrow check-in for the mandatory two hours before flight guideline. I have a full breakfast in the first class lounge, surrounded by the American twang reminds me I'm heading back to their territory.

The United States of A, gun totting, world economy controlling always at war self absorbed state. Yet the land of freedom and opportunity. If you don't step out of line you have a good shot at success that is if you can avoid getting shot face to face, via drive by or accidentally by the cops.

Loneliness my constant companion now makes himself known, a familiar friend as I ease my car out of LA lax and head towards home. Living in opulence driving top of the range cars eating the best food top class medical care that money can buy yet I'm still little me. Who is your friend now? A big fat nobody, me myself and shadow for company.

Digging deep I try and recall good things that took place, meeting up with my buddies, bucket brigade. The success stories the triumphs the poor judgment but all in all acquiring that red passport. Each of us has paid a price. Tolerated not accepted abroad, at home tolerated envied our place in society taken and not given back on arrival, living within two cultures yet belonging to none.

What a price to pay yet everyday round the world another wave make their way to the west, who put it in our mind we have to come to the west to be successful? there are millions round the world who remain in their country of origin and make it rich beyond their dreams. This brain drain to the west should have a name an ICD (International Classification of Diseases) recognized internationally as a disease in its very own category.

I laugh the first time since leaving Heathrow; electronic gates open a system that is triggered by the car as mine approaches, technology in the west, programmed to the household car, no pointing and pressing remote control.

The twinkling sound of the fountain the green of the perfectly manicured lawns the standing fish pond one of my favorite piece rather than crane my next to see the fish they are sitting in a raised pond, no danger of a toddler falling in, that had been my thought thinking my daughter been the only child will hatch like a chicken and I'll be overrun with grandchildren but zilch to date...oh well

My Mexican maid comes out smiling a welcome, she is the niece of one of my workers, English so bad on arrival we communicated in a mad sign language that had me laughing my head off with the muddle she got herself in, I ask for a drink and get fresh cut watermelon or a plate of spicy beans with the Mexican flat bread. Catholic to the point of obsession Almundina whose name refers to the Virgin Mary crosses herself and says hail Mary's as if afraid she will forget the words.

Allowing me to call her Dina I suggested evening English classes which I paid for, Dina would have been perfect for ITV's sitcom Mind your Language, I would get confused and spoke like she did to make sense of what she wanted to communicate. Dina is a perfect example of invest in me and I'll make sure you don't regret doing so. Her little piece of madness is entertaining.

I accept first the small glass of water and then the Margarita; taking a long pull I smile a hello as she speaks as good the American twangy English as the natives do. Following her directive I head upstairs with my drink, in five minutes I am reclining in a scented bath, easing and soothing bones that were now complaining of a thirteen hour flight, my nail throbs and my back passage feels somewhat sore not totally recovered from the hot chilli enema.

I sip the Margarita and press the remote access to the phone punching in the option for messages, I have been away for three weeks and have three messages, one from my absent husband, totally impersonal asking if I'm back, my daughter gushes her love while her husband calls out his from the background, they sound happy, Claire's voice is next can I give her a call when I'm rested and can meet up. What now, has Kirk Stapleton said something, oh well; unless someone is planning to exhume bodies I know I am home safe.

Best get it over with, I call both family members and then Claire, Kirk has been in touch to say how distressed I was he recommended grief counseling, as I don't just pay her per session but also a retainer amount that enables her to fast track me should I be in crisis she has been proactive and found one for me here in Bel-Air, it's a closed group and runs for 7 sessions with individual follow-up as needed.

First session is in three days time, that will be fine, I thank her and we agree to meet in two months time which will be after grief therapy sessions. Touching base with my PA to let her know I'm back I eat a light brunch and hit my bed sleeping solidly for 21hours.

When I wake up just before noon, something has shifted, I didn't feel refreshed, my dreams littered with images of my mother laughing at me telling me my efforts are the usual clumsy mess, an Aunt kept surfacing, I remember overhearing her say they should tell me and her been told not to start anything, a small collection made up of my Dad's two younger sisters and that Aunt a cousin of my dad, at the time I had thought it was linked to money request now in my dream her words are amplified.

Dragging myself up I remember and miss the joys of the in-house masseuse at the Savoy. I place a call to Hotel Bel-Air requesting a home visit by their top masseuse you cannot go wrong with La Prairie a case of what the rich want they provide, an unhurried but totally professional contact. I don't do small talk. I jump in the shower and wander downstairs, Dina meets me with one of her nasty green smoothie she insists I drink trice a week, they are not that bad just look nasty.

I down it quickly and look through my mail, nothing important mainly fund raising invitations as a good 90% of communication is now done online. I have an hour to kill before my massage. Getting up I take a slow stroll around the house everything is in its place all is as it should be except the in habitant, I have changed, leaving this house three weeks ago I had such high hopes of coming back home like a victorious Boadicea against the Romans, I feel nothing like that, is my mother going to make me miserable from her grave. Shaking this thought off I think how lucky I am. In a good financial position, my business practically runs itself, if we were to float shares, I will be drowning in money, as things are I can retire anytime I want but my old demons won't let me, nightmares of poverty lack of love, warmth and money are never far away.

I catch my reflection as I move past the mirror and stop to look at myself it occurred to me my staff know I have just buried my mom but not seen any grief, this is where Dina found me a minutes later tears streaming down my face, not a hard thing to do as I only need to think of Mum and Tayo. Genuine tears come when I think of my father.

Supporting me and forgetting to speak English she lapses into Spanish saying soothing words that meant everything and more. I point her in the direction of the guest bedroom downstairs, I don't like strangers in my private quarters, and I sit in the chair and wait for my massage team to arrive. La Pairie has a speciality in which two people mass you simultaneously one the top and the other your torso a wonderful feeling compared to each part of the body waiting its turn. I put a damp towel on my face and leave $200 on the sideboard, their tip, La Pairie sends a quarterly electronic bill. It's so good I call them back daily for the three days I'm at home 'catching my breath time'.

Returning to work is uneventful I might as well had never been away, for this lack of chaos I thank God, but I am feeling loose, the knot that drove me and spurred me on is gone replaced by an irritation for my sister, the sort you get when a fly is trapped in the room and you hold the door open wide but it doesn't fly out so you swat it, that is how I feel she is buzzing round in my head taking up valuable space but not yet creating the level of intensity I felt for mum. Main thing I do not feel like self harming my finger is also throbbing less, recovered for now until the next time.

At the designated evening choosing a modest car the Toyota Camry I drive to the grief support group. We are asked to bring a picture of the loved one we lost. Thus begins seven sessions of excruciating pain, how I tolerated it, I reminded myself this is America big brother and sister are watching you. I paid attention spoke when I it was expected of me, said the right comforting words, shared with the group my relationship with mine had been shitty but we made up, I described her listening to me, validating me accepting her mistakes and finally apologizing to me, all the stuff I wanted that did not happened I fed them in that meeting.

On our last session when one of the men mentioned the guy who runs the group is a Police Psychologist/Criminal Profiler, I knew I had made the right decision about being cautious. Well whatever he feeds back to Claire I will find out next week and with that my grief resolved.

Murder is no longer on the card when you read their risk assessment on me. The first time I saw the document I realized I had said too much of what was inside me eating me away, a professionals meeting followed with the only way out for me assuring the risk panel I had no plans to go home and my thoughts were just my way of coping with deep rejection, based on the no travel to Nigeria plan I got away with things by a thin strip.

Always the will she won't she question, until after many years they relaxed but my hope thoughts fantasy and planning did not relax for one day. Be very careful what you share they do not destroy records, it's stored away like salted breeze dried beef Jerky for times of need. Well I hung on to my business and contracts by arguing saying it didn't mean I wanted to do it and pointing out everything had gone well when I had visited. I guess somewhere in the belly of the US Embassy in Nigeria they did a sneaky welfare check on my mother.

Claire McCluskey, I could have written the script to my meeting with her myself. With encouragement I should make contact should my dark thoughts resurface towards anyone in the future I am to make contact so I can be supported through whatever crisis has brought them on. The grief counseling feedback showed I had been able to work through my loss and so on the evaluation went. When she asked for feedback comments from me I thank her and the Psychotherapy services for always being there in the background and supporting me in Naija when I hit crisis point, on that note of reminding me of reaching out if the need arose we parted company. I believe I am no longer on the radar of those who are likely to commit a specific crime to an intended person/ persons. Claire and her clever so full of it cronies are out of my hair and breathing space.

Chapter 69

Its three months since I left Nigeria the bungalow is at the roofing stage, ready to move into in ten weeks maximum that will be two weeks ahead of schedule. I think of all my preparations before I left Naija three months ago, scouting Ikorodu I had decided on Labis Oasis Hotel where reservation is possible without the hassle of a credit card, I had gone in and booked a room for 12 days this will cover Worm-man, days when I am in the country and no one knows except worm-man, the hotel is 12.4 miles to the airport, a 10 bed roomed hotel, I can see me going about my business without anyone showing any interest in me. I need the receipt to show worm man so he'll think he's heading to a whole load of sex. I go over my plans and tick off what else needs doing.

A ping that a message has arrived on my phone interrupts my train of thoughts its instant messenger from Kike, she's coming to LA for a medical conference next month, and hubby will be accompanying her they would love to take me to dinner. I bombard her with texts saying how delighted I would be to see her, would they like to stay with me, no, what a shame the Nigerian Medical Association has sent her so lodging taken care of. They arrive two weeks before I head back to Lagos. What more can a girl want.

I jump off the bed and undress, standing naked I look at myself in the mirror, first I don't look my age, my breasts are firm, I only breast feed for six weeks before I needed to introduce bottle feeds. Nil stretch marks, my skin is nice and quick glance looks unblemished, I look very okay to hot until you look closely or part my legs but that's not visible if I keep my legs together. Worm man will take the bait, predators always do thinking they are one step ahead of their victim.

The next few days pass in a flash, I am busy again in my mind I am so busy I have to still my thoughts or they race ahead of me. I begin to pack the two bags I will take to Naija with me. I take out the bubu's and long Ankara dresses I bought for my encounter with worm man, the Naija shoes and slippers all designed so I blend in unnoticed and head scarf's black and brown only, adding two pairs of prescription glasses I picked up at the swap meet. I already bought the chains and padlocks, heavy duty but thin, explained away as needed for gates back home. I pop in one roll of masking tape, tub of carpet freshener, a plastic tie adding the portable low level hand held light and a packet of Diazepam my choice of tranquilizer then with Tayo in mind a small bottle containing a few berries Deadly Nightshade (Atropa Belladonna). Today the keys for the property gated and left alone as I requested arrived via DHL. I don't need anyone to let me in.

Worm man and Kike arrived last night, Kike and I have spoken twice I sent flowers and a bottle of Bollinger over to their hotel Montage Beverly Hills, the Nigerian government is not doing bad if it can house the attending medics at the Conference hotel good show. As they are in town for 4 days with the dinner and dance on the last night I agreed to be their guest, it is the only time I want to spend with them, I need to get worm man's business card or it will be impossible to make contact with him when I arrive in Nigeria. I plan to make quite an impression.

I dress with care, summoning my Fashion Fair makeup artist I feel confident and look stunning in a pastel green full length Lavin Grecian dress that ebbs and flow in all the right places, I wear Wale's emerald set with a shoe and bag set from Clio in New Bond Street. If unsure expose your neck, I have my hair plaited up and beautifully done in the million dollar sweep, giving me an elegant neckline and profile. I am ready, cocktails is at 6pm with dinner sitting at 7. The dance is billed to end at 2 am; I don't plan to stay that long. My mission tonight is simple...lay the bait.

Keen to see me Kike must have made worm man and her not stray too far from the entrance, as soon as I swept in they were in my line of vision...worm man bowed and kissed my hand, smiling down at me, I forgot how tall he is compared to me, smiling at me I can see his brain working overtime. In his dinner jacket I can see he's thickening in the middle, evidence of good living as we say. Hello and introductions to the small group of Nigerian delegates, I hand Kike a small gift bag, she protests while worm man looks on, when Kike opens the slim box and sees the tennis bracelet, she says diamonds and no at the same time. I show her mine on the wrist that should have a watch on and stated looking at worm man "sister's let's enjoy this wealth".

Kike hugs me and orders worm man to, as soon as he does I quietly say 'your business card' and step away, then I purposely ignore him for the rest of the evening, making sure I sat on Kike's side rather than between them, I avoid eye contact and show a kin interest in what others round the table had to say. One of the doctors compared me to someone called Ediosere a lady who had been given the contract for military wear during Nigeria's first junta and did very well for herself. We agreed I had more money than all of them put together, I modestly reminded them no one takes it with them when death says pack your bags.

Excusing myself I head to the bathroom I can bet my last dollar that when I walk out worm man will just happen to be coming out of the men's his contact card in his hand. Bang on cue he is there, I take the card from him without a word and head back into the ladies, tucking it in my purse I join the others, the rest of the evening flew past pleasantly but I had lost interest the moment I achieved what I came for, giving my excuse of flying out to Cincinnati tomorrow morning I take my leave at midnight promising to call Kike the moment I set foot in Lagos for the reading of the will.

Good things come to those who wait, today I am heading back to Lagos, no calls to or from Tayo who interestingly has gone rather quiet. Nil hanging around Europe. Northwest Airline into Heathrow and British Airways from Terminal 3. London to Lagos leg of my journey I use my Nigerian passport, I must not bring any attention to myself. Arriving in Lagos at 4.20am I am through customs and have got my bag and suitcase, declining porter help I come through to the first set of doors, turning left I head past the cafe to left luggage and deposit my suitcase there paying the 12,000 naira and tipping the guy 500 naira a modest amount that will ensure he doesn't remember me for tipping big.

Heading to the ladies I quickly change out of my jeans top into a kaftan, I wrap my head hijab style and having donned one of the fake prescription glasses even I don't recognize myself. I am make up and jewellery free apart from the dark smudge on my forehead which I used my mascara to create and associated with prayerfulness from touching one's head to the ground, my locs plaited flat is not visible. I purchase 2 very basic Nokia phone and another more modern phone so I can use the video/camera facility and put some credit on all three, as its second hand the guy is able to give me fully charged batteries. There is nothing about my appearance that say's I have just stepped off a plane.

Heading to my chosen clearing and forwarding agent I present the paperwork to pick up the bag I had sent ahead. A black one favored by lots of Nigeria it's a bag that draws no attention, I head out the airport unnoticed. Joining the early morning crowd I do the short taxi ride to Maryland then another taxi to Ikorodu ensuring I am dropped off by college bus stop then walking quickly head down I am in my compound gate locked behind me by 06.15hrs.

The 1 packet of drinking water totaling four bottles I unpack as well as the meal supplements energy bars and some boiled hard sweets. To any early bird, who have seen me they will describe a middle aged medium build Muslim woman returning early from travel or business. I look round the house, nice and compact, nil neighbors.

I love the coolness of the tiled floors, I try the tap, water flows already pumped up to the tank to make sure all is in working order. A small generator is available but I won't be using it. I seat for a while in the room I have chosen to be worm man's place of judgment. Waiting quietly like this until 7.30 I call worm man's mobile, he answers on the third ring "can you talk are you alone I arrived this morning", "give me a moment I'll call you back in a bit" comes the swift reply.

Worm man calls back faster than a bit, I tell him I'm in Ikorodu at a hotel planning to visit a property I just had built when will I see him, he was going away for a few days work he can spend those few days with me. "Dress down I say", let the driver take you to the domestic airport as usual then get a taxi and head to Beach Road the hotel is at Ewuala, call me and I'll meet you close by. "Expect me in two hours" he says. I am all set.

Switching off the phone I take two bottles of water and head to the hotel Labi Oasis, showing them my reservation under the name Alhaja Ramota Dada and payment slip, I am quickly shown into my double room, my first task I chuck one of the bottled waters in the freezer compartment of the fridge in my room. Unpacking my clothing and bits and pieces, I want the room to look lived in whenever the cleaners come in. Now I wait.

An hour fifty minutes later he calls he is on Beach road, I advise him to lose the taxi at the college junction and wait for me. As I walk towards him I adjust my scarf slightly and take the glasses off, when I walk up to him he is shocked, "what do you expect from me to come her dressed to the nines and be a target for every crook within miles" he burst into laughter when I hand him the chilled bottled of Evian as I guide him towards my bungalow, he drinks long and hard not tasting the 6mgs of diazepam, I need us to reach the bungalow and be inside before the drug takes effect.

As we hurry along me with nothing but the keys him with a weekend bag, I ask how he is and ask for his opinion on whom should do the furnishing of the property for me, in reply he yawns several times and states he didn't realize he was so tired. I open and lock the gate behind us while he stands there trying to clear his head, I lead him into the house by the hand, come and have a seat I say, we make it into the room before he slumps on the mackintosh sheet loving laid with bitter leaves a look of surprise on his face.

I set to work quickly, tussling him up like a Christmas turkey I know he will be out for some hours but he is a strong man and I don't want him to be injured in his effort to loosen his chains, to ensure very little struggle I have interlocks so that if he struggles too much he will choke himself. It is natural he will try but once he connects the pressure on his windpipe to struggling he will try and stay perfectly still.

I put the masking tape across his mouth and then undo his trousers ease them down, taking both testicles in hand I twist the attachment skin holding the sack away from the body, holding both balls this way I used the masking tape like a tourniquet winding it round them as tight as I can I then use the gardening tie, feeding the plastic through the eye I pull as hard as I can get it and look on in amusement at my handiwork, his balls are hanging tight in no time I know they will begin to swell from the lack of blood flow, it is the pain and helplessness of abuse I want this shitty man to feel, he came to me believing he was going to spend quality time with a friend same way I went willingly at his invitation years ago believing I was going to have lunch with a friend, well I'll treat him to a surprise just like he gave me. I let myself out and am back in the hotel in no time, returning to the hijab style scarf and adding the glasses.

I order yam and corned beef stew for breakfast, while waiting I check the amount of Naira I have on me 350 thousand, I should be fine, nil overhead and not planning to go far from the hotel. I eat quickly and put the tray outside the room; taking a quick shower I look at the time it is 11.05am. It is surreal to think I got off a flight from the USA less than seven hours ago but this is evidence of good planning. I lie down and sleep deeply and peacefully waking up 4.30pm, only because the electricity cut out, the heat in the changeover minutes to the generator woke me up.

I pick up the phone and order a Chapman, I itch to login to view my emails to see if I have any messages but I had told folks in the States I am heading to Europe for a week and then Nigeria next week I most leave no cyber foot prints. I dress in a black kaftan with a brown scarf and head to the bungalow, using my shoulder wrap to shield my face as I walk through reception. The streets are quiet, the rush to get home has not yet started, I turn down the familiar road and quickly let myself in locking the gate after me.

Why are bullies such wimps who can't take a dose of their own medicine. You all need to see worm man, scared is an understatement it is reeking from all pores and orifice. He does not struggle having worked out if he does so he cuts off his own supply of oxygen, I seat on the floor cross legged, I open the bottle of palm wine I had bought at the airport before changing gabs, it's cool in the room as we are at the back of the room, he looks wild angry eyes communicating everything he will do to me once free of his restrains. I position the phone and switch on the video.

I get comfortable and smile sweetly at him for the first time I address him directly " I built this house for you, from the moment I saw you at the Yacht club I knew the lunch at your house in 1979 needed reciprocation, I truly felt happy when you started to talk to me, phoning our house visiting been friendly whenever our paths cross at home or abroad, talking to me finding out information what I like my dislikes my hopes fears what makes me laugh, then you delivered, I gave you the ammunition you needed and you used it against me very well, you broke me.

Look at you looking like you want to kill me do you not realize you already killed me, think where you are right now, you are at my mercy, I plan to kill you and roll your shitty body down the valley but before you die physically I will make you wish you died long before then. Didn't you pay any attention when we walked here, nil neighbors, not even a footpath beyond the house, the buck stops here on the edge of the forest.

First of all I intend to ensure you lose all functioning in your balls at some point the tissue will break down because of the poor blood flow, hopefully it will necroses' quickly, the smell of your own rotten flesh should make you gag, the filth of not washing changing your cloths and cleaning yourself after a bowel movement, it will never match the dirty way you left me feeling. The belief that suicide is better than being alive will quickly follow. You had no right to do what you did to me, no right at all.

Just in case it's crossed your mind, no one but you knows I am in the country, absolutely no one; I am here only for you. When you are dead I will either burn this place down and walk away or tip you down the valley for the animals to devour. Noooooo! that is not urine is it, you must save it, try not to pee you need all the fluids in your system to remain hydrated, I don't plan to give you any nourishment so hang on to what's in your system.

You sure are an undiagnosed sociopath, I often wonder if I am your only victim or there are others, poor little rich girls like me who just wanted to be friends but ended up been raped and violated traumatized by you. It's your identifying, recruiting, planning and reeling in, your friendly face, that masks a violent nature, so cold and intent only on what you want, my begging pledging fell on deaf ears yet you had a sister my age under the same roof, didn't you remember I am someone's sister what if someone treated your sister to what you subject me to. It just occurred to me, did you abuse your sister? Is that what her death was about, we all know she committed suicide it just wasn't talked about".

He actually reacts, straining and trying to do what I really don't know, his eyes roll as he struggles against the lack of oxygen he's created, settling down he lies panting having achieved nothing. I move close and look at his balls, nicely redden swollen and shiny smooth, I don't need to touch to know they are hot temperature wise.

"By the way I say you won't be missed yet not for the days you said you'll be away. I promise you this you will roe the day you forced yourself on me. However many women you destroyed the buck stops here. Let me remind you in case there have been so many your memory fails you. After having lunch with your very pretty step-mum your pimply faced sister and you, we moved to your sitting room where your sister stayed for a few minutes before disappearing, there was music playing which I later realize was possibly to drown me out should I scream. I didn't even realize you had gone to get undressed thinking you were discreetly using the bathroom. When you emerged in your dark blue paisley dressing gown, my brain refused to register your nakedness, what I registered quickly is the small plastic container with a lid which you opened to show a wiggling mass of worms and your command that day 'don't make any noise or I will throw this on you', on the settee I was sitting you made me take off my underwear and forced yourself on me, the bowl of worms inches from my face, I dare not move, just laid there. Thinking it was over and I was free when you said go in the room and clean up, I didn't realize I was in for more this time on your bed again with the bowl of worms almost touching my cheek you brutalized me again. When you got off me I tried the sitting room door it was locked, that was when I went to the balcony and made the decision to jump down to the ground we were only on the first floor. You must have sensed I was serious and promising not to bring the worms near me pledged with me not to jump, you unlocked the door and I left. I remember the cab drive home, hurting and hurting, look at you now the same member or violator now shriveled up surrounded by your disgusting grey pubic hair".

Taking his penis in my hand I insert the drinking straw I had brought along from the hotel into his urethra. "What did you think; you will get away with what you did? Nope, justice is here on earth. This is heaven this is hell. It's still strange to me you didn't make me take my clothes off, I guess you wanted to be able to get dressed quickly and push me out should you be disturbed. I'm sure this was your modus operatus, you had nothing to fear been the popular spoilt rich boy at college. Debating, Sports, Cultural evening events these were your recruiting field, the famous handsome dude making friends with young gullible girls like me who were starved of attention. Clever guy.

Oh well its late, I'm going to make a move, I'll see you again at some point". Switching off the phone which was the only light I make my way out letting myself out unobserved, head down at a fast trot I am back in the hotel in no time, no one gave me a second glance, checking the time it's 8pm, I order a heavy meal of efo riro and semolina with a bottle of Crest Bitter Lemon and a large Eva water. Keeping my tip low at 500 naira I leave the tray outside, watch Nollywood movies and call it timeout in the early hours of the morning, sleeping in until 2pm.

Chapter 70

I cannot go online, can't communicate with anyone I'm in the country. I stay in the room whenever the cleaning crew come in I took to seating on the small prayer mat I bought and hold the prayer beads in my hand, born into mixed religion with Muslims and Christians peppered throughout the family, my faith and belief shattered at an early age by the Imam and church scout master who wouldn't keep their hands to themselves, I detach myself from any faith once I left home, I believe if there is a heaven I will make it there, I wrong no one only taking revenge when wronged, that I feel I can account for. Those I helped and whose life I have made a difference far outweigh the 3-4 people who will die at my hands. Should there ever be a question of the guest in room 10, I want the description to be a Muslim business woman, prayerful and quiet.

I do not return to Bassey and the Bungalow until Friday evening, I do not want to go there over the weekend as the risk of someone seeing me will be increased, Nigerians value their weekends after being stuck in classrooms and offices week days, the weekend is spent outdoors, visiting or simply seating outside their houses, worm-man has been in the bungalow for five days.

No nice smells of after shave and perfume pampered bodies. His musky smell hits me as soon as I walk in, switching the low light on I check the chains, they fit smugly, perfectly even I have given room for weight loss due to dehydration, keeping the chain slightly tight on Monday, today I adjust the knots to ensure as he shrinks the chains do not come loose. It will be a disaster if he freed himself; I know for sure I will be the dead body left in this place.

Removing the masking tape I caution worm-man I will leave it in place if he dares makes a noise, I chuckle to myself as a good chunk of his moustache comes away with the tape having had a few days to embed itself and his cracked lips a strange grey color. His eyes are like someone left behind and captured in Beirut during the unrest, shrunken and red like a ganja smoker, his hair seems to have become more peppered with grey. I open one of the bottles of water I left and drink.

Switching the phone video on I capture him as he croaks the word please, holding my hands up I say "please for what" "everything" he says "everything I did to you", "what did you do to me I ask" "I forced you, I didn't ask you I didn't know you were not having sex, all the boys said you are good for it, I thought you had sex with any of the boys that wanted, it was after that I realized they were wrong, you were so tight and frightened but I couldn't stop myself once I started. I'm sorry about the worms".

"Who told you I was easy, which boys because I had no friends so I'm unsure who you mean". Eager to appease me names tumble forth. "Stop" I interrupt him, "these are guys who were on the debating team, we met at such functions twice a year, the only thing in common each had asked me to be their girlfriend, I had said no, so did they make up stories so they looked good". "Yes he answers eagerly that must be where the stories came from.

Oh well never mind let's have a look at the rest of you", switching off the video, I look at what is festering in his half pulled down trousers, interesting he has not opened his bowel, the urea stench is from Monday. Oh that you could be with me and see his balls, magnificent, the cracks in the skin are all seeping, not yet infected but well on the way, he keeps his legs very still the pain must be excruciating. I know in a day or two pressure sores will begin to make him wish he was dead from lying on the same side. You can see the whiteness of the muscle bag of the scrotum, anytime now the skin will simply burst. The rash from the bitter leaf is a joy to see, his skin is like a prickled fruit. Fumes from the palm wine make him wretch.

Switching the low light off I sit across him in the dark, I ignore his ramblings his promises pledging falling on deaf ears the same way mine fell on his deaf ears, I can barely make out what he's saying anyway, his throat so dry he crows the words out. Switching the low light on again, and I put the phone video back on. Worm-man is not terrified enough by my books, so I begin to tell him.

"I need to go to Abuja tomorrow morning, pray all goes well and I return quickly, if my business is delayed then I'll be delayed in returning to you, by the way I'm aware you should be returning home at some point this weekend, do try and stay alive I might let you talk to Kike when I return", with that I left amused by the fact this huge man cannot even struggle. Hopefully he is beginning to understand what the word hopeless means a feeling he gave me by the truck load that faithful day I went to lunch.

It's just after 8pm the streets are beginning to empty as I hurry back to the hotel. This is why I picked Ikorodu, it's such a stew pot with lots of scary beliefs about witchcraft and voodoo that no one hangs around long enough to see what business you're up to. Pulling my scarf close I walk through holding my prayer beads by my side I have stripped the bottle label off and simply drop the bottle knowing those who collect plastics for recycling will be grateful, further along the road I throw the label in the gutter.

Ordering yam pottage with spicy palm oil mixed meat soup I eat a hearty evening meal, I view the two video clips twice knowing this may be insurance up until the moment I fly out of the country, I know Worm-man belongs to some powerful orders and cults with far reaching hands, as long as I have him on tape, what am I thinking what will it matter he will be dead anyway, or won't he? That moment I realized my plans had changed somewhere in the past few days. How and why I struggle to understand the moment of change but here goes something else. I pray I succeed else all this will have been a waste. As the new plans unfold inside me I sign with a sudden rush of contentment. I will not kill the fool that will be an end yet there is no ending for me, no escape why give him one.

With this I spend a quiet weekend in the room, Aljazeera and CNN plus Nollywood my constant companions. To keep any chance of being spotted going in and out the bungalow, I wait until Tuesday afternoon at the height of the heat at 1pm I left the hotel make my way to the bungalow, making sure no one followed me. The smell of rotten flesh is the new deodorant at the bungalow, don't get worried worm man is not dead, people like him don't die easy, I check the chains at a distance, they look firmly in place, moving close I make the necessary adjustments as he struggles to open his now infected eyes, I remove the masking tape, the smell when he opened his mouth to attempt to talk makes me gag. Taking out the phone I put the video on and place it close to his face, talk I signal, all he can do is look and try to croak out please that comes out sounding like piss or peace. Keeping the video to a 15 second clip. I type the first of many texts to Kike and read it out to the moron lying at my feet.

Dear Kike, If you are not alone then make sure you are before you read the next message.

I ran into some problem but I am okay, alive that is all that matters.

Please do as these guys say they mean business.

They have said they will release me if we pay a ransom of 2 million naira.

You are not to go to the police or discuss this with anyone else.

They are keeping the amount low so you can raise it without asking anyone for help.

Make haste please. I love you.

They give you four days so if you withdraw 500 thousand each day it won't raise suspicion, no new notes.

They will contact you in four days time, please don't try calling them on this number and don't go to the police if you do they guarantee I am going to die. Don't tell anyone Please.

I am okay don't worry about me just do what you need to bring me home.

Saving each message I cover my nose with my scarf because of the stench and sit across from him back to the wall just staring at him, when I am used to the stench I move forward to his private part, the penis lays shriveled a faultless organ with a straw stuck in stretching and keeping his urethra open for some nice tract infection to begin, using my finger I poke him in the side "you a sociopath came into my life to wreck my belief in the word friendship".

Worm-man's scrotum is from another planet tissue has finally broken down, it's remains attached to his body by a small connection. I carefully use the small carpet cutter blade I had with me to cut the masking tape and plant tie in his groin area away while bodily fluid surges forth. I pack the tape in a little black bag so common in Nigeria if you buy something small, I will chuck it in the gutter on my way to the hotel, no one I guarantee will touch it out of fear it contains voodoo stuff.

9 days without nourishment and Worm-man looks like he's lost a good few kilos, well it will do him some good. He's no longer moving, just lying looking at me from time to time, mouth so sore he doesn't bother to try to talk, tongue so swollen it gets in the way. I must have dozed off because I can hear voices, faintly but I can hear

voices all the same, I listen trying to make out what direction it's coming from I can't see worm-man's face it's nearly dark in the room, crawling I move in the direction of the voices out into the corridor towards the side of the house, the voices are louder now, somewhere in the distance but shouting across to each other, within a moment I relax, they are hunters, coming back from checking the traps they laid with their catch. They are bidding each other farewell until Friday when they meet at the edge of the valley in the cool of the evening.

If realize I have been holding my breath a bit and exhale long and hard, if worm-man heard them he clearly did not have the strength to call out. The bugger looks so frail yet I struggle to find any compassion for him, a run over cat would get sympathy from me not this monster, black as the night and wicked in his entirety. Replacing the masking tape with a small piece that just held his lips together, I make sure he sees me send the first text to Kike rapidly followed by the 10 second video clip to give authentication to the rest of the texts that quickly followed. Taking the phone apart keeping the sim in my bra, I hurry away from the bungalow, the battery went into one gutter, the front casing in another the main body of the phone flung into a different gutter on the other side of the road.

Going to my room I use a scissor to cut up the sim card and flush the pieces down the toilet. Ordering Togolese beans and do-do for dinner, I pack my bags ready to depart at first light.

6.30am finds me on a local bus heading to mushin, I again kept my tip to a minimum at the hotel giving the front desk staff a 1,000 naira note. I confirmed I had enjoyed my stay and will be back, when they asked what I did I stated a dry fish trader who had come to oversee delivery and distribution of the largest consignment yet at Mile 12. With my prayer beads in sight I left to the murmur of one tell the other ' you'll never guess how rich she is and so prayerful too'

Getting out of the cramped danfo I walk into the teeming crowd and put my bag down for a moment knowing it will not be there by the time I finished reading my pretend address on a piece of paper, it all goes like clockwork, my bag is gone stolen in seconds I make no noise just quietly walk away and hail a taxi for the short ride to the airport. In the back of the taxi I put my hand out the window and discreetly drop off the pieces of the mobile I had used to call worm-man on arrival. Retrieving my luggage and changing into my pant suit I emerge from the ladies and mingle with the new arrivals. Switching my phone on I call AHI hotel's residence driver Mr Peter to say I've arrived and will wait for him to come and pick me up from International arrivals.

I spend the hour eating toast and reading Ovation magazine or rather looking at picture, just in case things go pear shaped I need to create an arrival trail, so tip my waitress generously with $20 as well as give her the magazine once I spotted Mr Peter outside. On the ride to Lawal Street I call Tayo to say I've arrived she's expressed delight but seems subdued, I ask if all is well, 'oh yes fine, I'm fine you know the wahala's of Lagos. I call Kike to say I'm in town it rings and goes to voicemail, I guess my number is not the one she's expecting. I make the final call to the family lawyers to say I am in town and will be at the reading of the will at 11.00 in their offices as agreed.

Checking in I ask Mr Peter to take me to Tejuosho market. There I purchase another set of black with brown accessories kaftan, this time adding an ankara outfit to my ensemble. I return to the Hotel and rest, checking my mail on their in-house system I want as many people to remember me arriving as possible, smiling and chatting in my America accent Nigerians like so much. Tomorrow after the reading of the will I will call my buddies and their wives for now all is well. I order a meal of fresh fish and rice, setting my alarm for 5pm I sleep. Tonight I will call Wale when I return to the hotel.

Chapter 71

5.15pm finds me on a bus to mile 12, from there another bus into Ikorodu town, taking a danfo I head towards the bungalow, I have timed things well it is 7pm. I work quickly, worm-man is alive and very feather weight, pulling the straw out easing his trousers up over his festering balls the pain makes his eyes roll back and at some point pass out for a few minutes. I clean up quickly rolling the plastic sheet I tie it in a small knot, I take off worm-man's chains and put them in my small carrier bag, I drink the small bottle of water I had left for tonight, empty the palm wine down the toilet and flush, returning to the room I pour the contents of a bottle of shake and vac in the room in time it will absorb the smell, slinging his small weekender on I lead him out, lock the gate with the original padlock and put my temporary one in my pocket.

Walking along at a brisk pace with worm-man barely conscious and dragging one leg I cut through the grass at the back of houses, my target is waiting for me a few streets away, leaving worm-man in the grass area I had chosen I put his bag on his body to weigh him down, he is pretty disorientated but just to be safe, I walk away quickly I have a few minutes and one try only. Walking to my target I use a hairpin to open the door of the Peugeot 504, I am banking on no alarm and there isn't, I quickly hot wire the car, it comes to life, driving away I double back down the road where I left worm-man, he is in the same spot I left him, throwing the bag in the front passenger seat I lay him across the back seat, sitting him first and then simply pushing him sideways, I drive off quickly, it's 10 minutes to 8pm.

I am on target, heading towards Lagos, I keep to the left and stay at a steady 40miles an hour while those who are petrified of armed robbers zoom past. I am at my destination in another 10minutes spotting where I want I switch the car lights of and bump off the road letting the car roll about 50meters, I have stopped at a shack used by crab sellers during the day, its right next to the swampy river and ideal. I sit for a moment eyes adjusting to the shacks around me no movement that is good.

Getting out I squat and quickly change into my ankara dress tucking all other clothing into the plastic bag. I ensure my hair is fully covered with the ankara material and throw a long wrap round my shoulder. I am sweaty and smell which is what I want when I go round the corner where there is a transport stop. Winding down my window a bit so there is fresh air, I know he will be discovered at first light.

I hurry away towards the road where though cars are flashing past there are regular intervals of no vehicle. Switching the third mobile on with the screen light switched off, I send the text already saved to Kike "we don release he dey too sick, find am'" switching the phone off and dismantling it as I walk, I throw all pieces into the river followed by the mackintosh loosening the knot before I throw it. I follow this with the kaftan and hijab, empty bottles the chains then let the black carrier bag float off in the breeze.

Hurrying forward I join the body of people who are in a hurry to make it into the safety of city lights, I pay my 300 naira and pretend to doze until we are in Yaba, taking a taxi for the short drop to Lawal street I stop at the chemist to make several purchases again to ensure I am seen at some point in the hours away from the hotel.

Jumping in the shower having requested for the ankara outfit to be picked up for laundry, I leave it outside the room and heard footsteps a few moments later. I emerge from the shower and dress in a duck blue long linen dress, switching on my phone I head down stairs and go across the road to Solitude hotel, nil alcohol where I'm staying; tipping the security men money on arrival they are delighted to see me.

I enjoy my meal and watch as different groups come in, men with men business talk and deals brokered, men with young chicks the age of their granddaughters feel pleased they can pull such young talent oblivious to the faces the young girls pull behind their back. I see family groups who are clearly in town for functions and through it all see the looks from the men unsure whether to approach me clearly put off by the top of the range phones in front of me, I enjoy mixing a generous amount of Dubonnet with my Chapman and call it a day at 01.00 hours after speaking to Wale and asking him to accompany me to the reading of the will. He'll pick me up at 10.00.

If you've ever climbed a mountain attained that which has always seemed impossible removed a thorn from your side that's how I feel, a degree of accomplishment. Nearly there I tell myself as I fall asleep.

Wale arrives at 9.30, I tell them to show him to my room and let him in while in my underwear, "American woman he shrieks without coming near me, abeg get cloths on before you blind me or I lose my senses", I ignore him and carry on getting dressed while he leans against the door pretending not to enjoy the view. Once dressed I go over and hug him hug him tight, you know that kind of hug that goes on and on, not sexual just connection. Wale sighs as our hug carries on and on. "I love it" he says "I'm glad you're a part of my life" I say, "me too" he replied "now come on before my fast is ruined for the day".

Post morning traffic the ride to the lawyers office is pleasant, Tayo and her husband are waiting, at the sight of my sister I touch the small pillbox containing the crushed night shade berries, I have got it down to as fine a powder as possible. Throwing herself in my arms she begins to cry 'oh sis this is so final isn't it' I comfort her and say my hello's at the same time. Such drama what is final?

Nothing in the universe prepared me for what came next. After cutting through the legal jargon, the entire estate is mine to do as I wish. I don't understand when I look at my sister she just cries and cries. I am not stupid but need clarification. Broken down this is what it means.

My father left his entire estate to me, why? I am his only blood relation, my mother his Ghanaian partner was killed in a car crash when I was 4 months, I was 18 months old when my father met Tayo's mother, newly pregnant and freshly abandoned by her man God knows where. Showing great compassion he agreed to marry her, the disgrace for her as the daughter of a Pastor would have been too much, alliance with one of the young successful lawyers in town is a win-win situation all my father asked was she should never give me cause to feel motherless.

Realizing his mistake a few years into the relationship my father quietly changes his will making sure I am well provide for. My sister is not my sister, we have no blood ties, her mother who has never worked since the day she met my father has lived off my money all these years yet today despite whatever Tayo and her squandered there is an unbelievable amount of cash and solid investments left.

I look at the sniveling woman in front of me and have one question, keeping my emotions in check I put on a gentle voice and ask "Tayo did you know" she shakes her head affirmative, "how long have you known"? "Mum told me when I was young", I thank her for her honesty thanking the lawyers I ask for a visit to the various buildings identified in Lagos State I will think of what to do with the rural land and properties later, bidding them good day Wale and I take our leave.

I ask Wale to take me to Kike's office, at the hospital we are told she is off sick, I ask Wale to take me to the home address, suggesting we take her out to lunch or just eyeball her to cheer her up, we send her staff in with my business card and are told to come in, Kike looks as bad as her husband weight-wise, she looks rough like a heroin addict going cold turkey. She stands looking at me eyes wild trying to talk but emitting a strangled cry instead, rocking on her heels she bursts into tears, I gather her in my arms and lead her to the couch.

"Whatever is the matter have you seen the doctor", "I can't tell you I'm not allowed to tell you" I ask where worm-man is and she starts to wail my "what is wrong" gets no answer I do what I know, I slap her hard on the face she is so surprised she stares at me open mouthed, "what is wrong tell me right now I demand", with tears flowing she tells me how he went away last week Monday she thought it strange he didn't call home but excused that thinking he may have a tight schedule or bad signal where he's working.

Few days ago she got a text and a short video clip from an unknown phone saying they had kidnapped him and wanted two million naira giving her instructions to stand by for further instructions in four days time. They were clear if I go to the police they will kill him. There is no one to talk to I didn't know what to do so I just waited and waited, then last night a text came saying they've freed him to collect him but it didn't say where and with that she collapses.

I look at Wale for directive, he is calling someone, I ask who with my head he states the Inspector of Police Alhaji Musilu Smith, he quickly relates events to the man who tells him he'll send some officers round and get people investigating. 20 minutes later two plain cloth officers pick up a picture of worm-man and leave. We are still there two hours later when Wale's phone rings, he is alive but in a bad way, he was found at dawn by fishermen returning from night fishing and taken to Ikorodu Hospital as we speak an ambulance with a police escort has been dispatched to bring him back to Lagos.

I get Wale to call BA for me and change my travel date giving me an additional few days in town rather than leave this Sunday an idea forming in my mind. Turning to Kike I tell her I can't leave her during such time of crisis and instruct her to go and have a bath and tidy up for when her husband sees her.

With instructions to the ambulance crew to head to Parklande Hospital in Surulere we wait for Kike to join us and head there, stopping briefly at my hotel where I pick up $10,000. Getting to the hospital we are told the ambulance is a few minutes away. Taking Kike with me we complete registration and relay the information the ambulance staff are able to give us to the medics, with a cash deposit amounting to several million I know the best care available will be delivered, good hospitals don't run on thin air.

As he is unloaded Kike is close to collapse again, I can see they've done their best to clean him up at Ikorodu, his face has been washed, eyes no longer closed but still grungy with infection and on a double drip to rehydrate him, there is a raise cage for the torso which is covered but the smell yea God's the smell is something else, you cannot mask the smell of rotten flesh.

With my arm round Kike I lead her forward, when worm-man opens his eyes he groans alarmed by my presence but unable to do much closes them again Kike kisses his head over and over when she moved back I stepped forward and pretending to put my cheek against him I quietly say "you know the score" moving away I murmur "you will be fine, best medical care awaits you".

Turning to Wale I release him, he has spent the day with me putting on hold whatever he needs to do, Wale departs saying the same driver will be back for us. For two hours we wait, them we are called in. Incredible people they have given him a low haircut, trimmed his nails, given him a really good bath, attended the festering mass added two more IV fluids, antibiotics, nourishment and the remaining two electrolytes and pain killers you can tell the man has been given pain relief.

We meet with the Doctors who say he is doing well considering, putting his better condition down to his previous fitness. When I suggest Kike goes in alone she refuses, we walk in together I am on the lookout for any close circuit cameras in the room, this hospital is that modern, I see none but remain very cautious all that was stationed in the room are two policemen and a nurse. I watch the reconciliation drawing a seat close I sit just behind Kike and watch the scene.

His speech remains slurred he can't remember anything except been dropped at the airport he must have been drugged, no idea what part of town or state he was held, the men didn't let him see their face, they were not Yoruba from their accent. They left him alone for long periods he thinks he not sure if they were there but didn't speak and so on and so forth. Once the policemen were satisfied and congratulated Kike on her good fortunes they left promising to follow instructions to leave things out of the news. I had earlier discreetly passed a bundle of money to Kike to give to the officers. Oh well sooner or later I have to leave worm-man and his wife alone so here goes, I step out and leave them to it.

Once outside I switched my phone on Tayo has left message after message, tearfully asking what my plans are, are we still okay as sisters she sorry she didn't say anything but her mum swore her to secrecy. I listen to all 13 messages, going into the guest loo I flush the nightshade powder down the toilet, then using the toilet brush to help the small container I flush that too. What do you do with someone who worships money, deny them money, I don't need to kill Tayo. Tayo with no access to large reserve of money is a living dead.

Kike comes out to call me in to say goodnight to worm-man, I do so and we both leave, he has been sedated again, I wonder what his iodine covered scrotum looks like. He will never live a day without thinking about me. As we walk towards the driver I ask Kike what she wants to do stay with me or I stay with her. She asks me to stay with her, we swing by the hotel and I pack a small case taking additional funds with me. This is going to be fun.

With Wale's car and driver at my disposal I drop Kike at the hospital and meet with the Lawyers by the end of the afternoon I am staggered by what I owe, buildings I have walked past driven past belong to me, I am worth oddles of money, if combined with my $

purse I am truly a Multi Billionaire in every currency sense. Another call from Tayo interrupts me, I ask for clarification of what she wants is she asking for Dad's assets or speaking about sisterly bonds, she splutters as she chooses sisterhood recovering quickly to say she has no idea who her father is the way I haven't had the pleasure of knowing my mum. Bad move bad taste, I cut the call off and switch off my phone. Relief to find I'm not the child of a cold heartless woman. Tayo doesn't need to die, Dad's will totally favored me, his instruction is simple, all control to me as his child, to share as I see fit. Even in death my father valued and loved me. It is enough.

The weekend is spent back and forth at the hospital, there is a review on Monday morning, I have to say he is looking much better, I have to accept I won't be able to see the end of my handy work but I know things are bad as decision had been made to let them dry and fall off rather than operate as the infection has responded well to antibiotics, If nil new complication he will be coming home on Monday with daily visits from the community nurse every day for the next 10 days. Worm-man a eunuch, I am sure that will be a secret guarded closer than the crown jewels of the Queen of England. He will grow plump and feminine if male hormone injections are not given. Revenge is a desert truly served long term.

With a Wednesday morning flight I spend Monday with Kike leaving late on Tuesday night, sharing with Kike the details and outcome of a will I was not expecting and assuring her not to worry about medical bills, checking with the hospital we are still in credit when medication physio and the community visits fees are included. I advise Kike whatever sum is left at the end of treatment she should tell the hospital to keep aside and use to offset the bills for those who are unable to pay thus helping a helpless soul.

I spend a few moments with Worm-man before I leave, to my horror he quietly says the word "sorry" this time I know the bastard means it. I look at him for a long time he is unable to hold my gaze after a moment he pretends to be asleep moving close to him I whisper "I will never forgive you in the future if you piss me off again I will sneak back in the country find you and send body bits to Kike" With that I walked out of the room conscious of his eyes on me I didn't waste my time looking back.

I leave Kike feeling I have someone close to sister material for the first time in my life. I ask Wale to ring Mr Smith once I've checked in the following morning and express my gratitude pilling on the American accent and promising to visit next time I'm in Lagos. Doing our usual prolonged hug Wale and I draw admiring glances, I've asked him to figure out what Country is not looking for him in relation to drug trade and we meet there, shaking his head he reiterates he is now a hommie apart from yearly trips to Mecca he has no interest in leaving the Country everything I need is here he says patting his belly. With a final hug I head towards customs.

24 hours later I walk into my house, with a drink in my hand I recall life, the unhealthy appetite for things that bring me pain, vulnerability, wanting to belong, be loved feel needed. My daughter is the only one who has truly needed me; I have always been a stepping stone to something for others. In the space of seven months I have untied the two most painful knots in my chest knots that stopped me living breathing enjoying constricting me all the time. What do I do with the others identified, how many times can I enter Nigeria kill someone and get away with it. Am I a serial killer hell no. How and why do killers get caught they kill once too often. I have too much to lose to risk getting caught. There are other ways to create a living dead. Firing up my laptop I send off messages to my four abusers who responded to the face book request I sent.

Tonight I make a decision to sell my business go back to Nigeria and get into what will suit me perfectly.... Politics it's the one thing you can do and get away literally get away with bad behavior. No more killing I say not convinced, I need to track down those who hurt me and are still available in Lagos. Maybe set up an NGO as well to give something back to the community, using the opportunity to work for me and earn big money as a lure to reel those guys in. Taking a sip of my drink I remember my parting words when I left worm man at the crab sellers shack.

'You can speak but you will not. I left your tongue intact to show you a complete power reversal, the barbed wire you wound round my tongue then now wind itself tightly round yours' Remember this, I will be back.

Printed in Great Britain
by Amazon